JOE PICKETT

ORDINARY MAN,
EXTRAORDINARY HERO

"Writing genius... on a par with James Lee Burke."
Library Journal

"I read one book and then hunted out
four more... Box has it all."
Toronto Globe and Mail

"Joe doesn't let us down... exhilarating."
New York Times

"Box gets better and better with each novel."
Bookreporter.com

"Absorbing... Relentlessly paced powder keg of a thriller."
Publishers Weekly

"Exquisite descriptions... Box's story moves smoothly
and suspensefully to the showdown."
Washington Post

"An absolute must."
Kirkus

"Riveting."
USA Today

"The suspense tears forward like a brush fire."
People Magazine

"A superb mystery series."
Booklist

FREE FIRE
C.J. BOX

CORVUS

First published in the United States of America in 2007
by Penguin.

This paperback edition first published in Great Britain in 2011
by Corvus, an imprint of Atlantic Books Ltd.

9 8 7 6 5 4 3

A CIP catalogue record for this book is available from
the British Library.

Paperback ISBN: 978-1-84887-991-1
E-book ISBN: 978-0-85789-446-5

Printed and bound by CPI Group (UK) Ltd, Croydon, CR0 4YY

Corvus
An imprint of Atlantic Books Ltd
Ormond House
26-27 Boswell Street
London WC1N 3JZ

www.corvus-books.co.uk

For Becky, who finally saw her bear
... and Laurie, always

Acknowledgments

The author would like to thank those who contributed to this novel. First and foremost, Brian C. Kalt, Michigan State University College of Law, for writing "The Perfect Crime," a Legal Studies Research Paper Series. Those interested in the official citation (Georgetown Law Journal, vol. 93sss, pg. 675) can look it up at http://papers.ssrn.com/sol3/papers.cfm?abstract_id=691642. Mr Kalt's assistance with technical aspects of the law and his theory were invaluable. Additionally, thanks to U.S. District Judge Alan Johnson in Cheyenne for reviewing the premise and Wyoming game wardens Mark and Mari Nelson, as always, for reading the manuscript and offering their expertise.

In Yellowstone, I thank those who provided background and documentation, including Cheryl Matthews, Brian S. Smith, Judy M. Jennings, Mike Keller, Bob Olig, and my friend Rick Hoeninghausen. The wonderful book Old Faithful Inn: Crown Jewel of National Park Lodges, Karen Wildung Reinhart and Jeff Henry, Roche Jauene Pictures, Inc., 2004, was a helpful resource as well.

My deepest appreciation for the hard work, loyalty, and dedication of Team Putnam: Ivan Held, Michael Barson, Katie Grinch, Tom Colgan, and my new editor Rachel Kahan.

And thanks to Don Hajicek for www.cjbox.net and the wonderful Ann Rittenberg for being Ann Rittenberg.

Yellowstone National Park

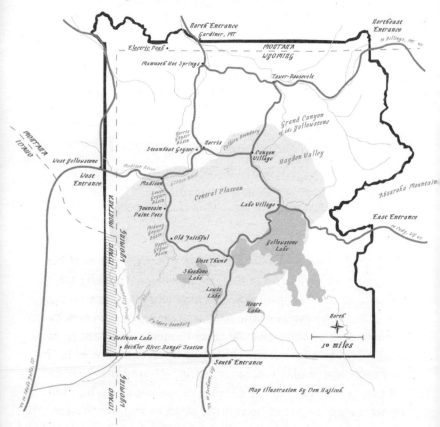

Map Illustration By Don Hajicek

PART ONE

YELLOWSTONE ACT, 1872

AN ACT TO SET APART A CERTAIN TRACT OF
LAND LYING NEAR THE HEADWATERS OF THE
YELLOWSTONE RIVER AS A PUBLIC PARK
Approved March 1, 1872 (17 Stat. 32)

Be it enacted by the Senate and House of Representatives of the United States of America in Congress assembled, That the tract of land in the Territories of Montana and Wyoming, lying near the headwaters of the Yellowstone River ... is hereby reserved and withdrawn from settlement, occupancy, or sale under the laws of the United States, and dedicated and set apart as a public park or pleasuring-ground for the benefit and enjoyment of the people; and all persons who shall locate or settle upon or occupy the same, or any part thereof, except as hereinafter provided, shall be considered trespassers and removed therefrom. (U.S.C., title 16, sec. 21.)

1

Bechler River Ranger Station
Yellowstone National Park
July 21

A HALF-HOUR after Clay McCann walked into the back-woods ranger station and turned over his still-warm weapons, after he'd announced to the startled seasonal ranger behind the desk that he'd just slaughtered four campers near Robinson Lake, the nervous ranger said, "Law enforcement will be here any minute. Do you want to call a lawyer?"

McCann looked up from where he was sitting on a rough-hewn bench. The seasonal ranger saw a big man, a soft man with a sunburn already blooming on his freckled cheeks from just that morning, wearing ill-fitting, brand-new out-door clothes that still bore folds from the packaging, his blood-flecked hands curled in his lap like he wanted nothing to do with them.

McCann said, "You don't understand. I *am* a lawyer."

Then he smiled, as if sharing a joke.

2

Saddlestring, Wyoming
October 5

J OE PICKETT WAS fixing a barb-wire fence on a boulder-
strewn hillside on the southwest corner of the Longbrake
Ranch when the white jet cleared the mountaintop and halved
the cloudless pale blue sky. He winced as the roar of the
engines washed over him and seemed to suck out all sound
and complexity from the cold mid-morning, leaving a vacuum
in the pummeled silence. Maxine, Joe's old Labrador, looked
at the sky from her pool of shade next to the pickup.

Bud Longbrake Jr. hated silence and filled it immediately.
"Damn! I wonder where that plane is headed? It sure is
flying low." Then he began to sing, poorly, a Bruce Cockburn
song from the eighties:

If I had a rocket launcher ...
I would not hesitate

The airport, Joe thought but didn't say, ignoring Bud Jr.,
the plane is headed for the airport. He pulled the strand of wire

tight against the post to pound in a staple with the hammer end of his fencing tool.

"Bet he's headed for the airport," Bud Jr. said, abruptly stopping his song in mid-lyric. "What kind of plane was it, anyway? It wasn't a commercial plane, that's for sure. I didn't see anything painted on the side. Man, it sure came out of nowhere."

Joe set the staple, tightened the wire, pounded it in with three hard blows. He tested the tightness of the wire by strumming it with his gloved fingers.

"It sings better than you," Joe said, and bent down to the middle strand, waiting for Bud Jr. to unhook the tightener and move it down as well. After a few moments of waiting, Joe looked up to see that Bud Jr. was still watching the vapor trail of the jet. Bud Jr. looked at his wristwatch. "Isn't it about time for a coffee break?"

"We just got here," Joe said. They'd driven two hours across the Longbrake Ranch on a two-track to resume fixing the fence where they'd left it the evening before, when they knocked off early because Bud Jr. complained of "excruciating back spasms." Bud Jr. had spent dinner lobbying his father for a jacuzzi.

Joe stood up straight but didn't look at his companion. There was nothing about Bud Jr. he needed to see, nothing he wasn't familiar with after spending three weeks working with him on the ranch. Bud Jr. was thin, tall, stylishly stubble-faced, with sallow blue eyes and a beaded curtain of black hair that fell down over them. Prior to returning to the ranch as a condition of his parole for selling crystal methamphetamine to fellow street performers in Missoula, he'd been a nine-year student at the University of Montana, majoring in just about every one of the liberal arts but finding none of them as satisfying as pantomime on Higgins

6

Street for spare change. When he showed up back at the Longbrake Ranch where he was raised, Bud Sr. had taken Joe aside and asked Joe to "show my son what it means to work hard. That's something he never picked up. And don't call him Shamazz, that's a name he made up. We need to break him of that. His real name is Bud, just like mine."

So instead of looking at Bud Jr., Joe surveyed the expanse of ranchland laid out below the hill. Since he'd been fired from the Wyoming Game and Fish Department four months before and lost their state-owned home and headquarters, Joe Pickett was now the foreman of his father-in-law's ranch—fifteen thousand acres of high grassy desert, wooded Bighorn Mountain foothills, and Twelve Sleep River valley. Although housing and meals were part of his compensation—his family lived in a 110-year-old log home near the ranch house—he would clear no more than $20,000 for the year, which made his old state salary look good in retrospect. His mother-in-law, Missy Vankueren-Longbrake, came up with the deal.

It was the first October in sixteen years Joe was not in the field during hunting season, on horseback or in his green Game and Fish pickup, among the hunting camps and hunters within the fifteen hundred-square-mile district he had patrolled. Joe was weeks away from his fortieth birthday. His oldest daughter, Sheridan, was in her first year of high school and talking about college. His wife's business management firm was thriving, and she outearned him four to one. He had traded his weapons for fencing tools, his red uniform shirt for a Carhartt barn coat, his badge for a shovel, his pickup for a '99 Ford flatbed with LONGBRAKE RANCHES painted on the door, his hard-earned authority and reputation for three weeks of overseeing a twenty-seven-year-old meth dealer who wanted to be known as Shamazz.

All because of a man named Randy Pope, the director of the Game and Fish Department, who had schemed for a year looking for a reason to fire him. Which Joe had provided.

When asked by Marybeth two nights ago how he felt, Joe had said he was perfectly happy.

"Which means," she responded, "that you're perfectly miserable."

Joe refused to concede that, wishing she didn't know him better than he knew himself.

But no one could ever say he didn't work hard.

"Unhook that stretcher and move it down a strand," Joe told Bud Jr.

Bud Jr. winced but did it. "My back ..." he said.

The wire tightened up as Bud cranked on the stretcher, and Joe stapled it tight.

THEY WERE EATING their lunches out of paper sacks beneath a stand of yellow-leaved aspen when they saw the SUV coming. Joe's Ford ranch pickup was parked to the side of the aspens with the doors open so they could hear the radio. Paul Harvey News, the only program they could get clearly so far from town. Bud hated Paul Harvey nearly as much as silence. and had spent days vainly fiddling with the radio to get another station and cursing the fact that static-filled Rush Limbaugh was the only other choice.

"Who is that?" Bud Jr. asked, gesturing with his chin toward the SUV.

Joe didn't recognize the vehicle—it was at least two miles away—and he chewed his sandwich as the SUV crawled up the two-track that coursed through the gray-green patina of sagebrush.

"Think it's the law?" Bud asked, as the truck got close

8

enough so they could see several long antennas bristling from the roof. It was a new-model GMC, a Yukon or a Suburban.

"You have something to be scared of?" Joe asked.

"Of course not," Bud said, but he looked jumpy. Bud was sitting on a downed log and he turned and looked behind him into the trees, as if planning an escape route. Joe thought how many times in the past his approach had likely caused the same kind of mild panic in hunters, fishermen, campers.

Joe asked, "Okay, what did you do *now*?"

"Nothing," Bud Jr. said, but Joe had enough experience talking with guilty men to know something was up. The way they wouldn't hold his gaze, the way they found something to do with their hands that wasn't necessary, like Bud Jr., who was tearing off pieces of his bread crust and rolling them into little balls.

"She swore she was eighteen," Bud said, almost as an aside, "and she sure as hell looked it. Shit, she was in the Stockman's having cocktails, so I figured they must have carded her, right?"

Joe snorted and said nothing. It was interesting to him how an old-line, hard-assed three-generation rancher like Bud Longbrake could have raised a son so unlike him. Bud blamed his first wife for coddling Bud Jr., and complained in private to Joe that Missy, Bud's second wife and Marybeth's mother, was now doing the same thing. "Who the fuck cares if he's *creative*," Bud had said, spitting out the word as if it were a bug that had crawled into his mouth. "He's as worthless as tits on a bull."

In his peripheral vision, Joe watched as Bud Jr. stood up from his log as the SUV churned up the hill. He was ready to run.

9

It was then that Joe noticed the GMC had official State of Wyoming plates. Two men inside, the driver and another wearing a tie and a suit coat.

The GMC parked next to Joe's Ford and the passenger door opened.

"Is one of you Joe Pickett?" asked the man in the tie. He looked vaguely familiar to Joe, somebody he might have seen in the newspaper. He was slightly built and had a once-eager face that now said, "I'm harried." The man pulled a heavy jacket over his blazer and zipped it up against the cold breeze.

"He is," Bud Jr. said quickly, pointing to Joe as if naming the defendant in court.

"I'm Chuck Ward, chief of staff for Governor Rulon," the man said, looking Joe over as if he were disappointed with what he saw but trying to hide it. "The governor would like to meet with you as soon as possible."

Joe stood and wiped his palms on his Wranglers so he could shake hands with Ward.

Joe said, "The governor is in town?"

"We came up in the state plane."

"That was the jet we saw, Joe. Cool, the governor," Bud Jr. said, obviously relieved that the GMC hadn't come for *him*. "I've been reading about him in the paper. He's a wild man, crazy as a tick. He challenged some senator to a drinking contest to settle an argument, and he installed a shooting range behind the governor's mansion. That's my kind of governor, man," he said, grinning.

Ward shot Bud Jr. a withering look. Joe thought it was telling that Ward didn't counter the stories but simply turned red.

"You want me to go with you?" Joe asked, nodding toward the GMC.

10

"Yes, please."

"How about I follow you in?" Joe said. "I need to pick my girls up at school this afternoon so I need a vehicle. We'll be done by then, I'd guess."

Ward looked at him. "We have to be."

Joe stuffed his gloves into his back pocket and picked up his tools from the ground and handed them to Bud Jr. "I'll ask your dad to send someone out here to pick you up."

Bud's face fell. "You're just leaving me here?"

"Get some work done," Joe said, gesturing toward the fence that went on for miles. "Come on, Maxine," he called to his dog.

Bud Jr. turned away and folded his arms across his chest in a pout.

"Quite a hand," Ward said sarcastically as Joe walked past him toward the Ford.

"Yup," Joe said.

THE GOVERNOR'S PLANE was the only aircraft on the tarmac at the Saddlestring Regional Airport. Joe followed Chuck Ward to a small parking lot at the side of the General Aviation building.

Joe had heard the stories about the drinking contest and the shooting range. Rulon was an enigma, which seemed to be part of his charm. A one time high-profile defense lawyer, Rulon became a federal prosecutor who had a 95 percent conviction rate. Since the election, Joe had read stories in the newspaper about Rulon rushing out of his residence in his pajamas and a Russian fur cap to help state troopers on the scene of a twelve-car pileup on I-80. Another recounted how he'd been elected chairman of the Western Governors' Association because of his reputation for taking on Washington bureaucrats and getting his way,

11

which included calling hotel security to have all federal agency personnel escorted from the room of their first meeting. Each new story about Rulon's eccentricities seemed to make him more popular with voters, despite the fact that he was a Democrat in a state that was 70 percent Republican.

Governor Spencer Rulon sat behind a scarred table in the small conference room. Aerial photos of Twelve Sleep County adorned the walls, and a large picture window looked out over the runway. The table was covered with stacks of files from the governor's briefcase, which was open on a chair near him.

He stood up as Ward and Joe entered the room and thrust out his hand.

"Joe Pickett, I'm glad Chuck found you."

"Governor," Joe said, removing his hat.

"Sit down, sit down," Rulon said. "Chuck, you too."

Governor Rulon was a big man in every regard, with a round face and a large gut, an unruly shock of silver-flecked brown hair, a quick sloppy smile, and darting eyes. He was a manic *presence*, exuding energy, his movements quick and impatient. Joe had seen him work a crowd and marveled at the way Rulon could talk with lawyers, politicians, ranchers, or minimum wage clerks in their own particular language. Or, if he chose, in a language all his own.

Ward looked at his wristwatch. "We've got fifteen minutes before we need to leave for Powell."

"A speech for the Community College Commission," the governor said to Joe before settling back in his chair. "They want more money—now that's a shocker—so they'll be willing to wait."

Joe put his hat crown down on the table. He was suddenly nervous about why he'd been summoned because there was no way to anticipate what Rulon might do or say. Joe had assumed on the drive into town that it had something to do with the circumstances of his dismissal, but now he wasn't so sure. It was becoming clear to him by Ward's manner that the chief of staff didn't really like the purpose of the meeting, whatever it was.

"Everybody wants more money," Rulon said to Joe. "Everybody has their hand out. Luckily, I'm able to feed the beast."

Joe nodded in recognition of one of the governor's most familiar catchphrases. In budget hearings, on the senate floor, at town meetings, Rulon was known for listening for a while, then standing up and shouting, *"Feed the beast! Feed the beast!"*

The governor turned his whole attention to Joe, and thrust his face across the table at him. "So you're a cowboy now, eh?"

Joe swallowed. "I work for my father-in-law, Bud Longbrake."

"Bud's a good man." Rulon nodded.

"I've got my résumé out in five states."

Rulon shook his head. "Ain't going to happen."

Joe was sure the governor was right. Despite his qualifications, any call to his former boss, Randy Pope, asking for a job reference would be met with Pope's distorted tales of Joe's bad attitude, insubordination, and long record of destruction of government property. Only the last charge was true, Joe thought.

"Nothing wrong with being a cowboy," Rulon said.

"Nope."

"Hell, we put one on our license plates. Do you remember when we met?"

"Yes."

"It was at that museum dedication last spring. I took you and your lovely wife for a little drive. How is she, by the way? Marybeth, right?"

"She's doing fine," Joe said, thinking, *He remembered her name*. "She's got a company that's really doing well."

"MBP Management."

Amazing, Joe thought.

"And the kids? Two girls?"

"Sheridan's fifteen, in ninth grade. Lucy's eleven, in fourth grade."

"And they say I have a tough job," Rulon said. "Beautiful girls. You should be proud. A couple of real pistols."

Joe shifted in his chair, disarmed.

"When we met," the governor continued, "I gave you a little pop quiz. I asked you if you'd arrest me for fishing without a license like you did my predecessor. Do you remember me asking you that?"

"Yes," Joe said, flushing.

"Do you remember what you said?"

"I said I'd arrest you."

Chuck Ward shot a disapproving glance at Joe when he heard that.

The governor laughed, sat back. "That impressed me."

Joe didn't know it had. He and Marybeth had debated it at the time.

Rulon said, "So when we were in the air on the way to Powell, I was reading through a file that is keeping me up nights and I saw the Bighorns and I thought of Joe Pickett. I ordered my pilot to land and told Chuck to go find you. How would you like to work for the state again?"

Joe didn't see it coming.

Chuck Ward squirmed in his chair and looked out the window at the plane as if he wished he were on it.

14

Joe said, "Doing what?"

Rulon reached out and took a thick manila file off one of the stacks and slid it across the table. Joe picked it up and read the tab. It read "Yellowstone Zone of Death."

Joe looked up, his mouth dry.

"That's what they're calling it," Rulon said. "You've heard about the situation, no doubt."

"Everybody has."

The case had been all over the state, regional, and national news the past summer—a multiple homicide in Yellowstone National Park. The murderer confessed, but a technicality in the law had set him free.

"It's making me crazy and pissing me off," Rulon said. "Not just the murders or that gasbag Clay McCann. But this."

Rulon reached across the table and threw open the file. On top was a copy of a short, handwritten letter addressed to the governor.

"Read it," Rulon said.

Dear Gov Spence:

I live and work in Yellowstone, or, as we in the Gopher State Five call it, "the 'Stone." I've come to really like the 'Stone, and Wyoming. I may even become a resident so I can vote for you.

In my work I get around the park a lot. I see things, and my friends do too. There are some things going on here that could be of great significance to you, and they bother us a lot. And there is something going on here with the resources that may deeply impact the State of Wyoming, especially your cash flow situation. Please contact me so I can tell you what is happening.

I want to tell you and show you in person, not by letter.

This correspondence must be held in complete confidence.
There are people up here who don't want this story to be
told. My e-mail address is yellowdick@yahoo.com. *I'll*
be waiting to hear from you.

It was signed Yellowstone Dick.

Joe frowned. He noted the date stamp: July 15.

"I don't understand," Joe said.

"I didn't either," Rulon said, raising his eyebrows and leaning forward again. "I try to answer all of my mail, but I put that one aside when I got it. I wasn't sure what to do, since it seems like a crank letter. I get 'em all the time, believe me. Finally, I sent a copy over to DCI and asked them to check up on it. It took 'em a month, damn them, but they traced it with the Internet people and got back to me and said Yellowstone Dick was the nickname of an employee in Yellowstone named Rick Hoening. That name ring a bell?"

"No."

"He was one of the victims murdered by Clay McCann. The e-mail was sent to me a week before Hoening met his untimely demise."

Joe let that sink in.

"Ever hear of the Gopher State Five?"

Joe shook his head.

"Me neither. And I'll never know what he was talking about, especially that bit about deeply impacting my cash flow. You know how serious that could be, don't you?"

Joe nodded. The State of Wyoming was booming. Mineral severance taxes from coal, gas, and petroleum extraction were making state coffers flush. So much money was coming in that legislators couldn't spend it fast enough and were squirreling it away into massive trust funds and only spending the interest. The excess billions allowed the governor to feed the beast like it had never been fed before.

Joe felt overwhelmed. "What are you asking me?"

Rulon beamed and swung his head toward Chuck Ward. Ward stared coolly back.

"I want you to go up there and see if you can figure out what the hell Yellowstone Dick was writing to me about."

Joe started to object but Rulon waved him off. "I know what you're about to say. I've got DCI and troopers and lawyers up the wazoo. But the problem is I don't have jurisdiction. It's National Park Service, and I can't just send all my guys up there to kick ass and take names. We have to make requests, and the responses take months to get back. We have to be *invited* in," he said, screwing up his face on the word *invited* as if he'd bitten into a lemon. "It's in my state, look at the map. But I can't go in unless they *invite* me. The Feds don't care about what Yellowstone Dick said about my cash flow, they're so angry about McCann getting off. Not that I blame them, of course. But I want you to go up there and see what you can find out. Clay McCann got away with these murders and created a free-fire zone in the northern part of my state, and I won't stand for it."

Joe's mind swirled.

"You're unofficial," Rulon said, his eyes gleaming. "Without portfolio. You're not my official representative, although you are. You'll be put back into the state system, you'll get back pay, you'll get your pension and benefits back, you'll get a state paycheck with a nice raise. But you're on your own. You're nobody, just a dumb-ass game warden poking around by yourself."

Joe almost said, *That I can do with no problem,* but held his tongue. Instead, he looked to Ward for clarification. "We'll

17

tell Randy Pope to reinstate you as a game warden," Ward said wearily, wanting no part of this. "But the administration will *borrow* you."

"Borrow me?" Joe said. "Pope won't do it."

"The hell he won't," Rulon said, smacking his palm against the tabletop. "I'm the governor. He will do what I tell him, or he'll have *his* résumé out in five states."

Joe knew how state government worked. This wasn't how.

"Without portfolio," Joe said, repeating the phrases. "*Not* your official representative. But I am."

"Now you're getting it," the governor said, encouraging Joe. "And that means if you screw up and get yourself in trouble, as you are fully capable of doing based on your history, I'll deny to my grave this meeting took place."

Chuck Ward broke in. "Governor, I feel it's my responsibility, once again, to advise against this."

"Your opinion, Chuck, would be noted in the minutes if we had any, but we don't," Rulon said in a tone that suggested to Joe that the two of them had similar disagreements as a matter of routine.

The governor turned back to Joe. "You're going to ask me why, and why you, when I have a whole government full of bodies to choose from."

"I was going to ask you that."

"All I can say is that it's a hunch. But I'm known for my good hunches. I've followed your career, Joe, even before I got elected. You seem to have a natural inclination to get yourself square into the middle of situations a normal thinking person would avoid. I'd say it's a gift if it wasn't so damned dangerous at times. Your wife would probably concur."

Joe nodded in silent agreement.

"I think you've got integrity. You showed me that when you said you'd arrest me. You seem to be able to think for yourself—a rare trait, and one that I share—no matter what the policy is or conventional wisdom dictates. As I know, that's either a good quality or a fatal flaw. It got me elected governor of this great state, and it got you fired.

"But you have a way of getting to the bottom of things, is what I see. Just ask the Scarlett brothers." He raised his eyebrows and said, "No, don't. *They're all dead.*"

Joe felt like he'd been slapped. He'd been there when the brothers turned against each other and went to war. And he'd performed an act that was the source of such black shame in him he still couldn't think about it. In his mind, the months of feeding cattle, fixing fences, and overseeing Bud Jr. weren't even close to penance for what he'd done. And it had nothing to do with why he'd been fired.

"When I think of crime committed out-of-doors, I think of Joe Pickett," Rulon said. "Simple as that."

Joe's face felt hot. Everything the governor said seemed to have dual meanings. He couldn't be sure if he was being praised or accused, or both.

"I don't know what to say."

Rulon smiled knowingly. "Yes you do. You want to say YES! You want to shout it out!" He leaned back in his chair and dropped his voice an octave. "But you need to talk to Marybeth. And Bud Longbrake needs to hire a new ranch foreman."

"I do need to talk to Marybeth," Joe said lamely.

"Of course. But let me know by tonight so we can notify Mr. Pope and get this show on the road. Take the file, read it. Then call with your acceptance."

Ward tapped his wrist. "Governor ..."

"I know," Rulon said, standing and shoving papers into his briefcase. "I know."

Joe used the arms of his chair to push himself to his feet. His legs were shaky.

"Tell the pilot we're ready," Rulon said to Ward. "We need to get going."

Ward hustled out of the room, followed by Governor Rulon.

"Governor," Joe called after him. Rulon hesitated at the doorway.

"I may need some help in the park," Joe said, thinking of Nate Romanowski.

"Do what you need to do," Rulon said sharply. "Don't ask me for permission. You're not working for me. I can't even remember who you are. You're fading from my mind even as we speak. How can I possibly keep track of every state employee?"

Outside, the engines of the plane began to wind up.

"Call me," the governor said.

JOE'S HEAD WAS still spinning from the meeting as he wheeled the Ford into the turn-in at Saddlestring Elementary. Lucy was standing outside with her books clutched to her chest in the midst of a gaggle of fourth-grade girls who were talking to one another with great arm-waving exuberance. When all the girls turned their faces to him and watched him pull up to the curb, he knew something was up. Lucy waved goodbye to her friends—Lucy was a popular girl— and climbed in. As always, Lucy looked as fresh and attractive as she had at breakfast.

"Sheridan's in big trouble," Lucy said. "She got a detention, so we'll have to wait for her."

"What do you mean, big trouble?" Joe asked sharply.

He wished Lucy hadn't told him her news with such obvious glee. He continued to drive the four blocks to the high school, where Sheridan had just started the month before.

"Some boy said something at lunch and Sherry decked him," Lucy said. "Knocked him right down to the floor, is what I heard."

"That doesn't sound like Sheridan," Joe said.

"It would if you knew her better." Lucy smiled. "She's a hothead when it comes to her family."

Joe pulled over to the curb and turned to Lucy, realizing he had misread his youngest daughter. She was proud of her sister, not happy with the fact that she was in trouble. "What exactly are you telling me?"

"Everybody's talking about it," Lucy said. "Some boy made a crack about you in the lunchroom, and Sheridan decked him."

"About me?"

Lucy nodded. "He said something about you not being the game warden anymore, that you got fired."

"Who was the boy?"

"Jason Kiner."

That stung. Jason was Phil Kiner's son. Kiner was the game warden who had been assigned Joe's district by Randy Pope. Joe had always liked Phil, but was disturbed that Kiner never called him for background or advice since assuming the post and moving his family into Joe's old house near Wolf Mountain. Joe assumed Pope had told Phil to steer clear of the former inhabitant.

"And Sheridan hit him?"

Lucy nodded eagerly, watching him closely for his reaction.

Joe took a deep breath and shook his head sadly, thinking

it was what he should do as a father when he really wanted to say, *Good for Sheridan*.

JOE AND LUCY waited a half-hour in front of the high school for Sheridan to be released. Lucy worked on homework assigned by her teacher, Mrs. Hanson, and Joe thought about how he would present the opportunity the governor had given him to Marybeth. He had mixed feelings about it, even though Rulon had been right that Joe's first reaction had been to yell *Yes!* The "Yellowstone Zone of Death" file was facedown on the bench seat between them.

"Mrs. Hanson says Americans use up most of the world's energy," Lucy said. "She says we're selfish and we need to learn how to conserve so we can help save our planet."

"Oh?" Joe said. Lucy loved her teacher, a bright-eyed young woman just two years out of college. Joe and Marybeth had met Mrs. Hanson during back-to-school night and had been duly impressed and practically bowled over by her obvious enthusiasm for her job and her passion for teaching. Since Lucy's third-grade teacher had been a weary, bitter twenty-four-year warhorse in the system who was counting the days until her retirement, Mrs. Hanson was a breath of fresh mountain air. Over the past month, Lucy had participated in a canned-food drive for the disadvantaged in the county and on the reservation, and a candy sale with profits dedicated to Amazon rainforest restoration. Lucy couldn't wait to go to school in the morning, and seemed to start most sentences with, "Mrs. Hanson says …"

"Mrs. Hanson says we should stop driving gas-guzzling cars and turn the heat down in our houses."

"Gas-guzzling cars like this?" Joe asked, patting the dashboard.

"Yes. Mrs. Hanson drives one of those good cars."

"Do you mean a hybrid?"

"Yes. And Mr. and Mrs. Hanson recycle everything. They have boxes for glass, paper, and metal. Mrs. Hanson says they take the boxes to the recycling center every weekend."

"We have a recycling center?" Joe asked.

"It's in Bozeman or Billings."

Joe frowned. "Billings is a hundred and twenty miles away."

"So?"

"Driving a hundred and twenty miles to put garbage in a recycling bin doesn't exactly save energy," Joe said.

"Mrs. Hanson says the only way we can save the planet is for all of us to pitch in and work together to make a better world."

Joe had no answer to that, since he didn't want to appear to Lucy to be in favor of actively contributing to a worse world.

"Mrs. Hanson wanted me to ask you a question."

"Really?"

"She wants to know why, if you're a cowboy now, you don't ride a horse? She says horses are much better for the environment than trucks and ATVs."

"Do you want me to pick you up from school on a horse?" Joe asked, trying to keep his voice calm.

Lucy started to say yes but thought better of it. "Maybe you can still come get me in a truck, but you can ride a horse around all day on the ranch to help save the planet."

"What are you reading?" he asked, looking at her open spiral notebook.

"We're studying the Kyoto Protocol."

"*In fourth grade?* Don't they teach you math or science at that school?"

Lucy looked up, exasperated with her father. "Mrs.

23

Hanson says it's never too early to learn about important issues. She says, 'Think globally and act locally.'"

ON THE STATE highway to the Longbrake Ranch. Sheridan stared out the passenger window as if the familiar landscape held new fascination for her. Lucy continued to do her homework with the notebook spread open on her lap.

"Do you want to talk about it?" Joe asked finally.

"Not really," Sheridan said.

"We'll need to discuss it, you know."

Sheridan sighed an epic sigh, and without seeing it, Joe knew she performed the eye roll that was such a part of her attitude these days.

Joe glanced over at his oldest daughter, noting again to himself how much her profile mirrored Marybeth's. In the past six months, Sheridan had become a woman physically, and borrowed her mother's clothing sometimes without asking. Joe had trouble believing she could possibly be fifteen already. How had it happened? When did it happen? How did this little girl he knew so well, his best buddy while she was growing up, suddenly become a mysterious creature?

"Did you really knock him to the floor?" Lucy asked her sister.

After a long pause, Sheridan said, "Jason Kiner is an ass."

Joe wished the reason for the lunchroom argument had been something besides him. He hated thinking that his daughters could be ashamed of him, ashamed of what he did, what he was now. A cowboy. A cowboy who worked for his father-in-law.

But, he thought, *a cowboy with an offer.*

3

J OE, MARYBETH, AND their daughters trekked across the hay meadow for dinner in the main ranch house with Bud and Missy Longbrake and two sullen Mexican ranch hands. As they walked across the shorn meadow the dried hay and fallen leaves crunched under their feet, the sounds sharp. The brief but intense light of the dying sun slipped behind the mountains and lit up the yellow-gold leaves of the river bottom cottonwoods, igniting the meadow with color. Despite the fact that there wasn't a high-rise building within 200 miles and Sheridan had never been to New York, she referred to this magical moment each evening as "walking down Broadway."

The light doused just as they approached the main house. The evening was still and cold, the air thin, the sky close. A milky parenthesis framing the slice of moon signaled that snow could come at any time. Joe had brought a flashlight for the walk back to their house after dinner.

Because Marybeth had arrived home later than usual, Joe had not yet had a chance to talk to her about his meeting with the governor.

Lucy told her mother about Sheridan's detention. Marybeth nodded and squinted at her oldest daughter, who glared at Lucy for telling.

"No talk about Sheridan or the detention during dinner," Marybeth told Lucy.

"You mean not to tell Grandmother Missy?" Lucy said.

"That's what I mean."

Joe agreed. He preferred internal family discussions to remain internal, without Missy's opinion on anything. It pleased him that Marybeth felt the same way. In fact, Joe thought he detected a growing tension between Marybeth and her mother lately. He stifled the urge to fan the flames. Joe and Marybeth had talked about buying a house of their own in town and had met with a realtor. In the realtor's office, Joe was ashamed to admit he had never owned a home before—they had always lived in state housing—and therefore had no equity. The meeting concluded quickly after that. He had no idea how expensive it was to buy a house with no track record, and they knew they needed to save more money in order to build up a deposit and get good financing. To relieve his guilt on the drive back to the ranch, Marybeth had pointed out the comfort of the situation they were in—a home, meals, the undeniable beauty of the ranch itself. But Joe found himself too stubborn to concede all her points, although she certainly was practical. Looming over the argument, though, was the specter of Missy, Marybeth's mother.

"I wish that stove would get here," Sheridan said as they approached the ranch house. "It would be nice to eat dinner in our own house for once."

It had been only a week since the ancient stove in the log home quit working. But Marybeth didn't point it out because she was getting smarter about choosing her battles with Sheridan, Joe thought. In fact, it seemed as if the two were starting to come to a new understanding in regard to each other. Mysterious.

26

Joe opened the door for everyone.

As Marybeth passed him she raised her eyebrows, said, "I heard the governor's plane was at the airport today."

"We can talk about that after dinner too," Joe said.

That stopped Marybeth for a moment and she studied his face. He stifled a grin, but she could read him like a book.

EVEN WITH THE other employees and the whole Pickett family in the dining room, the table still had plenty of empty chairs since it had once been where a dozen ranch hands ate breakfast and dinner, back when the Longbrake Ranch was in its heyday. Maria, the ranch cook and housekeeper, served steaming platters of the simple ranch fare Bud Sr. liked best, inch-and-a-half-thick steaks, baked potatoes, green salad (lettuce and tomatoes only), white bread, apple cobbler. Bud Sr. called it "real food," as opposed to anything that didn't include beef. Joe tended to agree with Bud Sr. on that one. There was a time when real food was served five nights a week. Since Missy had arrived, it had been cut down to once during the week and on Sunday.

They sat down at the table in the seating arrangement that had come about since they moved to the ranch. Bud no longer sat at the head of the table. His old chair was now occupied by Missy. The only explanation for the change was a single throwaway line by Missy earlier in the summer, saying, "I need to be closer to the kitchen door so I can help Maria serve." But, as far as Joe could tell, Missy had never helped Maria do anything except provide tips on her makeup. Not that Bud Sr. seemed to care about the power shift. That was one thing about Bud, Joe thought. He was so in love with his bride of one year that he was blind to everything else. He had conceded authority with almost giddy enthusiasm.

"Where's Bud Jr.?" Joe asked.

"In his room," Bud Sr. said, spearing a thick steak with his fork and sliding it onto his plate. "His back's hurting. He says he may never walk again."

Lucy looked up in alarm.

"Not really, darling," Bud Sr. said. "That's just how Bud Jr. is. Everything's a big deal."

"It's called creativity," Missy said softly.

Eduardo, Maria's husband and one of the ranch hands at the table, described driving out to the fence line that afternoon to retrieve Bud Jr. He found him lying on his back in the cheater grass, moaning. He brought him home.

"Shamazz, eet look like he was dead," Eduardo said in a heavy accent. Pascal, the other hand, tried to disguise a sudden bout of laughter by coughing into his hand. Pascal made no secret of his contempt for Bud Jr.

Missy seemed distracted, and had hardly looked up. Joe had to admit how attractive she was for her age, and she looked especially good tonight as she sat there and picked at the tiniest portions possible of everything on her plate. She wore a charcoal cashmere sweater and a thin rope of pearls, dark lipstick. Her hair was perfect, not a strand of gray. When she caught Joe watching her, she glared back for a second before breaking the gaze.

Joe wondered what he had caught her thinking about.

"You're dressed up," Marybeth said to her mother. "Are you going out?"

"I've got a meeting in town tonight," Missy said dismissively. "Just the county arts council thing."

"My little artiste." Bud Sr. grinned and reached over and stroked Missy's shoulder. "Don't you want some more steak?"

"No, thank you. You know how I feel about red meat."

28

Bud shook his head. "She's as tiny as a bird, my little artiste."

Now Sheridan coughed in her hand. Marybeth shot her daughter a look.

"Good steak," Joe said.

"Damned good steak." Bud Sr. nodded. "Real food."

"Ees good," Eduardo said, and Pascal agreed.

Marybeth looked at Joe, her eyes saying, *Get me out of here*.

ON THE WAY back to their house, Joe shone his flashlight on the path and everyone followed him holding hands in a line: Marybeth, Sheridan, Lucy.

"Come along, my little ducklings," he said.

"Come along, my little artistes," Sheridan said. "My tiny little birds."

Joe laughed.

"Sheridan," Marybeth said sternly. "Don't mock." Then: "Joe, you're not helping the situation."

"Sorry."

The stiff grass had a sheath of beaded moisture. It would frost tonight, Joe thought.

"Look," Sheridan said after a moment, "you don't have to say anything about what happened today at school. I know I screwed up. I never should've taken the bait from that ass Jason Kiner. I'll never do that again, not because he doesn't deserve a good ass kicking, but because it embarrassed me and it embarrassed you. I'm better than that. Okay? Can we drop it now?"

Joe waited for Marybeth to answer. This was her department.

"Okay," Marybeth said in a way that made it clear the discussion was over.

"She said 'ass' twice," Lucy whispered, and Joe laughed again. Luckily, so did Marybeth and Sheridan, both relieved that a confrontation had been averted.

As they approached their house, Joe squeezed his wife's hand in the dark and she squeezed back.

"I KNOW THAT look in her eye," Marybeth said later, once the girls were in their rooms, Sheridan doing biology homework and Lucy working on another project for Mrs. Hanson.

"What look?" Joe asked from the couch. The file the governor had given him was in his lap. The woodstove was lit and ticking as it warmed, the television was off. He'd been waiting for his wife to change clothes after they returned from dinner. She hadn't had time earlier. Even in her worn baggy sweats, Joe felt a *zing* when he saw her come down the hallway. He liked how she walked across the floor to him. His wife was blond, trim, attractive. Although she was the same age as Joe, when he looked at her he saw the image of the girl he had seen for the first time on the campus of the University of Wyoming, the girl he knew, that instant, he wanted to marry. It was the best decision he ever made, and he still felt that he could be exposed at any time as not being worthy of her. She brought a purpose to his life. And he was as crazy in love with her as Bud was with Missy.

"That determined look in her eye," she said, "combined with the sweater and the pearls."

Joe finally got it that Marybeth was talking about her mother.

She said, "It's like a knight putting on his armor or an Indian painting his face. She's getting ready to take action."

"What action?" Joe asked, patiently waiting for Marybeth to finish with her theory so he could tell her about the offer.

"I don't know for sure, but I'm suspicious. I think we're looking at the opening phase of another round of trading up."

Joe nodded. Bud Longbrake was Missy's fourth husband. The first, Marybeth's father, was a small-time defense attorney in Denver. The second was the owner of a real estate company. The third was a developer and state senator in Arizona who was eventually convicted of fraud. Each man had more social status than the last and a bigger bank account. Missy had each new potential husband lined up, thoroughly smitten, and locked-in before announcing her intention to divorce. As a game warden, Joe had observed predators like coyotes, eagles, and wolves for years. None of them held a candle to his mother-in-law.

"Who do you suppose is the target?" Joe asked as Marybeth joined him on the couch. The log home was sturdy, dark, and comfortable, despite its age. Generations of ranch foremen and their families had lived there before Joe and Marybeth, and they'd taken good care of it and, like so many old ranch structures, added on. There were three bedrooms. The kitchen was bright and sunny and looked out over the Twelve Sleep River, and the living room where Joe sat—the original room of the home—had elk and deer antlers on the walls and cattle brands burned into the logs. A rarely used stone fireplace dominated the north wall. A family photo covered a section of the wall where, for a reason never explained, someone had fired six bullets into a log from inside. Walking through the house in the dark was an adventure. Interior corners were out of square and floors weren't level from room to room. The house had character and was filled with the benevolent legacy of past cowboys and their families. Joe loved the place, despite the circumstances of how they had come to live there.

31

Marybeth said, "I've been thinking about it, and I can come up with one man. Earl Alden."

"Ah," Joe said. They called him the Earl of Lexington. Alden was a Southern multibillionaire media mogul who had recently bought the former Scarlett Ranch. He divided his time between the ranch and three other residences in Lexington, New York City, and Chamonix. The rumor was that Mrs. Alden didn't like their ranch, and she rarely came with him. The fact that there was a Mrs. Alden had never posed much of a hurdle to Missy before.

"The Earl just gave a couple hundred thousand to the Twelve Sleep County Arts Council," Marybeth said. "So it's possible he'll be at the meeting tonight."

"Where Missy can begin her charm offensive," Joe said.

"Exactly."

Joe said, "How did you turn out so well?"

Marybeth smiled. "My mother wouldn't agree. She wonders where she went wrong." Missy made no secret of how she had hoped Marybeth—the smartest of her children—would become a corporate attorney or a U.S. senator, or at least follow her example and marry one.

Joe patted himself on the chest. "I was your downfall."

Marybeth sat back and facetiously looked him over, nodding. "Yes. Marrying you doomed me. Then you made me have our children. Now I'm trapped."

Joe thought, *She's kidding but her mother is not.*

JOE TOLD HER about the offer from the governor. He gauged her reaction carefully as he laid it out. He noticed that while he spoke, she glanced several times at the file folder in his lap.

When he was through, she hesitated for a beat and said, "Can we trust him?"

32

"The governor?"

"Yes."

He wasn't sure how to answer. He said, "If we can't trust our governor, who can we trust?"

She rolled her eyes. "I need a glass of wine."

Joe thought about her question while she was gone. He dug deep. Did he trust Spencer Rulon?

When she came back with two glasses, he said, "No, not completely."

"The deal as you describe it makes me uncomfortable," she said. "They either hire you back or they don't. From what you tell me, you'll be operating on your own with no backup and no support. If you get into trouble, you're on your own. *We're* on our own. What is that phrase politicians like to use?"

"Plausible deniability."

"Right. And how do we know Randy Pope won't do everything he can to undermine you at every turn?"

"I expect him to do that," Joe said.

She sighed, sipped her wine. "Remember how frustrated you were with the bureaucracy, with fighting against the system? Do you think you could live within it again—do you think it's changed at all?"

Joe shook his head. "Not a bit."

"Do we move back to our house?"

"I don't think so. He never mentioned it. Would you want that?"

"No, although I wouldn't mind a change of scenery if that meant we could get our lives back."

Me too, he thought.

"The last time you had to leave us it wasn't very good," she said, not meeting his eyes.

When he was assigned temporarily to Jackson, Joe

thought. No, it wasn't very good for them. In fact, his absence and the things that happened with both of them had damaged their marriage. It was only now healing. Time and their joint determination to right the ship had created scar tissue. But the wound was still there, and would always be there, he supposed.

"I'd want you to come this time," Joe said. "Bring Sheridan and Lucy every chance you get. It'll be tough with school and activities, but let's make sure we stay close and in contact."

She nodded, thinking it over. "I've always wanted to go to Yellowstone, as you know."

"I know."

"But we've never gone."

Joe sighed, and found himself staring at the woodstove.

"Are you going to be able to do this?" she asked.

He looked back. "I have to."

Yellowstone, a place so special and awe-inspiring that after exploring it in 1871, the Hayden Expedition conceived of the original concept of the world's first national park—a set-aside of 2.2 million acres containing more than ten thousand thermal features, canyons, waterfalls, and wild-life—so no man or corporation could ever own it. As a boy, Joe had been to Yellowstone dozens of times. Many of his earliest memories were of geysers, mud pots, bears, and tourists. He had once loved the park unlike anywhere else, and announced to his parents he wanted to live there, to fish, hike, and camp for the rest of his life. It was a magical place and he had preferred it to heaven because at that age Joe didn't think there could be trout streams in the clouds.

His father shared his love for the park, which was the reason they vacationed there year after year. Their mutual love for it was one of the few things they ever agreed on, other than the movie *Shane*. It was the one place, Joe recalled, where his father came alive, stopped drinking, and played at being an amateur geologist—explaining to his two young sons that there were three kinds of thermal features in the world: geysers, mud pots, and fumaroles (steam vents), and Yellowstone featured them all. He remembered his father running down a boardwalk in the Upper Geyser Basin—actually running!—and shouting over his shoulder to his boys to follow him because Old Faithful itself was about to erupt. It was a place where one could look into the cruel molten heart of the earth itself, and Joe had once done exactly that. Or thought he had. It was in a huge lung-shaped hot pool, the water vivid aquamarine, steam hovering above the calm surface. A shaft of sunlight plunged deep into the pool, which looked so inviting but was nearly two hundred degrees, illuminating bleached-white bison bones resting on rock shelves as far down as he could see. Bones! And no bottom to the pool; it simply descended far past where the sun could reach. For years, he had nightmares about those bones, about falling into the pool, about sinking slowly as the water got hotter and hotter, his bones coming to rest on an outcropping.

His brother loved it too, but in a different way.

But he couldn't remember Yellowstone without what came next: the darkest period of his young life.

He'd never been back.

He'd attempted to defeat the demons nine years before, when Sheridan was six and Lucy a baby. Joe had borrowed a tent, and their plan was to spend a week camping in Yellowstone, just as he had done when he was a child. He would cook meals over a campfire, and they'd see the sights: Old Faithful, Mammoth Hot Springs, Norris Geyser Basin, the Grand Canyon of the Yellowstone, the Lower and Upper

Falls. Everything had been ahead of them then and nothing seemed daunting. He'd actually looked forward to going back to the park and putting all the bad memories about it behind him for good. But the week before they went, Marybeth discovered she was pregnant, and the early weeks would mean morning sickness and misery. Although she was willing to gut it out, they postponed the trip for later. It was the year they had been assigned the Saddlestring District, a year before violence entered their lives. And never went very far away.

MARYBETH WAS THE most practical woman Joe had ever known. She ran the finances for the family, her business, her clients. She could see things clearly. Yet she had not even mentioned that if he went back to the state—with a raise—their situation would dramatically improve. That a house in town away from Missy would be within reach.

She looked up and studied his face. He tried not to give his thoughts away. He didn't succeed.

"You really want to do this, don't you?"

Joe said nothing.

"You want to get back into it. You want to carry a badge and a gun again, don't you?"

"I don't like to be a failure," he said.

"Stop it. You're not a failure."

He let that lie. The last thing he wanted was to make her tell him why he wasn't a failure. He could counter every argument.

"Joe, what do you want to do?"

There were so many reasons not to accept the offer. Pope. Bureaucracy. The chance, once again, that the evil he encountered would affect his family.

But ...

36

"Yes, I want to do it."

"Then it's settled," Marybeth said. "Call the governor."

"I love you," he said.

She reached out and squeezed his arm. "I love you too, Joe."

"I don't know why."

She laughed, said, "Because you want to do good, even when you should know better."

WHEN THE KNOCK came at her door, Sheridan quickly typed "Gotta Go" on her computer screen, ending the stupid IM conversation she was having with Jarrod Haynes, and turned back to her biology book as if deep in thought. Jarrod, she thought, liked to talk about Jarrod. Too bad she wasn't as interested in the subject as he was.

"Yes?"

"Can I come in for a minute?"

"Sure, Dad."

Her father entered and shut the door behind him.

"I tried to use the phone," he said. "The line was busy. I need to make a call."

Caught, Sheridan said, "I was on the Internet for a minute."

"For an hour, you mean."

"I'm off now."

"I thought you were studying."

She gestured to her open book. But she could tell that wasn't really why he had knocked.

"Sheridan, I want to tell you that the governor offered me a job today. I'm going to be a game warden again, sort of."

Her first reaction was a mixture of joy and desperation. She was thrilled that her dad had gotten his job back because, well, that's what he was: a game warden. *The* game warden, as far as she was concerned. She had been with him many times while he worked, and she knew how dedicated he was.

Sheridan remembered when she had been an apprentice falconer to Nate Romanowski. Nate had been given a prairie falcon that had been hit by a car. The bird was either aggressive—likely to bite or strike out—or moody, sulking for days in the mews and refusing to eat. It was her opinion that the bird should be set free, that it would never be any good. Nate proved her wrong by taking the bird out and working with it, letting its natural instincts reemerge. The falcon soon became swift and efficient, eager to fly, hunt, and return to Nate. "He just needed a job," Nate told her. "He needed to do what he was born to do. Falcons, like some people, need to *do* things. They can't just exist."

"Does that mean we have to move?" she asked.

"Not this time," he said.

"So will that ass Jason Kiner go away?"

Her dad seemed confused for a minute. He said, "No. Phil Kiner will still be the Saddlestring game warden. I won't really have a district. I'll sort of be working freelance."

"Like a secret agent or something?"

He smiled. She could tell he liked that characterization but didn't want to admit it. "No, more like I'm on loan for special projects."

She felt good about this news, but didn't want to show it too much because that would betray the embarrassment she'd kept hidden since he lost his job.

"Sheridan," her dad said, "I know it's been tough on you with me being out of work and all."

"You're the ranch foreman," she said quickly. "Nothing wrong with that."

"The governor said the same thing. But we both know it's bothered you. With Jason Kiner saying things and all. It's bothered *me*."

She couldn't deny it outright. She said, "Dad, it doesn't matter ..."

But he waved her off. "Don't say it. It's not necessary."

She found herself beaming.

"So you're back," she said.

He grinned. "I'm back."

Her dad, she thought, needed to *do* things.

JOE STUMBLED OVER something in the dark kitchen of their home and nearly crashed to the floor. He righted himself on the counter, turned on the light, and beheld Lucy's project. Three cardboard boxes marked PAPER, GLASS, and METAL. On each, she had written "To Be Recycled." And beneath the writing, she'd drawn a stylized globe with a word balloon reading "Save me."

"Save *me* from falling on my face," Joe grumbled, and moved the recycling boxes into the mudroom so no one else would trip over them.

He dialed the governor's residence in Cheyenne. Spencer Rulon listed his number in the telephone book, something he never tired of announcing to his constituents.

Voicemail: "This is Gov Spence. Please leave your name and number and I'll get back to you. I'll only return calls to my constituents. If you aren't from Wyoming, you need to call *your* governor."

Joe said, "Governor, Joe Pickett. I accept the job. I do need to get a little more information, though. Like whom I work with in your office, how you want me to stay in contact ..."

The governor picked up. He'd obviously been listening.

"Don't call me again," he said brusquely.

"But ..."

"Chuck Ward will be in touch with you. Deal with him for everything."

"Yes, sir."

"And don't call me sir." Joe could hear the governor smacking his receiver with the palm of his hand, or hitting it against the wall. "This is a bad connection. Who did you say was calling?"

JOE WENT INTO the bedroom with a vague sense of unease after his conversation with the governor. He set the feeling aside when Marybeth shut off the lights, came to bed, and started kissing him with an intensity and passion that surprised and delighted him.

He turned toward her and soon they were entwined. With each movement, the old bedsprings squeaked.

When they were through, she said, "I feel like I need a cigarette," although she had never smoked.

"How about another glass of wine?"

"No, I'm tired. Aren't you tired?"

"I'm jazzed up," he confessed.

"You haven't been jazzed up in a while."

"Thanks to you."

She smiled and stroked his jaw. "Good night, Joe."

"I'm going to read for a few minutes."

"What, the file?"

He nodded.

"Not too long," she said, and rolled over.

HE KNEW ABOUT the crime in general. What he didn't know until he read the file were the specifics. He read over the incident reports filed by the national park rangers, as well as clippings from the *West Yellowstone News,* the *Idaho Falls Post-Register,* the *Bozeman Chronicle,* the *Billings Gazette,* the *Casper Star-Tribune,* and a long feature in the *Wall Street Journal* that summarized them all. It was the worst crime ever committed in Yellowstone National Park. But that was only half the story.

On July 21, a West Yellowstone lawyer named Clay McCann parked his car at the Bechler River Ranger Station in the extreme south-west corner of the park, checked in with the ranger at the desk of the visitor center, and hiked in along the trail that followed, and eventually crossed, Boundary Creek. Later that morning, he returned to the center and confessed to shooting and killing four people in a backcountry campsite.

Investigating rangers confirmed the crime.

The victims were found near the bank of Robinson Lake, two miles from the ranger station. All were pronounced dead at the scene, although the bodies were airlifted out to the Idaho Falls hospital.

Jim McCaleb, twenty-six, was a waiter in the Old Faithful Inn and a five-year employee of the park's concessionaire, Zephyr Corporation. Zephyr ran all the facilities and attractions in the park under contract to the government. McCaleb was shot four times in the torso and once in the back of the head with a large-caliber handgun. His body was found half-in and half-out of a dome tent.

Claudia Wade, twenty-four, managed the laundry facility near Lake Lodge. Wade's body was in the same tent as McCaleb's. There were two shotgun blasts to her back, and she'd been shot once in the head with a handgun.

Caitlyn Williams, twenty-six, was a horse wrangler at Roosevelt for Zephyr. Williams's body was sprawled over the campfire pit with a shotgun blast to her back and a single large-caliber wound to her head.

Rick Hoening, twenty-five, was a desk clerk at the Old Faithful Inn. His body was located twenty yards from the others in the campsite, near the trail. Investigators speculated that he'd been the first to encounter the gunman and the first one killed. He'd been shot three times with a handgun, twice with a shotgun, and, like the others, had an additional single shot to the head.

Wade, Williams, and Hoening were also Zephyr Corp. employees. All four victims listed their original home addresses in St. Paul, Minnesota—the Gopher State— although they lived in Gardiner, Montana, or within the park at the time of their murders. The forensic pathologist in Idaho Falls noted that while each had sustained enough wounds to be fatal, the single shots to the head were likely administered after the initial confrontation.

They were the coup de grâce, fired close enough to leave powder burns and guarantee that no one survived the initial assault.

Joe thought, *The Gopher State Five*. But there were only four of them. He read on.

The scene was littered with .45 brass and fired twelve-gauge shotgun shells. The newspaper articles called the incident "overkill," a "senseless slaughter" with "the fury of a crime of passion." One of the rangers who found the bodies was quoted as saying, "He killed them and then he killed them again for good measure. He was a mad dog. There is nothing at the scene to suggest that the guy [McCann] didn't just lose it out there."

There was no question then, and no question now, who had killed them.

Clay McCann willingly handed over two SIG-Sauer P220 .45 ACP semi-automatic handguns and a Browning BT-99

Micro twelve-gauge shotgun to the park rangers. Then he shocked the rangers by asking for them back. They refused.

When asked why he did it, McCann made the statement that became infamous, the words that became the subhead of every story written about the slaughter at the time:

"I did it because they made fun of me, and because I could."

At the time, no one imagined the possibility that Clay McCann would be released from jail three months later to return to his home and law practice.

That he'd committed the perfect crime.

4

"Explain this to me again," Nate Romanowski said to Joe over coffee in the small dining room of Alisha Whiteplume's home on the Wind River Indian reservation.

"It's about jurisdiction and venue, and what they call 'vicinage,'" Joe said. "It's a hidden loophole in the federal law. Or at least it was hidden until recently."

A large-scale map of Yellowstone was spread out on the table between them with cups of coffee and the pot holding down the edges.

"Yellowstone was established as the first national park in the world in 1872 by an act of Congress. The boundaries were drawn before Wyoming, Idaho, and Montana were granted statehood," Joe said, pointing at the strips of national park land that extended beyond the square border of Wyoming—which contained more than 92 percent of the park—north into Montana and west into Idaho. "About two hundred and sixty square miles of Yellowstone is in Montana, and about fifty in Idaho. The law in Yellowstone is federal law, not state law. If a crime is committed there, the perp is bound over under federal statutes and tried either inside the park at a courthouse in Mammoth Hot Springs, or sent to federal district court in Cheyenne. The states have no jurisdiction at all."

Nate nodded while he traced the boundary of the park with his finger on the map. He was tall with wide shoulders and a blond ponytail bound with a falconer's leather jess. He had clear ice-blue eyes and a knife-blade nose set between twin shelves of cheekbones. A long scar he received three years before from a surgical knife ran down the side of his face from his scalp to his jawbone.

Joe continued. "Because Congress wanted to keep Yellowstone all in one judicial district, it overlaps a little bit into two other states, these strips of Montana and Idaho. Got that?"

"Got it," Nate said, a little impatiently.

"That's where the problem comes in with Clay McCann and the murders," Joe said. He'd read most of the file the night before and finished it before breakfast that morning before taking the girls to school and driving to the reservation. "Article Three of the Constitution says the accused is entitled to a 'local trial,' meaning a venue in the state, and a 'jury trial' but doesn't say where the jury has to come from. The Sixth Amendment of the Constitution specifies a 'local jury trial'—that's the vicinage. That means the jury would have to come from the state—Idaho—and the district—Wyoming—where the crime took place."

Nate stopped his finger on the thin strip of Idaho on the map. Boundary Creek separated Wyoming and Idaho within the park. "You mean the jury would have to come from here? Within these fifty miles?"

"Right. Except no one lives there. Not one person has a residence in that strip of the national park. So no jury can be drawn from a population of zero."

"Shit," Nate said.

"Clay McCann declined to be tried in Cheyenne, which

was his right to decide. He demanded to be tried where the crime was committed, by a jury from the state and district, as the Constitution states. The federal prosecutors in charge of the case couldn't get around the loophole in the law, and still can't. It was never an issue before, and there is no precedent to bypass it. The only thing that can be done is to change the district or change the Constitution, and I guess there is going to be legislation to do that. But even if it's passed …"

Nate finished for Joe, "Clay McCann still walks. Because they can't create a law after the fact and then go back on the guy."

Joe nodded.

"The son of a bitch got away with it," Nate said. "Did he know what he was doing?"

Joe said, "That's not clear. He claims the campers insulted him and he lost his cool. He said in the deposition he'd never seen or heard of the people he killed before he killed them."

Nate shook his head slowly. "There has to be something to get him on. I mean, I couldn't just grab you right now and drive you up to the Idaho part of the park and put a bullet in your head, can I?"

"You better not try," Joe said, smiling. "And it wouldn't work for you. That would be kidnapping and you could be tried and convicted of that in Wyoming because you planned and carried out a major felony on your way to commit the murder."

"So McCann's defense is that he didn't know the victims were there and hadn't planned to kill them when he went on his little hike, so what happened … happened. He just went on a little day hike armed to the teeth?"

Joe said, "That's what he claimed in his deposition. And

that's what he said to the court in Yellowstone, where he served as his own lawyer."

"So the murder of four people isn't a crime?" Nate asked with a mixture of disgust and, Joe noted, a hint of admiration.

Joe said, "Oh, it's a crime. But it's a crime that can't be tried in any court because no one has the power to give him a proper trial. The only thing they can legitimately get him on is possessing firearms in a national park, and they booked him for that and he was tried and convicted of it. But that's just a Class B misdemeanor, no more than six months or a fine of five thousand dollars, or both. So there's no jury trial and the Sixth Amendment doesn't apply."

"Jesus."

"They even tried to get him on a federal statute called Project Safe Neighborhoods that was set up to really nail guys who have a gun on federal property. That would have at least sent him to prison for ten years. But to qualify for that"—Joe dug a sheet out of the file and read from it— "McCann had to be a felon, a drug user, an illegal alien, under a restraining order, a fugitive, dishonorably discharged, or committed to a mental institution." Joe lowered the sheet and looked up at Nate. "McCann didn't qualify for any of those. Hell, he's a lawyer with no past criminal record at all."

Nate drained his cup and leaned back in his chair.

"I have a feeling he knew about the loophole," Nate said. "Maybe he just decided to go hunting."

Joe shrugged. "Could be. Or maybe there's some kind of connection with the victims, but nobody's been able to establish one. I want to get more information on him, and I want to talk to him."

Nate said, "I ought to just drive up there and blow his

48

head off. Everybody would be happy. Hell, he's a murderer *and* a lawyer."

Joe smiled grimly. "That's not why I'm here."

"So, why are you here?" Nate asked, knowing the answer.

"I want to ask you if you'll help me out with this one."

"You didn't even need to ask."

Joe hesitated before he said, "I wanted to see if you were still on your game."

"Meaning what?" Nate asked, offended.

Joe sat back and gestured around Alisha Whiteplume's kitchen. "Meaning *this*."

Nate was in love.

Alisha Whiteplume taught third grade and coached at the high school on the reservation. She had a master's degree in electrical engineering and a minor in American history and had married a white golf pro she met in college. After working in Denver for six years and watching her marriage fade away as the golf pro toured and strayed, she divorced him and returned to the reservation to teach, saying she felt an obligation to give something back to her people. Nate met her while he was scouting for a lek of sage chickens for his falcons to hunt. When he first saw her she was on a long walk by herself through the knee-high sagebrush in the breaklands. She walked with purpose, talking to herself and gesticulating with her hands. She had no idea he was there. When he drove up she looked directly at him with surprise. Realizing how far she had come from the res, she asked him for a ride back to her house. He invited her to climb into his Jeep, and while he drove her home she told him she liked the idea of being back but was having trouble with re-entry.

"How can you find balance in a place where the same boys who participate in a sundance where they seek a vision and pierce themselves are also obsessed with Grand Theft Auto on PlayStation Two?" she asked. Nate had no answer to that.

She said her struggle was made worse when her brother Bob intimated that he always knew she would come back since everybody did when they found out they couldn't hack it on the outside. She told Nate that during the walk she had been arguing with herself about returning, weighing the frustration of day-to-day life on the reservation and dealing with Bobby against her desire to teach the children of her friends, relatives, and tribal members. Later, Nate showed her his birds and invited her on a hunt. She went along and said she appreciated the combination of grace and savagery of falconry, and saw the same elements in him. He took it as a compliment. They went back to her house that night. That was three months ago. Now he spent at least three nights a week there, and it was Alisha's house where Joe located Nate.

Nate was still wanted for questioning by the FBI but thus far had eluded them. Apparently, the FBI had its hands full with more pressing matters. It had been months since Special Agent Tony Portenson had been in the area asking Joe if he'd seen his friend lately.

"What, you think I've been domesticated?" Nate asked, incredulous. "You think I've lost my edge?"

Joe didn't answer. He had noticed how Nate's middle had gone soft as a result of Alisha's good cooking. Before Alisha, Nate had survived at his stone house on the banks of the river by hacking off cuts of antelope that hung in the meat cellar and grilling the steaks. Now, he sat down to real meals at least twice a day.

"I didn't say that."

"I'll never go back on my word," Nate said, in reference

to the vow he'd made to help Joe when he asked or when he simply needed it whether or not he asked. Nate had made the promise years before when Joe proved his innocence after Nate had been charged with a murder he didn't commit.

"I'm leaving tomorrow," Joe said.

At that moment, the door opened and Alisha Whiteplume entered carrying two bags of groceries. Joe and Nate stood, and each took a bag and put it on the counter.

"Hello, Mr. Pickett," Alisha said cautiously. "It's good to see you again."

"Alisha."

She was slim and dark, with piercing, always amused eyes and a good figure. Joe could see why Nate was enchanted.

"Are you here to take my boy away?" she asked, arching her eyebrows.

"If he's willing," Joe said.

"Are you willing?" she asked Nate softly.

He hesitated, looking from Joe to Alisha.

Joe thought, *He's got it bad. Don't tell me he's going to ask …*

"What do you think?" Nate said to her.

She began to pull cans out of a sack and put them away in the cupboards. "I think Joe wouldn't ask for your help if he didn't think he needed it, and I'd be disappointed in you if you refused because you wouldn't be the man I know and love."

Nate said to Joe, "It'll take me a couple of days to finish up some business. Where will you be staying in the park?"

"I'm not sure yet," Joe said, choosing as always not to ask Nate what his business was. "It's about to close for the season. Either Mammoth, Old Faithful, or West Yellowstone.

Those are the only places still open. I'll call when I know."

Nate nodded. "Come with me for a minute."

Alisha said goodbye to Joe and resumed putting groceries away. Joe followed Nate outside to Nate's Jeep.

"She's something," Joe said.

"Damned right," Nate answered, swinging up the back hatch and flipping open the lid on a large metal toolbox. He removed the tray of tools on top to reveal a stash of weapons underneath. Nate's .454 Casull, manufactured by Freedom Arms in Freedom, Wyoming, was a heavy five-shot revolver of incredible power and accuracy in Nate's hand. It was on top.

"What are you carrying up there?" Nate asked.

"My shotgun, I guess," Joe said. He hadn't given weapons any thought. "And I'm not even sure about that. It's illegal to have a firearm in the park, like I mentioned."

Nate's look of disdain was epic. "Fuck the Park Service," he said, digging into the box. "We're Americans last I looked. That's the only thing about this situation that causes me heartburn: helping out the Feds."

"Actually, I'm working for the governor."

"They're all the same," Nate grumbled, digging into the box and handing Joe a semi-automatic Glock-23 .40.

"You've used one of these, right? Thirteen in the magazine and one in the chamber, so you've got fourteen rounds of high-caliber hell. Buy some shells, practice a little so you get familiar with it. It's a damned good weapon, and practically idiot-proof. Rack the slide and start blasting. No hammer to get caught in your clothes, no safety switch to forget about."

"Fourteen misses," Joe said, alluding to his ineptitude with a handgun. "That's why I'm bringing my shotgun."

"Twenty-seven misses," Nate said. "There's an extra full

magazine in a pocket on the holster. Take it anyway. You never know. It'll make me feel better if you have it."

Joe started to protest, but Nate's expression convinced him not to start an argument. He'd carried a Glock .40 before since it was the assigned weapon of the Game and Fish Department. His last weapon was thrown into the Twelve Sleep River after the situation with the Scarlett brothers. At the time, Joe had thought he'd never carry a handgun again, and that was fine with him then, and fine with him now. Handguns were good for only one thing: killing people.

"What about this letter to the governor," Nate said. "Can you figure anything out about it?"

Joe shook his head.

"Or the fact that four of the Gopher State Five got whacked? Who is Gopher State One?"

"No idea."

"The governor is okay with me assisting?"

"He doesn't want to know about it."

"I can't say I blame him," Nate said, reaching for the .454.

JOE FOUND BUD Longbrake in the Quonset hut working on the engine of his one-ton truck. Bud was perched high on the front bumper, leaning in over the engine. Eduardo stood on the dirt floor next to the truck handing up tools as Bud called out for them. They'd not fired up the propane heater in the corner of the building, so it was colder inside than it was outside. Bud had a policy about not turning on the heaters before November, as if to defy the coming of winter until its proper time on the calendar. Joe noticed he wouldn't even use the heater in the truck until then.

"I'll take over if you don't mind," Joe said to Eduardo.

"No *problema*," Eduardo said, stepping away from the

toolbox and blowing on his hands. "I need to eat some hot lunch."

"Seven-eighths socket," Bud called down.

Joe snapped the attachment on the wrench and handed it up.

"Goddamn mice get in the engine and chew up the belts," Bud grumbled. "I gotta put new belts on every year."

Although Bud hired contractors in semitrucks to haul cattle to buyers, he liked to move his brood stock to lower pasture himself behind the one-ton. His plans were always delayed until he got the truck running again.

"Bud, I got offered my old job back," Joe said.

There was a slight hesitation in Bud's hand as he reached down for the socket wrench.

"I took it," Joe said.

Bud cranked on a bolt. "I figured you probably would."

"I'm sorry."

"Don't be," Bud said. "You need to do what you're good at."

"Thank you."

Bud worked for a while without saying anything and called for the fresh belt. Joe unwrapped it from the packaging and handed it up.

"You've always got a job here if you want it," Bud said. "You're a good hand."

It was the ultimate compliment on a ranch, Joe knew, and it made him feel guilty for leaving. Worse, he had to ask, "I was hoping we could come to an arrangement for Marybeth and the kids to stay here for a while longer. At least until we can get a house in town."

Bud snorted. "Why do you even ask me that?"

Joe didn't know what Bud meant and froze up.

Bud said, "Of course they can stay. I'll work up some

kind of rent deal and let you know. I don't want you even thinking about moving for a while. I like having you around here and I'd miss the hell out of those girls of yours."

"Thank you, Bud," Joe said, genuinely grateful.

"I'll give Eduardo a raise," Bud said, as much to himself as to Joe. "Make him the foreman and see how he works out. I think he can do it, as long as the immigration people don't come sniffing around."

"Sorry to spring this on you now," Joe said.

"There's never a good time on a ranch," Bud said. "But with winter coming, this is as good a time as any, I guess."

Bud fit the belt on and tightened the bolts. "They giving you a vehicle?"

Joe and Marybeth had only the family van. "I've got to pick one up in town," Joe said.

"You need a ride to go get it?"

"Sure," Joe said, feeling bad about letting this good man down.

"I'll finish up here and give you a ride," Bud said.

AS THEY WALKED to the main house, Bud turned with his grease-stained finger to his lips and said, "Shhhh. Missy is taking a little nap. That art meeting went until all hours last night."

Joe felt a tingle in his heart.

"She didn't get back until three this morning," Bud said in all innocence. "They must have had a lot to discuss."

Joe bit his lower lip to keep from saying anything. He waited on the porch while Bud went inside for his keys.

Five minutes later, Bud came out, said, "Missy wants to talk to you for a minute."

"To me?" Joe asked. Missy rarely wanted to talk to him, which was a good thing.

55

"I'll pull the truck around," Bud said, walking away across the gravel.

Joe sighed and went inside, looking first in the living room for her. Missy wasn't in her chair, or in the kitchen with Maria. He found her in her bed.

The bedroom was large and recently redecorated. Missy had stripped the walls, replaced the fixtures, and refurnished it with tasteful antiques. Nothing remained of Bud's first wife, not even the floors. Missy lay under a comforter on top of the bed. The shades were pulled, which she did when she wasn't wearing makeup and didn't want to be seen closely. *She looks so tiny*, Joe thought. Even in the gloom, though, she was a startlingly, undeniably beautiful woman, even if she was at war with her true age.

"I hear it was a late meeting," Joe said. "How's the Earl of Lexington?"

"He's fine …" she said, then quickly bit off her words and glared at him. Marybeth was right. He *was* at the meeting. Missy propped herself up on an elbow, fixing her big eyes on him.

"I heard the news," she said with an edge in her voice, quickly regaining the upper hand.

Joe said nothing.

"I also heard that you might be thinking of a house in town."

"Maybe."

She shook her head slowly. "Let my people go, Joe."

"What?"

"Let them *go*," she said sharply, sitting up and swinging her feet to the floor. "Everything is perfect as it is. For the first time, Marybeth is comfortable. She has a fine place to live. She's moving up, finally. Quit dragging my daughter and my granddaughters down with you."

Joe felt his neck get hot.

"They deserve better than to be handcuffed to a mid-level state employee who brings danger they don't deserve into their lives," Missy said, the words dripping with disdain. "Don't you dare take them away from me again. Step aside, and let them ... blossom."

"*Blossom*?"

Her eyes flashed. "I've said my piece. I wish you would think about it while you run around in the woods again like a schoolboy."

Joe knew he was one of the few to see her occasionally in her full, evil, stripped-down honesty. He doubted Bud Sr. ever really had. It was the one thing they had together, he and Missy: icy moments of bitter, hateful truth.

"I'll think about it," Joe said. "While I'm thinking about it, I'd like you to come to Yellowstone so I can show you around. One place in particular, way on the western side of the park, in Idaho. I hear it's beautiful."

"What are you talking about?" she asked, narrowing her eyes and frowning.

He turned and left, his hands shaking.

5

West Yellowstone, Montana
October 7

CLAY MCCANN DIDN'T like how the reporter from the *Wall Street Journal* had described his hair as "pink." The description denigrated him, made him sound less serious, like a circus clown. No one wanted to have pink hair. The reason for the description in the *Journal,* and this was patently unfair, was that his hair—once a deep red—was now streaked with silver-gray hairs. The silver made it look from a distance (if the observer was a jaded Eastern reporter) like he dyed his hair pink. *Which he did not!*

He confirmed it once again in the rearview mirror of his car as he drove through Yellowstone Park. While looking at himself in the mirror instead of watching the road, he nearly collided with a herd of buffalo. McCann cursed and slammed on his brakes, bringing his car into a skidding stop three feet from the front quarters of a one-ton bull. The animal swung its woolly triangle head toward the car, stared through the windshield at him with black amoral prehistoric eyes, snorted with what sounded like indignation, and slowly joined the rest of the herd.

A buffalo jam. Anyone driving through Yellowstone Park had to get used to them. The dank smell that hung in the air, the *clip-clop* of ungulate hooves on the pavement.

Wouldn't that have made a hell of an ironic story, McCann thought, saying the headline aloud: "Freed Murderer Killed in Park Collision With Bison."

While he waited he studied his face again in the mirror. The same reporter had described him as "pale, paunchy, and past his prime" in a flowery alliterative rhetorical flourish filled with popping P's. *That prick*, McCann thought.

The buffalo herd seemed endless. Dozens of them, maybe a hundred dark woofing behemoths. None of them cared that he was there, only that they needed to cross the road to get to the Madison River. McCann had no choice but to sit and wait. He had tried to push through a herd once, but a bull swung its head and dented his driver's door with a horn.

The heavy buck-brush near the river blazed red with fall color in the last half-hour of dusk. It was a great time and season to see the park, if one cared. But the tourists were all but gone. The roads were virtually empty. And Clay McCann, who had been the focus of so much attention, the center of so many conversations, was now utterly alone except for the buffalo.

Finally, as the last cow crossed, leaving blacktop spattered with steaming piles of viscous dung, McCann shifted into drive and accelerated.

McCann was nearly out of the park. He was going home.

THE RANGER AT the West Yellowstone gate waved a cheery "Goodbye!" from her little gatehouse as he slowed to leave the park. The town of West Yellowstone was just ahead.

Although she waved him through, McCann stopped next

to the exit window, powered down his window, and thrust his face outside so she could see him.

She began to say, "You don't need to stop ..." when she recognized him. Her eyes widened and her mouth pulled back in a grimace and she inadvertently stepped back, knocking a sheaf of *Yellowstone News* flyers to the ground outside her box. "My God," she mouthed.

"Have a pleasant night," he said, basking in her reaction, knowing now, for sure, he'd entered the rarified air of celebrity.

HE'D BEEN AWAY for nearly three months. During that time, Clay McCann had gone from a semi-obscure small-town lawyer specializing in contracts and criminal defense law to being known both nationally and internationally. For a brief time, every utterance he made to reporters inside the tiny jailhouse at Mammoth Hot Springs made the wire services. Profiles of him and the *Yellowstone Zone of Death* appeared in a half-dozen national publications. For a delicious week or two, his face and the crime were as familiar to viewers of twenty-four-hour cable networks as any celebrity criminal or victim. His arguments before the court were dissected by celebrity lawyers who predicted, correctly, that he'd win, which he did. Although the federal prosecutors threatened loudly to appeal the decision to the Tenth Circuit and the Supreme Court, the thirty days allowed to file had lapsed and he'd received no notification. McCann banked on the assumption that the Feds didn't want the case to go further with the very likely possibility that higher courts would have to declare that the Zone of Death actually existed.

He was as free as those buffalo back on the road. Originally, the news of the murders burned bright and his face was everywhere. Reporters and cameramen camped out on the lawn of the old Yellowstone jail, sharing the grass with grazing elk. But the story soon became eclipsed by the circumstances. He faded out of it, and other crimes that had more appeal—like blondes found missing on islands or cruise ships—overtook the hard-to-understand concept of vicinage and the Sixth Amendment, and he was discarded onto the electronic landfill of old news. It was expensive, a reporter told him, for the network to keep a team out there in the middle of nowhere with little to report. Plus, he complained, there was nothing to do at night for the crew. Eventually, they all left. But McCann had no doubt he was still hot stuff up and down the Rocky Mountains.

HE DROVE THROUGH the empty, familiar streets of West Yellowstone as the few overhead lights charged, hummed, and lit against the coming darkness. His house was located in a cul-de-sac within a stand of thick lodgepole pines west of town. His neighbors were a doctor and a fly-fishing guide who had turned his name into a well-known brand. The doctor and guide were among the elite in town and it was an exclusive, if tiny, neighborhood. McCann had acquired his house in a foreclosure auction, but nevertheless.

As he pulled into his driveway he saw immediately that his house had been vandalized. The windows were broken and FILTHY FUCKING MURDERER was spray-painted in red on the front door, drips of paint crawling down the wood like dried blood.

He charged up the walk and kicked through weeks of porch-delivered newspapers and entered his dark house to find the power and water shut off. He experienced a moment of overwhelming despair: *How could they expect me to keep up with the local bills when I was incarcerated?*

Retrieving a flashlight from his car, he returned to his home as despair sharpened into quiet rage. His house reeked of spoiled food from inside the refrigerator and freezer. He didn't even open them. Long-dead tropical fish floated in a slick of scum on the top of his fish tank. His cat was long gone, although he'd shredded most of his living room furniture and sprayed the carpet in his bedroom before finding his way out.

Drawers and closet doors were agape, clothing thrown across the floors by investigating cops. His telephone was ripped from the wall for no good reason at all. His bookcase was ransacked, emptied, law books tossed into piles along with the military thrillers he liked to read. Holes were punched into his walls as they looked for … what? What were they trying to find and why were they trying to find it? The case wasn't a mystery, after all.

What made him angriest was to visualize the slow-witted local cops and park rangers rooting through his personal belongings, reading his mail, laughing, no doubt, at his collection of pornography in the drawer of his nightstand and finding—*Jesus*—the cardboard box containing the stuffed animals from his childhood that he just couldn't make himself throw away. He wondered how many people knew about that. If somebody said something about the box in town, he vowed, he'd sue their ass so fast it would leave skid marks.

No note of apology, no crime-scene tape, no acknowledgment of what they'd done. They simply trashed the place and left it for vandals.

He would need protection. Some yahoo might try to take him down, try to become famous for killing the man who beat the system. These people here liked that kind of rough frontier justice. Unfortunately, the Park Service hadn't returned his weapons and he'd have to threaten a suit to get them back. As he drafted the action in his head, he remembered something. Months before, a client charged with a third DUI had paid him a retainer consisting of cash and a .38 snub-nosed revolver. The lawyer had dropped the gun into a manila envelope and filed it among his casework portfolios in his home office. Remarkably, the cops had missed it. He retrieved the gun and checked the loads, more familiar with weapons than he used to be, and slid it into his jacket pocket. It felt solid and heavy against his hip. He liked how it felt.

Pausing on the porch among the litter of unopened mail and newspapers, McCann took a deep breath of cold air. It tasted faintly of pine-cone dust and wood smoke. He fought against the dark specter of being absolutely alone.

BECAUSE IT WAS late in the year, only locals were out. McCann drove to Rocky's, a local favorite they all raved about like it was Delmonico's, but he found more or less passable. It was both a bar and a restaurant, one big room. He wanted a beer and a burger, something they couldn't mess up. Ninety days of jail food had screwed up his system.

The place was humming with raucous conversation as he entered, and it took a moment to get the bartender's eye. When he did, the man simply looked at him with tight-lipped trepidation as if he were a ghost, a demon, or Senator Teddy Kennedy.

Then the din started to fade, and it continued to diminish until it was almost silent inside. McCann felt nearly every set of eyes in the restaurant on him. He heard whispers:

"Oh my God, look who's here."

"It's Clay McCann."

"What's he think he's doing here?"

A few of the men's faces hardened into deadeye stares, as if challenging him to start something. A young mother covered the eyes of her child, as if she thought simply seeing him would scar the little tyke for life.

Even though he'd expected this reception, it still came as a sour jolt. Sure, he was used to indirect derision and whispered asides because he was a lawyer. Lawyers made enemies. But this was full-scale, almost overpowering. His only solace was the knowledge that it would be short-term and that he had a .38 in his pocket.

He looked back at them, not without fear. *8 percent*, he thought. *Look for the 8 percent. Take comfort in the 8 percent.*

Early in his career, before he messed up, McCann had been a criminal defense attorney in Minot, North Dakota, after he'd fled Chicago to avoid that ethics charge. He'd been lucky enough to land a deep-pockets client almost immediately—a North Dakota banker accused of hiring thugs to kill his wife. The case was considered a slam-dunk conviction by the prosecution, and it looked hopeless to McCann. Because splitting the fee was better than losing the case outright, McCann brought in Marcus Hand, the flamboyant Wyoming trial lawyer who was famous for four things: long white hair, buckskin clothing, delays that sweetened the payout for the lawyers, and his ability to persuade a jury. McCann watched Hand perform in the courtroom and the Wyoming lawyer nearly convinced McCann himself that his client didn't do it. Eventually, the jury deadlocked at 10–2, and couldn't reach a unanimous verdict. In the retrial a year later. Hand managed to create almost the same result, with an 11–1 hung jury. Although the embarrassed prosecutors let it be known that they would bring the case to trial a third time, it never happened. The banker walked away into bankruptcy and into the arms of his pretty, new twenty-five-year-old wife.

Over victory drinks, Hand explained the 8 Percent Rule to McCann. "It's really very simple," he said, using the same melodic voice he used to pet and stroke the jury. "I have to convince one juror out of twelve to vote with us. One of twelve is eight percent, give or take. Not that I need to convince him our client is innocent, understand. I just need to establish an intimate partnership with that one fellow or lady in a crowd who is *contrary*. The man or woman who has an ax to grind. My theory, and you saw it happen twice, is that in any group of people forced to be together, at least eight percent of them will go against the majority if for no other reason than to shove it up their ass—if they have an authority figure they can trust to be on their side. I am that leader in the courtroom. I talk only to my soul mate, Mr. Eight Percent. That man—or woman, in the case today—will follow me into hell, just so we can put one over on the rest. Remember, Clay, we aren't running for election. We don't care if ninety-two percent of the voters want the other guy. Who cares about them if we have our pal, Mr. Eight Percent? We just want our evil partner, Mr. Eight Percent, who hates the guts of the majority and always will, to show his true colors. He just wants to be bad, unique—an *individual*!—and I'm there to show him the way."

McCann remembered that conversation as he tried to boldly return the stares. Sure enough, when he studied the dinner and bar crowd, he detected two or three people who looked back not with horror, disgust, or revulsion, but with guarded neutrality. All were former clients.

Gavin Toomey, a local miscreant best known for poaching violations and his palpable hatred for the federal government, sat alone at the opposite end of the bar. Toomey actually nodded a discreet greeting.

Butch Toomer, the former sheriff who was recalled by angry voters for accepting bribes, looked at him coolly and raised his beer bottle. Toomer would be pleased McCann was back because McCann owed him.

And Sheila D'Amato, the dark-eyed former vixen who had shown up on the arm of a reputed mafioso en route to the park only to be dumped on the street after an argument, met his eyes while wetting her lips with the point of her tongue.

She was with him, for sure. Good enough for now.

McCann said with a tone of triumph, "*West Yellowstone's most infamous resident has returned.*"

Someone in the back mumbled, "Let's see how long he lasts."

A few men snorted in assent.

McCann visualized the room standing en masse and charging him. He inconspicuously lowered his right hand and brushed the dead weight of the .38 in his jacket pocket with his fingertips.

Les Davis, owner of the Conoco station, said, "I don't think you're welcome here."

"So get the hell out," another man rasped.

McCann found his voice, said, "We don't want this to get out of hand."

Davis mumbled something inaudible.

"We can be friends or we can be enemies," McCann said. "I'd prefer to be friends. That way none of us winds up in court."

He turned to the bartender. "I'd like a cheeseburger, medium rare, and a Yellowstone Pale Ale." His voice didn't quaver and he was thankful.

The barman attempted to stare McCann down, but he couldn't hold it. Sheepishly, he glanced over the bar at the still-silent crowd. They were all watching him to see what he'd do.

McCann said softly, "Are you refusing me service? I'd hate to bring a discrimination suit against this place since everyone loves it so much."

"Give him some fucking food," Butch Toomer growled from his corner table. "The man's got to eat."

The barman looked down, said, "I just work here."

"Then place my order."

"I don't think that's such a good idea."

McCann nodded his appreciation to Toomer, who raised his beer in silent partnership. Sheila was practically devouring him with her dark, mascara'd raccoon eyes. She smiled wickedly at him, her eyes moist. And not just her eyes, he hoped.

"Tell you what," he said to the barman, "I'll order it to go. You can have someone bring the order to my office. That way your patrons can reel their eyes back in."

"Good idea," the man said, visibly relieved.

As he opened the door, McCann shot a glance over his shoulder at Les Davis and his crowd of burghers and fought the impulse to say, *"Losers."*

ON THE WAY to his office two blocks away on Madison, McCann bought two six-packs of local Moose Drool beer from the dingy convenience store and carried them to his office. He fished the gun from his pocket and placed it on his desk, then sat in his chair and waited for his dinner to arrive. His nerves were still tingling.

The *Journal* reporter had made fun of his office location too, that his practice was on Madison Avenue, but not *that*

Madison Avenue. This Madison Avenue, in West Yellowstone, Montana, saw more wandering elk on the sidewalks than it did men in three-piece suits.

There was a huge pile of unopened mail on his desk and he rifled through it. Hate mail, mostly, he assumed. He swept the pile into the garbage can. He'd done the same with letters sent to him while he was in jail.

The only letters McCann took seriously were from other lawyers threatening civil actions against him on behalf of the murdered campers. McCann knew they'd have a good case. Luckily, he thought, it could take years to get to trial, and he didn't plan to be available when and if it did.

While he waited, he imagined hearing the sounds of a mob building outside on the street. Pitchforks and torches being raised. Guttural shouts morphing into a chant: "*Justice … Justice … Justice …*" Then the door would burst open and dozens of dirty hands would reach for him across his desk …

So when there was a knock on his door he gripped the .38 with one hand before reaching for the handle with the other. Sheila D'Amato stood in the threshold with a large foam container and a tray with two tap beers in mugs covered by plastic.

"Why you?" McCann asked.

"I offered."

"I don't remember ordering two beers."

"I thought maybe I'd drink one with you."

He nodded, let her in after checking the street to confirm there was no mob, and shut the door behind them. He gestured to the sack with the six-packs. "I've got more."

"What you did to those people in Yellowstone," she said, "it was just so *baaaaad*." Her eyes glistened as she drew out the word. "And the way those people reacted in Rocky's—wow."

Wow, he knew, was probably the best she could do.

She drank beer after beer and watched him eat. He was grateful for her company, he admitted to himself, which was proof of his desperation.

He'd represented Sheila after she was arrested for shop-lifting $200 worth of makeup from the drugstore. That was when she'd been around town for a few months, long enough that merchants had learned to watch her closely. He employed a "high-altitude" defense, claiming to the judge that Sheila's brain was out of whack because she came from New Jersey and her brain had yet to adapt to the altitude and lack of oxygen. It made her forgetful, he said, and she had simply forgotten to pay the clerk. The judge was amused with the argument but still would have convicted her if the drugstore owner hadn't forgotten to show up and testify. Sheila credited McCann for her acquittal.

Sheila D'Amato admitted to McCann after the trial that she was getting old and her clothes were too tight. All she wanted was her old life back, before she'd been dumped. She was pathetic, he thought, but he enjoyed her stories of being a kept woman in Atlantic City, being passed from mobster to mobster for fifteen years. She claimed she hated Montana and all the tight-assed people who lived here. She'd left town with men a few times since her arrival, but had drifted back after they cut her loose. She said she didn't know why she kept ending up here.

"Do you plan to stay around?" she asked him. Sheila had an annoying little-girl-lost voice, he thought.

"Why are you asking?" But he knew why.

She shrugged and attempted to look coy. "Well, everybody hates your guts."

"Not everybody," he said, saluting her with his beer bottle.

"Don't flatter yourself," she said, letting a little hard-edged Jersey into her voice, but cocking her head to make sure he knew she was teasing.

"I won't be here long," he said. He knew not to tell her too much. But she could be of use to him, even if he couldn't trust her. She probably didn't trust him either. They had that in common.

"Where will you go?" she asked, trying not to be obvious.

"Someplace warm."

"What's keeping you?"

That, he couldn't tell her. "I'll leave when the time is right."

She nodded as if she understood. He drank another beer and she started to look better.

"What was it like?" she asked, her eyes glistening. She wanted him to tell her killing was a rush, a high. He wondered what the mobsters used to tell her it was like.

"It solved the problem," he said, measuring his words, letting her interpret them however she wished. How could he tell her it meant nothing to him? That, in fact, it was hard work and unpleasant but simply a means to an end?

He waited her out until she finally asked if he would take her with him when he left.

Of course not, he said to himself, *not in a million fucking years.* To Sheila, he said, "It depends."

"On what?"

"On you."

She had paid her legal bill to him for the shoplifting charge in blow jobs. They'd haggled and determined $50 per. She was pretty good. He'd been in jail for three months. He'd make her keep those too-tight clothes on.

EARLY THE NEXT morning, after shaving in his office and

71

deciding that maybe he would look into some sort of hair coloring that would drown out the gray, McCann dropped the .38 into his coat pocket and went outside into the chill. Sheila had been gone for hours, but not before they'd made a date for later that night. At least she was someone to talk to, he thought, although he preferred her with her mouth full. Maybe she wasn't so pathetic after all. She'd do until he left, at least.

West Yellowstone was called a gateway community; it existed almost solely as a staging area or overnight stop for tourists en route to the park. With a permanent population of less than two thousand people, the little town swelled to seven or eight thousand on summer nights and about half that with the snowmobile crowd in the winter. The place was unique in that they didn't plow the roads so snowmobiles could be used legally on the streets.

West, as it was called, was rough-hewn and blue collar, consisting of motels, fly-fishing shops, and souvenir stores. Winters were severe and the people who lived there were rugged. Of the five places McCann had practiced law— Chicago, Minot, Missoula, Helena, and now West Yellowstone, West was by far the bottom of the barrel for a lawyer. Not that he'd had any choice, of course, after the trouble he'd had. For McCann, West was the place he ended up, like something washed up on the shore of the Madison River. Sheila's story was similar. He could go no farther. He liked to tell people that when they brought him their problems.

A sheen of frost covered the windshields of parked cars and stiffened the dying grass between the cracks in the sidewalk. His breath billowed as he walked down Madison. There were no cars on the streets except those parked haphazardly around Bear Trap Pancake House. Locals, most of them. He bought a newspaper from the stand and went in.

He sat alone in a booth with his back to the front door and surveyed the crowd. Men wore cowboy hats or caps proclaiming their allegiance to fly shops or heavy equipment. They were sullen, waking up, waiting for the caffeine to kick in. In contrast were the four bustling waitresses who seemed unnaturally cheery. McCann figured it out: the staff were happy because today would be their last day for the season. Like most businesses in West, the Bear Trap would close until December when there was several feet of snow and the snowmobilers would be back.

A middle-aged waitress with a name tag that read "Marge" practically skipped across the restaurant toward him with a pot of coffee. McCann pushed his empty mug across the table toward her.

As she began to pour, she looked up and her eyes locked on his, and she froze.

"Yes, please," he said, gesturing toward his cup.

Her face hardened and she righted the pot without pouring a drop. Then she turned on her heel and strode into the kitchen.

A few moments later, McCann saw the face of the cook above the bat wing doors, then the face of the owner of the Bear Trap. The lawyer nodded toward the owner, who acknowledged him cautiously, then returned quickly to the kitchen.

A young waitress (nameplate: Tina) had apparently not witnessed Marge's reaction and came over with a pot.

"No," Marge said out the side of her mouth from two tables away.

Tina stopped, unsure of what to do.

"No," Marge said again.

Tina shrugged apologetically at McCann and retreated to the far end of the restaurant to take care of other tables.

McCann sat quietly for twenty minutes as customers came in and placed their orders. Nothing was said to him. He was simply being frozen out, as if he didn't exist. His coffee cup remained empty.

As Marge passed with another fresh pot, McCann reached out and tugged on her apron and she jumped back as if he'd goosed her.

"I'd like breakfast," he said.

"In hell," she answered, swinging her large hips away from him.

McCann stood up angrily and reached for his coat. The .38 thumped against his side and for a second he considered reaching for it. Several patrons watched him furtively between forkfuls of pancakes. Most didn't even look up.

He slammed the door so hard that the bells on it swung and hit the glass, punctuating his exit. He stormed halfway across the street before stopping and turning around. Marge glared back at him from behind the window, her face distorted by condensation on the glass. His eyes slipped from Marge to the rust-tinged FOR SALE sign on the door of the building. Every place in West, it seemed, was always for sale. That went with the transient nature of the town.

But it gave him an idea.

Maybe he could buy the goddamned place and fire Marge. He could buy Rocky's too. He could own the whole fucking town; then they'd *have* to respect him.

MCCANN COULDN'T FEEL his feet as he walked back toward his office to make a call. His insides boiled, and he kept his mouth clamped shut so tightly that his jaw ached. His brief revenge fantasy of buying the town faded quickly. Despite his hunger for reprisal, the last thing he wanted was to stay a minute longer in this place than he had to.

He looked at his wristwatch, calculating the time difference. He needed to make a call. As he began to open the door to his office, he changed his mind. Who knew who might be listening on his line?

At a payphone outside the supermarket he dropped in coins and dialed. It was answered on the third ring and he gave his account number from memory. The receptionist transferred him to his banker.

The banker asked him to repeat the account number and asked for a password. McCann gave both and waited a moment, listening to a keyboard being tapped.

"Yes," the banker said in a clipped Islands/English accent.

"Has the transfer been made?"

Hesitation. "There's been a problem."

The words cut through him like a sword. He swooned, and the sky seemed to tilt to the right, causing him to reach out to steady himself on the frame of the phone booth. "What do you mean. *There's been a problem*?"

"The bulk of the funds didn't arrive when you said they would. We don't know when the remainder will arrive."

He tried to stay calm. "How much?"

More tapping. "Approximately five percent of what you told us to expect."

"Five percent?" He did the math. Five percent was nothing. Five percent would barely cover his current debts.

Fighting panic, he asked the banker to check it again. While he waited, he backed away from the booth as far as the cord would let him. He looked down the empty street. Walls of dark pine closed in. Even the crooked sky seemed to push down on him.

"I'm sorry," the banker said. "It is correct."

"How fucking long do I have to stay here in this shithole and wait?" he said, his voice rising to a choked shout.

"It is not the fault of our institution, sir," the banker said defensively. "The problem is with the sender. You should talk to him and find out what is the cause of the delay."

McCann wanted to plead to the banker, *This was not the plan.*

"Your issue is not with us," the banker said.

"I'll check back with you," he said, biting his lip hard enough to draw blood and slamming down the receiver.

Stunned, he turned to walk away. But to where? How could this be happening?

And to think, three months ago he'd been famous.

PART TWO

YELLOWSTONE ACT, 1872

AN ACT TO SET APART A CERTAIN TRACT OF
LAND LYING NEAR THE HEADWATERS OF THE
YELLOWSTONE RIVER AS A PUBLIC PARK
Approved March 1, 1872 (17 Stat. 32)

Sec 2. that said public park shall be under the exclusive
control of the Secretary of the Interior, whose duty it shall
be, as soon as practicable, to make and publish such rules
and regulations as he may deem necessary or proper for the
care and management of the same. Such regulations shall
provide for the preservation, from injury or spoliation, of
all timber, mineral deposits, natural curiosities, or wonders
within said park, and their retention in their natural condition. The Secretary may in his discretion, grant leases for
building purposes for terms not exceeding ten years, of small
parcels of ground, at such places in said park as shall require
the erection of buildings for the accommodation of visitors;
all of the proceeds of said leases, and all other revenues that

may be derived from any source connected with said park, to be expended under his direction in the management of the same, and the construction of roads and bridlepaths therein. He shall provide against the wanton destruction of the fish and game found within said park, and against their capture or destruction for the purposes of merchandise or profit. He shall also cause all persons trespassing upon the same after the passage of this act to be removed therefrom, and generally shall be authorized to take all such measures as shall be necessary or proper to fully carry out the objects and purposes of this act. (U.S.C., title 16, sec. 22.)

6

On the morning Joe was to leave for Yellowstone he took the girls to school in the white Yukon the state had assigned him. It was the same one that had delivered Chuck Ward to the ranch. There was a brief flare-up between Sheridan and Lucy regarding who would get the front seat and who would have to cram into the backseat along with his duffel bags of clothes and outdoor gear. Sheridan won the battle with the oldest trick in the book—pointing toward the horizon and saying, "Look!"—thereby distracting Lucy and Joe while she scrambled into the front.

It was a brilliant crisp fall day, no wind, colors in the river bottoms igniting as the sun lit them like lantern mantles. Although it wasn't a green pickup with the pronghorn antelope Game and Fish logo on the door and a light bar on top, Joe acquainted himself with his new vehicle. The Yukon was unabashedly big, tall, roomy, heavy, and powerful. He felt only slightly guilty about liking it so much. Joe prayed he could return it in one piece.

From the backseat, Lucy asked, "Does this car waste a lot of gasoline?"

Like sailors on shore leave "waste" beer, Joe thought. But he simply said, "Yes."

"Why can't you have something that's better for the environment?"

"Because I'm taking it into some pretty rough country and it's nearly winter, so I might need four-wheel drive."

"Hmmpf."

Sheridan ignored the exchange and picked up a FedEx box near her feet. "Can I look inside?"

"Sure," he said. The box had arrived the previous afternoon from headquarters in Cheyenne. As he had anticipated, there was no "Welcome Back, Joe!" note inside from Randy Pope.

But there was a badge, and credentials.

Sheridan looked through the embroidered shoulder patches, a new name tag, newly issued statute booklets, recent memos paper-clipped together, a handheld radio. She opened the plastic box with the small gold shield inside.

"Number fifty-four," she said. "Didn't you used to have a lower badge number?"

Joe smiled ruefully, surprised she had paid attention. "I used to have number twenty-one."

There were only fifty-four game wardens in the state, and the higher the seniority, the lower the number. Even though Pope had been ordered to restore his salary and pension, the governor probably hadn't thought of asking to reassign his number. The high badge number was usually given to trainees fresh out of college, and it sent an obvious message.

"That's so unfair."

"It's all right," he said, thinking, *Yes, it was a slap in the face. But not unexpected.*

"I used to look at your badge every morning at breakfast," she said. "That's how I remembered."

Joe felt a sentimental pang. He had no idea.

"We're going to visit you in Yellowstone Park, right?" Lucy asked.

"Yup."

"Mom told me we almost went there once," she said. "Mrs. Hanson says it's a great place but people are ruining it."

"You were a baby," Joe said, choosing not to comment on what her teacher had said.

"You're *still* a baby," Sheridan said, getting in a dig when the opportunity presented itself, which was in the job description of being an older sister.

"Dad!" Lucy protested.

He admonished, *"Sheridan ..."*

As they neared Saddlestring, Joe said, "Be good for your mom while I'm gone. Help her out."

"We will," they mumbled.

He didn't look at them because he didn't want them to see mist in his eyes. "I'm going to miss you girls."

And he wished, for a moment, that he wasn't so damned thrilled about getting his job back.

MARYBETH WAS STILL at home when he returned, which was unusual. So was the fire in the seldom-used stone fireplace. Joe noted that the curtains were drawn, and recalled opening them that morning.

When she came down the hall in her robe, Joe understood.

"The girls are gone, Bud and Missy went to town, and I called the office and told them I'd be late," she said. Her blond hair fell on her shoulders, her eyes caught the flames of the fire.

"I was thinking of a proper send-off," she said, smiling. "But I decided on an improper one." She gestured toward

81

a jumble of quilts that were spread out in front of the fireplace. He hadn't noticed when he entered.

"What, again?" he said, instantly regretting his choice of words.

"Mr. Romantic," she said, shaking her head.

"Please ignore what I just said," he said, stepping toward her.

"I already have."

"You make it tough to go."

"Exactly."

AS HE CLEARED the timber, mountain meadows opened up and so did the view. Dark folds of wooded slopes stretched in all directions and the pale sky fused into the horizon, giving Joe a once-familiar "top of the world" view that now matched his attitude. The two-lane ribbon that was U.S. Highway 14 was rolled out straight and narrow before him. As he approached Burgess Junction, in the heart of the Bighorn National Forest, he had a decision to make. He could stay on 14 all the way to Yellowstone via Greybull and Cody, or take 14-A, the high-altitude route that included the Medicine Wheel Passage. Remembering that when he went to Jackson two years before he chose 14-A and bad things followed, he opted to stay on 14 this time. Superstition.

On top, he got a cell signal again and his phone burred. Chuck Ward was calling from Cheyenne. Joe eased off the highway onto the shoulder and parked.

"We've notified the National Park Service that you want to meet with the investigating rangers," Ward said. "They've assembled the principals for a meeting at four this afternoon at their offices. The chief ranger, James Langston, will be there as well. They didn't seem real excited about the prospect of meeting with you, but they agreed."

"I thought I was going incognito," Joe said, puzzled at the change in strategy.

"The governor had a slight change of mind," Ward said flatly. "He didn't want to risk them finding out about you after the fact and raising hell with us. Our relationship with the Feds is bad enough without that. We told them you were up there to write a report about the crime and the investigation for the state attorney general's office. A summary of what's happened."

"You mean there isn't already a report?"

"If there is such an animal," Ward explained, "the Feds have kept it all to themselves, which isn't unprecedented. All we've got is what was in the file the governor gave you. Lots of pieces, but no definitive white paper. The Park Service has agreed to cooperate with you as long as you don't interfere with them."

Joe held the phone away for a moment and looked at it as if it would provide more information. Then: "Won't the Park Service wonder why the governor isn't sending the AG or one of his lawyers? Why send a game warden?"

"Because," Ward said, changing his voice and cadence to imitate Rulon's rapid-fire speaking style, "'You're well versed in many facets of outdoor issues including law enforcement and resource management.'"

"I am?"

"I'm quoting, so don't ask."

Joe didn't.

"Also, don't wear your uniform. It might spook 'em. They don't like state interlopers up there in their park. They consider the place their own little private fiefdom."

Joe nodded, although he knew Ward wouldn't know he had.

"And, Joe, nothing about that letter from Rick Hoening should be brought up, understand?"

"Not really," Joe said, feeling as if Ward was already tugging at the rug he was standing on.

"And if they want to make you a 'special policeman,' don't do it," Ward said. "You can't divide your loyalty."

"What's a special policeman?" Joe asked, the image of a helmeted Keystone Kop appearing in his mind.

"Who the hell knows? Something the Park Service does for local law enforcement. Like deputizing you, I guess. The guy who set up the meeting, Del Ashby, suggested it. He's your contact. His title is supervisory special agent, Branch of Law Enforcement Services, Office of Investigations. How's that for a mouthful?"

"Sounds official," Joe said.

"Just wait," Ward laughed. "They'll need to order bigger business cards up there if their titles keep getting longer. Anyway, ask for Del Ashby."

"They won't like me second-guessing their investigation," Joe said.

"Nope, they won't."

"Four o'clock," Joe repeated.

"Yes. And remember, nothing about the letter."

Joe found himself frowning. "So, what is it I'm supposed to report?"

"You'll have to figure that out on your own. The governor said to do what you do and try not to create any problems. You'll be there as our representative, but it's federal and they have the right to throw you out anytime."

"I'm confused," Joe said.

He could hear Ward sigh. "So am I," he confessed.

"It seems like you're really hanging me out there."

"We are. Why did you ever think different?"

As Joe started to close the phone, he heard Ward say, "Don't contact me unless it's an emergency. And whatever you do, don't call the governor."

AT BURGESS JUNCTION there was a gas station, a restaurant, a gift shop, a sporting goods store, and a saloon all located in the same weathered log building. The owners also rented cabins. As Joe pulled into the parking lot, it appeared that the place was busy. Of course it was, he thought, it's hunting season.

Unshaven men in camo coats and blaze orange hats milled on the wooden porch and around the cabins in back. Four-wheel drive vehicles and ATVs were parked wherever the trees were cleared. The air smelled of wood smoke, gasoline, and tallow. Field-dressed mule deer and elk carcasses hung in the trees, rib cages opened to the air to cool, the view inside the cavities red-white-red like split and flattened barber poles.

"Those yours?" Joe asked one of the hunters on the porch.

"The elk? Got 'em this morning."

"Mind if I take a look?"

"Feel free."

He couldn't help himself; old habits die hard. The first thing he noticed as he inspected the hanging carcasses was that the elk were well taken care of. Hides had been removed, cavities scrubbed clean, tags visible. He searched for entrance and exit wounds and could see that only one of the animals had taken a body shot. The others, apparently, had been killed by bullets to the head or neck. Very clean kills. The hunters knew what they were doing and they took pride in their work. The elk were big and healthy, another good thing. The inch-thick layers of fat along their

85

backbones, white and scalloped, was proof of the excellent habitat and resource management.

"Nice," Joe said to the hunter who had accompanied him from the porch.

"Want to see the antlers?"

"Nah, that's all right."

Joe didn't care about antlers, just that the herd was healthy and the job of harvesting done right.

"Good work," he said, nodding.

"We take it seriously," the hunter said. "If you're going to take an animal's life, you owe it to that elk to take responsibility."

"Exactly." Joe smiled.

Nodding at the rest of the hunters on the porch as he passed them, he reached for the door handle.

"Got your elk yet?" one of them asked.

"Nope," Joe said pleasantly. In Wyoming, "got your elk yet" was a greeting as ubiquitous as "good morning" was elsewhere, but Joe was momentarily struck by it. For the first time he could remember, he was taken for a hunter and not the game warden. In the past, his arrival would have been met with stares, sniggers, or the over-familiar banter of the ashamed or guilty.

Inside, he bought water, jerky, and sunflower seeds because he had forgotten to pack a lunch. While he was paying for the items at the counter, a stout, bearded man in the saloon eyed him, slid off his bar stool and entered the store. Joe assessed him as the man pushed through the half-doors. Dark, close-cropped hair, bulbous nose, wind-burned cheeks, chapped lips. Watery, bloodshot eyes. A hunter who'd been at it for a while, Joe guessed. No other reason for him to be up there this time of year. The hunter had rough hands with dried half-moons of dark blood under his fingernails. Joe could tell from his appearance that he wasn't a member of the group out on the porch. Those men were sportsmen.

"Got your elk?" the man asked, keeping his voice low so the clerk wouldn't hear him ask.

Joe started to shake his head but instincts kicked in. "Why do you ask?"

The hunter didn't reply, but gestured toward the door with his chin, willing Joe to understand.

Joe shook his head.

Frustration passed across the hunter's face because Joe didn't appear to get it.

"Come outside when you're through here," the hunter said, sotto voce, and went out the door to wait.

While the clerk bagged his snacks, Joe shook his head. He knew what the hunter was telling him but had played it coy. Over the years, he'd learned that deception, unfortunately, was a necessary trait for a game warden. Not open dishonesty or entrapment—those ruined a reputation and could get him beaten or killed. But in a job where nearly every man he encountered in the field was armed as well as pumped up with testosterone—and calling backup was rarely an option—playing dumb was a survival skill. And Joe, much to Marybeth's chagrin, could play dumb extremely well.

The bearded hunter was not on the porch when Joe went outside, but was waiting for him near a cabin at the side of the building. Joe shoved the sack of snacks into his coat pocket as he walked down the length of the wooden porch onto a well-worn path. As he approached the hunter, he wished the .40 Glock Nate had given him wasn't disassembled in a duffel bag in his Yukon.

The hunter studied Joe with cool eyes and stepped on

87

the other side of his pickup and leaned across the hood, his bloodstained fingers loosely entwined, the truck between them.

The hunter raised his eyebrows in a greeting. "You might be a man who's looking for an elk."

"Think so, huh?" Joe said, noncommittal.

"Me and my buddies jumped 'em this morning early, down on the ridge. They was crossing over the top, bold as you please."

Joe nodded, as if to say, "Go on."

"That's the thing about elk hunting. Don't see nothing for five straight days, and all of a sudden they're all around you. Big herd of 'em. Forty, fifty. Three of us hunting."

Joe glanced behind the cabin, saw three big bulls hanging from the branches, their antlers scraping the ground, hides still on, black blood pooling in the pine needles. Despite the distance, Joe could see gaping exit wounds on the ribs and front quarters. Even in the cold he could smell them.

"Yeah, three good bulls," the hunter said, following Joe's line of sight. "But my buddy went a little crazy."

"Meaning," Joe said, "there are a few more killed down there than you have licenses for."

The hunter winced. He didn't like Joe saying it outright.

"At least four cows if you've got a cow permit," the hunter whispered. "A spike too. That's good eating, them spikes."

Spikes were young bulls without fully developed antlers. Cows were female elk. Five extra animals wasn't just a mistake, it was overkill. Joe felt a dormant sense of outrage rise in him but tried not to show it.

He said, "So a guy could drive down there with an elk tag and take his pick?"

The hunter nodded. "If a guy was willing to pay a little finder's fee for the directions."

"How much is the finder's fee?"

The hunter looked around to see if anyone could hear him, but the only other people out were back at the building.

"Say, four hundred."

Joe shook his head. "That's a lot."

The hunter grinned. "How much is your time worth, is what I think. Hell, we've been up here five days. You can go get you a nice one without breaking a sweat."

"I see."

"I'd go three seventy-five. But no less."

"Three hundred and seventy-five dollars for a cow elk?" Joe said.

Again, the hunter flinched at Joe's clarity. Again, he looked around.

"That's the deal," he said, but with less confidence than before. Joe's manner apparently created suspicion.

Joe glanced down at the plates on the hunter's pickup. Utah. He memorized the number.

"Would you take a check?" Joe asked.

The hunter laughed unpleasantly as his confidence returned. "Hell, no. What do you think I am?"

"I'll have to run back to Dayton to get cash from the ATM," Joe said. "That'll take me an hour or so."

"I ain't going anywhere. Them elk aren't either."

"An hour, then."

"I'll be in the bar."

Joe leaned across the hood and extended his hand. The hunter took it, said, "They call me Bear."

Joe said, "They call me a Wyoming game warden, and I've got you on tape." With his left hand, he raised the microcassette recorder from where he always kept it in his pocket. "You just broke a whole bunch of laws."

89

Bear went pale and his mouth opened, revealing a crooked picket fence row of tobacco-stained teeth.

"Killing too many elk is bad enough," Joe said. "That happens in the heat of battle. But the way you take care of the carcasses? And charging for the illegal animals? That just plain makes me mad."

JOE CALLED DISPATCH in Cheyenne on his radio. He was patched through to Bill Haley, the local district warden.

"GF-thirty-five," Haley responded.

"How far are you from Burgess Junction, Bill?"

"Half an hour."

Joe told him about the arrest.

"His name is Carl Wilgus, goes by Bear," Joe said, reciting the license plate number. "Cabin number one. Five extra elk, Wanton Destruction, attempting to sell me an elk and the location. You can throw the book at him and confiscate his possessions if you want. We've got him down cold, on tape, telling me everything."

While Joe talked on the mike, Bear was handcuffed to the bumper of his pickup, embarrassed and angry, scowling at him.

"You going to stick around?" Haley asked. "Grab a burger with me?"

"I'm here just long enough to give you the tape and turn him over," Joe said. "I've got a meeting to get to in Yellowstone."

"I heard you were back," Haley said. "How's it going, Joe?"

"Outstanding," Joe said.

"We're all trying to figure out what's going on with you. Did Pope give you a district?"

"Nothing like that," Joe said, not wanting to explain the situation further.

90

"What are you up to, then?"

Joe thought. "Special projects," he said, not knowing what else to say. Special projects sounded vague yet semi-official.

"Well, welcome back."

"Thanks, Bill."

"See you in a few."

"GF-fifty-four out."

"Fifty-four? They gave you fifty-four? For Christ sake."

THE SPEED LIMIT through the Wapiti Valley en route to the East Entrance of Yellowstone dropped to forty-five miles per hour and Joe slowed down. He checked his wristwatch. If he kept to the limit and didn't get slowed by bear jams or buffalo herds, he should be able to make it to the park headquarters at Mammoth Hot Springs by 3.30 P.M., enough time to locate Del Ashby and get the briefing.

As he drove on the nearly empty road, winding parallel to the North Fork of the Shoshone River, Joe thought again about the murders and how they'd taken place because the circumstances of the crime bothered him. All those shots, multiple weapons. That's what jumped out. Most people reading the reports would come to the conclusion the park rangers apparently had, that the crime had been committed in anger, in passion. Joe wasn't sure he agreed with that assessment, despite all the blasting. Just because Clay McCann fired a lot of shots didn't mean he had gone mad. It might mean he wanted to make sure the victims were dead. Most of the wounds Joe read about could have been fatal on their own, so they were well-placed. There was nothing in the reports to suggest McCann had shot at the victims as they stood in a group, or peppered the shore of the lake with lead. Just the opposite. Each shot, whether

91

by shotgun or pistol, had been deliberate and at close range. Although there were no facts in the file to suggest McCann was anything other than what he was—an ethically challenged small-town lawyer—Joe couldn't help thinking the murders had been committed by a professional, someone with knowledge of death and firearms. Since McCann's biography didn't include stints in any branch of the military and didn't include information that he was a hunter, Joe wondered where the lawyer had received his training.

Joe had spent most of his life around hunters and big game. He knew there was a marked difference between the way Bear and his friends killed those elk and the way the men on the porch hunted. Bear and his friends were clumsy amateurs, firing indiscriminately at the herd and finding out later what fell. In contrast, the men on the porch were careful marksmen and ethical hunters.

Simply pointing a long rod of steel (a gun) and pulling the trigger (*Bang!*) didn't instantly snuff the life out of the target. All the act did was hurl a tiny piece of lead through the air at great but instantly declining speed. The bit of lead, usually less than half an inch in diameter, had to hit something vital to do fatal damage: brain, heart, lungs. To be quick and sure, the bullet had to cause great internal damage immediately. Rarely was a single shot an instant kill. That only happened in the movies. In real life, there was a good chance a single jacketed bullet would simply pass through the body, leaving two bleeding holes and tissue damage, but not doing enough harm to kill unless the victim bled out or the wounds became infected. Pulling the trigger didn't kill. Placing the bullet did. McCann had placed each and every shot.

In a rage, a man like Clay McCann would much more likely start pointing his weapons and shooting until all his victims were down and consider the job done. But to have the presence of mind to walk up to each downed camper and put a death shot into their heads after they were incapacitated? That was pure, icy calculation. Or the work of a professional. And if not a pro, someone who had reason to assure himself that all his victims were dead, that no one could ever talk about what had happened, or why it happened. Vicinage and jurisdiction aside, the murders had been extremely cold-blooded and sure.

Joe couldn't put himself into Clay McCann's head on July 21. What would possess a man to do what he did with such efficient savagery? What was his motivation? An insult, as McCann later claimed? Joe didn't buy it.

AT THE EAST entrance gate, the middle-aged woman ranger asked Joe how long he'd be staying. Until that moment, he hadn't really thought about it. He was thinking that he was glad he had never had to wear one of those flat-brimmed ranger hats.

"Maybe a couple weeks," he said.

"Most of the facilities will be closing by then," she said. "Winter's coming, you know."

"Yes," he said, deadpan.

He bought an annual National Park Pass for fifty dollars so he'd be able to go in and out of the park as much as he needed without paying each time. While she filled out the form, he was surprised to see the lens of a camera aiming at the Yukon from a small box on the side of the station.

"You've got video cameras?" he asked.

She nodded, handing him the pass to sign. "Every car comes in gets its picture taken."

"I didn't realize you did that."

She smiled. "Helps us catch gatecrashers and commercial

93

vehicles. Commercial vehicles aren't allowed to use the park to pass through, you know."

"I see," he said, noting for later the fact about the cameras.

He listened to her spiel about road construction ahead, not feeding animals, not approaching wildlife. She handed him a brochure with a park road map and a yellow flyer with a cartoon drawing of a tourist being launched into the air by a charging buffalo. He remembered the same flyer, the same cartoonish drawing, from his childhood. He could recall being fascinated by it, the depiction of a too-small buffalo with puffs of smoke coming out of his nostrils, the way the little man was flying in the air with his arms outstretched.

"Are you okay?" she asked because he hadn't left.

"Fine," he said, snapping out of it. "Sorry."

She shrugged. "Not that you're holding up traffic or anything," she said, gesturing behind him at the empty road.

7

THE LAW ENFORCEMENT center for the Park Service, known informally as "the Pagoda," was a gray stone building a block from the main road through the Mammoth Hot Springs complex in the extreme northern border of the park. Joe turned off the road near the post office with the two crude concrete bears guarding the steps. Mammoth served as the headquarters for the National Park Service as well as for Zephyr Corp., the contractor for park concessions. Unlike other small communities in Wyoming and Montana where the main streets consisted of storefronts and the atmosphere was frontier and Western, Mammoth had the impersonal feel of governmental officialdom. The buildings were old and elegant but government's version of elegance—without flair. The architecture was Victorian and revealing of its origin as a U.S. Army post before the National Park Service came to be. Elk grazed on the still-green lawns across from the Mammoth Hotel, and the hot springs on the plateau to the south billowed steam that dissipated quickly in the cold air. When the wind changed direction, there was the slight smell of sulfur. A line of fine old wood and brick houses extended north from behind the public buildings, the homes occupied by the superintendent, the chief ranger, and other administrative officials, the splendor of the homes reflecting their status within the hierarchy of the park.

In the height of summer, the complex would be bustling with traffic, the road clogged with cars and recreational vehicles, the sidewalks ablaze with tourists displaying bone-white legs and loud clothing. But in October, there was a kind of stunned silence after all that activity, as if the park was exhausted and trying to catch its breath.

Joe parked the Yukon on the side of the Pagoda. It wasn't well marked. The Park Service didn't like signs because, he supposed, they looked like signs and the park was about nature, not people trying to go about their business in the world outside the park. He circled the building twice on foot before deciding that the unmarked wooden door on the west side was, in fact, the entrance.

The lobby was small and dark and he surprised the receptionist, who quickly darkened the screen of whatever Internet site she had up. She raised her eyebrows expectantly.

"Don't get many visitors, eh?" he said.

"Not this time of year," she said, chastened, guilty about whatever it was she had been looking at and obviously blaming Joe for making her feel that way. "May I help you? Do you know where you're at?"

"I'm here to see Del Ashby. My name is Joe Pickett."

"Del is off today," she said.

"Excuse me?"

She nodded toward a whiteboard on the wall. It listed the names of ranking rangers, with a magnetic button placed either "in" or "out." Del Ashby was marked "out." So was the chief ranger, James Langston, who Chuck Ward had said would also be in the meeting.

96

The receptionist started going through papers from her inbox. It took a moment for Joe to realize he had been dismissed.

"Hold it," he said. "I've got a meeting with them at four. Can you check to see if they'll be there?"

She gave him a withering look, but put the papers down and huffed away, pointedly closing the door behind her desk so he couldn't follow.

While he waited, trying not to become frustrated with the situation that seemed to be developing, he studied another whiteboard on the wall above her desk. Painstakingly, in intricate detail, someone had drawn a multicolored flow-chart of all the park rangers in Yellowstone, starting with James Langston at the top, Del Ashby under him, and a spiderweb of divisions and units including SWAT, interpretation, and other units. He counted about a hundred park rangers assigned to law enforcement, more than he would have guessed.

The door opened and a short, wiry, intense man came through, head down as if determined to cross the room as efficiently as possible. He was wearing a sweatshirt and sweatpants.

"Del Ashby," he said, firing out his hand.

"I thought for a minute my information was wrong," Joe said, flicking a glance at the receptionist, who smoldered behind Ashby.

"It's my day off," he said. "I had to come in just for this, so I hope we can get to it and get out."

Joe nodded.

"We've got a conference room upstairs," Ashby said. "The others are already there."

"The chief ranger? James Langston?" Joe asked.

"Nah, it's his day off."

"Doesn't he live just a block away?" Joe asked, recalling the stately line of old brick homes.

Ashby turned and his expression hardened. "Not everyone will come in on their day off, like me. But don't blame Chief Ranger Langston; he's a busy man. He's got a lot on his plate, you know."

Joe nodded non-committally. The chief's absence told Joe how seriously his presence and the meeting itself was being taken by the park administration. Nevertheless, he was grateful Ashby was there.

Ashby turned and hustled through the door. Joe followed. While they climbed the stairs, Joe looked at his watch. Three-fifty-five. Right on time.

ASHBY STEPPED ASIDE in the hall so Joe could enter a windowless room with a large round table crammed into it. Two men and a woman stood as Joe entered. Ashby shut the door behind them.

"This is Joe Pickett," Ashby said, "from Wyoming governor Rulon's staff."

Joe didn't take the time to consider the introduction—his staff, huh? Is that what Chuck Ward had told them?—but leaned across the table to greet the others. The atmosphere was instantly tense and uncomfortable and Joe surmised quickly that no one really wanted to be there. He recognized Special Agent Tony Portenson of the FBI out of the Cheyenne office. Portenson rolled his eyes at Joe as if to say, *Here we are again*. Then he smiled, which always looked like an uncomfortable sneer on him, like he was trying it out for the first time.

"No need to introduce us," Portenson said to Ashby. "We know each other from way back."

"Hi, Tony."

"I thought I'd gotten rid of him for good," Portenson said in a way that didn't reveal if he was joking or not. "But here he is again, like a bad penny. Wherever I go I seem to run into Joe Pickett and then something goes wrong."

Joe knew Portenson had been seeking a transfer out of Wyoming for years. He hated the state, its people, the quality of crimes he was in charge of. While the rest of the FBI was reshaping itself into a counterterrorism agency, Portenson had to oversee cattle rustling, crime on the Wind River Indian Reservation, and other mundane, career-advancement roadblocks. He'd complained mightily to Joe about it.

Portenson said, "What in the hell is going on now? You're working for the governor of Wyoming?"

Joe nodded, not sure how much to reveal. He hadn't expected someone from his past to be in the room, especially not Portenson, who had made it a life's goal to send Nate Romanowski to prison.

"Sort of," Joe said.

"I've heard Rulon is a loose cannon, a damned maniac. He and the director have been going at each other for two years, ever since the election," Portenson said. "The guy—Rulon—is power-mad, is what I hear. He thinks the Bureau should march to his orders. He probably thinks the same thing about the Park Service."

With that, Portenson looked around the room, having quickly established Joe as an agent for someone who threatened everyone in it.

Joe winced. "Thanks, Tony."

"You bet," Portenson said, satisfied.

"Eric Layborn," said a man in an impeccably neat park ranger's uniform. "Special investigator, National Park Service." Joe reached out, and Layborn gripped his hand so

99

hard Joe winced. Layborn had a heavy brow and a lantern jaw, a close-cropped military haircut, and a brass badge and nameplate that reflected the single light above the table. Even his gun belt was shiny. Layborn's eyes were unsettling to Joe because one bored into him and the other was slightly askew, as if it were studying his ear.

"Ranger Layborn headed up the criminal investigation," Ashby said to Joe.

"Whatever you want to know I can tell you," Layborn said. "We've got nothing to hide."

Joe thought it odd that Layborn would lead with that.

"This is Ranger Judy Demming," Ashby said, gesturing toward the woman at the table who had not launched herself at Joe as Layborn had. "She was first on the scene."

"Nice to meet you," Joe said, flexing his fingers to get the feeling back in them before shaking hands with her.

Demming was a few years older than Joe with medium-length brown hair, wire-framed glasses, a smattering of freckles across her nose. She seemed pleasant enough, gentle, and it was clear to Joe she was ill at ease. He couldn't tell if she was uncomfortable with him, with others in the room, or with her role in the case. After shaking his hand she seemed to withdraw and defer to Ashby and Layborn without really moving.

Portenson and Ashby sat back in their chairs, signaling they were ready to start the meeting. Demming saw them and sat too. So did Joe. Layborn remained standing, his eye fixed on Joe and Joe's ear. He didn't say anything, but it wasn't necessary. The stare was a challenge. Joe had seen it before from local sheriffs, police chiefs, Director Randy Pope. The look said, *"Don't cross me, don't second-guess me, don't step on my turf. And I'm bigger and tougher than you."*

"Eric," Ashby said sharply, "let's get started."

100

Layborn held the scowl for a moment longer, then eased back into his chair with the grace of a cat.

Message delivered.

Joe had brought the file folder the governor had given him. The letter from Rick Hoening was on the bottom of the documents, facedown. He didn't want them to see it.

"Before we get started," Ashby said, "I thought you might need some background on our job here and how we work. That way, we can save some time later."

Out of the corner of his eye, Joe noticed Portenson had immediately drifted away and was studying the large-scale map of the park behind Joe's head.

"Yellowstone National Park is a federal enclave," Ashby said. "You are no longer in the state of Wyoming, or Montana, or anywhere else. This is literally the last vestige of Wyoming Territory, and we're governed as such. There are two U.S. marshals up here, just like the frontier days, and we've got a hundred rangers including four special investigators. Eric here is our top investigator."

At that, Layborn leaned forward. Joe was still stinging from the "message" and fought the urge to ignore the man. Instead he acknowledged Layborn with a quick nod.

"Think of the park as a city of forty thousand people any given day in the summer and fifteen thousand people in the winter," Ashby said. "But unlike a city, everyone is passing through, turning over. We'll have over three million in the summer, a few hundred thousand in the winter. It's a brand-new scenario every day, a whole new cast. Our job is to serve and protect these people and enforce the laws, but at the same time to protect the resources of the park itself. This place is like a church; nothing is to be disturbed. It's a national shrine and no one wants to see harm come to it. It's a hell of a tough job, unlike anything else in law enforcement. Park rangers are the most assaulted federal officers of all of the branches because of the public interaction that comes with the job. No one has jurisdiction over us in the park, including your governor and the FBI," he said, indicating Portenson.

Portenson, Joe noticed, appeared to be counting holes in the overhead ceiling tiles in boredom.

"Because we're federal," Ashby said, "we operate under two sets of laws—the Code of Federal Regulations and the Federal Criminal Code and Rules statutes—and we can pick and choose depending on the violation. Most violations are Class B misdemeanors, meaning six months in jail and or a five-thousand-dollar fine. Half of the violations are 'cite and release'—we give them a ticket and let them proceed. But the other half are the serious ones, and they include felonies, poaching, violations of the Lacy Act, and so on. Because of the transient nature of the population here, all sorts of scum pass through. Last year we nailed a child molester who'd brought a little girl into the park in his RV. On average, we make two hundred to two hundred fifty arrests a year and issue four thousand tickets."

Joe raised his eyebrows. There was more action than he realized.

Layborn broke in. "Don't be fooled by the numbers, Mr. Pickett. We aren't just arresting tourists. Half of the arrests are of permanent residents—meaning Zephyr Corp. employees. I spend most of my time tailing those people. Some of them act like they left the law at home when they moved out here." He said it with a vehemence that seemed out of place after Ashby's sober recitation of facts, Joe thought.

Layborn continued even though Ashby admonished him with his eyes to stop.

"There are seven thousand Zephyr people. They come from all over the world to work in the park. Too many of them come to think they're on the same level as we are. They forget they're here because we allow them to be. They're contractors for the Park Service, nothing more. They work in the hotels, change the bedding, cook, unclog the sewers, wrangle horses, whatever. Some of them are renegades. We used to call 'em savages—"

"Eric, *please*," Ashby said, sitting up, cutting Layborn off. "We're getting off track."

"The hell we are," Layborn said to Ashby. "If we got rid of the bad apples in Zephyr, we'd get rid of most of our crime."

"That may be, but that isn't why we're here."

"The hell it isn't. The campers who got shot were Zephyr people camping in a place they shouldn't have been camping." He turned back to Joe. "See what I mean about their attitude? And you can only imagine what they said to get themselves killed. I knew those people very well. I didn't get along with 'em either. They had no respect for anyone or anything, those people. They liked to call themselves the Gopher State Five because they were all from Minnesota, like that made them special somehow."

Joe observed that Demming had subtly pushed her chair farther away from Layborn. Portenson observed Layborn as if the ranger were an amusing, exotic specimen.

"You know," Portenson said, "I bet you guys could really run this damned park properly if you could just get rid of all of the people in it. We feel the same way about the reservation. If we could ship all those damned Indians off somewhere, we wouldn't hardly have any trouble at all."

Layborn turned his scowl on the FBI agent. Demming looked mortified by both Layborn's and Portenson's language. Joe felt sorry for her.

"Maybe we can get back to the issue here," Joe said, and received a grateful nod from Ashby.

"And maybe," Layborn said to Joe, "we can start with why you're really here. Why we all had to show up for this damned meeting in the first place."

"I'm a little curious about that myself," Portenson agreed.

Joe felt his neck get hot. He had been expecting the question and couldn't lie or mislead them. Not that he was any good at lying anyway. He felt it was his assignment to tell them the truth but leave a couple of things out. The specter of Governor Rulon stood in the corner, it seemed, listening closely to what Joe said.

"Spencer Rulon was the U.S. Attorney for the District of Wyoming before he ran for governor, as you know," Joe said. "So if he still had his old job, he would have been the one trying to prosecute this case. He's got a vested interest in it. He'd like to see Clay McCann thrown in prison because he doesn't like the idea of a man getting away with murder in his state, despite the weird legal circumstances of this one. So he asked me to come up here and talk to you all and write a report summarizing the case. If he reads something that interests him, he may go to the new U.S. Attorney, or have the Wyoming AG take a look at it. He wants to help, not interfere. That's what he told me. He asked me to come up here and poke around, see if I can figure anything out from a fresh perspective."

Layborn snorted, sat back, and crossed his arms over his chest. "What do you expect to find that we haven't already gone over?"

Joe shrugged. "I have no idea."

"This is pointless," Layborn said. "You're wasting my time and everybody's time in this room."

"Maybe," Joe agreed.

Ashby said, "I suppose it can't hurt. Sometimes the best thing to do is start fresh."

Joe could tell by the way Ashby said it that he really didn't believe what he was saying. He was playing peacemaker and he wanted to move the meeting along so he could get out of there.

"Doubtful," Layborn said.

Ashby sighed and looked squarely at Joe. "The particulars of this case have been reviewed ad nauseum. We've never had a case with a higher profile, and frankly, we don't appreciate the publicity that's come from it. We saw more national press up here last summer than we've seen since we reintroduced the wolves, and it wasn't very good press."

"Is that why the chief ranger isn't here?" Joe asked.

Ashby tried not to react to Joe's question, but there was a flicker behind his glare.

"The National Park Service is funded by federal appropriation," Ashby said flatly. "Congressmen want to feel good about the parks. We want to be the agency everybody feels all warm and fuzzy about. They don't like this kind of controversy, and neither do we."

Layborn shot his arm out and looked at his wristwatch. "I've got to go," he said.

"I have some questions," Joe said quickly.

"This is stupid," Layborn said, looking to Ashby for a nod so he could have permission to leave. "He has the files. He should read 'em."

Ashby wouldn't meet Layborn's eye to dismiss him.

"I read over the file more than once," Joe said, forging ahead. "I read everything in it, but I'm not sure all of the information was in there. Not that anything was withheld deliberately, but there are things I'm just unclear on. So I thought I'd start with those so I have a better picture of what happened."

The room was suddenly silent except for a loud sigh from Layborn.

"The sooner we do this the sooner I'll get out of your hair," Joe said quickly. Ashby acquiesced and sat back in his chair. With his fingers, he signaled, *Go on*.

"It looks to me like everybody involved did everything exactly right," Joe started, hoping to relieve some of the doubt they might have. "By the book, down the line. From the initial call to throwing McCann into the Yellowstone jail. I have no questions about the procedure at all. In fact, given the crime, I was damned impressed with how restrained and professional you all were."

He looked up to see Layborn nodding as if to say, *What did you expect?*

"The things I don't get have nothing to do with how you handled the arrest. They have to do with other aspects of the case."

Joe didn't like talking so much. He had already used more words in this room than he had in the past month. But he had no choice but to continue. Self-doubt began to creep into his consciousness, like a black storm cloud easing over the top of the mountains. He wasn't sure this was a job he could do well, a role he could play competently. Joe liked working the margins, keeping his mouth shut, observing from the sidelines. He did his best to block out the image of the thunderhead rolling over.

He asked Demming, "You were the first to respond, correct?"

For the first time, Demming sat up. Her expression changed from embarrassed to interested.

"Yes," she said, nodding. "I was actually off-duty at the

time. I was coming back from Idaho Falls with my daughter, who had to see the orthodontist. I was out of uniform, but I had the cruiser and my weapon. I heard the call from dispatch and realized I was just ten to fifteen minutes away from the Bechler ranger station, so I responded."

Ashby cut in. "That corner of the park is by far the least visited," he said, his voice monotone, as if he'd explained it countless times, which he likely had. "You can't even get there from the park itself. In order to get to Bechler, you've got to drive into Idaho or Montana and come back in. The road down there doesn't connect with any of our internal park roads. That's why we didn't—and don't—have a constant law enforcement presence there."

Joe said, "I've read the file, Mr. Ashby. I know where Bechler is located. What I'm asking about are things that aren't in the incident report."

Ashby sat back slightly chastened.

Demming continued, "When I got to the station, McCann had turned over his weapons and was sitting on the bench waiting. He didn't put up any kind of struggle, and he admitted to what he'd done. I took him outside, cuffed him, and waited for backup."

"Which was me," Layborn said. "I was there within the hour."

"How did McCann act?" Joe asked Demming.

Demming shook her head, as if trying to find the right words. "He was easy to get along with, I guess. He didn't say all that much. He wasn't ranting or raving, and didn't act like he was crazy or anything. In fact, he seemed sort of stunned, like he couldn't really believe it was happening."

"So he didn't deny the murders?"

"Not at all. He described what happened down at Robinson Lake. That he'd been hiking and the campers

107

harassed him, so he defended himself. That's how he put it, that he was defending himself."

"Asshole," Layborn whispered. Joe ignored him.

"So at the time you arrived, he didn't indicate to you he knew anything about the Zone of Death?"

"No."

Ashby looked pained. "We don't like that term and we don't use it."

Joe acknowledged Ashby but pressed Demming. "So he found out about it later? After he was in jail?"

Demming shook her head. "I had the feeling he knew about it at the time," she said. "It's just an impression, and I can't really prove it. He was just so cooperative. I got the impression he knew that he was going to walk eventually. He acted like he had a secret."

Joe nodded.

"You never told me that," Layborn said to Demming, his voice threatening.

"I did so," she said, looking back at him. "I told you when you arrived. But it didn't fit with anything then, so you probably just forgot about it."

Layborn rolled his eyes and turned to Joe. "What difference does it make?" he asked.

"Maybe none," Joe said. "I'm just trying to figure out if he went trolling for targets or if there was more to it."

Joe asked Demming, "Did McCann check in at the ranger station before he went on his hike that morning? Did anyone see him?"

Demming hesitated, trying to recall. "Yes," she said, "he even signed the register, listing his destination as Robinson Lake."

"I didn't see a copy of the registration page in my file," Joe said. "That's why I asked."

"Why does it matter?" Layborn cut in.

Joe said, "Because if McCann checked in that morning he could have looked on the register to see who was already in the park before him. I assume the victims registered the day before. McCann could have seen their names on the sheet and known who was at Robinson Lake. If he knew their names and where they were camping, that might suggest some familiarity with them after all—that he didn't just bump into complete strangers like he claimed."

Layborn, Ashby, and Portenson exchanged looks. Joe had hit on something. He felt a little trill in his chest.

"What about that?" Ashby asked Layborn.

The chief investigator started to answer but stopped. His face reddened as he looked back at Joe.

"I'm sure the sign-in sheets are still at the station," Demming said, unsure where Joe was headed.

"It would be interesting to take a look at them," Joe said.

Portenson reacted by furiously rubbing his face with his hands. "We've been down this road for months, Joe," he said. "The FBI has been working on the Gopher State angle. We interviewed everyone the victims knew in Minnesota, their parents, teachers, friends, fellow environmental activists. Environmental terrorism is high priority with us and we pursued that angle. What we found is a bunch of granola eaters who hate George Bush. No surprises there. But we couldn't find a single thing that connected the victims with Clay McCann. Not a damned thing. We've gone over it a thousand times. Nada."

Joe said, "So none of them had ever been to West Yellowstone?"

"Not that we could find," Portenson said with impatient finality. "And we couldn't find any record of McCann in the park either. Like maybe he stayed at Old Faithful and one of them spit in his food or something so he wanted revenge. Believe me, we've been all over this."

"We think they were involved in drugs," Layborn cut in.

Joe looked up at him. That wasn't in the file.

"Meth, dope," Layborn said. "There's a goddamned pipeline from somewhere into the park. We think half the Zephyr people are users, and we don't think they travel to Jackson or Bozeman to get it. We think they buy it locally."

Ashby cleared his throat. "*Half* is too much, Eric."

"I wouldn't be surprised if it was more than half," Layborn said, ignoring his boss. "I'm convinced if we ever find out why those four people were murdered, if there was even a reason other than Clay McCann having target practice, it'll have something to do with the drug ring."

Joe looked to Ashby and Portenson for clarification. Portenson rolled his eyes. Ashby looked away, said, "We don't have any evidence that the crime had to do with drugs."

Layborn smirked. "Drugs and environmental terrorism," he said. "I'll bet the house they'll have something to do with this. We'll just never fucking know, I'm afraid."

Layborn's conspiracy had silenced the room.

"And I'll tell you something else," he said, leaning across the table toward Joe. Ashby saw what was happening and was too late to intervene. Layborn growled, "Getting rid of those four assholes was not the worst thing to ever happen to Yellowstone National Park."

"*Eric!*" Ashby said. Then quickly, to Joe: "That is *not* our policy."

"But I bet you wish it could be." Portenson grinned.

"No, we don't," Ashby said heatedly.

Demming had shrunk back into her chair as if trying to become one with the fabric.

Joe didn't know what to say. He looked back down at the list he had made several days before and continued as if nothing had happened.

"There are several references to the Gopher State Five," he said. "Four are dead. Who survived?"

"His name is Bob Olig," Demming said quietly. "We haven't been able to find him."

"There's a nationwide BOLO for him," Portenson said, meaning Be On The Lookout. "No solid hits yet."

"He worked here also?" Joe asked.

Layborn said, "Another Zephyr scumbag."

"He was employed at the Old Faithful Inn," Ashby said wearily, having lost all control of Layborn and given up trying. "He vanished the day after the murders were reported."

"Where was he the day of the murders?" Joe asked.

"Giving tours of the Old Faithful Inn," Ashby said. "That's been verified by the site director, Mark Cutler. Olig was a tour guide, and a pretty good one."

Joe sat back, thinking. "So three of the five—Rick Hoening, Jim McCaleb, and Bob Olig—all worked together at Old Faithful?"

Ashby nodded. "In the area, anyway. But it's a big complex with hundreds of employees, nearly a thousand in the summer. It wasn't like they did the same job."

"But I assume they lived in employee housing together?"

"Correct."

"And it's been searched?"

"Torn apart," Layborn said. "We found some meth, some dope, like I said. A bunch of books about environmental sabotage, monkey-wrenching, that sort of crap. And e-mails from their fellow loons around the world. But nothing about Clay McCann, or anything we could use."

111

"Can I look at them?" Joe wondered how many of the e-mails were to and from Yellowdick, and what they were about.

When he asked the question, he saw Layborn, Portenson, and Ashby all smile paternalistically. Portenson leaned forward on the table. "You can quit the charade, Joe."

Joe didn't respond but he knew his face was flushing because it was suddenly hot. The thunderhead of doubt rolled across the sky, blacking it out.

"We know about the e-mail to your governor," Portenson said. "It was sent by Hoening. He was Yellowdick. He sent messages to the governors of Montana and Idaho too." He paused, letting that sink in before continuing. "And the president, and the secretary of the interior, and the head of the EPA. None of them make any sense. All of the e-mails have references to resources and cash flow. The best we can determine is the guy objected to some aspects of management up here and liked to be a scaremonger. The Park Service is an easy target, you know. Everyone's a critic. Hoening liked to stir things up, is all."

Joe was embarrassed. They had known all along why the governor sent him and had been waiting for him to come clean. His duplicity shamed him.

"We know all about his e-mail traffic; we know everything there is to know about the victims," Portenson said. "We didn't just fall off the fucking turnip truck. But what we can't figure out is if there is anything more to this case than what is staring us right in the face: that Clay McCann walked into Yellowstone Park and shot four people in cold blood and got off. That's bad enough, but I'm afraid that's all there is."

Joe swallowed.

Portenson said, "This is the strangest case any of us have

112

ever been involved in because everything's transparent." The FBI agent raised his fist and ticked off his points by raising his fingers one by one: "We know what happened. We know who did it—the son of a bitch admits it. We think we know the motivation. And we know there isn't a god-damned thing any of us can do about it."

Joe said, "Unless we can prove McCann went there specifically to kill those four people as some kind of bigger scheme, then we can get him on conspiracy to commit murder."

Portenson sighed. "You think we haven't tried?"

"You're welcome to follow up with me and my staff with any questions you might have," Ashby said, taking back control of the meeting as Joe gave it up. "But we resent the idea that your governor thinks we're a bunch of incompetents up here and he needs to send a game warden to figure things out. We resent the *hell* out of it."

Joe's ears burned, and he needed a drink of water because his mouth was suddenly dry.

Ashby said, "Everything that could be investigated has been investigated. We're sick to death of reporters, and questions, and second-guesses. We didn't write the law that created this loophole and there's nothing we can do about it now. The chief ranger wants this whole episode to *go away*."

"Meaning," Layborn said, "do what you have to do and then get the hell out. We don't need your help and we don't need your governor to check up on us."

Ashby looked at his wristwatch again. For all intents and purposes, the meeting was now over.

"Thank you," Joe said, and his voice sounded hollow even to him.

Layborn was up and out of the room before Joe could

gather his papers and put them back into his file. Demming gave Joe a sympathetic nod and was gone.

"My daughter has a volleyball game in Gardiner," Ashby said. "It started at five." He held out his hand and Joe shook it.

"I've got daughters too," Joe said. "I know how that goes."

Ashby stood aside so Joe and Portenson could leave, then locked the room after them.

Joe and Portenson went down the stairs. The receptionist, who had to stay five minutes beyond quitting time because of the meeting, glared at Joe as he passed her desk.

The evening was cool and still. Joe didn't realize Portenson was following him until he reached the Yukon.

"You ought to just go home, Joe," Portenson said. "Save yourself the aggravation. This case has beaten me to death."

Joe turned around and leaned against his vehicle. "You really think we know all there is to know?"

Portenson shook his head. "Sometimes, it's all there right in front of you. We all want to find something else, figure it out, be heroes. But in this case, there's nothing to figure. It is what it is."

Joe wasn't sure he agreed. "So where's Bob Olig?"

"Who the fuck knows? Or cares? He probably just felt guilty because his friends died and he didn't, so he went to Belize or someplace like that."

"Shouldn't the FBI be able to find him?"

Portenson snorted. "Man, haven't you been reading the paper?"

Joe didn't want to go there. "The other thing I can't wrap my mind around is this Clay McCann. The story just doesn't ring true. He just happened to go on a hike armed like that? Come on."

"The story's so bizarre that it might just be true. And even if the guy knew about the Zone of Death, so what? He committed the perfect crime."

Joe mulled that over.

"Those guys up there," Portenson said, nodding toward the law enforcement building, "they don't know you very well, do they?"

"I don't know what you mean."

The FBI agent grinned wolfishly. "They don't know you've got a knack for getting yourself in the middle of trouble. I wouldn't really call it a talent, exactly; it's more like a curse, like I'm cursed to never get out of this fucking state." He laughed. "It might be just their bad luck that you'll bumble onto something we missed. Poor fucking them."

Joe shook his head and thought Portenson had more confidence in him than he had in himself, especially after having his head handed to him in the conference room.

"Are you going to be needing any help up here?"

Joe misunderstood. "Are you offering?"

"Fuck no. I'm through with this case. What I was wondering about was whether you might ask your old buddy Nate Romanowski to show up with his big gun and his bad attitude."

Joe looked away, hoping his face didn't reveal anything.

Portenson read him. "So he might show, eh?"

Joe said nothing.

"I still want to talk to him, you know."

"I know."

"I may never get out of this state," Portenson said, "but it'll make my sentence more pleasant if I know Romanowski is in a federal pen."

"Don't you have real terrorists to chase?" Joe asked.

Portenson snorted and opened his arms to embrace all of

Mammoth Hot Springs, all of Yellowstone, all of Wyoming, and shouted, "I fucking *wish*!"

With that, Portenson turned on his heel and stomped across the small parking lot to his Crown Vic with U.S. Government plates. The FBI agent roared away with a spray of gravel.

Joe sighed, looked around. Cumulus clouds became incendiary as the setting sun lit them. The quiet was extraordinary, the only sound the burble of a truck leaving Mammoth Village and descending the switchbacks toward Gardiner.

It occurred to him that he hadn't made arrangements for where he would stay that night. His choice was to drive down the switchback roads from Mammoth out the North Gate and find a motel in Gardiner, Montana, or cross the street, the lawns where the elk grazed, to the rambling old Mammoth Hot Springs Hotel.

8

J OE'S, BOOTS ECHOED on the hardwood floor of the lobby of the Mammoth Hotel. The lobby had high ceilings, a cavernous sitting area overlooked by a massive mural, dozens of empty overstuffed chairs. Two check-in clerks huddled around a computer monitor behind the front desk and looked up at him as he approached.

"Can I get a room?"

The clerk said, "Sorry, sold out," then smiled to show he was kidding.

"Very funny, Simon," the other clerk said in a British accent, then to Joe: "Don't worry, we're at the end of our season. There are plenty of rooms available. We get a little punchy when the end is near."

"When the *end is near*," Simon mimicked with an intonation of false doom while he tapped on a keyboard.

"You know what I mean," the other clerk said.

Joe drew his wallet out and fished for a credit card. Although the state had sent him his credentials, a state credit card wasn't in the package. He'd need to ask about that, and soon. The family credit card had a low maximum, and Joe didn't know the limit.

The two clerks worked together with a jokey, easy

rapport that came from familiarity. Joe noted that both wore Zephyr Corp. name badges with their first names and residences. While both were undoubtedly British, their name tags said "Simon" and "James" from Montana.

"You aren't really from Montana," Joe said, while Simon noted the name on his credit card.

"How did you guess that?" James asked slyly.

"Actually, when you work for Zephyr long enough and get hired on in the winter, you can claim Montana or Wyoming for your residence," Simon said. "Better than Brighton, I suppose."

"Definitely better than Brighton," James said.

"Or Blackpool, James." To Joe: "You've got a reservation," Simon said, looking up from the screen.

"I do?"

Simon nodded. "And it's covered. By a Mr. Chuck Ward from the State of Wyoming."

Joe liked that and appreciated Ward for taking care of details. Simon handed over the keys to room 231.

"Are you familiar with the hotel?" Simon asked.

Joe was, although it had been a long time. Despite the years, the layout of the building was burned into his memory.

ROOM 231, ALONG with the rest of the rooms and the hallway, had been renovated since Joe was there last. The lighting wasn't as glaring and the walls not as stark as he remembered, he thought, musing how years distorted memory and perception. It was still long though, and he struggled down it with too many bags. A sprinkler system now ran the length of the ceiling, and the muted yellow paint of the ceiling and walls was restful. Still, it gave him a feeling of melancholy that was almost overwhelming.

While they could change the carpeting and the fixtures, they couldn't change what had happened there more than twenty-five years ago, or stop the memories from flooding back to him.

His room was small, clean, redone. A soft bed with a brass headboard and a lush quilt, a pine desk and chair, tiled floor in the bathroom, little bear-shaped soap on the sink. There was no television. A phone on the desk was the only nod toward the present. Otherwise, the room could have been something out of the 1920s, when the hotel was built. He looked out the window and was pleased it overlooked the huge stretch of lawn known as the parade ground.

He sat on the bed, his head awash with overlapping thoughts. He tried to convince himself the meeting had not gone badly, that he hadn't embarrassed himself, that he'd learned a few things to help him carry out his assignment. That was true, but he couldn't get over the moment when Portenson said, "Cut the charade, Joe," and he realized they had all been waiting for him to fess up.

Joe stood and surveyed his room. There was a two-foot space between the bed and the curtained window. He stared at the space, thinking it must have been larger once, since that was where he'd spent his time when he was here last. His parents had put down blankets and he slept there on the floor. But it had seemed so much bigger at the time, just like the room had seemed bigger, the hallways longer, the ceilings higher, the lightbulbs brighter. He could recall the musty smell of the carpet and the detergent odor of the bedspread. He remembered pretending to sleep while his father drank and raged and his mother sobbed. It was the first time in his life he'd been without his brother, and his brother was the reason they were in Yellowstone then. But most of all, he could remember the feeling of loss in the room, and what he thought at the time was the dawning of his own doom, as if his life as he knew it was over after only eighteen years. And not so great years either.

Long after his family had stayed at the Mammoth Hotel, Joe saw the movie *The Shining*. In one scene the camera lingers on an impossibly long, impossibly still hallway when a wave of blood crashes down from a stairwell and floods the length of it. At the time he had thought of the hallway of the Mammoth Hotel. He thought of it now. He needed a drink.

Joe dug through one of his duffel bags for a plastic bottle—a "traveler"—of Jim Beam and poured some into a thin plastic cup. He remembered the hum of an ice machine in the hall and grabbed the bucket.

He opened the door cautiously, half expecting the wave of blood he'd imagined to slosh across the floor. It didn't, and he felt foolish for letting his mind wander. As he stepped out there was a bustle of clothing and a sharp cry from the end of the hallway where the stairs were. He turned in time to see two men scrambling out of sight from the landing down the stairs. He glimpsed them for only a second; they were older, bundled in heavy clothes, not graceful in their sudden retreat. He hadn't seen their faces, only their backs.

Puzzled, he considered following them but decided against it. Their heavy footsteps on the stairs pounded into silence and they were no doubt crossing the lobby. Had he frightened them? He wondered what they had been doing that they felt it necessary to flee like that when he emerged into the hallway.

Joe filled his bucket and went back to his room. Although he generally liked solitude, what drew him was the quiet of being outside, where he could see, hear, and feel the landscape around him. It was different in a huge, virtually unoccupied hotel, where he longed for the hum of conversation behind doors he passed, and the assurance that he wasn't totally alone on his floor. He paused at his door and shot a suspicious glance back where he'd seen the men. There was no one there now, although the empty hotel seemed clogged with ghosts.

THE MAMMOTH DINING room was the only restaurant still open in the village and it was a short walk from the hotel. Although Joe disliked eating alone, he had no choice so he grabbed his jacket and the Zone of Death file to read over, yet again, while he ate. Simon and James were still at the desk when he descended the stairs.

Joe asked Simon, "About a half hour ago, did two old men come running across the lobby from the stairs?"

Simon and James exchanged glances. Simon said, "I remember that, yes. But they weren't running when I saw them. They were walking briskly toward the front doors."

"Do you know them?"

Simon shook his head.

"Were they Zephyr employees?"

James laughed. "Who knows? It's the time of year when the nutters really come out, you know? We don't pay any attention to them unless they bother the guests. Were they bothering you?"

"Not really," Joe said.

AS JOE CROSSED the street to the restaurant he noticed a park ranger cruiser at the curb. The door opened and Judy Demming got out.

"Del Ashby asked me to give you something," she said, popping open the trunk with a remote on her key chain.

Demming was out of uniform, in jeans, a turtleneck, and

a sweater. She looked smaller and more scholarly in street clothes, Joe thought, her eyes softer behind her glasses.

"Were you waiting for me?" Joe asked.

"I just pulled in."

He followed her around her car as she lifted a cardboard box out of the trunk.

"All of those e-mails printed out," she said, holding the box out to him. "The ones you said you wanted to look at."

Joe tossed the Zone file into the box and took it from her. It was heavier than he would have guessed.

"That was pretty efficient," he said. "I hope you didn't have to do this on your time off."

"No bother," she said. "My husband's home with the kids. I called him and told him I'd be late. He's a saint."

"I've got one of those at home too."

She didn't rush to jump back into her cruiser, but seemed to be waiting for Joe to say something.

"Can I buy you dinner?" Joe asked. "I've got lots more questions."

She looked at her watch and shook her head. "Lars is cooking something, so I don't have time for dinner," she said. "But maybe we could have a glass of wine in the bar."

"Sounds good," he said, wishing he hadn't had the bourbon already. He wanted to be sharp.

Less than a quarter of the tables were occupied in the dining room, Joe noticed, as they entered and turned right toward a small lounge. Several men sat at the bar drinking draws and watching SportsCenter on a fuzzy television, the first set Joe had seen in the park. The men looked like they'd been there awhile, and Joe discounted them as being the strangers in the hallway. Demming chose a small dark table in the corner farthest from the bar and sat with her back to the wall. He guessed she didn't want to be seen but didn't ask why. Since it was a slow night they waited for the bartender to top the glasses of the viewers before coming to take their orders himself. Joe ordered another bourbon and water and Demming a red wine.

"Thanks for the e-mails," Joe said. The box was near his feet.

She shook her head sadly. "I don't think you'll find anything very useful in them. I read them myself, hoping against hope that there would be some kind of reference to Clay McCann, but there isn't. You'll learn all kinds of things about environmental activism and how horny those poor guys got being out here all alone, but I don't think you'll find anything valuable. There are some messages planning their trip to Robinson Lake, mainly who is to bring what alcohol and food. I'm afraid the e-mails are another dead end."

"If nothing else," Joe said, "maybe I'll get a better feel for Hoening and the other victims."

She agreed. "They weren't bad people, just young and misguided. You'll find that the five of them had a yearly reunion at the end of the season."

Joe was interested. "Was it always at Robinson Lake?"

"No, but all of the reunions were in that little corner of the park," she said, her tone low but amused. "It's kind of a funny story, really. When the five of them left Minnesota to come out here together to try and get jobs in Yellowstone, they didn't have a road map with them, I guess. They entered the park for the first time at the Bechler entrance, coming from Idaho. They had no idea they couldn't go any farther into the park from there, so they camped out their first night in that area. Apparently, a ranger told them they'd need to go back out of the park and drive up to West or down to Jackson to get on the right road to Mammoth to apply for jobs. So, because of that inauspicious beginning, they held a reunion of the Gopher State Five every year down there where they first showed up, even though it was the wrong place to enter the park."

"So," Joe said, as the bartender arrived with their drinks, "it's possible that McCann knew where they'd be and when."

"It's possible," she said, sipping, "but we can't prove it. He denied knowing them, you know. He said they just happened to be there at the time."

"Which brings us back to the guest register," Joe said.

She nodded. "That's why I'm here now," she said. "I'd like to go down to Bechler with you tomorrow, if that's okay."

Joe said, "I'd be honored."

"Of course, Ashby wants me to keep an eye on you as well."

"I figured that."

Now that it was out, a heavy silence hung between them.

"Why does Layborn hate Zephyr employees so much?"

Demming rolled her eyes. "I wish he wasn't so strident about it, but he is. Layborn used to be a SWAT assault team captain for the Bureau of Alcohol, Tobacco, Firearms and Explosives, and he brings too much of that gung-ho training to his job. He's like a lot of real-world cops I've met. Day after day, he only sees the worst side of human nature, you know? He never gets calls to watch thousands of them serving food, or doing laundry, or giving tours. He only encounters the employees who get into trouble, so he assumes they're all like that. And some of them really are. The Gopher Staters used to drive him crazy. They made it personal."

"How so?" Joe asked, leaning forward with his elbows on his knees and steepling his fingers.

"They were like frat boys. He caught them hot-potting more than once and he gave them tickets for it."

"Hot-potting?"

"Sorry, we have so much lingo up here. Hot-potting is soaking in thermal pools. It's illegal, but lots of people do it at night. It's relaxing and a way to wind down—a natural hot tub. Because there aren't any movie theaters or night-clubs or anything like that up here, some of the Zephyr employees go hot-potting for date night. Alcohol is usually involved, of course. Most of us look the other way because it's basically harmless. There's even a spot called Ranger Pool, if you catch my meaning. But we leave them alone unless they're being particularly loud or blatant about it. Not Eric Layborn, though. He busted the Gopher State Five a few times and they got to know him, and to know him is to dislike him, as you learned today. It escalated from there."

Joe encouraged her to go on.

She said, "Once they found out Layborn suspected them of dealing, they declared all-out war on him. They'd let the air out of his tires when he was at lunch, or they'd put a potato in his exhaust. Stink bombs, stuff like that. Once they acted like a big drug deal was going down in employee housing at Old Faithful—they put the word out to people Layborn used as informants—so Layborn put a huge squad together to raid it. It turned out to be a birthday party for a seventy-year-old waitress who'd worked in the park for forty-some years. Layborn was reprimanded, and it made the local papers. They set him up. And I'm sure you noticed his eye?"

Joe said he had.

"One time, they did that trick from *American Graffiti*, the movie? Layborn was hiding in the trees watching for speeders near Biscuit Basin. Somebody snuck up behind his car and put a chain around his axle and attached the other end to the trunk of a tree. Another guy raced by on the road. Layborn took off after the speeder and the chain ripped the axle off. Poor Layborn lost an eye on the steering column when that happened."

"That explains it," Joe said.

"It's glass," she said. "Rumor has it Eric had the National Park Service logo engraved and painted on the inside of his glass eye, so when it's in his socket it points at his brain. But that's just a rumor—I've never seen it."

Joe was taken aback. "You're kidding me."

"I wish I was."

Demming was so deadpan when she said it they both burst out laughing.

She covered her mouth with her fingers. "We shouldn't laugh."

"No, we shouldn't."

"So," Joe said, recovering, "no one was ever caught?"

"No. Nobody would fess up. We all knew it was the Gopher Staters, but we couldn't prove it."

Joe shifted uncomfortably. "Judy, did Layborn have any dealings with McCann?"

Demming wasn't shocked by the question. "I know what you're asking. But no, I don't think so."

"Everything's on the table," Joe said. "Maybe eye-for-an-eye kind of revenge, so to speak?"

Demming nodded, uncomfortable. "I'm probably not helping my career talking to you so much," she said. "You're not exactly the most popular guy in the park right now."

"Who knows I'm here?" Joe asked, thinking of the two old men at Mammoth.

"You'd be surprised how word gets around," she said,

taking a generous drink of wine. "This is a big park, but a really tiny community. Information and gossip are the way to get ahead, so there's always a lot of buzzing about what's going on, who's talking to whom, that sort of thing. A newcomer like you raises suspicion." She tossed her hair girlishly and continued. "There are *so* many factions. A lot, I mean *a lot,* of conflicts. Zephyr versus the Park Service. Environmentalists against resource users. Hunters outside the park versus park policy. The three states fighting with the Feds. Even in the Park Service, it's law enforcement versus interpretation, and seasonal rangers against full-timers. It's bureaucracy run amok, with too many small-minded department heads trying to advance. It's cutthroat, Joe."

"Sounds a whole lot like government," Joe said. "I speak from experience."

"I shouldn't be telling you all this. You must have ordered truth serum instead of wine," she said, gesturing toward her empty glass.

"Would you like another?"

"No!" she laughed. "I've done enough damage for one night. Plus, I've *got* to get home."

"Sorry," he said. "I hope talking with me doesn't do you any harm."

She stood and held out her hand. "You never know, and frankly I don't care anymore. I'm forty-two and Lars works for Zephyr. Up here, that means I'm in a mixed marriage, Yellowstone-style. We have two kids and live in a busted-down Park Service house, and I'm getting tired of playing the advancement game, because after eighteen years I've realized I'm going nowhere fast. Maybe the best thing that could happen would be for them to try and get rid of me."

Uh-oh, Joe thought.

127

"I'll see you tomorrow," she said, suddenly flustered. He watched her go. As she opened the front door, she shot a furtive glance into the dining room to see, he assumed, if there was anyone in there who recognized her.

AS HE ATE, Joe skimmed through the stack of e-mails. The messages to Governor Rulon and the other politicians were on top. They were similarly vague in regard to details and the request to contact him in "the 'Stone." Joe found it significant that the phrase "cash flow" was used only in Rulon's e-mail. He set it aside for later and went through the printouts. They all fit roughly into three categories.

The first was environmental activism. Saving the wolves, grizzlies, bison. Lots of back-and-forth with other activists about the upcoming buffalo hunt that would take place in Montana. Yellowdick, or Rick Hoening, was as passionate an advocate for endangered species as he was disdainful of hunters, ranchers, uninformed visitors, and certain factions of the Park Service, mainly law enforcement. His newest cause was something he called "bio-mining."

While learning of Hoening's political leanings and contacts within the environmental community, Joe detected a softening in his stance in the more recent exchanges. Often, Joe had found that people's extreme views weakened when they moved to the heart of the controversy and were exposed to the other side. It didn't happen with everyone, but many. It was easier to stay away and keep a rigid ideology when not mugged by reality. Although Hoening was certainly an environmentalist to the end, his more recent arguments to activists suggested that perhaps some of their policies and methods could be more reasonable and less harsh.

The second category was park gossip and news. These

e-mails composed the bulk of the box. Yellowdick was a chatty guy. The messages consisted of which employees were moving up and down the corporate ladder, who was moving where (the five hubs of activity were Old Faithful, Grant Village, Roosevelt Lodge, Lake Hotel, and Mammoth), who said what to whom, who was sleeping with whom, where parties were going to be after work and on weekends, who would drive, who would bring what. Demming was accurate about the insular nature of Zephyr employees. Like college students on campus, they had their own culture, rituals, words, and phrases. Their social lives existed in a separate universe from what millions of tourists experienced at the park. Visitors encountered waiters, servers, maids, front-desk staff. There was probably little thought as to what these people who served the tourists did with their lives when not in uniform, when the Zephyr name tag was off. Joe found the secret world fascinating and made himself stop reading and move on.

The third rough category he classified as *Desperate Pleas to Women*. In these, Joe found himself smiling and cringing at the same time. Men away from home in their early twenties could be shameless, and Hoening was no exception. Yellowdick was relentless, equal parts charm, desperation, and rakishness. He seemed to have tried to revive every friendship and chance meeting he had ever had with a female while growing up in Minnesota, stretching back to childhood. In each correspondence, he started out recalling the particulars of their meeting, often citing what she wore and the cute things she said. He said he missed her. If she replied, he continued the long-distance back-and-forth, writing about Yellowstone and what he and his friends were doing and seeing, extolling the clean air and healthy lifestyle or, if she liked the darker side, how great the parties were.

A girl named Samantha Ellerby apparently liked parties so much she had moved from Minnesota to L.A. to find really good ones. Hoening claimed the events he staged in Yellowstone rivaled anything she had found. She doubted it, she wrote. He said he'd prove it if she came to see him, and closed with the same line that he apparently felt was the clincher: "We'll have some cocktails and laughs, watch the sun set over Yellowstone Lake, go hot-potting and light a couple of flamers." Another e-mail said, "I can't wait to see you. I'll be at the airport in Jackson."

From what Joe could tell, she was the only woman Yellowdick had successfully persuaded. Based on the last two e-mails between them, one to him that said "A-Hole!" and his reply, "Bitch!", their time together had not gone well. But despite his low batting average, Yellowdick never stopped swinging for the fences. In the most recent e-mails, he had turned his sights on visitors he apparently had met and exchanged e-mail addresses with, having exhausted his list of females from Minnesota.

Although there were still plenty of e-mails to go through, Joe admitted to himself that what Demming had told him was essentially correct. There were no references to Clay McCann or anyone like him, and nothing revealing about their plans for the annual reunion at Robinson Lake. Except one thing, Joe thought. Bob Olig had been copied in on every message. It meant, Joe thought, Hoening had no reason to assume Olig wouldn't be there.

A thought struck him.

What if Olig *was* at Robinson Lake? What if the employee records at Old Faithful were wrong on that fact, or Olig had manipulated them to appear as if he'd been working that day?

Joe retrieved his file from the box and reviewed the

crime-scene report in detail once again, looking for something that would confirm his suspicion. Like finding five sleeping bags instead of four.

After reading and rereading the report and going over the inventory of items found at the scene, Joe could come up with only one conclusion: either Olig or McCann had removed every single shred of evidence of Olig's presence, or he'd never been at the camp at all, just like Layborn had said.

JOE LOOKED UP and realized he was the last diner in the restaurant. A knot of workers, busboys and waiters, had gathered near the kitchen door, pretending they weren't waiting for him to leave.

Joe stood, said, "Sorry!" and left a big tip he couldn't afford.

Carrying the box outside, Joe noted how incredibly dark it was with no moon, and no ground glow from streets, homes, or traffic. The cool air had a slight taste of winter.

HE CALLED MARYBETH from a payphone in the lobby of the hotel, having learned in Jackson not to rely on his cellphone in remote or mountainous places. Plus, he liked the intimacy of closing the accordion doors of the old-fashioned booth and shutting everything out so he could talk with her.

She covered the home front. Everyone was doing fine and it was too soon to really miss him. An employee in her Powell office had gotten angry and walked out for no good reason. Missy was snubbing her because, Marybeth assumed, her suspicions about Earl Alden and the arts council were correct.

"Fine with me," Marybeth said.

Joe recounted his day: the drive up, the arrest of Bear, the meeting, drinks with Judy Demming.

As he told her, he could feel her mood change, not by what she said but by the silence.

"You'd like her," he said. "She's trying to help me out up here even though her bosses probably wish she wouldn't. You'll need to meet her when you come up."

She asked for a description.

"Early forties, married, mother of two," he said. "She and her family live in broken-down federal housing and she says she's lost in the system. Kind of sounds familiar, huh?"

"She sounds nice," Marybeth said.

Changing tack, he asked, "Have you heard anything from Nate? Any idea when he's leaving?"

"He's already gone," she said. "He left a message on our phone tonight. I meant to tell you about that earlier."

"Did he say when he'd get up here?"

"No. Just to tell you he was on his way but he needed to tend to something in Cody first."

"So maybe tomorrow," Joe said.

"I'd assume."

She waited a beat. "How are you doing, Joe?"

He knew what she was referring to. He described his room, the hotel, the feeling he'd had since he arrived of the presence of ghosts.

"Does anyone know about your brother?"

"No. It's not important that they know."

They made plans for Marybeth to bring the girls to the park in a week.

ALTHOUGH TIRED, JOE couldn't sleep for more than an hour at a time. He couldn't determine if it was the strange bed, the unfamiliar night moans of an old building, or the

132

particularly vivid dream he'd had of sleeping on the floor at the side of the bed, knowing his parents were tossing and turning two feet away. He awoke to the foul, sour odor of his dad's breath after a night of drinking.

He sat up and found his duffel bag with his equipment in it, assembled his Glock and put it on the nightstand.

When he opened the window to let in the cold night air, he thought he saw two figures down on the lawn in the shadows, hand-cupping tiny red dots of lit cigarettes. When he rubbed his eyes and looked again, they'd been replaced by a cow elk and her calf.

PART THREE

YELLOWSTONE GAME PROTECTION ACT, 1894

AN ACT TO PROTECT THE BIRDS AND
ANIMALS IN YELLOWSTONE NATIONAL
PARK, AND TO PUNISH CRIMES IN SAID PARK,
AND FOR OTHER PURPOSES,
Approved May 7, 1894 (28 Stat. 73)

Be it enacted by the Senate and House of Representatives of the United States of America in Congress assembled, That the Yellowstone National Park, as its boundaries are now defined, or as they may be hereafter defined or extended, shall be under the sole and exclusive jurisdiction of the United States; and that all the laws applicable to places under the sole and exclusive jurisdiction of the United States shall have force and effect in said park: *Provided, however,* That nothing in this act shall be construed to forbid the service in the park of any civil or criminal process of any court having jurisdiction in the States of Idaho, Montana, and Wyoming. All fugitives from justice taking refuge in said park shall be subject to the same laws as refugees from justice found in the State of Wyoming. (U.S.C., title 16, sec. 24.)

SEC. 2. THAT said park, for all the purposes of this act, shall constitute a part of the United States judicial district of Wyoming, and the district and circuit courts of the United States in and for said district shall have jurisdiction of all offenses committed within said park.

9

THE NEXT MORNING, joe waited alone in the hotel lobby for Demming to arrive. There were no other guests up and around so early and he had the entire lobby to himself. He sat in an overstuffed chair and read a day-old *Billings Gazette*—newspapers from the outside world didn't arrive in the park until later in the day—whilst sipping from a large cup of coffee. Morning sun streamed through the eastern windows, lighting dust motes suspended in the air. The old hotel seemed vastly empty, the only sounds the scratch of a pen on paper and occasional keyboard clacking from Simon behind the front desk. On the lawns outside the hotel he could see that a herd of buffalo had moved in during the night and both the elk and buffalo grazed. The presence of wildlife larger than he just outside the hotel humbled him, as it always did, a reminder that he was just another player. When an official-looking white Park Service Suburban pulled aggressively into the alcove in front of the hotel, Joe assumed it was Demming and started to gather his daypack and briefcase.

Instead of Demming, a uniformed man of medium build pushed through the front doors. He had the aura of officialdom about him. Joe watched him stride across the lobby floor with a sense of purpose, his head tilted forward like a battering ram despite his bland, open face, his flat-brimmed ranger hat in his hand whacking against his thigh, keeping time with his steps. The ranger's uniform had crisp pleats and shoes shined to a high gloss. He had a full head of silver-white hair, thin lips, a belt cinched too tight, as if to deny the paunch above it that strained against the fabric of his shirt. He looked to be in his mid-fifties, although the white hair made him seem older at first. Beneath a heavy brow and clown-white eyebrows, two sharp brown eyes surveyed the room like drive-by shooters. The ranger saw Joe sitting in his Cinch shirt and Wranglers, dismissed him quickly as someone of no interest to him, and approached the front desk.

"I need to check on a guest," the ranger said in a clipped, authoritative voice.

"Name?" Simon asked without deference.

"Pickett. Joe Pickett."

"He checked in last night."

"How long is he staying?"

Tap-tap-tap. "The reservation extends through next week."

"A week! Okay, thank you."

The ranger turned on his heel and began to cross the lobby.

"Can I help you?" Joe asked, startling the ranger. "I'm Joe Pickett."

The man stopped, turned, studied Joe while biting his lower lip as if trying to decide something. He held out his hand but didn't come over to Joe. Meaning if Joe wanted to shake it, he'd need to go to *him*. Joe did.

"Chief Ranger James Langston," the man said, biting off his words. "Welcome to Yellowstone."

"We missed you at the meeting yesterday," Joe said.

"I had other matters to tend to."

138

"I thought it was your day off."

Langston nodded. "In my job, you never have a day off."

"That's too bad," Joe said, not knowing why he said it.

Neither did Langston. He released Joe's hand and stepped back, said, "I hope you got all the information you needed and everybody's been helpful and cooperative."

"So far."

"Good, good. Nice to meet you," Langston said, starting to head for the door.

"Why did you want to know how long I was staying?" Joe asked pleasantly.

"Just curious," Langston said. "We'd like to get this whole McCann thing behind us and move on. What's done is done. There isn't anything you or anyone else can do about it."

"Ah," Joe said.

"I've got to go. My motor's running."

"It sure is," Joe said.

Langston looked at him curiously, clamped on his hat, and went outside. The Suburban roared off all of two blocks to the Pagoda.

Demming came in the front door. "Was that Chief Ranger Langston?" she asked Joe.

"Yup."

"What did he want?"

Joe said, "I'm not real sure."

DEMMING PARKED HER cruiser and they took Joe's Yukon to the Bechler ranger station. Because of an overnight rock slide near Obsidian Cliff that likely wouldn't be cleared until that evening, Demming suggested they exit the park through the north entrance at Gardiner, drive to Bozeman, and double back south through West Yellowstone and on to Bechler.

"That's a lot of driving," Joe said as they cleared Mammoth.

"Get used to it," she laughed. "This is a *huge* place. You learn not to be in a hurry. Four or five hours to get somewhere is pretty common. The park forces you to slow down, whether you want to or not."

Joe drove down the switchbacks toward Gardiner. As he did, a growing sense of dread introduced itself to his stomach.

"Do you notice how laid back the pace is here?" Demming said, unaware of Joe's increasing trepidation. "No one is in a hurry. Rangers, waiters, desk clerks ... everybody moves at a slower pace than the outside world. We're like a tropical island in the middle of the county—everything is different here. Slower, more deliberate. Nothing can't wait until tomorrow. It drives you crazy at first but you get used to it. You know what we call it?"

They cleared the switchbacks and the terrain flattened out. The road became a long straightaway of asphalt across a grassy meadow. In the distance he could see the stone arch that signified the north entrance to the park. At one time, when the railroads delivered tourists like Rudyard Kipling, it was the primary gateway to Yellowstone.

"Joe, did you hear me?" she asked.

"I'm sorry, what?"

"I said, do you know what we call it?"

"No."

"Yellowstone Time. Everybody here is on Yellowstone Time."

"I see," he said, distracted.

They drove under the arch with the words FOR THE BENEFIT AND ENJOYMENT OF THE PEOPLE carved into the rock. The corner was still scarred and had not been patched. It receded in his rearview mirror.

140

"Joe, are you okay?" Demming asked.

"Why?"

"Your face is white. Are you sick?"

"No."

"Are you okay to drive?"

"Yes."

She settled back in her seat, silent, but stealing looks at him.

"I haven't seen that arch for twenty-one years," Joe said finally. "It brings back all kinds of bad memories. I'm sorry, but it sort of took me by surprise."

"A stone archway took you by surprise?" she said gently.

He nodded. "My family used to vacation in the park. This is the way we came in. I still have pictures of us standing by the arch, my dad and mom, my brother and me. Victor was two years younger. We were close. The park was our special place, maybe because it was the only place where my dad was happy. He loved Teddy Roosevelt's words: *'For the benefit and enjoyment of the people.'* He used to say it all the time."

Joe hesitated, surprised how hard it was to tell the story, surprised he wanted to tell it.

Demming didn't prompt him for more. They drove north through Paradise Valley in Montana as the morning sun poured over the Absaroka Mountains.

He swallowed, continued. "I was in college. On my brother's sixteenth birthday he called me in my dorm room at two in the morning. He was drunk and real upset. His girlfriend had dumped him that day and he was, well, sixteen. Everything was a crisis. He wanted to talk but I told him to go home, get some sleep, I had a test in the morning."

Joe slowed while a rancher and two cowboys herded cows down the borrow pit next to the highway. Puffs of

141

condensation came out of their mouths like silent word balloons. Calves bawled. When they were past, Joe sped up.

"After I hung up on him, Victor went home like I told him but took my dad's car. Stole it, actually. He drove five hours in the middle of the night and crashed it head-on into that arch. The police said later they estimated he was going a hundred and ten miles an hour."

She said, "My God."

"We stayed at the Mammoth Hotel for the funeral. Victor's buried in the Gardiner cemetery somewhere. My dad said he didn't want him back. I haven't been to his grave since."

Tears formed in his eyes and he didn't want them there. He wiped brusquely at his face with the back of his hand, hoping she didn't see them.

"Do you want to turn around and go there?"

Joe turned his head away from her. "Later, maybe."

"I'm sorry."

He shrugged. "I'm sorry I started your morning out with such a downer."

"Don't apologize."

"Okay."

What he didn't tell her, couldn't tell her, was that when his family returned home after the funeral his mother never unpacked. She left without saying goodbye. His mother and father blamed each other for Victor's death, although Joe knew it was his fault. The implosion had been on the cards for years, fueled by alcohol. He went back to college after that. While he was gone, his father sold the house and vanished as well. Getting back at her, Joe supposed. He'd not heard from either of them in years, although an Internet search by Marybeth indicated his mother had remarried and moved to New Mexico. His father's name produced no hits. Joe tried not to think of them at all, and asked Marybeth to stop searching. His parents could be happy, or dead. His family consisted of Marybeth and the girls. Period.

AFTER THEY CLEARED Bozeman, Joe said, "Really, I'm sorry about telling you that story. Don't pay any attention to me. Forget you heard it."

She was puzzled. "You probably needed to get it out."

"No, I didn't."

"It's okay, Joe."

"No, it isn't," he said. "I'm not really a touchy-feely guy and I don't want you to think I'm sensitive."

She laughed and shook her head, reached over and patted him on the arm. "Don't worry—your secret's safe with me."

He glowered at her.

JOE SAID, "YOU mentioned last night that the park has its own language. What are some of the other terms you can think of unique to here?"

She smiled. "Over the years, I've kept a list of them. 'Bubble queens' are laundry room workers; 'pearl divers' are dishwashers; 'pillow punchers' change sheets on the beds; 'heavers' are waiters and waitresses. All guests are called 'dudes' behind their backs long before everybody called everybody dudes."

"What are flamers?" Joe asked.

"Excuse me?"

"When I read Hoening's e-mails to prospective women, he always wrote, 'We'll go hot-potting and light a couple of flamers.'"

Demming shrugged. "I'm not sure. Zephyr people have their own language within a language."

"Is he talking about dope?"

"I assume."

"Maybe Layborn was on to something," Joe said.

"Maybe."

THEY STOPPED FOR lunch at Rocky's in West Yellowstone. It was one of the few places open. The streets were deserted, most businesses closed until the winter season. While they waited for their sandwiches, Joe surveyed the crowd. Everyone looked local and had the same logy listlessness about them as the people he saw in Mammoth; no doubt recovering from the tourist season, he thought.

"James Langston," Joe asked Demming, "what's he like?"

"The chief ranger? He's a bureaucrat of rare order. I've always found him arrogant and very political. He didn't get to where he's at by being everyone's friend, that's for sure. I heard him say once he thinks he's underappreciated given all he has to put up with. By *underappreciated* he meant underpaid. Ha! He should take home *my* government paycheck."

Joe said, "Maybe he should quit the Park Service and work in the private sector if he wants more money."

"What—and have to be accountable to shareholders? Work past five? And not live in a mansion that's financed by taxpayers? Are you crazy, Joe? What are you saying?"

She caught herself and looked horrified. "But I shouldn't be saying that."

"Your secret's safe with me," Joe said slyly. "Why do you suppose he was checking up on me?"

She sighed. "I'm sure he just wants you gone. He doesn't want this McCann thing in the news again."

"Speaking of McCann," Joe said. "We're in his hometown. Have you guys kept track of him since he was released?"

"I assume he's back here," she said, "that he came home. If he left I haven't heard. Why, do you want to check up on him?"

Joe nodded.

"Now?"

"I'm curious. Aren't you?"

IN THE CAR, Joe turned onto Madison.

"This isn't the road to Bechler," Demming said.

"Nope."

"Then what ..."

He gestured out the window. "Look."

The law office of Clay McCann was a simple single-story structure made of logs. It looked like the type of place that was once an art gallery or a Laundromat.

"Think he's in there?" she asked.

Joe shrugged, but felt a tug of anxiety. He stared at the law office as if he might get a better read on McCann by studying it. The news photos of McCann made the lawyer look bland and soft. Joe wanted to see him in the flesh, look into his eyes, see what was there. Joe parked the Yukon on the other side of the street.

"Maybe we should go in and say hello," Joe said.

As they climbed out, Joe dug the Glock out of his daypack and shoved it into his Wranglers behind his back.

"Did you have that gun in the park?" Demming asked.

"Yes."

"You're breaking the law. You can't have firearms in the park."

"I know."

"Joe ..."

"It's okay," he said. "I can't hit anything with it."

She continued to shake her head at him as they crossed the street.

Joe entered the office, Demming behind him. A dark-haired, dark-eyed woman sat at a reception desk reading a glossy magazine. She looked as out of place as a nail salon in a cow pasture and she raised a face filled with undisguised suspicion.

"Is Clay McCann in?" Joe asked.

"Who are you?" she asked in a hard-edged East Coast accent.

"I'm Joe, this is Judy."

"What do you want?"

"To see Clay McCann."

"Sorry, he's not in at the moment and you don't have an appointment," she said, running a lacquered nail down a calendar on her desk. Joe noted there were no appointments at all written on it.

"When will he be back?"

"He's off making a call at the supermarket," she said, apparently unaware how odd that sounded. "That takes him hours sometimes. So, Punch and Judy, if you want to meet with him you can schedule an *appointment*."

"You're his secretary?"

She performed what amounted to a dry spit take. "Secretary? Hardly. I'm Sheila D'Amato and I'm stuck in this one-horse town. I'm filling in because his real secretary quit."

Joe and Demming looked at each other. Joe didn't want to wait, neither did Demming.

"We'll be back," Joe said, handing Sheila his card, as did Demming. He used the opportunity to steal a look through an open door behind Sheila into what was undoubtedly McCann's office. One entire wall was filled with Montana statute books. There was a messy desk stacked high with unopened mail. On a credenza behind McCann's desk were binders emblazoned with corporate names and logos: Allied, Genetech, BioCorp, Schroeder Engineering, EnerDyne. The names rang no bells, but the collection of them struck the same discordant note as Sheila.

"A game warden and a park ranger," Sheila said, curling her lip with distaste. "Punch and Judy. I bet I know what you want to talk to him about."

Outside, Joe paused on the sidewalk to scribble the company names into a notebook he withdrew from his pocket. While he did, Demming said, "Let's go, Punch."

"WHY WOULD HE be making a call at the supermarket?" Demming asked as they cleared West Yellowstone. "I assume he's using a payphone. Why not just call from his office?"

"Probably thinks his lines are tapped," Joe said. "Or he doesn't want Sheila D'Amato to know what he's up to."

"What *is* he up to?"

10

To get to Bechler ranger station, they drove south toward Ashton, Idaho, skirting the western boundary of the park, which loomed darkly to the east and was constantly in sight. The terrain opened up into plowed fields, and they caught a glimpse of the Tetons on the horizon before turning back toward Yellowstone. The Bechler area was dense and heavily wooded. Stray shafts of sunlight filtered through the tree branches to the pine needle floor. Deadfall littered the ground. There was no traffic on the road. Joe pulled into the ranger station and parked facing an old-fashioned hitching post.

The station had the feel of a frontier outpost, very much unlike the government buildings at Mammoth. There were five rough log structures built on short stilts, including a barn with horses in the corral, a long bunkhouse with a porch, and a small visitor center the size of a large outhouse. At the western corner of the complex was a trailhead for a narrow rocky path that meandered into the forest. No one was about, but a generator hummed in one of the buildings.

They clomped up the wooden stairway and entered the station, surprising a young seasonal ranger behind the counter.

"Wow," the man said, "I didn't see you pull in."

Joe smiled. "It gets lonely here, huh?"

The ranger, whose name tag said B. Stevens, nodded. "You're the first people here today. It gets real slow this late in the season."

B. Stevens hadn't shaved for a couple of days and hadn't combed his hair that morning. He was the polar opposite of the spit-shined James Langston Joe had met that morning.

Demming took over, telling Stevens they were following up on the murders, that Joe was with the State of Wyoming and she was providing assistance. While they talked, Joe flipped through the guest register, going back to July 21.

"Stevens was working that morning," Demming told Joe. "He was here when Clay McCann checked in."

"I was here when he came back too," Stevens said with unmistakable pride. "He put his guns right here on this counter and told me what he'd done. That's when I called for backup."

Joe nodded, asked Stevens to recall the morning. Stevens told the story without embellishment, replicating the chain of events Joe had studied in the incident reports.

"When he checked in before going on his hike," Joe asked, "did you see any weapons on him?"

Stevens said he didn't, McCann must have left them in his car. What struck him, though, was how McCann was dressed, "like he'd just taken all of his clothes out of the packages. Most of the people we see down here are hard-core hikers or fishermen. They don't look so ... neat."

"He didn't seem nervous or jumpy?"

"No. He just seemed ... uncomfortable. Like he was out of his element, which he was, I guess."

"Can you remember how much time he spent signing

in? Did he do it quickly, or did it take a few minutes?"

Stevens scratched his head. "I just can't recall. No one's asked me that before. He didn't make that much of an impression on me. The first time he was in here, I mean. When he came back with those guns, that's what I remember."

"Can I get a copy of this page he signed in on?"

Stevens shot a look at Demming, said, "We don't have a copy machine here. We've been requesting one for years, but headquarters won't give us one."

"Bureaucracy," Demming mumbled.

Joe asked if he could borrow the register and send it back, and the ranger agreed.

"We can't even get a phone line," Stevens said. "In order to call out we use radios or cellphones that get a signal about an hour a day, if that."

Joe said, "Does this entrance have a camera set up at the border like the others?"

Stevens laughed. "We have a camera," he said, "but it hasn't worked for a few years. We've requested a repairman, but ..."

"We were thinking of hiking to the crime scene," Joe said. "Is it straight down that trail out there?"

"We were?" Demming asked, slightly alarmed.

Stevens nodded. "There's a fork in the trail right off, but it's well marked." The ranger hesitated. "Are you sure you want to do that?"

"Yup."

Stevens looked at Demming, then back at Joe. "Be damned careful. This area has become pretty well known with all of the publicity. They call it the Zone of Death once you cross the line into Idaho. Lots more people show up here than they used to. Some of them get as far as the border but chicken out and come back giggling. But others are just plain scary-looking. The Zone draws them, I guess. They want to be in a place with no law. It's not my idea of a good time, but we can't stop them from walking into it if they've paid their fee and signed in. Personally, I think we ought to close the trail until the situation is resolved, or everybody just forgets about what happened."

Demming asked, "Are there people in there now?"

Stevens shrugged. "It's hard to say. More folks have signed in than have come out. Of course, the stragglers could have gone on from here, or come back after we're closed. But you never know. Our rangers are a little reluctant to patrol in there now, if you know what I mean. They're afraid of getting ambushed by somebody who thinks they can't ever be prosecuted for it."

"You're right," Demming said. "We should close the trail."

"We'll be okay in a few weeks," Stevens said, "when the snow comes. We've had twelve feet by Halloween in the past. That'll give us the winter to make our case."

Joe thanked Stevens and left with Demming. "Why did you take the register?" Demming asked.

Joe showed her the page with Clay McCann's name on it. Above his name were signatures from the day before for R. Hoening, J. McCaleb, C. Williams, and C. Wade. They listed their destination as "Nirvana."

Joe said, "If he wanted to make sure they were here, all he had to do was read the register."

As they stood near the Yukon they both looked at the trailhead, as if it were calling to them.

"I don't know, Joe ..." Demming said cautiously.

"I want to see the crime scene," Joe said. "It'll help me get my bearings. You can wait for me here if you want."

She thought about it for a few seconds, looking from Joe

152

to the trailhead and back before saying. "I'm going with you."

THE SIGN AT the fork in the trail indicated it was thirty miles to Old Faithful on the right, two miles to Robinson Lake on the left. The trail on the right fork was more heavily traveled. They went left.

The forest closed in around them. Because there was no plan or program to clear brush in the park, the floor of the timber on both sides of the trail was thick and tangled with rotting deadfall. Joe was struck by how "un-Yellowstone-like" this part of the park was. There were no geysers or thermal areas, and they'd seen no wildlife. Only thick, lush vegetation and old-growth trees. He studied the surface of the trail as he hiked, looking for fresh tracks either in or out, and stopped at a mud hole to study a wide Vibram-soled footprint.

"Someone's been in here recently," he said.

"Great," Demming whispered.

There was no delineation sign or post to indicate where they crossed the Idaho border. Joe assumed they had because the line, according to his map, was less than two hundred yards from the ranger station and they'd gone much farther than that. The trail meandered at a slight decline, but it was easy walking.

He heard it before he saw it.

"Boundary Creek," Joe whispered. They were now in the Zone of Death.

Joe felt his senses heighten as they crossed the creek, which was wider and more impressive than he'd guessed from looking at the map. He hopped from rock to rock, spooking brook trout that sunned in calm pools, their forms shooting across the sandy bottom like dark sparks. On the other side, as they pushed farther into the trees, he tried to will his ears to hear better and his eyes to sharpen. His body tingled, and he felt, for the first time in months, back in his element.

ROBINSON LAKE WAS rimmed with swamp except for the far side where trees formed a northern stand. The trail skirted the lake on the right and curled around it to the trees where, Joe guessed, the campers had set up their tents and been murdered. As they walked, he tried to put himself into Clay McCann's head. How far away did he see their tents? Where did he encounter Hoening? Did he smell their campfire, hear them talking before he got there?

As they approached the stand of trees and an elevated, grassy flat that had to be where the camp was located, Joe heard Demming unsnap her holster behind him. She was as jumpy as he was.

The camp had been cleared months before but the fire ring revealed the center of it. Logs had been dragged from the timber to sit on around the fire. Tiny pieces of plasticized foil in the grass indicated where a camper—or Clay McCann—had opened a package of snacks.

In the campsite, Joe turned and surveyed the trail they had taken. From the camper's perspective, they must have seen McCann coming. There was no way he snuck up on them unless they were distracted or oblivious, which was possible. Since Williams had been found near the fire ring and McCaleb and Wade had been killed coming out of their tent, he assumed McCann was literally in the camp before he started shooting. So was Hoening, whose body was found on the trail, the first or last to die? Again it struck him that the sequence of events really didn't matter. There was no doubt who'd done it.

"Joe ..." Demming whispered.

She was staring into the timber, her face ashen, her hand on her gun. Joe followed her line of sight.

The man aiming his rifle at them was dressed in filthy camouflage fatigues and had been hiding behind a tree. At fifty feet, it was unlikely he would miss if he pulled the trigger.

"That's right," the man said to Demming, "pull that gun out slow and toss it over to the side."

She did as she was told.

Because his back was to the lake, Joe figured the man with the rifle hadn't seen the Glock in his belt. Not that it would help them right now, since in order to use it he'd need to pull it, rack the slide, and hit what he was aiming at. In the time that would take, the rifleman could empty his weapon into the both of them.

"I seen you coming half a mile away," the man said, stepping out from behind the tree but keeping the rifle leveled. "I was in the trees taking a shit when you showed up."

He was short, stout, mid-thirties, with a blocky head, wide nose flattened to his face, dirt on his hands. His eyes sparkled with menace. Behind him, in the shadows of the timber, Joe now saw a crude lean-to shelter, a skinned and half-dismembered deer hanging from a cross-pole lashed to tree trunks. A survivalist, living off the land in a place with no law.

"You need to lower the weapon," Demming said, her voice calmer than Joe thought his would be at that moment. "Let's talk this over before you get yourself into any more trouble."

"What kind of trouble?" he said. "There ain't nothing you can do to me here."

"It doesn't work that way," Demming said.

"Sure it does," he said, and showed a tight smile. He was missing teeth on both top and bottom. "It worked for Clay McCann."

Joe and Demming exchanged a quick glance.

"I wrote him a letter but he never answered," the man said. Joe tried to determine the man's accent. His words were flat and hard. Midwestern, Joe guessed.

"Where you from?" Joe asked. "Nebraska?"

"Iowa."

"You're a long way from home."

The Iowan looked hard at Joe for the first time and narrowed his eyes. "This is my home. And you two are trespassing. And the way I got it figured, I could shoot you both right now and walk 'cause no court can try me."

"That's where you're wrong," Demming said. "How long have you been here?"

"Month."

"Then you don't know that Congress passed a law," Demming said. "You're now in the Idaho district. This is no longer off the map."

Joe admired Demming's quick thinking. The lie sounded credible. It produced a flicker of doubt in the Iowan's eyes and the muzzle of his rifle dropped a few inches.

"Let us leave," Demming said, "and no harm will come to you. There was no way you could have known."

"They really passed a law?" he asked.

Demming nodded. Joe nodded.

"And the president signed it?"

"Yes."

The Iowan looked from Demming to Joe and back, digging for a clue either way. Joe hoped his face wouldn't reveal anything. Seconds ticked by. A bald eagle skimmed the surface of the lake and just missed plucking a fish out.

"Naw," the Iowan said, raising the rifle butt back to his shoulder, "I don't believe you. If that was the case there would have been some rangers patrolling out here, and I ain't seen nobody."

The heavy boom, an explosion of blood and fingers on the forestock, and the rifle kicking out of the Iowan's hands happened simultaneously and left the wounded man standing there empty-handed and wide-eyed.

Demming screamed, Joe froze.

Another shot took the Iowan's nose and part of his cheekbone off his face. When he instinctively reached up with his now-shattered left hand, a bullet ripped through the back of his camo trousers at knee level, no doubt slicing through tendons, collapsing him backward into the grass like a puppet with strings clipped.

Joe saw movement on his left in his peripheral vision, a flash of clothing darting from the reeds along the shoreline into the cover of the trees. He fumbled for his weapon, racked the slide, trained it on the writhing, moaning Iowan as Demming retrieved her pistol.

He approached the Iowan and squatted, patting down the man and finding a .44 revolver, bear spray, and the half-gnawed leg bone of the deer. He tossed them aside, adrenaline and the after-effects of fear coursing through him. The leg plopped fifteen feet out into the lake.

He heard Demming shout into her radio, telling the ranger back at the station to call in a helicopter for an air-lift to Idaho Falls before the man bled out.

"Is he going to make it?" she asked Joe, her eyes wide, her hands trembling so badly she couldn't seat the radio back into its case on her belt. She glanced nervously in the direction the shots had been fired.

"I think so," Joe said, grimacing at the Iowan's split and disfigured face and the pool of bright red blood forming in the grass behind his knees. "We can tie his legs off with tourniquets and bind his hand and face to stop the bleeding," he said, taking off his shirt to tear into strips.

"What happened?" the Iowan croaked, mouth full of blood, shock setting in. "Who did this to me?"

Joe didn't recognize the flash of clothing, but the marksmanship was familiar.

"His name's Nate Romanowski," Joe said.

"Who?" Demming asked.

"Friend of mine," Joe said to the Iowan. "If he wanted to hit you in the head and kill you, you wouldn't be talking right now."

11

"How long ago were they here?" Clay McCann asked Sheila while picking up the business cards. He was agitated.

"I don't know—three hours, maybe."

"What did they want?"

"Gee, Clay," she said, rolling her eyes, "maybe they wanted to ask you about shooting four people dead."

Annoyed, he looked up at her from the cards. He recognized the woman's name—Demming. She was one of the first on the scene at Bechler. She was no heavy hitter within the park, he knew that. Nothing special. But ... a *game warden*?

Sheila looked back at him with insolence. She was a poor fill-in for the receptionist who quit. Too much attitude, too much mouth. He wanted to tell her to tone down her act or he'd lose what few clients he still had. Then his focus changed from Sheila to the open door behind her, to the credenza and the notebooks that were clearly displayed on his desk.

"Why is my door open?" he asked, his voice cold.

"I wanted some light out here so I could read," she said defensively. "If you haven't noticed, it's dark in here. You need to replace some bulbs. And there's a nice big window in your office that lets in the light. Besides, the room needed airing out."

He glared at her. It wouldn't take much to drag her out from behind the desk by her hair. "Did they go into my office?" he asked.

"Of course not."

"Did you?"

"Just to open the door and the curtains. I told you that. Jesus, calm down."

"Did either of them *look* into my office?"

She glared back. "No. What's your problem, anyway?"

Instead of answering, he strode around her desk into his room. Shutting the door, he said, "Keep it closed."

She knocked softly on the door. "Clay, what's wrong?"

"Nothing's wrong."

ACTUALLY, EVERYTHING WAS wrong.

He sat heavily in his chair and rubbed his face and scalp with both hands, stared at his desk without really seeing it.

Everything was wrong. He tried not to think he'd been played. He was the player, not the playee, after all, right?

But the money still hadn't been wired. The banker was getting ruder each time he called, and had even insinuated that morning that "perhaps Mr. McCann should consider another financial institution, one more enthusiastic about such a small deposit, one that would be more in tune to servicing such a meager balance. Maybe one in the States?"

The banker had turned McCann from an angry customer demanding answers into a pitiful two-bit wannabe, begging for just a few more days of patience. The money *would* be wired, he assured the banker. He guaranteed it, knowing the value of his word, like his big talk months before, was being devalued by the day.

Even worse was that the man who was supposed to deposit the funds wouldn't take his call. McCann couldn't get past the secretary. How could this be?

Had he been conned? McCann couldn't believe that. He was too smart, too street-savvy to fall for it. He knew too much. But why wouldn't his business partner take his call? Why wouldn't he pay up, as promised? If this was a legitimate transaction, McCann could slap a suit on the bastard and take him to court to get his money. A contract was a contract, and this was Contract Law 101. But in this circumstance, McCann couldn't handle the problem through the courts. The irony of his situation gave him the sweats.

He'd spent hours waiting by the payphone on the side of the supermarket for the callback that never came, his frustration and anger building by the minute. He debated with himself whether to go back and try again.

"Fuck it," he said to himself as he reached out and picked up his desk phone and dialed.

"EnerDyne, Mr. Barron's office," the receptionist answered.

"This is McCann, again. I need to speak to Layton Barron immediately. Tell him."

"Mr. McCann, I told you earlier. Mr. Barron is in a meeting and he can't be disturbed. I'll give him your message when—"

"Tell him *now*," McCann said. "It's a matter of life and death."

My life, McCann thought. His death, if there wasn't some cooperation.

The receptionist hesitated, then put him on hold.

Okay, McCann thought. Either Barron came on the phone and explained himself, which meant the deal was still in play, or he sent the receptionist back with another delay or refusal. If that happened, there would be hell to pay.

Minutes ticked by. The lawyer began to wonder if the receptionist had chosen to place him on permanent hold.

Finally, Barron came on the line, angry, and said, "You agreed never to call me here. Is this a secure line?"

McCann was relieved. "No. I'm calling from my office."

"Goddamn it, we agreed—"

"I'll go to a secure location, but I'm not going to stand around in the cold all day again. Call me in ten minutes." McCann read off the number of the supermarket payphone. Barron repeated the number back.

At last, he thought, gathering his coat and hat. Finally, he would find out why the funds hadn't been deposited into his account, as promised. He'd done his part, certainly. Now it was time for them to do theirs.

"Going again?" Sheila asked, sighing heavily.

"I'll be back soon," he said. "Keep—"

"*Your goddamned door shut!*" Sheila finished for him in a screech.

MCCANN THOUGHT ABOUT Sheila as he walked down the sidewalk to the supermarket. His feelings were mixed, which surprised him.

Even though she was a piss-poor receptionist, he liked to look at her. She was more than a cartoon after all, he'd decided. She brought experience, sexual knowledge, and unabashed dutifulness to his needs and desires. Her reputation as a former mafioso kept woman excited him. He liked being seen with her because it was scandalous and only added to his infamy in town. Her features were severe: very black hair, very white skin, fire-engine red, pillow-soft lips. She was a combination of sharp, soft, ethnic, sensual, and in-your-face. Even if she was on the summit of over-the-hill.

He'd always thought her exotic and amusing, but he was beginning to wonder if there was more going on with him. Was he falling for her? How could that be? He knew he couldn't trust her.

She was a puzzle, though. How she went on and on about getting out of there but never seemed to pull it off. It made no sense. Leaving wasn't that hard. An hour to Bozeman and the airport, that's all the time it would take. And it couldn't be just lack of money. What did a Bozeman-to-Newark plane ticket cost? Five hundred bucks? Surely she could afford that. So why she keep leaving just to end up back in West Yellowstone?

The only thing he could figure out was that, despite her constant complaints, she liked it. She liked being the wildest vamp in town, the fish with the biggest, reddest lips in the small pond. He started to admire her a little and feel sorry for her at the same time.

Maybe, just maybe, he would take her with him after all.

First things first, though. He needed his money.

AS HE TURNED the corner he saw the payphone blocked by a dirty white pickup. A big woman with a loud voice was on the phone. His heart sank. McCann approached the vehicle slightly panicked and checked his wristwatch. In two minutes, Barron had agreed to call.

She had curlers in her hair and was wearing an oversized parka. There was a cigarette in the stubby fingers of her free hand, and she waved it around her head as she talked. Her pickup was twenty years old, the bed filled with junk, the cab windows smeared opaque by the three big dogs inside, all of them with their paws on the glass and their tongues hanging out. He was vaguely familiar with her and had seen her deathtrap of a pickup rattling through town before. She collected and sold junk and hides. She had a sign on a muddy two-track west of town that offered ten dollars apiece for elk hides, seven-fifty for deer. Her name, he thought, was Marge.

When she saw McCann standing there, obviously waiting for her and checking his wristwatch, she flicked her fingers at him. "It'll be a while," she said. "There's a phone down the street outside the gas station."

"No, I need *this* phone."

Marge looked at him like *he* was crazy. "I told you it'll be a while, mister. The phone service is out at my place. I got a bunch of business calls to make."

She turned away from him. "I'm on hold."

In a minute, Barron would call.

"Look," McCann said to her back, "I'm expecting a really important call on this number. Right here, right now. You can call whoever it is you're waiting for right back. Hell, I'll give you the money. In fact, if you want to sit in my office and use the phone there, you can *make calls all day*."

She turned slightly and peered over her massive shoulder with one eye closed. "If you've got a phone in your office, mister, why don't *you* use it?"

He couldn't believe this was happening.

"Lady ... *Marge* ..."

She ignored him.

Furious, he reached out to tap her on the shoulder to get her attention when the dogs went off furiously, barking and snarling, gobs of saliva spattering the inside of the cab window inches from his arm. He recoiled in panic, and she yelled for her dogs to shut the hell up.

Then she turned on him. "What the hell is wrong with you, mister? I'm on the phone."

"I'm a lawyer," he said, his heart racing in his chest from the shock of the barking and the flash of teeth. "I'm expecting an important call. It's a matter of life and death. *I need that phone.*"

She assessed him coolly. "I know who you are, Clay McCann. I don't think much of you. And you're not getting it."

He shot a glance at his watch. Past time. He prayed Barron would be a few minutes late. Or call back if it was busy the first time. But what if he didn't?

The .38 was out before she could say another word. McCann tapped the muzzle against the glass of the passenger window in the drooling face of a dog. "Hang up now," he said.

"You're threatening my dogs," she said, eyes wide. "Nobody threatens my dogs."

Then she stepped back and jerked the telephone cord from the wall with a mighty tug.

"There!" she yelled at him. "Now nobody can use it!"

"Jesus! What did you do?"

"I just got started," she said, swinging the phone through the air at him by holding the severed metal cord. The receiver hit him hard on the crown of his head.

McCann staggered back, tears in his eyes, his vision blurred. But not blurred enough that he couldn't see her whipping the phone back and swinging it around her head like a lariat, looking for another opening.

He turned and ran across the street, hoping she wouldn't follow. On the other sidewalk, he wiped at his eyes with his sleeve, stunned. Marge glared at him, as if contemplating whether or not to give chase.

"Don't ever threaten my dogs!" she hollered.

Then she jammed the useless receiver back on the cradle,

lumbered into her pickup, which sagged as she climbed in, and drove down the street, leaving a cloud of acrid blue smoke.

Before reaching up and touching the lump forming beneath his scalp, McCann put the gun back in his pocket so no one would see it. He hoped she wasn't headed for the sheriff's department.

On the wall of the supermarket, the telephone box rang.

He closed his eyes, leaned back against the front of a motel that was closed for the season, and slowly sank until he was sitting on the concrete.

The street was empty and Clay McCann listened to his future, for the time being, go unanswered.

HE WAS STILL sitting on the sidewalk, eyes closed, his new headache pounding between the walls of his skull like a jungle drum, when Butch Toomer, the ex-sheriff, kicked him on the sole of his shoe. "You all right?"

McCann opened one eye and looked up. "Not really."

"You can't just sit there on the sidewalk."

"I know."

Toomer squatted so they could talk eye-to-eye. McCann could smell smoke, liquor, and cologne emanating from the collar of the ex-sheriff's heavy Carhartt jacket. Toomer had dark, deep-set eyes. His mouth was hidden under a drooping gunfighter's mustache.

"You owe me some money, Clay, and I sure could use it."

McCann nodded weakly. Now this, he thought.

"Tactics and firearms training don't come cheap. And it looks like it paid off for you pretty damned well. Four thousand dollars, that's what we agreed to back in June, remember?"

"Was it that much?" McCann said, knowing it was. He had never even contemplated, at the time, that money would be a problem. He did a quick calculation. Unless he sold his home or office or suddenly got a big retainer or the money he was owed came through, well, he was shit out of luck.

Then he thought of the business cards in his pocket. And his so-called business partners who had hung him out to dry. They could use some shaking up.

He said, "How would you like to turn that four thousand into more?"

Toomer coughed, looked both ways down the street. "Say again?"

McCann repeated it.

"Let's talk," Toomer said.

12

T HE IOWAN'S NAME was Darren Rudloff, he told Joe and Demming over the roar of helicopter rotors, and he was from Washington, Iowa, which he pronounced "*Warsh*-ington." He'd lost his job at a feed store, his girlfriend took up with his best bud, and his landlord insisted on payment in full of back rent. He felt trapped, so he figured *what the hell* and headed west armed to the teeth to live out his fantasy: to be an outlaw, to live off the land. He liked Robinson Lake. There had been dozens of hikers on the trail over the summer, but he'd avoided them. None were brazen or stupid enough to walk right into his camp, as Joe and Demming had done. When asked about the murders or the murder scene, he said he knew nothing other than what he'd read before he came out. All this he told Joe and Demming while the IV drips pumped glucose and drugs into his wrists to deaden the pain and keep him alive, while EMTs scrambled around his gurney replacing strips of Joe's shirt with fresh bandages until they could land in Idaho Falls and get him into surgery.

Joe found himself feeling sorry for Rudloff, despite what had happened. Rudloff seemed less than dangerous now. In fact, he seemed confused, childlike, and a little wistful.

Joe had a soft spot for men who desired the simplicity of the frontier that no longer existed, because he'd once had those yearnings himself. And, like Rudloff, he'd thought that Yellowstone was the place to seek them out. They'd both been wrong.

Demming confessed to Rudloff that she'd lied to him about Congress passing a law.

"I figured that out," Rudloff said through bandages on his face that muffled his voice. "That's the only good thing about today, I reckon. We don't need no more laws. I'll head back up there when I'm patched up."

"I'd advise against it," Demming said.

"You gonna press charges?"

"Maybe."

"Where you gonna have the trial?" Rudloff chided.

Demming had no answer to that, and she ignored him for the rest of the trip.

Joe asked the helicopter pilot to take them back to the Bechler station to get his vehicle after they'd admitted Rudloff. The pilot agreed.

THEY LANDED ON the only clear, flat surface at the Bechler ranger station—the horse pasture—at dusk. Joe and Demming thanked the pilot and scrambled out. Joe was happy to be out of the air and back on the ground. Stevens was there to meet them and handed Demming a message.

In the Yukon, Demming unfolded the piece of paper. "I need to call the Pagoda," she said. "Ashby wants a full report on what happened."

"Do we need to get back to Mammoth, then?" Joe asked, contemplating the five-hour drive.

Demming seemed lost in thought. He wondered if the shock of what happened at the camp had been held at bay

170

in her mind and was just now releasing. He'd seen that kind of delayed reaction to violence before, and had experienced it himself.

"Are you okay?" he asked.

She shook her head. "I guess so. That was a new one for me, I must say. I don't think I've ever been so scared as when I was looking into the muzzle of that rifle. His eyes— Jesus. They looked crazy and scared at the same time, which is never a good combination. And I feel ashamed that my first reaction when he got shot was pure joy—followed by nausea."

"I understand."

"I hate to feel so happy to see a man shot up."

"He'll be okay," Joe said.

"I know. But to see that kind of violence up close like that … I don't think I'm cut out for it."

"You were magnificent," Joe said. "You saved our lives when you told Rudloff about that law because it delayed him long enough for Nate to aim. You nearly had *me* believing it. That was quick thinking."

"If only it were true," she said. "Joe, do you think there are many more like him? I mean, more crazy survivalists in the Zone of Death?"

"Probably."

"Whoever saved us, is he one of them?"

Joe smiled. "Nate? Yes, he is. But he's been that way since I met him. He doesn't live in Yellowstone, though. He lives in Saddlestring, where I come from. He once told me he values what he considers justice over the rule of the law."

"That scares me."

Joe nodded. "Me too. Luckily, he's on our side."

*

171

RATHER THAN DRIVE all the way to Mammoth in the dark, they decided to go halfway, to the Old Faithful area instead, into the heart of the park. Since the next item on Joe's list was to question employees about the Gopher State Five, the diversion worked out. Demming used her radio to notify her husband that she wouldn't be home and said she'd call him when they got to Old Faithful.

"That probably won't go over very well," she said, as much to herself as to Joe.

"I understand," he said.

"I told him last night you were a nice guy, a family man."

He flushed. "I said the same about you to Marybeth."

"Now is the time for an uncomfortable silence," she said.

He agreed, silently.

THEY BACKTRACKED NORTH and entered the park proper through the gate at West Yellowstone, following the Madison River. The absence of any kind of streetlights made the moon and stars seem brighter and made Joe concentrate on driving, since bison or elk could appear on the road at any time. Demming had been trying to nap but couldn't get comfortable. She gave up trying with a sigh.

"When this is over," she said softly, "I think I'm going to quit. I don't ever want to be that scared again, and I've got a husband at home and two great kids."

"What would you do?"

She shrugged. "Well, maybe I won't quit outright. I probably can't. I'm the primary breadwinner in the family, you know."

"Believe me," Joe said, "I know what that's like. My wife is in the same boat, unfortunately."

"Maybe I'll transfer out of law enforcement into interpretation," she said. "I'd like a life of pointing out wildflowers and bison dung to tourists from Florida and Frankfurt. That sounds a lot less stressful than what I'm doing."

"Same bureaucracy, though."

"Yeah, I know. And as an added bonus, less money."

THE OLD FAITHFUL area was the largest complex in the park, consisting of hundreds of cabins, the Snow Lodge, retail stores, souvenir shops and snack bars, a rambling Park Service visitor center, and the showpiece structure of the entire park: the hundred-plus-year-old Old Faithful Inn that stood in sharp, gabled, epic relief against the star-washed sky.

Since Old Faithful was the most heavily visited area, there were a few dozen vehicles in the parking lot despite the lateness of the season. Joe drove under the covered alcove of the hotel, which framed the famous geyser as it puffed exhausted steam breaths. The sides of the cone were moist with water, and steaming rivulets snaked downhill to pour into the river.

"Postcoital geyser," Demming said, rubbing sleep out of her eyes. "It just went off. We missed it."

Joe smiled in the dark but chose not to respond.

They unloaded their gear, pulled open the heavy iron-studded seven-foot wooden doors and entered the most magnificent and bizarre lobby Joe had ever seen. He froze, like hundreds of thousands of visitors had before him, as he did when he first encountered the place two decades ago, and tilted his head back and looked up.

"Wow," Joe said.

"Gets you every time, doesn't it?" Demming said.

"I'd forgotten."

"Does it seem smaller, now that you're older?"

173

Joe shook his head. "It seems bigger."

His memories came flooding back, the sense of awe he'd felt then and felt now just as strongly, as if he'd been gone only minutes. At the time he first entered the inn and looked up, he'd never seen anything like it—it was the biggest log room he'd ever been in and it seemed to rise vertically forever. At least three levels of balconies lined the sides, bordered by intricate knotty pine railings and lit by low-wattage bulbs in candlestick fixtures, culminating high above in obscure catwalks and a fanciful wooden crow's nest nearly obscured by shadow. Fires crackled from hearths in the massive four-sided fireplace that rose in a volcanic stone column from the central lobby into darkness. Then, as now, Joe felt he was looking into the vision-come-true of a genius architect with a fevered and whimsical mind, and it took his breath away.

He marveled at both the beauty and the brashness of the construction, something that rarely interested him because he was not a fan of the indoors. The inn was built on an epic scale to inspire awe, like great European palaces or castles. But instead of stone, it was built of huge logs, and rather than gilded carvings for decoration there was functional but eccentric rococo knotty pine and natural wood. It had been built not for a small royal family but for the masses. There was something very American about it, he thought.

And it was emptier than he remembered. When Joe stayed at the inn as a boy his father had chosen a cheap, faraway "room without bath" accessed by dark hallways like cave tunnels and what seemed, at the time, to be hours from the lobby and a wrong turn away from certain death due to poor navigation skills on his part. The only thing that kept him alive and on the right course, he remembered, were the growing sounds of voices from hundreds of visitors milling in the lobby, either waiting for the next eruption or having just returned from the last one. Getting back to their room through those circuitous pathways was another matter.

This time, though, Joe requested a single room with a bathroom on the second level within sight of the lobby balcony. He got one because the hotel was nearly vacant. A smattering of visitors sat reading in rocking chairs near the fireplace, a few more talked softly on the balconies. The absence of conventional background sound—televisions, radios, Muzak—was striking.

The Zephyr front desk people and bellmen were friendly but worn out from the summer.

"We'll get you checked in and we can grab a bite," Demming said, "then I've got to get on the phone to Ashby and my husband."

"You aren't staying here?" Joe asked.

She shook her head. "We aren't allowed. The Park Service has housing across the road next to the Zephyr housing. I'll stay there and meet you early tomorrow."

Joe nodded and took his key. He threw his bags on the bed in a refurbished room that was nothing like the dark hovel he remembered, and met her in the vast empty dining room.

He watched her leave after dinner and found himself feeling a little sad she was gone. He liked her. He hoped she would be able to make the transfer she wanted into inter-pretation.

SINCE HE DIDN'T have a cell signal, Joe used a payphone from a bank of them in a room off the first-floor balcony to call Marybeth. Her day had been filled with shuttling

Sheridan and Lucy to the bus, from the bus, to Sheridan's volleyball practice and Lucy's piano lesson. Hectic but normal. Joe told her about Darren Rudloff.

"So Nate is there?" she asked.

"Yes, but we haven't really met up."

"He just saved your life and vanished."

"Same old, same old," he said, smiling at the statement as he made it.

"I'm glad he's there."

"Me too. I just wish working with Nate was more conventional."

"Then he wouldn't be Nate, would he?"

"Nope."

She said they would leave early Saturday morning to get to Yellowstone by early afternoon.

"I can't wait," he said.

IN HIS ROOM, Joe poured himself a light bourbon from his traveler and reviewed the growing file. It had helped to see McCann's office and the murder scene, to feel them, to re-create the crime in his mind. But there had been no eureka! moments. He read the rest of Hoening's e-mails and found several more references to hot-potting and flamers, but nothing that helped advance any kind of theory. He kept hoping he would find a reference to McCann that would link the victims to the lawyer. Nope.

Hoening's superior was a man named Mark Cutler, who was area manager of the Old Faithful complex. Joe made a note of the name and intended to interview Cutler in the morning.

He transferred his notes from the day onto a legal pad for his report to Chuck Ward and the governor. While he wrote, he heard a roaring and splashing sound and at first thought an occupant in the next room had flushed his toilet. But it came from outside.

Joe parted the curtains, threw open the window and watched Old Faithful erupt. The wind shifted as the geyser spewed and filled his room with the brackish aftereffect of the steam that smelled slightly of sulfur.

AS TIRED AS Joe was, he couldn't sleep. When he closed his eyes, scenes from the previous two days replayed in a herky-jerky video loop: the meeting at the Pagoda, the two old men scrambling from his sight in his hallway, the long day in the car with Demming, Clay McCann's office, Darren Rudloff, the fruitless look into the mind and motivations of Rick Hoening's e-mails, his own repressed memories of his brother's funeral and the subsequent breakup of his family.

He opened his eyes and looked at his wristwatch, shocked it was only 10:30 p.m. Without television, radio, or the routine of home, his body clock was thrown off. He considered going back over the file to see if something jumped out at him that hadn't before, now that his subconscious had asserted itself. Instead, he rooted through the desk and read about the Old Faithful Inn in Zephyr brochures.

A HALF-HOUR LATER he dressed, thinking he would go for a walk, hoping the physical activity would help shut down the video loop in his brain. Maybe he'd watch Old Faithful erupt again. He grabbed a jacket, considered taking the Glock, decided against it.

The hallway was dark but not as dark as he remembered it, and he felt familiar relief as the warm glow of soft light on the logs lit his path to the open, empty lobby. Even the desk clerks seemed to be taking a break. The strange mechanical clock on the fireplace ticked, and his boots echoed on the wooden stairs to the lobby floor.

As he reached out for the iron latch on the studded door something made him pause and turn around.

Not every rocking chair in front of the hearth was empty. Nate Romanowski was asleep in one of them, his hands hanging at his sides, his boot soles splayed, his head back and mouth open.

Joe crossed the lobby and nudged Nate's boot with his own. "Tag, you're it," Joe said.

Nate cracked an eye. "Hey."

"Thanks for today, Nate. I mean that."

His friend sat up and rubbed his face, waking up.

"Why didn't you stick around?" Joe asked.

"I heard what that ranger said about the new law," Nate said. "I believed her."

Joe chuckled. "She's good, isn't she?"

"Yeah."

"That was good shooting."

"I'm a good shot."

Joe pulled a chair over and sat down next to Nate. The fire was nearly spent, but the heated stones of the fireplace radiated warmth.

"I wanted to see the murder scene," Nate said, "find out if I could get any vibes from it. I got nothing. But I was glad I was there when you and the ranger walked up."

"Me too."

"Are you figuring anything out?" Nate asked.

Joe thought about it before answering. "Overall, I'd have to say … nope."

Nate simply nodded. Joe filled Nate in on what had happened so far, where he was headed. As Joe talked, he studied his friend. Nate appeared to be only half listening, as if there was something else on his mind.

When Joe was through, he asked, "Any questions? Any ideas?"

"Not yet."

"Okay, then."

Nate stood up, checked the front desk to confirm there was still no one there, then stepped over a metal barrier and approached the fireplace. "Watch this," Nate said, and started climbing the chimney using the outcrops of volcanic stones for hand- and footholds.

"Nate ..."

He scaled the fireplace until he vanished into the gloom. Above, in the shadows, Joe could hear Nate's heavy breathing and the scuffle of his boots on rock. Ten minutes later, Nate rejoined him after scrambling from the chimney onto a catwalk and taking a series of rickety, ancient stairs back to the lobby.

"I used to do that when I worked here," Nate said in explanation. "Every night if I could."

Joe shook his head. "When did you work here?"

"Many years ago."

"I never knew that."

"There are a lot of things about me you don't know."

"And I'm not sure I want to know them."

"No," Nate said, "you probably don't."

Joe sat back in his chair. "This is quite a place, isn't it? I read that it was built in 1903 and 1904, in the middle of winter. Some days it was fifty below. The guy who built it had a sixth-grade education, but he was a self-taught genius."

Nate agreed. "He was a wizard too. If you noticed, the windows on the building don't correspond with particular rooms or floors. They're scattered against the outside like they were just thrown up there and stuck. That's intentional. The architect wanted the look of the hotel to be random and asymmetrical, like nature itself. And it's just as interesting inside. There are secret stairways, hidden rooms, and a crazy dead-end hallway called Bat's Alley. They're closed to the public, of course, and very few people know about them."

Joe looked over. "But you know about them."

Nate nodded *Of course* but didn't meet Joe's eye.

"Nate, what's going on? There's something wrong, I can tell. You didn't climb that chimney to impress me, although it did. You climbed it because something's eating at you and you need to think."

Nate sighed but didn't disagree.

"What is it?" Joe asked.

"I was over in the Zephyr housing area earlier," Nate said. "I was wondering if there was anybody still here who I knew when I worked here."

"Yes?"

Nate leaned forward, rested his elbows on his knees, and cocked his head. "Joe, there's somebody you probably ought to see."

Joe was puzzled.

"Did you bring the Glock?" Nate asked.

"I left it in my room."

"Good," Nate said, rising. "You probably don't want a weapon around afterwards."

13

Joe followed Nate through a back door and they crossed a meadow of dry, ankle-deep grass on a well-worn path. Because a curtain of clouds had shut out the stars and moon and there were no overhead lights, the darkness was palpable. It was still and cold. Joe tracked Nate ahead of him by the slight white whisps of Nate's breath in the utter blackness. The lights of the inn receded behind them.

When the path stepped up onto blacktop, Joe knew where he was—crossing the highway toward employee housing, which was hidden away from tourists. There were no cars in either direction. They plunged into the trees on the other side and Joe stumbled into Nate, who had stopped.

"What?"

"There's something in front of us," Nate said. "Something big."

Joe looked over Nate's shoulder. Despite the lack of light, he could see a huge black triangle shape blocking the path. There was a strong odor of fur, dust, and manure. With a guttural snort, the buffalo spooked and crashed ahead through the timber.

"Are there more?" Joe asked.

"I don't think so. He was a loner."

"Like you."

Nate didn't respond. Behind them, far away in the basin, a geyser erupted. The sound was furious, angry, the roar of a boiling waterfall shooting into the air.

"Nate," Joe asked, "where are we going?"

"Employee housing," Nate said.

"But where specifically?"

"The bar."

THE ZEPHYR EMPLOYEE bar was hidden in the center of a long barracks-like building that fronted the dark employee dormitories. Steam hissed from a dimly lit laundry facility in one part of the building, and Joe caught a glimpse of several employees inside folding linen sheets. There were no neon beer signs to mark the bar and no cars outside, just a window leaking low light through a curtain and two middle-aged women smoking cigarettes on either side of the door. The women stubbed out their smokes as Joe and Nate approached, and started walking heavily toward the dormitories. Joe followed Nate inside.

The place was rough and crude, Joe thought, with the feel of a secret frat house drinking room. It was paneled with cheap laminate, and small bare lightbulbs hung from wires behind the bar. A crooked and stained pool table glowed under a pool of light, battered cues lying on it in a *V*. An entire wall was covered with curling yellowed Polaroids of Zephyr staff who had graced the place. Two tables were occupied with young employees who had been there for most of the night—it was obvious by the collection of empty drinking glasses and pitchers—and only two men were at the bar, one standing and glaring at them with a hand on the counter as if to hold himself back from attacking, the other slumped forward and asleep with his

182

face nestled in his arms.

"Nate Romanowski!" the standing man boomed. "You're back!"

"I said I would be," Nate said.

The bartender, who was washing glasses in a sink behind the bar, looked up and nodded to Nate and Joe.

"Joe," Nate said, "meet Dr. Keaton, or, as he's known around here, Doomsayer."

Joe extended his hand. Keaton was slim, tall, unshaven, and jumpy, with deep-set eyes and a sharp face like an ax blade. He looked to be in his sixties. He had stooped shoulders and a malleable mouth that twitched to its own crackling rhythm. Just being next to him made Joe tense up.

"Welcome to hell on earth," Keaton said, and cackled.

"Don't mind him," the bartender said to Joe, "he always says that. What can I get you two?"

Joe shot a glance at Nate, who ordered a pitcher of beer for the three of them.

"Is your partner going to join us?" Nate asked, nodding toward the man next to Keaton, who appeared to have passed out.

"He's sleeping it off," Keaton said. "He hit it a little hard earlier this evening, but when he awakes I'm sure he'll join right in again. We are both disciples of the Louis Jordan song 'What's the Use of Getting Sober (When You're Gonna Get Drunk Again).'"

Joe noticed the cadence of Keaton's phrasing: effete, affected. Educated. It played against his tramplike appearance.

The pitcher appeared. "Drink up," Keaton said, grabbing it before Nate could and pouring it into the glasses, "for tomorrow we die."

"That's why they call you Doomsayer, huh?" Joe said.

Keaton glared at Nate. "Who is this man, exactly?"

Nate said, "Friend of mine. He's up here investigating the Zone of Death murders."

Joe wondered why Nate blurted it out like that.

"Ah," Keaton said, turning his eyes to Joe and studying him from a new angle by listing his head to the side. "Another one up here to try and solve the *great mystery* ..." He said it with condescension that dripped.

"The amount of time and angst that has gone into this puzzle," Keaton said, sighing, "trying to figure out why the shabby lawyer killed the insolent Minnesotans. It amazes me."

"Why is that?" Joe asked, taking a sip.

Keaton shook his head. "Because it's indicative of a tired mindset. It's nothing more than mental jerking off: puffed-up officials trying to make order out of random acts when all around them their world is about to explode—but they just don't know it, or care. It's like trying to find the fly shit in the pepper. I mean, who cares?"

Joe had no idea how to respond, and he was angry with Nate for bringing him in here when he should have gone up to bed. Nate's fondness for the otherworldly and mystical grated on his nerves, and this, Joe thought, was a waste of his time.

"He has a Ph.D. in what, geology?" the bartender explained to Joe. "He's one of the founders of EarthGod, the big environmental activist group. He came up here twelve years ago to protest snowmobiles and never left."

Joe nodded. He'd heard of EarthGod. Even ardent environmentalists considered the group extreme.

Nate picked up on Joe's discomfort. "He isn't like that anymore," he said.

"Oh?"

184

"There's no point," Keaton said, "because we're all going to die."

"Maybe I ought to get a good night's sleep then," Joe said, not all that interested anymore.

Keaton jerked back, offended. His eyes narrowed. "You don't seem to understand, *Joe*," Keaton said, his voice dripping with contempt. "You've misread me entirely. You've made assumptions that I'm some crazy old man who is diverting you from your mission. But what you don't seem to understand, *Joe*, is that your mission doesn't matter. Nothing matters. Your laws don't matter, you don't matter, and neither do I. We're all on borrowed time, and have been for tens of thousands of years."

Over the next twenty minutes, Keaton laid it out. As he talked, his tone swooped while he made his arguments, then descended into whispers to drive home the gravity of what he was saying. Joe found himself getting sucked in.

"We are drinking this beer right now in the middle of a massive volcanic caldera," Keaton said, leaning across Nate to address Joe directly. "Do you know what a caldera is? It's the center of a dormant volcano. The Yellowstone caldera encompasses most of this so-called park. The edge of the caldera is all around us; we're in the bowl—in the mouth—of it right now. That's why we have all of our lovely attractions—the geysers, the steam vents, the mud pots. Magma from the center of the earth has pushed through the seams in the crust"—he demonstrated by making a bony fist and shoving it into his other palm, pushing it up—"right here, right below us. It's heaving upward trying to get out. There are only thirty places in the world where the center of the earth is trying to get out, and this is the only one of them on land, not water. When it does, when it finally blows, it will be a super volcano of a magnitude never even

185

contemplated by man. It will be two and a half thousand times more powerful than Mount Saint Helens! And it won't erupt slowly, it will explode!"

To demonstrate, Keaton slammed his fist down on the bar so hard the beer glasses danced.

Keaton screwed up his face with menace. "When it goes, when the Yellowstone super volcano goes, it will instantly kill three million people—every human life and all animal life for two hundred miles in every direction. Ash will cover the continent, asphyxiate the wildlife, and clog all the rivers. There'll be nuclear winter in New York City, and the climate truly will change as the world enters a vicious, sudden ice age. America will be over. Southern Canada, Northern Mexico—wiped out. The continent will resemble a postmodern wasteland, even more than it does now. This time, it will be real and not social."

Keaton paused to sip his beer, but he was so wound up that most of it dribbled out of his mouth onto his chin whiskers, which didn't seem to bother him.

"It has happened every six hundred thousand years through geologic history, at least four times that we can determine. Each super volcanic eruption changes the world. The last time it erupted was six hundred forty thousand years ago." Keaton's voice dropped to a whisper. "We're forty thousand years overdue."

"Then maybe it won't happen," Joe said.

Keaton showed his teeth. "Typical," he spat. "Just ignore it, wish it away. That's what people do best. But the signs are all around us that it will come sooner instead of later. You have to wake up and look at them!"

Joe now knew that he wouldn't be going back to the inn and tumbling into a restful sleep.

"In the past decade," Keaton said, "the ground has risen

fourteen centimeters in the Yellowstone caldera. That's right, the dirt beneath your feet is five inches higher in elevation than it was ten years ago. That's because the magma has forced it up, putting tremendous pressure on the thin crust. It's just like filling a tire with more and more air until it finally ruptures. And do you know, Joe, what is likely to cause the ground to rupture and release all that pressure, to turn the world inside out?"

"No."

"Earthquakes," Keaton said. "A tremor that will weaken and part the tectonic plates beneath us. That's all it will take … a crack, an opening. And do you know how many earthquakes there were in Yellowstone this past year?"

Joe shook his head.

"Three thousand. Think about it: *three thousand*. Over five hundred just in the Old Faithful area alone!"

To demonstrate, Keaton made himself tremble and his eyes blinked rapidly: *"We're starting to shake apart."*

With that, Keaton calmed himself, sighed, and settled back on his stool. "So drink up, Joe, for tomorrow we die."

Joe looked at Nate. Nate shrugged.

"It doesn't matter about the tiny little things you're concerned about," Keaton said, his voice moderating so he sounded almost reasonable, "your murders and your laws. Your jurisdiction. Once I realized that, the snowmobile emissions in Yellowstone Park seemed so … trivial. So stupid. So pointless. Nothing matters. We're trivial pissants in the big scheme of things, fleas, fly shit in the pepper."

Joe sipped his beer but it tasted bitter. He stanched a wild impulse to call Marybeth and tell her to grab the girls and flee to the root cellar.

"So I don't concern myself with laws or causes anymore," Keaton said. "I don't get worked up about what used to be

187

my passions—emissions, or recycling, or the trashing of the environment. We humans have such a high opinion of ourselves—especially my old brethren in the movement. We think we're gods on earth, that by merely changing our behavior or, more important, changing the behavior of the heathen industrialists and capitalists, that we can actually affect the outcome of the planet. We're so unbelievably arrogant and elite, so blind, so stupid. We think we can control the world. It's so tremendously silly I laugh when I think about it. It would be as if all the germs on our bartender's head decided to get together to prevent him from farting. It makes no difference what they decide or what they think—he'll still fart like a heifer."

The bartender, who'd been listening, looked offended.

Doomsayer continued, "Such efforts are beyond quixotic—they're comically hopeless. So we take infinitesimal little actions like preventing oil exploration, or recycling our beer cans, or driving hybrid cars that cost twenty-five times what a Third World worker makes in a year, or shaming other people for their desire to live well and prosper ..."

Keaton paused, let the word trail off, then shouted: "Ha! I say ha! Because once this baby goes," he yelled, pointing at the floor between his dirty shoes, *"once this baby goes,* none of those things matter. Nothing matters. We're stir-fry."

The bar was absolutely silent. Even the Zephyr employees at the tables looked wide-eyed at Keaton. Only the old drunk next to him slept through the reverie.

"So," Joe said, "if you really believe all that, why are you here? Why aren't you on some island in the Pacific?"

"Because, Joe," he said in a sing-song voice, as if explaining fundamental truths to a child, "when it goes I want to go with it. Instantly, in a flash of light with a drink in my hand. I don't want to huddle, shivering, in my apartment in Brooklyn or Boston while ash and snow blankets the city until I freeze slowly in the dark. I don't want to be on an island watching the ocean turn slowly milk-colored with ash and dead fish. I want to be at ground zero, where I can watch and monitor the thermal activity so I can be right here ordering that drink with my so-called friends around me."

"You mean there are others who think like you do?"

"Dozens," he said. "We're known as the Geyser Gazers. We serve a true purpose for the Park Service—charting eruptions and thermal activity. It used to be an easy job—sedentary—sitting on a bench waiting for a geyser to erupt and noting it in a little book. But that was in the old days, before the ground started to rise. Now, it's crazy. Geysers that used to go like clockwork have stopped entirely. Meanwhile, long-dormant geysers—monsters, some of them—are shooting off all over the park like fifteen-year-old boys on vacation. It's like the earth's guts are churning, ready to vomit! The signs of the apocalypse are all around, but only a few of us—my compatriots in the Geyser Gazers—have the knowledge and foresight to realize what is happening right in front of our eyes."

As he spoke he turned toward the bar, in profile, and Joe suddenly knew where he'd seen Keaton before.

"So you try to keep up with what's going on in the park, huh?" Joe asked.

Keaton hesitated a moment. "Yes ..."

"So you probably knew Rick Hoening and his buddies?"

"Savages! Nonbelievers!"

"And you like to check out visitors," Joe said. "Is that why you and your buddy there were in the Mammoth Hotel last night? Trying to see what I was doing here?"

That stopped Keaton. His eyes narrowed until they were

nearly shut. "We were there," he admitted, "but it's not what you think."

"Then why?"

"In a moment," Keaton said. "I have to urinate. Which," he said, sliding unsteadily off his stool, "if you take my philosophy to its logical conclusion so it applies to absolutely everything—like pissing your pants instead of going to the restroom after you've drunk too much beer—one would go mad while being stinky as well. But there is still something to be said for simple human dignity, despite all that." And he staggered to the men's room in the back.

After a few beats, Nate turned to Joe. "I thought he might have been one of them. I heard him mention he came from the north this morning."

"I wonder what he wants," Joe said.

"My guess is it'll surprise you."

"Meaning what?" Joe said, his mind still reeling.

"If we want to understand motivation," Nate said, "we might want to step outside convention and procedure. We might need to consider that some things happen up here because it truly is different."

"What are you saying?"

Nate shook his head. "I'm not sure. But since dozens of people have studied this crime and come up with nothing, maybe we need to try and think about it differently. Maybe we need to consider that what happened was absolutely unique to this place, and for a reason we never even thought of before."

Joe nodded. "Maybe."

Nate drained his beer. The bartender pointed at the clock behind the bar, signaling it was time to close.

"I didn't like that bit about germs and me farting," the bartender said. "Didn't like it one bit."

As if on cue, the bartender reached out both hands to grip the bar and Joe felt suddenly unsteady but didn't know why. Then he heard the tinkling of liquor bottles on the shelf behind the bar, and he saw ringlets form on the water in the sink. Just as quickly as it happened, it was still again.

"Just an earthquake," the bartender said. "Little one."

"My God," Joe whispered, turning to Nate. "So that's who you wanted me to meet, Doomsayer."

"No, not really."

"Then why did you bring me here?"

Nate took a deep breath and his eyes flitted away for a second. Joe was confused.

Nate walked over to Keaton's companion, who was still sleeping on the bar.

"You said you saw two men in the hallway up in Mammoth," Nate said. "Two old guys. Doomsayer was one of them, I think we know now. Is this the other one?"

He grabbed a fistful of thin hair on the head of the companion and pulled his face up. Joe felt as if a lightning bolt of bile had surged up into his throat. His boots seemed spot-welded to the floor.

Oh, how he recognized that face.

"Dad ..." Joe said, but the word croaked out.

Two bloodshot, rheumy eyes cracked open, wobbled, focused.

"Son," George Pickett said thickly.

"This is why I wanted you to leave your gun," Nate said.

14

Joe awoke to the sound of Old Faithful erupting outside his window, which for an instant he thought was his stomach. Assured that it wasn't, he threw back the sheets, padded barefoot to the window, and parted the curtains to watch the geyser once again, wondering if it would ever be possible to get tired of seeing it. He didn't think so. He marveled at the furious churning of steam and water, the angry noise that accompanied the eruption, and was struck how some gouts of water punched through the billows into thin, cold air and paused at their apex, breaking apart into fat droplets that caught the sun, and plunged back down to earth.

As he dressed he recalled the events of the night before and was still numbed from them. It was as if his world had tilted slightly to the left into unreality.

His father had been too drunk to maintain a conversation and could barely stand. With Keating on one side and Joe on the other, they walked George Pickett home. Nate followed silently.

"I see you haven't changed much," Joe said to his father as they cleared the dormitories and steered him toward a crooked line of rickety shacks hidden even farther in the trees.

"I'm happy you're here," his father slurred, taking three tries to get it out. "I'd like to get to know you, Son."

"You had eighteen years for that," Joe mumbled, knowing the conversation would likely be forgotten by George when he woke up the next morning.

After they'd lowered George into a disheveled single bed in a coffin-shaped cabin strewn with papers and garbage, Keaton said something to Joe about organizing a get-together for the Picketts very soon, so they could talk.

"Nothing to talk about," Joe had said, turning for the door.

"And it should be sooner rather than later," Doomsayer intoned as Joe stepped outside. "We're on borrowed time as it is, you know ..."

DEMMING WAS IN the dining room waiting for him at breakfast. He could feel her eyes on his face, trying to discern what was wrong. He ordered eggs from a waiter with the name badge "Vladimir—Czech Republic" and told her about meeting his father the night before in the Zephyr bar.

"He's one of the Geyser Gazers," Joe said, trying to sound casual. "He lives in a hovel and drinks like a fish, waiting for the Yellowstone caldera to blow up."

After Vladimir brought breakfast and talked to them about how beautiful it was outside this morning—"a vision of a dream of nature"—in broken but charming English, Demming said, "So where is your friend Nate?"

"Oh, he's around," Joe said, not wanting to tell her that Nate was staying somewhere inside the inn, likely in one of the sections that were officially off-limits to visitors. Nate had mentioned something about a tree house far up in the rafters, and Joe fought the urge to look up and see if he was there.

194

Before separating the night before, Nate had told Joe he intended to spend the day talking to old Zephyr friends to see if he could learn anything about the Gopher State Five.

"Around, huh?" she said, put off. "I'm beginning to think he doesn't exist. Like he's your special secret friend. My son has one of those too, Joe. He calls him Buddy."

JOE REVIEWED HIS notes and scribbled questions in his notebook while Demming went to find Mark Cutler, the area manager of Old Faithful. She returned with a cherubic and avuncular man about Joe's age with a pillow of dark curly hair, red cheeks, and an air of cheery competence about him. He wore wire-framed glasses, a tie and a blazer, but looked as if he spent as much time outdoors as indoors, judging by his sunburned skin and the scratches on the back of his hands.

"Mark Cutler," he said. "I manage this joint."

"Joe Pickett. Nice to meet you."

"Judy said you have some questions, follow-up on Hoening and McCaleb."

"Yup," Joe said. "Bob Olig too."

"Ah, Olig," Cutler said, smiling at the name. "Quite the characters, those three."

"Do you have a few minutes?"

Cutler looked at his watch. "If you want to sit down and talk, I really don't, but if you're willing to tag along with me as I do my work today, I've got all the time in the world."

Joe looked at Demming and she nodded.

"We'll tag along," Joe said.

"Good, good. You'll see some really cool stuff," Cutler said, turning on his heel and gesturing in a "follow me" wave.

Joe instantly liked him for his affability and enthusiasm for his job. He guessed Cutler was a pretty good manager.

195

"I've got a couple of things to wrap up in my office," Cutler said, leading them outside on a wooden walkway that led, eventually, to some low-slung administration buildings painted Park Service brown and tucked into a stand of lodgepole pine. "We're winding down the season, as you can see. It's quite an operation. That means shutting down all the facilities and winterizing them, dealing with the reassignment of employees, year-end reports, too many things to count. It would almost be easier if we just stayed open all year, but we don't."

"So you knew the victims pretty well?" Joe asked.

Cutler shrugged. "Pretty well. I mean, I was their boss, not their buddy. But I got along well with them. They were good guys, despite what you might have heard." He nodded toward Demming when he said it, indicating the tiff they had had with particular rangers like Layborn. "They worked hard and they played hard. Hoening had a bit of an agenda, as you probably know, but a lot of new hires do. They come here to save the place, but the day-to-day work starts to make them forget that."

Cutler's office was small and nondescript, nothing on the walls or his desk of a personal nature except for a photo of him smiling with Old Faithful erupting in the background.

While Cutler fired off responses to e-mails, Joe turned to Demming.

"The Pagoda is a palace compared to this," Joe said. "Cutler manages hundreds of people, but his office ..."

"I know," she said, rolling her eyes. "That's how it is. Government employees are the royalty and the contractors are our serfs. Discussion over, Joe."

"Sorry."

She smiled to show she wasn't angry. Then: "I talked to Ashby for an hour last night. He's not happy. The news about Darren Rudloff is getting out, and he's gotten some calls already. Apparently, some reporters are asking him questions about the Zone of Death, like are there a bunch of armed outlaws in it, why isn't the Park Service patrolling the area, those kinds of things. He doesn't like it one bit and he's meeting with Chief Ranger Langston this morning to discuss the situation. I may get called back to Mammoth to help out."

"How can you go back and keep an eye on me at the same time?" Joe asked slyly.

She shook her head. "I'd rather stay here. I don't know where we're going, but it seems like we're headed somewhere."

"Story of my life," Joe said.

"If I get called back, you may be asked to leave."

"Oh."

"They don't trust you," she said, lowering her voice. "They think you'll do something to bring the whole Clay McCann–Zone of Death thing back into the headlines. In fact, it's already happening, isn't it?"

"I hope so."

Cutler tapped the keys on his keyboard with efficient violence and fired off the last e-mail, saying, "There! Chew on that, Park Service weenies!" As he did so, he glanced at Demming and said, "Sorry, ma'am. No offense."

"None taken," Demming said coolly.

Cutler leaned back. "I'm going off my shift here now and putting on a different hat. Follow me."

Cutler launched himself out of his chair and was out the door in a shot, Joe and Demming struggling to keep up. Cutler explained that his primary interest in life was geology, specifically geothermal activity. It was the reason he came to Yellowstone in the first place, twenty years before. Although he was area manager, his degree and background were in science, and he'd published scientific papers in international journals and kept a regular and ongoing correspondence with geologists around the world, wherever there were geysers. He had personally mapped more than two thousand geothermal sites within the park, and served as the secretary for the loosely organized Geyser Gazers, the volunteers who watched and recorded eruptions and hotspot activities.

"So that's what brought you out here," Joe asked, "the geysers?"

Cutler nodded. "I originally wanted to join for the Park Service, but that didn't work out."

"Why not?" Demming asked, a little defensively.

Cutler stopped, smiled gently. "This is the most active, unique, and fascinating geothermal area in North America. Everything is visible here because the center of the earth is closer to the surface than anywhere else. It's like a doctor meeting someone who has all his organs on the outside of his body—everything is right there to study. Do you know how many geologists are employed by the National Park Service in Yellowstone?"

Joe and Demming shook their heads.

Cutler raised a finger. "One. And he's too busy to get out in the field. Not his fault, just the structure of the bureaucracy. So," Cutler said, spinning on his heel and continuing to lead the way to a cabin compound where he lived, "without volunteers, without the Geyser Gazers, there would be no ongoing study of the caldera in the park. But it's not a chore, it's a passion. I love what I do, both at Old Faithful and especially out here in the field."

"Are you married?" Joe asked. "Kids?"

"Engaged, sort of," Cutler said. "It's hard to convince some ladies to live here, believe it or not."

"Kids would love it," Joe said, smiling. "Imagine being raised in this place. I wanted to live here, once."

Cutler nodded with instant kinship. "Takes a special kind of person," he said. "Or an outright fool."

"Which are you?"

"I straddle the line."

Joe said he'd met Dr. Keaton the night before.

"Doomsayer?" Cutler asked, squinting.

"Is it true what he says?"

"He never stops talking," Cutler said, "so that's a hard one to answer."

"That Yellowstone could blow up in a super volcano any minute?"

"Oh sure, that part's true," Cutler said cheerfully, pausing outside his cabin. "Give me a minute to change and we can go."

Joe and Demming looked at each other. Joe thought she looked pale.

"You haven't heard this before?" he asked.

"I've heard it," she said. "I just didn't believe it."

"Doomsayer says drink up, for tomorrow we die."

WHILE CUTLER CHANGED clothes and gathered his equipment, Joe and Demming looked idly through five-gallon plastic buckets filled with tourist debris Cutler had fished out of geysers and hot springs. Most of the collection was of coins, tossed in, no doubt, to bring luck. There were American coins by the thousands, but also Euros, yen, pence, pesos, Canadian coins. Another bucket contained nails, hats, bullets, batteries, lug nuts, and, interestingly, a 1932 New York City Police Department badge and an engagement ring.

"I'd love to know the story behind that ring," Demming said, holding it up.

"I want to know who walks around with lug nuts in their pocket," Joe said.

Cutler emerged in ranger green with a radio on his belt. He loaded a long aluminum pole with a slotted spoon on the end into a pickup, along with metal boxes containing electronics.

"Thermisters," Cutler explained when Joe looked at the boxes. "We hide them in geyser and hot springs runoff channels to track the temperature of the water. We learn a lot about which geysers are getting active and which ones are shutting down by the temps."

"What's with the pole and spoon?" Demming asked.

"I use that to pick the coins and crap out of the geysers to keep them clean."

Joe and Demming climbed into the truck and Cutler roared off.

"Hoening, McCaleb, and Olig were all proud members of the Gopher State Five," Cutler said. "Since I'm from Minnesota, we hit it off right away. They were just big old Midwesterners. They worked hard, loved their beer, loved the park. They used to come along with me sometimes to check geysers and clean out hot springs, like we're doing now. They'd come on their days off, when they could be screwing around. When Ranger Layborn came around to ask me about them, it was as if he was describing entirely different people. He seemed to think they were big into drugs and crime, that they were some kind of gang. I never saw that side of them."

"Were they illegal hot-potters?" Joe asked.

Cutler smiled. "I'm sure they were. We frown on it when it's our employees, but it's just about impossible to stop. We can't watch everyone twenty-four-seven, even though the rangers think we should. No offense, ma'am," he said to Demming.

"None taken," Demming said, tight-lipped.

"Any other problems with them? What about the drug allegations?"

"Nothing I know of, and I mean that. That's not to say all of my people are clean. It's like any other work situation; there's a percentage of bad apples. But no more than any workplace in the outside world and less than some. Hell, I went to school in Madison, at the University of Wisconsin. Ranger Layborn could really ply his craft there."

"Not even marijuana?" Joe asked. "There seemed to be drug references in the e-mails Hoening sent. 'Flamers,' he called them."

Cutler shrugged. "Again, I can't swear he wasn't smoking, but I never saw or heard anything that would confirm it. As you know, there's a certain attitude and culture that goes with drug use, and he didn't seem to be a part of it. He was pretty tightly wound at times—kind of naively idealistic about environmental issues. But drugs, that would surprise me."

Cutler turned the pickup off the highway at the Upper Geyser Basin and parked it in the empty lot. Joe trailed him while Demming remained in the pickup to report to the Pagoda on the truck radio. The smell of hot sulfur and water was overwhelming. Cutler explained that the pools on either side of the boardwalk were 190 degrees, and the water temperature could be gauged by the color of the bacteria in the runoff—white being hottest, green and blue cooler but still too hot to touch. Using the slotted spoon, he carefully picked up coins that had been tossed into the thermals and handed them back to Joe, who juggled them from hand to hand until they cooled off enough to inspect. Three pennies and a dime. The pennies were already gray with a buildup of manganese and zinc from the water, Cutler said, but the dime, being silver, was unblemished.

Cutler swung over the side of the railing and landed with a thump on the white-crust surface. He urged Joe to follow him.

"What about the 'Stay on the Boardwalk' signs?" Joe asked, knowing the ground was unstable near geysers and the crust was brittle. Horror stories abounded of pets and visitors who wandered off the pathway.

"And if I break through?" Joe asked.

"Third-degree burns at the minimum," Cutler said, businesslike. "Excruciating pain and skin grafts for the rest of your life. If you live, I mean. Worse, you'll deface the thermal. But it would be nothing like if you actually fell into a hot spring or geyser."

"What would happen?"

"You'd die instantly, of course; then your body would be boiled. I've seen elk and buffalo fall in over the years. Within a couple of hours, their hair comes off in clumps and the flesh separates from the bone. The skeleton sinks, the meat and fat cooks and it smells like beef stew. Sometimes, an animal body affects the stability of the thermal and it erupts and spits all that meat back out. Not pretty."

"Maybe I should stay up here," Joe said.

"Just step where I step," Cutler said. "Not an inch either way and you'll be fine. I've done this for years and I know where to walk and where not to walk."

Joe felt a thrill being allowed to go where millions of tourists couldn't go, and stepped over the railing. He wished Demming—or Marybeth—could see him now.

For the next hour, Cutler carefully removed coins and debris from the geysers and hot pools. Joe followed in his footsteps, gathered them and noted what was found in Cutler's journal.

Cutler explained how the underground plumbing system worked, how mysterious it was, how a geyser could simply stop erupting in one corner of the park and a new geyser could shoot up forty miles away as the result of a mild tremor or indiscernible geological tic. How the water that came from the geysers had been carbon-tested to reveal it was thousands of years old, that it had been *whooshing* through the underground works before Columbus landed in America and was just now being blasted into the air.

CUTLER TOOK A quick turn off the road and pulled over to the side. Ahead of them was a hugely wide but squat white cone emitting breaths of steam. Joe was unimpressed at first glance.

"What you're looking at is Steamboat Geyser," Cutler said. "It's by far the biggest geyser in the world. When this baby goes—and we never know when or why—it can be seen from miles away. It reaches heights of four hundred feet, three times Old Faithful, and drenches everything around here for a quarter of a mile. The volume of boiling water that comes out of it is scary. Nearly as scary as its unpredictability. We've waited years for an eruption, and almost declared it dormant when it proved otherwise."

"When's the last time it blew?" Joe asked.

"A year ago, in the winter. Three times. No one was there when it went, but the evidence of the eruption was a herd of parboiled bison found a hundred yards away. It seems to be getting more active. The eruptions used to be up to fifty years apart, but last winter they were four *days* apart."

Cutler whistled. "I'd give my left nut to see it erupt."

THE FIREHOLE RIVER was on their left as they departed the geyser basin and drove north on the highway. Bison grazed along the banks and steamy water poured from Black Sand Geyser Basin into the river.

Geyser Gazers, according to Cutler, numbered nearly seven hundred strong, although the hard-core, full-time contingent amounted to only about forty. They were all volunteers, and included scientists, lawyers, and university professors as well as retired railroad workers, laborers, and the habitually unemployed. The thing that brought them together was their love, knowledge, and appreciation for Yellowstone and the thermal activity within the Yellowstone caldera. Most showed up on weekends or took their vacations to help. Only a few stayed in or near the park on a full-time basis, like Doomsayer and George Pickett.

"How many ascribe to Keaton's philosophy that we're all going to die?" Joe asked.

"Maybe a couple dozen," Cutler said. "The rest recognize the threat but choose to go on and live their lives normally, like me."

"What about Hoening and the other Gopher Staters? Were they Keaton disciples?"

"No chance."

"Another theory shot down," Joe said, and smiled at Demming. That's when he noticed how introspective she was. She didn't appear to be listening to Cutler explain about geyser activities.

"Are you okay?" he asked.

She shook her head, indicating she would tell him later.

CUTLER PARKED AT Fountain Paint Pots and grabbed his pole and slotted spoon. Joe said he'd meet up with him in a minute. As Cutler strode away on the boardwalk, Joe turned to Demming.

"Ashby?"

"Yes. He met with Chief Ranger Langston and they're getting agitated and nervous. They want us to break it off here and come back up to Mammoth. Langston is quite adamant about it."

"Why?"

"Ashby said they don't like the direction we're headed, going to the Bechler station, interviewing Mark Cutler. He thinks we're going to open the Park Service to unwanted exposure."

Joe shook his head, felt anger well in him. " 'Unwanted exposure'? What does that mean?"

"I'm not sure, but they seem to think you have another agenda. And they don't like your friend being up here."

"How do they know about Nate?"

"I told them," she said. "I had to. It's my job."

Joe said, "How much time do we have?"

"They want us back by tonight."

"I'll think about it," Joe said, wondering what they'd done to suddenly warrant Ashby and Langston's concern, wondering if he'd need to call Chuck Ward to intervene, if possible. "I wish I knew what was going on here."

"Me too," she said. "What really seemed to upset them was us talking with Cutler. Maybe it's just a Park Service versus contractor thing, I don't know."

"Or maybe Cutler knows something they don't want us to find out," Joe said.

AS THEY DROVE, Joe noticed Cutler glancing more frequently in his rearview mirror.

"That's strange," he said. "I noticed that pickup back when we left Fountain Paint Pots. He was the only other vehicle in the lot, parked way over on the far side. Now I see it behind us."

"Don't turn around," Joe said to Demming, not wanting her to reveal to the driver of the truck that they were aware of him. "Let's check it out in the side mirror."

Joe leaned over Demming to see. The mirror vibrated with the motor, but he could see a glimpse of a pickup grille a third of a mile behind them. Over a long straightaway, Joe could see the truck better. Red, late-model 4x4 Ford. Montana plates. Single driver wearing a cowboy hat. As he looked, the pickup driver reduced his speed so it faded into the distance.

When Cutler turned off the highway at Biscuit Basin onto a one-lane road, he slowed down and watched his mirror.

"Don't see him now," he said. "He must have turned off. You guys are making me paranoid, I guess. I normally wouldn't notice something like that, but there are so few visitors in the park the truck sort of stood out."

The road rose into heavy timber and broke through onto a wide, remote plain dotted with dead but standing trees and steam rising from cratered mouths. The trees had no leaves and were bone-white in color.

"This is one of the hottest spots in the park," Cutler said. "We've watched it get hotter over the past four years. That's why the trees are dead; all of that hot mineral water got soaked up by their roots to fossilize them. There's lot of activity here, and some really great hot pots."

Joe glanced at his list of questions.

"What about Clay McCann?" Joe asked. "Did you ever meet him? Did they ever mention his name?"

Cutler shook his head. "I saw his name around but I never met him. And no, the Gopher Staters never mentioned him."

"What do you mean you saw his name?"

"On some papers, some bio-mining contracts."

Joe exchanged glances with Demming. "Bio-mining?" Joe said.

"What, you haven't heard of it?"

"No," Joe said. He asked Demming, "Have you?"

"Unfortunately, yes," she sighed.

THEY PARKED AT the end of a dirt two-track that culminated with a downed log blocking the road and a Park Service sign reading ACCESS PROHIBITED. AUTHORIZED PERSONNEL ONLY. Joe noticed that despite the sign there were clearly tire tracks in the crusty dirt beyond the log where someone had driven. He asked Cutler about it.

"Bio-miners, I'm sure," Cutler said. "They have a permit. Follow me."

It was midday and the sun was straight overhead in a virtually cloudless blue sky and the day had warmed considerably into the mid-sixties. Joe was struck by the utter quiet all around them as they hiked up a footpath and over a gentle rise. The only sounds were their boots, breath, and the occasional caw of a far-off raven.

"It's very controversial," Cutler said, swinging a thermister in a case next to his leg as he walked. "I'm surprised you haven't heard or read about these projects."

Joe confessed he'd been isolated the last few months, working on a ranch near Saddlestring.

"Lucky you," Demming said. He could tell by her demeanor that she felt strongly about the topic.

"I know I keep telling you how unique the Yellowstone caldera is," Cutler said, "but up here, wonders never cease, so what can I say? Over the last twenty years, biologists have discovered thermofiles—microbes—that are absolutely unique to anywhere else on earth. I'm no expert, but the

207

reason they find them here is a kind of biological perfect storm—the combination of the hot water, the minerals, and the ecological isolation of the area—that's produced all these rare species. Only real recently have companies discovered there are, um ... *properties* ... in some of the microbes that can be used for other purposes."

"What kinds of properties?" Joe asked.

"Well, one particular microbe has been found that radically assists bioengineers performing DNA typing. From what I understand, it's really advanced science in that area. Another microbe can apparently speed up the aging process in some mammals tenfold, or so they think. That's a scary one, if you ask me. And there are all kinds of rumors that I can't back up, like thermophiles that can help unlock a cure for cancer, to other microbes that can be weaponized. The government, legitimate companies, and bio-pirates are afoot up here these days."

"Bio-pirates?"

Demming moaned. "Yes, Joe. There have been reports of freelancers up here scooping up growth and plant species in the hot water runoff and trying to sell it to companies or other governments. No one's actually been caught at it yet, but every once in a while there's a report. As if we don't have enough to worry about up here, you know."

Joe felt a growing sense of discovery and excitement as Cutler and Demming talked. This was new. There was nothing in the "Zone of Death" file about bio-mining, or McCann's connection to it.

Ahead, he could see the trees parting and feel—if not yet see—their destination. It was a huge opening in the timber, walled on four sides by dead and dying trees. The odor of sulfur and something sickly sweet hung low to the ground.

"This is Sunburst Hot Springs," Cutler explained. "It's

called that because, from the air, the runoff vents come off of it like spikes in all directions. It looks like how a little kid draws the sun in art class, with spikes coming out of the circumference."

Joe could feel the heat twenty feet away and hear and feel a low rumbling, gurgling water sound somewhere beneath his feet. Sunburst was gorgeous, he thought, in a dangerous and oddly enticing way. The steaming surface of the water was nearly fifty feet across, held in place by a thin white mineral rim that looked more like porcelain than earth. The water inside was every shade of blue from aquamarine near the surface to indigo as it deepened. It was hard to see clearly into the open mouth of the spring because of scalloped ripples of steam on the surface, which dissipated into the air. Inside the spring the sun illuminated outcroppings, bronzing them against the blue, and Joe could clearly see a sunken litter of thick, stout barbell-shaped buffalo bones that had been caught on shelves along the interior walls. Again, he felt the pull of the water but not as strongly. The placid blue water seemed to beckon to him in the way that a warm bath or a Jacuzzi pulls a frozen skier at the end of the day. Beyond Sunburst Hot Springs was a smaller pool rimmed with dark blue and green, meaning much cooler water.

Cutler saw him looking at it, said, "That's Sunburst Hot Pot. It's much, much cooler than the hot springs, and it's a really nice pool to lounge in"—he grinned slyly at Demming—"if one were so inclined."

Joe checked out the hot pot. If God designed a natural jacuzzi, he thought, this would be it. It was waist deep, clear, and someone had fitted flat wooden planks into the walls to sit on. Obviously, the pool had been used for illegal hot-potting. Joe visualized Hoening sitting on one of the planks with a Minnesota female he had just lured out from L.A., and smiled.

"Nice place for a date," he said.

As he circled the hot pot he felt an odd sensation of someone blowing air up his pant leg. He stopped and turned, studied the ground. It took a moment before he saw the series of quarter-sized holes in the soil, each emitting a light stream. He squatted and held his palm out to one of them, feeling it on his skin. No doubt, he thought, the superheated earth under the surface had to release something, like a natural pressure cooker. He'd heard about visitors (and, more likely, Zephyr employees) burying chickens in the ground in secret places to bake them. He thought he could probably do that here. The idea intrigued him.

The ground in the little tree-lined basin was nearly white, as if it had been baked. The consistency of the dirt was crumbly. Joe noted a long dark line in the earth that extended from deep in the trees and topped an almost imperceptible rise. The dark streak ran past the side of the hot springs and out the other side.

"What's that?" Joe asked.

"Like I mentioned," Cutler said, "the cool thing about the park is that all of the insides are pushed out in places. That's a seam of underground coal. It's not very big, and it's hard to say how far down it extends. It's one of the few places in the whole park where there's any coal."

Joe had learned earlier not to wander away from the path established by Cutler for fear of breaking through and falling in, so he stuck close to him, as did Demming. He watched as the geologist went downhill from the spring itself along one of the troughs of runoff that came from the hot springs, where he pushed aside some ancient pitch wood stumps and revealed a thermister and a half-submerged wood-sided box of some kind in the water. He called Joe and Demming over, and they squatted near him.

With a small laptop computer, Cutler plugged into the thermister and downloaded the last two weeks of temperature readings. Joe noticed both the instrument and the wooden box were covered with what looked like long pink hair that wafted in the soft current of the warm water.

"I call this *'million-dollar slime,'*" Cutler said, pointing at the pink microbe growth. "This is the stuff used for genetic typing I told you about. I don't know how it works, of course, but the company that harvests it can't replicate it in a lab. They need to get it right here at Sunburst, and as far as they know, this is the only place on earth it can be found."

"Kind of pretty, but not very impressive," Demming said.

Cutler agreed. He told Joe that the bioengineering firm sent a truck into the park every month or so with a heated incubator in the back to harvest the microbes that had grown inside the box. The thermophiles were transported to Jackson or Bozeman and flown to the company laboratory in Europe.

"Okay," Cutler said, once again arranging the driftwood over the equipment so it couldn't be seen from the trail, "we're done here."

As they trudged back toward the pickup, Joe's mind raced with new possibilities. Demming eyed him suspiciously.

Joe said to Cutler, "You said Hoening and the others sometimes came along with you when you did your work. Did they ever come here?"

"Sure, a couple of times."

"Did they know about the million-dollar slime?"

"Definitely. It's no secret. The contracts are public record, even though more than a few people have a problem with the idea."

"Like me," Demming said.

"Rick Hoening did too," Cutler said. "Me, I keep my mouth shut and my head down. I don't want anyone mad at me enough to take away the opportunity to spend my time out here, doing the good work."

Joe could tell Cutler said it for Demming's benefit.

"What's the issue, anyway?" he asked.

"Think about it, Joe," Demming said. "It's illegal to take a *twig* out of the park. We don't allow oil or energy companies in here to drill, or lumber companies to come in and cut down the trees. This is a national park! But for some reason, we allow bioengineering firms to come in here and take the microbes. We're talking about thermophiles that have made millions and millions of dollars for the companies that use them. And who knows what other uses are being made of the species here? It's a damned crime. Hypocrisy too."

"Hoening got worked up for the same reason," Cutler said. "He talked to me about it several times. He thought it was outrageous that a big company could come in here and take resources from the public and profit from it. He was kind of a Commie at times, I thought."

Joe hadn't thought of it that way. "Who lets them?" he asked.

Demming and Cutler exchanged a look. "The Park Service," Demming said. "They negotiate contracts with them, two or three years' exclusive use of the microbes obtained from certain hot springs. The companies pay a few hundred thousand dollars for the rights."

"Does the Park Service or the government get a royalty on what's found?"

"Of course not," Demming said.

"Then why do they do it?"

She shrugged. "They just do. The NPS will do anything for cash since we're so underfunded. Or so we say."

"Who has the contract for Sunburst, then?"

She shrugged, looked at Cutler. "I can't remember the name," he said. "But it's foreign, I know that."

Joe stopped abruptly.

"What?" Demming asked.

"This might turn out to be something," Joe said. "If Hoening was worked up about bio-prospecting, and his complaints were too loud, it might be a reason to silence him."

Her eyes widened for a moment, then narrowed as she thought about it. "I'd like to think that, Joe. But as much as I don't like it, there's nothing illegal going on here. Nothing worth killing about, for sure. The bio-mining operation is perfectly legitimate, even though I think it's a stupid idea that goes against park policy."

Her words deflated him somewhat. He said, "Still, though, this is the only thing we've found that might be a motive."

She shrugged. "So where does Clay McCann fit into this?"

"He was the lawyer who filed the application for the permit."

"I can't imagine that kind of legal work would be so lucrative he'd kill to keep the business, can you? He was probably hired because he's local, and probably didn't have many billable hours."

"Let me think about it," he said.

IT WAS ALMOST evening as they approached the turnoff back to Old Faithful. Joe, Demming, and Cutler had batted around the theory Joe had advanced, but nothing new or solid came from the discussion. After a while, each lapsed into their own thoughts.

Joe wished Marybeth and his girls would be waiting for him, but their reunion was still days away. He wondered if Nate had turned up anything talking with Zephyr people. He tried not to think about George Pickett. Instead, he pushed his father's appearance out of his mind, as far away as he could push it. He was unsuccessful, though. He felt a sense of growing dread the closer they got to the inn.

He thanked Cutler for making the time that day.

Cutler didn't answer, his eyes on the rearview mirror.

"Damned if I don't see that red truck behind us again," Cutler said.

"Pull over after you've made the turn," Demming said. "Let's see who's been following us all day."

"Cool," Cutler said.

They took the turn to Old Faithful and in the first stand of trees that couldn't be seen from the highway, Cutler drove off the asphalt and hit the brakes.

Joe and Demming bailed out the passenger door. She drew her weapon, glanced at Joe.

"Where's your gun?" she asked.

He felt his face flush. "In my daypack in the truck."

Her eye roll was brief but damning.

"Let me get it," he said.

"Forget it, Joe," she said, stepping out onto the road and slipping her pistol back into her holster. "He's gone. The red truck never made the turn."

JOE WAS GREETED at the desk by two messages. The first was a flyer reminding all guests that the Old Faithful Inn would close for the winter the following day at noon. The second was from Dr. Keaton and George Pickett, inviting him to dinner at the employee cafeteria.

PART FOUR

YELLOWSTONE GAME PROTECTION ACT, 1894

AN ACT TO PROTECT THE BIRDS AND
ANIMALS IN YELLOWSTONE NATIONAL
PARK, AND TO PUNISH CRIMES IN SAID PARK,
AND FOR OTHER PURPOSES,
Approved May 7, 1894 (28 Stat. 73)

Sec. 3. that if any offense shall be committed in said Yellowstone National Park, which offense is not prohibited or the punishment is not specially provided for by any law of the United States or by any regulation of the Secretary of the Interior, the offender shall be subject to the same punishment as the laws of the State of Wyoming in force at the time of the commission of the offense may provide for a like offense in said State; and no subsequent repeal of any such law in the State of Wyoming shall affect any prosecution for said offense committed within said park. (U.S.C., title 16, sec. 25.)

15

"Dᴉᴅ ᴛʜᴇʏ ꜱᴇᴇ you?" McCann asked Butch Toomer after the ex-sheriff had returned from the park in his red Ford pickup and entered the law office. McCann had asked while ushering him into his office past Sheila, who eyed them both with open suspicion. When he closed the door he heard her cry, "Hey!" but ignored it.

Toomer had an annoying habit of wearing his aviator shades while he was working, so no one could see his eyes. He sat heavily in the chair across from McCann and lit a cigarette. "Yup," he said. "I'm pretty sure they saw me."

McCann felt a sharp pain in his chest. He placed his hand over his heart and rubbed it as he spoke. "I thought you were going to be inconspicuous."

Toomer waved his cigarette, dismissing McCann. "It couldn't be helped. There's no one in the park—no traffic. Of course they saw my truck, but I don't think they saw *me* or were close enough to make the plate. And there's no way they could be sure I was following them. There's only the one road system, you know. Any fool would notice the only other car on the road, for Christ sake."

McCann breathed a little easier. It made sense. "What did they do?"

The ex-sheriff withdrew a notebook from his jacket pocket. "Started the morning at Old Faithful, like we thought. Then they switched vehicles on me and I almost lost them. They got in a Park Service truck with the manager of the area by the name of Mark Cutler."

"You're sure it was Mark Cutler?" McCann asked, his mouth suddenly dry.

Toomer seemed to be studying him, but McCann wasn't sure. He wished he'd take off those damned sunglasses.

"Sure enough," Toomer said finally, as if annoyed at being questioned. "He'd changed into a Park Service uniform, though, sort of doing a switcheroo on me. But I'd seen him before and confirmed it was him by calling the hotel and asking if he was in. I guess Cutler volunteers for the Park Service when he's off-duty from Zephyr. He's some kind of expert on geysers. They said his shift was over at ten and he was going out on geyser duty, so that confirmed it."

"You didn't identify yourself when you called?"

"No," he said sarcastically, "I told them my name was Clay McCann, the infamous killer lawyer." Despite the sunglasses, McCann could tell Toomer rolled his eyes as he spoke. Toomer said, "Are you going to question everything I say? What, do you think I've never done surveillance before? Do you think I've never carried out an investigation?"

"Sorry."

Toomer grumbled and shook his head, then resumed his report. He outlined the tour Cutler had taken him on—the Upper Geyser Basin, the Firehole River, finally Biscuit Basin and Sunburst Hot Springs.

McCann felt himself go cold.

"What?" Toomer asked.

"They went to Sunburst? Why?"

"Damned if I know." He shrugged. "They carried some equipment from the truck in there but I didn't get out and follow them on foot. If I had, my cover would have been blown for sure, because that area is officially off limits. I waited until they got back to their vehicle, then followed them out."

"How long were they there?"

"An hour, hour and a half."

"But you didn't see what they did at the hot springs?"

"I told you that already."

McCann closed his eyes, felt his heart race.

"You want some water or something? A drink?" Toomer asked. "You look pale all of a sudden."

"No, I'm fine."

"Good, because I need some money for today."

Trying to recover, McCann opened a desk drawer and pulled out a binder of blank checks.

"I'd prefer cash."

"I don't have cash."

Finally, Toomer removed his sunglasses so he could glare at McCann. "I don't want to go down to the bank and cash a check from you. The rumors would start to fly. You're poison around this town, and I can't be associated with you. Don't you get that?"

McCann swallowed. "Yes. But I don't have five hundred in cash."

Toomer snorted. "You mean seven fifty. Don't try to mess with me. We agreed on a hundred an hour."

"If I don't have five hundred in cash, I don't have seven fifty either."

"Get it by tomorrow. And make it eight hundred for my trouble. Plus the four thousand you owe me for weapons training. I'm tired of working for you for free."

McCann pursed his lips and nodded in agreement, wondering where he would get the money. What could he sell, fast? He'd hoped he could send Toomer away with a check and have some money in the bank from his partners by the time the ex-sheriff tried to cash it.

"I'll have it tomorrow," McCann said.

"Good."

Toomer just sat there, his eyes narrowing. "What's the deal with Sunburst Hot Springs? When I said it I thought you were going to jump out of your chair. I thought this had to do with what happened down in Bechler."

McCann said, "It does. Don't worry about it. I didn't hire you to answer your questions, Butch."

"Why exactly did you hire me?"

"I think we're through here," McCann said. "I'll get you your fee tomorrow."

Toomer smiled a half-smile, put his sunglasses back on, and stood up and left without shaking McCann's extended hand.

"Don't mess with me, Clay," he said as he shut the door.

MCCANN'S INSIDES WERE burbling. This thing was coming apart. He should have been out of the country by now, on an island, sipping a drink and being petted by a woman he'd yet to meet. Instead, it seemed like the sky itself was crushing down and the walls were tightening in on him like jaws of a vise. He wondered what Cutler had told Pickett and Demming.

He punched the button for the intercom.

"Sheila, get me Layton Barron's home number in Denver."

No response.

"Sheila?"

"What do you think I am," she screeched. "*Your fucking secretary?*"

220

BARRON'S WIFE ANSWERED and McCann asked to speak to Layton. She covered the phone while she called to her husband but McCann could hear her through her fingers, which he imagined as bony but finely manicured.

Barron said, "Yes?" He didn't sound pleased.

"You know who this is."

"I can't believe you called me at home." His tone was angry, astonished. "I'm going to—"

"If you hang up on me, you're going to spend the rest of your life in prison," McCann said flatly. "Your bony-fingered wife will be alone with all of your treasure."

Pause. Then: "Honey, I need to take this in my office. Will you please hang it up in a second?"

There were no pleasantries once Barron picked up his private phone. "Look, I tried to call you back yesterday," Barron said, sounding as if he were speaking through clenched teeth. "I tried that number you gave me three times. First it was busy, then it rang and rang. And how do you know about my wife?"

"Forget that," McCann said.

"Then why are you calling me? How did you get my home number?"

"Forget that too," McCann said. "I want you to shut up and listen for once."

He could hear Barron take a breath. "Go ahead."

"We may have trouble up here. A couple of investigators"—McCann glanced at the business cards and read off the names—"went to Sunburst today with Mark Cutler. They may be too stupid to put things together, but that's getting too close for me."

"Jesus," Barron said softly.

"I want to get out of here," McCann said. "I want you to

live up to your end of the deal. I want my money, *now!*"

"Clay, it's not what you think. We're not trying to screw you, not at all. The SEC's been camped out in our building for three weeks. It has nothing to do with you at all, but I can't move any money right now. They're going over everything for the past four years. It's a fucking nightmare."

"You're right," McCann said, "this has nothing to do with me. I could care less about the SEC, or your company. I want my money. I did my part, you need to do yours."

"Look," Barron said, an edge of panic entering his voice, "I think they'll be gone by the end of the week. I really do. We're clean, I swear it. It's just that some of our accounting looks a little, well, *optimistic*. I'm sure we'll get it sorted out and when those assholes leave, I'll get that transfer to you within the hour."

"Not good enough," McCann said. "I need it now. Tonight."

"Tonight?"

"You have no idea what it's like for me," McCann said. "If Pickett and Demming start connecting the dots, I'm just sitting here."

"Can't you be more reasonable?"

Yes, McCann thought, the panic in Barron's voice was real. He'd cracked him.

"Listen to me," McCann said, pressing, deciding to show his hole card, "if I don't get my money, I'll go to the FBI and sing in exchange for immunity. They'll give it to me, I promise you. I've worked with them and they'd rather nail somebody high-level—somebody like Layton Barron of EnerDyne—than put me back in jail."

"My God, you can't be serious."

McCann nodded. "I'm serious."

"But I told you, I can't move the money. The SEC—"

222

"Then send me some of *your* money, you twit," McCann said. "Sit down at your computer and wire at least a ten-thousand-dollar down payment to my account tonight. I put my career and my life on the line for you. I expect some consideration."

He could hear Barron swallow. "But you wouldn't really go to the FBI, would you?"

"Absolutely."

"Okay," he said in a whisper, "I can do that."

"And you need to keep it coming," McCann said. "Ten thousand tonight, ten thousand tomorrow, ten thousand the next day until you can pay the balance from your company, whenever that is. It's not my problem, it's yours. I'll talk with my banker every morning. If you miss a single day, I sing. Got it?"

Silence.

"Got it?"

"Yes."

McCann felt some of the burden lift from his shoulders. "That's not all," he said, liking the way the power had shifted to him.

"What else?"

"It's time for you to contact your man on the inside," McCann said. "Tell him what's going on and see if he can do something about it. He's the only guy close enough to the situation on the ground to steer it away from us. It's time he got his hands dirty."

Barron moaned, as if McCann were torturing him. "He's not going to like it."

"I could give a shit," McCann said, starting to feel, finally, that he was making things happen in his favor. "He's had a free ride so far. Tell him to act or he'll be implicated as well. Tell him I'm serious."

"I wish it didn't have to be this way," Barron said, his tone strangely resigned, as if seeing McCann in an all new light as his enemy. Good, McCann thought. It's about time.

"All you had to do was your part," McCann said. "I did mine."

He hung up the telephone, sat back in his chair, looked at his reflection in the glass doors of his bookcase, and fell righteously back in love with the man who grinned at him.

He'd let the locals get to him. He'd even let one old cow whack him on the head with a telephone receiver. The power he'd built up since his time in jail had been pouring out of him since he'd returned, puddling at his feet. Now it felt like the wounds had healed. He was recharging.

"Jeez," he said, "I *missed* you."

HE WAS STILL smiling when Sheila D'Amato opened his door without knocking and leaned against the jamb with her hand on her hip and a sly smile on her face. Her eyes sparkled.

"You son of a bitch," she said with admiration.

"Don't tell me you listened," he said, shaking his head.

"Ten thousand a day," she said. "Damn, you're a better earner than the crooks I used to hang with."

"I'll take that as a compliment," he said, maintaining the grin somehow while part of his brain raced, trying to process the magnitude of what she'd done, how he would deal with it.

"I'm still confused," she said. "I don't get what it is you guys are trying to hide. I mean, it obviously has something to do with some Sunburst thing, but I don't get how that has anything to do with those four dead people."

"It's complicated," he said.

"I've got all night."

"Let's go have some dinner," he said. "I'll fill you in."

She beamed, and he was surprised how attractive she looked when she was full of joy. He hadn't known because she'd never been so happy in his presence before.

THEY STEPPED ONTO the sidewalk to go to Rocky's for dinner. He held the door open for her and smelled her as she came through. A nice scent. He liked the way her heels clicked on the pavement. It was rare to see a woman in the West in a dress and heels, and he found himself lagging behind her a little so he could look at her strong calves through the nylons.

"I've got to say," she said, shooting a come-hither look over her shoulder, "I'm more than a little surprised that you didn't bite my head off for listening in."

"I thought about it."

"But you didn't," she said. "I guess that means we really are in this together."

"I need allies," he said.

"I'd like to think I'm more than that."

"You are," he said.

"This all has to do with that company, doesn't it?" she asked.

"What company?"

"EnerDyne. I saw the binder on your credenza. You work for them, right?"

He whistled. "Boy, you don't miss a trick, do you?"

"I haven't yet," she purred. She'd knocked another fifty dollars off her legal bill before they went out on the street. He still felt a little light-headed.

DINNER TOOK HOURS. McCann ordered too many martinis. She looked good in the light from the single cheap candle on the table, which took ten years off her face and made her skin seem smoother and whiter and her lips more lush and red.

"Tomorrow we'll drive to Idaho Falls," he said. "We can check on flights, do a little shopping. You'll need some things to wear on the beach, I would guess."

"It must be nice to have money," she said. "Ten thousand a day."

"That's just a fraction of what they owe me."

"You turned that man into a quivering little squirrel," she said, holding her hand out toward him and pulling her sleeve back. "I got goose bumps listening."

He shrugged, flattered.

"Who is the man on the inside?"

"Tomorrow. I'll fill you in tomorrow … if you're a good girl until then."

"When I'm good, I'm very good," she said. "That's what they used to tell me …"

"And when you're bad …" he said, letting it trail off.

"I'm really fucking bad." She grinned.

He ordered another martini for both of them. He had to look down to see if he'd finished his steak. Nope.

She favored him with a smile so full-bore he could see her back teeth. "We really are partners in crime, aren't we?"

"We are," he said. "You now know more than anyone else."

"I'll keep my mouth shut," she said, "except when, well, you know."

It was as if she were melting for him before his eyes.

He'd never been with a woman like her, he thought. Too bad about tomorrow.

16

Iᴛ ᴡᴀs ᴏʙᴠɪᴏᴜs to Joe when he saw George Pickett waiting for him at a back table in the near-empty employee cafeteria that the old man had cleaned himself up. George looked dark and small, birdlike, fragile, his thick black hair slicked back wetly in jail-bar strings and his hands entwined in front of him. A tray of food sat off to the side. He wore a dingy but clean white shirt buttoned all the way up and dark baggy slacks Joe recognized from years before, which gave Joe an uneasy feeling and caused a hitch in his step that he powered through, as if his legs had thought better of the reunion and decided to flee.

The closer Joe got to his father, the angrier and more confused he became. The emotions came out of a place he didn't know still existed, as if a long-dormant tumor had ruptured. He felt eighteen again, and not in a good way.

Joe sat down across from George. They had the table to themselves. Outside the murky, unwashed windows, the last moments of the sun died on the pine boughs.

"You can grab a tray and get some dinner," George said, gesturing toward the buffet line at the front of the room.

"I'm not hungry."

"You've got to eat something."

"No."

George slid his tray before him—slices of dark meat covered with brown gravy, a mound of mashed potatoes with a hollowed-out, gravy-filled pocket on top. Joe remembered watching his father do that growing up—hollowing out the potatoes with the heel of his spoon, pouring gravy in the depression so it looked like a volcano about to erupt.

George halfheartedly cut a forkful of beef and raised it to his mouth. He chewed slowly, painfully, as if his gums hurt. Joe noticed that his hand holding the fork trembled as he raised it.

When he was through chewing, George washed it down with half a glass of ice water and winced as he drank. "You sure you don't want something?"

"I'm sure."

"Just so you know, I haven't had a drink all day."

"That's why you're shaking and drinking water," Joe said.

"I did it for you. It wasn't easy."

Joe nodded. He could not make himself thank his father for not drinking for the day. He couldn't think of a good thing to say about anything, and regretted that he'd come.

"It's good to see you, Son," George said softly, holding Joe's eyes for a fleeting second before looking away. Joe noticed George was having trouble keeping his mouth still, as if his teeth wanted to chatter.

"I guess I'm supposed to say it's good to see you too," Joe said.

"But you can't say that."

"I can't say that."

Still not meeting Joe's eyes, George nodded as if he understood how things were. He tried to eat a forkful of mashed potatoes but it hung there, inches from his open

228

mouth. With resignation, he dropped the fork to his plate. "I can't eat this."

The silence eventually turned into a kind of roar, Joe thought. He couldn't hear his father when he broke it.

"What?"

"I said I thought about giving you a call lots of times."

"But you never did."

"Tell me about my grandchildren," George said, his first genuine smile pulling at his mouth. "My daughter-in-law. What's her name again?"

"Marybeth."

"How old are my granddaughters?"

"Getting older all the time," Joe said.

His father stared at him. Joe remembered that stare, those eyes, that set in his mouth that could curl into a grin or, just as easily, bare and reveal tiny sharp teeth.

"You don't want to tell me about them," George said.

"They have nothing to do with you. You have nothing to do with them."

"I had hoped it wouldn't be like this."

Joe wanted to reach across the table, gather the old man's collar in his fist, and bounce him up and down like a rag doll. "At one time, I had a lot to say to you. For years, I rehearsed what I was going to tell you if I ever got the opportunity I have now. I'd go over it when I was by myself like it was a speech. I had sections about what you did to my mother, my brother, and me. It was a pretty good speech, and I'm not good at speeches. But now that you're sitting right there, I can't remember any of it."

George shook his head. "It wasn't all bad. I wasn't a monster."

Joe didn't disagree.

"Your mom and I, we—"

"I don't want to hear it," Joe snapped. "What's done is done. You can't justify it now."

"It was never about you," George said. "You probably think that. It was about your mother and me. I never had anything against you or Victor."

"You're right," Joe said. "It was never about us. Not a thing was ever about us."

"That's not what I meant."

"Yes, it was."

His father took a deep breath. Joe could hear it wheeze into his lungs. "Can't we put that all behind us now? You're a grown man. We're both grown men. I was hoping maybe we could talk."

"I'm not a big talker."

"I've got some things I'd like to say."

"Like what?"

"Like when I left, it was the best thing for all of us. Would it have been better if I'd stayed and continued to make everyone's life as miserable as mine?"

Joe said, "At least that would have showed that you tried to think of someone other than yourself."

"You're not hearing what I'm saying," George said, a familiar phrase from his father. What it meant to Joe was, *You're not agreeing with what I say, you're defective.*

"I needed space," his father said, "I needed to find out why I was put on this earth."

Joe stared at him with bitter contempt. "What a load of crap that is," he said.

George was startled.

"I get pretty sick of hearing people like you try to find good reasons for acting selfish," Joe said. "It's not about what you say, it's about what you do. You cut and ran."

"How did you get so hard, Son?" his father whispered.

"A few months ago," Joe said, "I put the muzzle of my Glock to a man's forehead and pulled the trigger. I think about it all the time, just about every night. I justify it to myself that he was threatening my family, which he was. That if I let him go he'd figure out a way to come back for me, which he would have. But it doesn't matter what I say to myself, I still did it. I didn't *have* to do it, I *chose* to. My words about it mean nothing, just like yours."

George sighed and it was as if all of his spirit was being expelled. He seemed smaller than when Joe sat down. Joe watched his father think. He knew he'd made him angry. Fine.

George looked up. "I might have done some stupid things, but at least I never killed a man."

Joe thought of Victor. "In a way, what you did was worse."

"And here I thought tonight might be nice," George said sadly.

"I've got a great wife and two great kids," Joe said. "I learned how to be a good father and a husband from them. Without them I'd fly off the planet."

"When Victor died—"

"Without them," Joe said, refusing to let George turn the conversation, "I might have turned out to be like you."

He stood up and walked out of the cafeteria. Joe wasn't sure why he'd confessed, and it confused him as much as anything. George didn't call after him.

MARYBETH WAS CLEANING up after dinner when Joe called, and the first thing she said was, "Three more days."

Which reminded him he needed to make arrangements for them, reserve rooms or a cabin in the only place that would still be open, Mammoth.

He asked her if she could get on the Internet and research some companies he had learned about but hadn't had the means to check out. She eagerly agreed, and he read them off: Allied, Genetech, BioCorp, Schroeder Engineering, EnerDyne.

"I'll see what I can find," she said.

He told her about George Pickett, putting a gloss on the meeting. Already, he was feeling guilty for being so hard on the old man. Too much had spilled out and too quickly.

"Joe," she said, "does he want to meet us?"

"I'm sure he does. But I don't think that's a good idea."

"I'm tough," she said. "Your girls are tough. They can handle it."

"But why should they?"

"Kids are always curious about where they come from," Marybeth said. "This is an opportunity for them to meet their grandfather."

Joe laughed nervously. "You're supposed to be the one with good judgment. Why should we introduce them to a sick old drunk who thinks the world will end any minute?"

She paused. "Honey, are you okay?"

"No," he said. "I'm not."

JOE SAT IN a rocking chair in front of the four-sided fire-place with the purpose of making notes for his report to Chuck Ward but finding himself staring at the dying flames until late into the night. The inn had the feel of melancholy and abandonment on its last night open, which precisely matched his mood. He could not get the image of his father out of his mind—sitting there in his shirt buttoned to his neck, eyes rheumy, hands shaking, saying, "How did you get so hard, Son?" At one point, from out of nowhere, he fought the urge to cry.

NATE ARRIVED HOLDING two stout logs, which he tossed into the fire after stepping over the railing designed to prevent visitors from doing exactly that. The lengths of soft dry pine took off as if they were angry, throwing out heat and light. Joe snapped out of his reverie and sat up.

Nate asked, "How'd dinner with Pop go?"

Joe said, "Badly."

"I had an interesting day," Nate said, settling down in the chair next to Joe. "But first, tell me about yours."

After Joe was finished, Nate slowly nodded his head. "I remember the hot pot at Sunburst," he said. "Nice place. I took a girl there once."

"I'm guessing that's where Hoening went also," Joe said, making a mental note to himself to try to contact several of the girls Yellowdick had corresponded with. As far as he knew, the investigators hadn't followed up with any of them because there appeared to be no reason to do so. But if they could tell Joe anything about trips to the hot springs, it might shed some light. Or, Joe thought, simply make the murky even murkier.

"You said today was interesting," Joe said. "How so?"

"Couple of things," Nate said, leaning forward. "Did you know you were being followed?"

Joe told him about their suspicions.

"I got the plate number," Nate said. "I saw his pickup parked on a side road watching you and Demming wait for Cutler to change clothes. Red oh-four Ford pickup, Montana. Owner is a guy named Butch Toomer, ex-sheriff from West Yellowstone. Likely associate of Mr. Clay McCann. I mean, you'd assume the sheriff and a lawyer would know each other, right? He stuck with you guys all day. Maybe you can ask your contacts to check up on him."

"I will," Joe said. "How'd you learn all that about Toomer? Did you call the DMV in Montana?"

Nate chuckled. "It wasn't necessary. Everybody knows everybody up here, don't you know that by now?"

Joe waited for the rest.

"There's a hard core of full-time Zephyr people," Nate said. "They're the ones who work different jobs all year-round, unlike the thousands of seasonal folks who go home for the winter. I found out I knew a few of the hard-core types from when I was here. They're still around, still crazy. But they keep track of what's going on. They know when that ranger Layborn is on the prowl for them, and they sure as hell know an ex-sheriff when they see him."

"Ah," Joe said, smiling.

"Something else," Nate said. "Bob Olig is still around."

Joe sat forward. *"What?"*

"I heard it three or four times today."

Joe and Nate leaned forward in their chairs until their heads nearly touched. "Either it's him or his ghost," Nate said. "He's been spotted, mostly here around the Old Faithful area. One man swore he saw him in the kitchen one morning but Olig ran off before he could stop him. A couple of fine ladies said they saw a guy who sounds like Olig just strolling along the boardwalk one night in the moonlight like he didn't have a care in the world. When he saw them, he ducked into the trees. And an old guy who has insomnia and wanders around swears he saw Olig standing behind the front desk one night about three-thirty going through the guest register. The old guy yelled at him because he knew Olig pretty well from Olig's days as a tour guide, but Olig ducked behind the counter and disappeared. But he swears it was him. He said Olig looked scared."

"Olig," Joe said, "or a guy who looks a lot like Olig? I

234

mean, this sounds like the kind of thing lonely people would come up with to keep themselves amused."

"Take it for what it's worth," Nate said.

"Were any of them interviewed by the Park Service or the FBI?"

"If they were," Nate said, "they didn't say anything about seeing Bob Olig. I think most of the sightings happened long after those murders, long after anyone was asking."

Joe sat back. "Do you believe them?"

Nate was stoic. "You know I believe this kind of shit," he said. "But that's just me."

They stopped talking when they heard the footsteps of a uniformed Zephyr employee crossing the wooden floor. Joe looked up, half-expecting to see Bob Olig.

Instead, it was a grizzled bellman with a full beard and a name tag that said Hérve from France.

"Are you Joe Pickett?" Hérve asked.

When Joe said yes, Hérve handed him a message. "Since we don't have telephones in the rooms, this is the way we deliver them."

"Thank you."

"I want to remind you, sirs, that the inn closes tomorrow at noon," he said.

"We know."

Hérve smiled, turned on his heel, and returned to the front desk, where his colleagues were packing up and closing down for the season.

Joe unfolded the note and read it aloud.

"Joe: I thought a lot about everything and may have figured something out. It's a doozy. Meet me at Sunburst Hot Springs tomorrow at seven. Best, Mark Cutler."

17

A$_\text{T}$ 6.45 $_\text{THE}$ next morning the thermals in the upper geyser basin created a wall of billowing steam across the highway that wetted the outside of the Yukon's windshield so Joe had to brake, turn on the wipers, and crawl through. For a moment, in the midst of the sharp-smelling steam, he was blinded and had the strange sensation of being in an airplane as it rose skyward through the clouds.

Demming was in the passenger seat clutching a large paper cup of coffee; Nate was in the backseat smelling of wood smoke. The two had met uneasily at the Yukon ten minutes before.

"Thanks for saving us," Demming had said.

"Anytime," Nate said.

It was crisp and cold, the first shafts of sun pouring over the western mountains as if assaulting the day. A heavy frost made the grass sparkle and coated the pine trees. Elk grazed in the open parks, wisps of steam curling up from their nostrils.

Joe's holstered Glock was on the console between him and Demming. He had watched her reaction when she saw it and detected no official warning. Maybe she hadn't awakened yet, he thought. Nate wore his .454 in a shoulder holster beneath a billowy, open fatigue jacket, the leather strap in clear view across his chest. He had no doubt she'd seen that too and said nothing.

They didn't encounter a single vehicle until they turned from the highway to Biscuit Basin and nearly hit a black SUV head-on that was coming out. Joe swerved sharply right, missing the front bumper by inches. The SUV turned away from the Yukon as well, and both vehicles went off the road into opposite shallow ditches. Joe stopped but the other continued on, the driver jerking it back onto the road and roaring away, heading north with a spray of pea gravel that peppered the back window of the Yukon. It happened so quickly that Joe didn't get a glimpse of the driver through the smoked glass windows of the SUV—only the gleaming grille like the bared teeth of a shark that had just missed an attack.

"Man!" he shouted. "Where'd he come from?"

Demming squirmed in her seat, lap soaked with spilled hot coffee.

"I'm all right," she said.

"I'm sorry," Joe said. "My fault. I wasn't expecting anyone because we haven't seen another car all morning."

Nate was half-turned in the seat, watching glimpses of the SUV wink through the trees. "Two in the car but I couldn't see them clearly," he said. "Wyoming plates, but I didn't get a number."

Demming said, "I look like I wet my pants."

"His driving does that to people," Nate said.

"I'm *sorry*," Joe said to Demming, shooting Nate a glance. Nate smiled back.

Joe breathed slowly until his nerves calmed, then pulled back onto the road.

CUTLER'S PARK SERVICE pickup was sitting where they had parked the day before. Joe pulled up beside it as Demming used the last of a box of tissues to absorb the coffee on her uniform pants. He put the close call behind him and climbed out.

The odor in the air was familiar, he thought, but it was from a different time and place. It reminded him of Sundays, growing up, and the smell that came from the kitchen while he lounged in the living room with his brother, Victor, watching football.

Joe wondered if the meeting with his father had skewed his mind, triggered reminiscences that had long been put away.

Nate got out, sniffed, squinted with puzzlement and said "Pork roast?"

Joe clipped the Glock onto his belt, cold dread gripping his stomach, remembering something Cutler had said the day before.

BY THE TIME they found Mark Cutler's body in Sunburst Hot Springs, his volunteer Park Service uniform and most of his flesh had separated from the skeleton and was floating free, boiling in the water. Commas of black curly hair were being carried down the runoff chute along with bouncing yellow globules of parboiled fat.

"No ..." Demming gasped, stuffing her fist in her mouth, turning away.

Joe froze, stared in absolute horror, and forgot for the longest time how to breathe. Finally, he unclenched himself and put his arms around Demming and held her. She didn't resist. He felt her hot tears on his neck.

He looked over her head at the scene. The trunk of the

body turned slowly in the hot springs and more pieces came loose. The spring boiled angrily. Joe made himself look away, despite a morbid fascination that shamed him.

"That poor son of a bitch," Nate said as he joined them. "When I go, I want it to be from a bullet to the head. I sure as hell don't want to be *stew*."

DEMMING WAS THE first to recall the encounter with the black SUV. Voice trembling, she tried to contact dispatch on her handheld to alert rangers on patrol as well as the personnel at the park gates. No one answered.

"Come in, anyone," she said.

Static.

"We're out of range," she said dully, indicating the radio. "Let's try Mark's truck radio."

"On the chance he left it unlocked and his keys in it," Joe said, clearly remembering how fastidious Cutler had been about taking his keys and locking the truck at every stop the day before.

As they trudged back toward the vehicles, Joe said, "That SUV can't be more than fifteen minutes away. Maybe we can catch it."

"Mark was such a nice guy," Demming said. "No one deserves what happened to him. If whoever was driving that SUV did this, I'll shoot and ask questions later."

"I like her style," Nate said to Joe.

"We don't know anything yet," Joe said. "We don't even know if the SUV driver even saw Mark, much less knocked him into Sunburst. But he sure was in a hurry to get out of here."

Nate said, "Luckily, there aren't that many roads. Whoever it is has three options: He could be on the way to the gate at West Yellowstone, or continuing north toward Mammoth.

Or he could have cut through the middle of the park by now toward Canyon Village. If he gets to Canyon, that would give him three other ways out."

"God, this is horrible," Demming said, shuddering. "I've never seen anything like that before."

Joe hadn't either. He couldn't get the scene out of his mind. He made a point not to look over at the rivulet of cooling springwater that bordered the path they were on in the chance he would see more of Cutler's body floating away. He imagined the truck keys were likely somewhere deep in the thermal pool, caught on a ledge, heating to over two hundred degrees. At what temperature would metal melt? He didn't know. How long would it take for Cutler's bones to boil clean white and sink, like the bison bones he had seen deep in the water the day before? He jolted off the trail into the trees and threw up.

"Sorry," he said, wiping his mouth with his sleeve.

He could tell by the look on Demming's face that she might be next, and she was.

THEY HEARD A roar ahead of them in the direction of the road. By now, the sound was familiar.

"Geyser going off," Joe said. "I wonder which one it is." He also wondered if the body in the spring had upset the delicate interconnected underground plumbing of the thermal basin enough to cause an unscheduled eruption. Cutler would have known the answer to that question, he thought.

Nate was in the lead and he topped the hill ahead of Demming and Joe, and was the first to see the geyser.

"Oh, no," Nate said, shaking his head.

"What now?" Joe asked.

"We won't be chasing any SUV," Nate said. "And, Joe, you aren't going to like this one bit."

241

Joe didn't.

A fissure had opened through the thin asphalt of the road directly under the Yukon. Steam and superheated water were blasting up from the ground into the chassis. The windows of the vehicle had been blown out, the paint was peeling off the sides in curled shards, and the tires and plastic grille were melting.

"Jesus," Demming said.

Joe thought, *How can this possibly be happening?*—although he knew that in Yellowstone, it happened all the time. Things just came out of the ground anytime, anywhere.

"Your old boss was right," Nate said. "You're really rough on trucks."

"Not now," Joe said.

"The SUV will get away," Demming said softly, shaking her head.

Joe found Cutler's pickup locked and the keys missing. There was nothing they could do to pursue the SUV, call for help, or get out of there.

"This place is kicking our asses," Nate grumbled.

IT TOOK AN hour for Joe and Demming to flag down a road maintenance truck on the highway. An old couple from Nebraska had swerved to avoid them and never slowed down, and an RV speeded up, despite the fact that Demming had flashed her badge and put her hand on her weapon. When the truck stopped, Demming crowded in and Joe said he would stay and wait.

"I'll call dispatch and get some rangers here as fast as I can." she said. "An ambulance too."

Joe didn't ask what she thought an ambulance would pick up.

*

NATE SAT ON an overturned dead tree trunk that was white with absorbed minerals. The morning had heated twenty degrees already with the rising sun, and the ankle-high grass was now wet instead of frozen. Three bison had emerged from a stand of trees and were slowly grazing their way up the trail toward Sunburst.

Joe sat down next to him and stared at the hulk of the Yukon. The fissure beneath it had stopped erupting, although he could hear burbling and see an occasional puff of steam.

"Man," Joe said, sighing, nodding toward the Yukon. "This keeps happening to me."

"I know," Nate said. "If you would have parked ten feet either way, it would have missed it."

"Cutler was a damned good guy," Joe said. "I really liked him."

Nate nodded. "Somebody didn't. Question is, who knew he'd be here?"

Joe hadn't thought of that. "Hérve," Joe said. "And whoever took the message or saw it before it was given to us."

"Or anyone you, me, or Demming told about the meeting this morning," Nate said.

Joe hadn't told anyone. There was no one to tell.

"I wonder if Demming called her bosses," Joe said, not wanting to go where his thoughts seemed to be taking him.

Nate nodded. "Maybe we've got a big problem on the inside. I can't say I'm shocked at the idea."

"Damn, you're cynical."

"You forget," Nate said, "I used to work for the Feds myself in another, um, capacity. No personal agenda in a closed bureaucracy can surprise me."

A black raven the size of a football cruised along the basin, calling out rudely. It skimmed the rivulet, saw something in the water, turned and landed. The raven quickly speared something in the stream—a piece of Mark Cutler—and ate it a second before it blew up in an explosion of black feathers.

"I hate ravens," Nate said, holstering his .454.

Joe hadn't even tried to stop Nate from drawing his weapon and firing because he agreed with the sentiment, given the circumstances.

A HALF-HOUR before approaching sirens split the silence, Nate patted Joe on the shoulder and said he had to go. "There will be lots of questions," Nate said. "Portenson might even be here. I don't have time for that now."

"I understand."

"Besides, you and Demming can cover everything," Nate said. "I'll catch up with you later."

18

T HAT AFTERNOON, CLAY McCann drove south from West Yellowstone and the sun streamed in through the windows but didn't take the chill off the inside of the car one bit, he thought. In fact, it felt like it was getting colder, despite the digital gauge on the dash that showed it was nearing sixty degrees.

Butch Toomer sat in the passenger seat, reaching incessantly to fiddle with the radio to try to find a station he liked. He had a toothpick in his mouth that never stopped dancing, and he was wearing his shades.

Sheila sat in the back, fuming. Her rage was palpable, an emotional cold front that could close schools and government buildings in seven states.

"Why the *fuck* is he here?" she asked McCann. "This was supposed to be a special day."

"I told you," McCann said. "I owe him some money. I told him I'd get it in Idaho Falls, and he insisted on coming along."

"I wish you two would stop talking like I'm not here," Toomer said. "It's getting on my nerves."

"*You're* getting on my nerves," Sheila said. "And don't get me started on Clay."

McCann shrugged. Fall colors were bursting like fireworks in the wooded folds of the mountains. Not that he cared. Scenery got old. Instead, he recalled how Sheila had looked that morning when he pulled into the parking lot of her shabby apartment building to pick her up. She had never looked better, he thought. Tight black sweater, charcoal skirt, black nylons, strappy shoes. And where in the hell did she get those pearls?

Oh, how her face fell when she saw Toomer in the car. Oh, the words she used. McCann was a little surprised when she was through that blisters had not formed on his exposed face and hands.

Several times, he had tried to catch her eye in the rearview mirror. He wanted to smile at her, have her know he was smiling at her. The only time she looked back her eyes were fearsome black daggers and when they connected with his he thought the temperature in the car dropped another ten degrees.

"DO YOU THINK we'll have time to look at a couple of horse trailers in Idaho Falls?" Toomer asked. They had just crossed the state line from Montana into Idaho.

"Why?" McCann said.

"Elk season," Toomer said. "Christ, don't you pay any attention around here? Haven't you seen all those men wearing orange and driving around with dead animals in their trucks?"

McCann didn't respond. He tried to catch Sheila's eye in the mirror again but she wouldn't look back.

"I got a two-horse slant load," Toomer said. "I want to upgrade to a four-horse stock, now that I'm coming into a little money. I like them stocks. They pull good and I got a mare that blows up when I try to get her to load into the slant."

It was as if he were speaking Martian, McCann thought.

"Clay," Sheila sighed from the back, "please take me somewhere without horses. Or hunters. Or ex-sheriff assholes who won't take their sunglasses off."

McCann noted that her anger had been replaced by despair. He felt sorry for her. All dressed up and stuck in a car with Butch Toomer. And him. She deserved better, he thought. He wished Toomer was gone and she'd take her sweater off.

"Make her shut up, or I'll do it," Toomer growled at him.

"Leave her alone," McCann said.

"Don't you tell me what to do."

McCann could tell the ex-sheriff meant it.

"Okay," McCann said. "Let's all settle down, please." He tried to catch Sheila's eye in the rearview. When he did she displayed her middle finger at him.

MCCANN HAD HEARD nothing from Layton Barron. That alone told him all he needed to know. If Barron and his partner were playing straight with him, there would have been at least a call that morning. And if Barron had been unable to reach his man on the inside, he should have let McCann know he was working on it and beg him not to carry out his threat.

And when his banker told him no money had been deposited into his account, McCann knew Barron had talked to his partner, and they'd decided not to pay up, but to take another course of action. Either they didn't believe he'd go to the police or they had plans for him. He guessed the latter.

Which meant, McCann decided, that his situation was desperate. And desperate men, well … they hire lawyers to think of ways to use the law to save themselves. Fortunately, he had that part covered.

THE ROAD GOT narrower, more rural. Straightaways turned into meandering turns through farmland. The Tetons sparkled in the distance, looking clean, white, and fake.

Toomer said, "It always pisses me off that the snooty bastards over there in Jackson Hole always refer to our side of the mountains as 'the back side of the Tetons.' Who in the hell gave them the 'front'?"

McCann watched for the turnoff and ignored Toomer. Sheila had seemed to make it her mission to ignore both of them now. Instead, she kept sighing.

"I need a drink," she said, breaking her silence. "Are there any bars ahead?"

"This is Mormon country," Toomer said. "No bars."

"Mormons drink," she said. "Especially if there's just one of them. I've seen 'em go at it at Rocky's. If there's two, they watch each other and neither one will drink. It cracks me up."

"That's what they always say in elk camp," Toomer said, laughing with loud guffaws. "If a Mormon comes and he's alone, *hide the whiskey*!"

They seemed to be getting along so well, McCann thought, neither noticed he had turned off the main road toward the east. Or that the bridge that crossed Boundary Creek was just ahead. Or that despite the absence of a sign or a gate, they were officially in Yellowstone Park.

With his left hand, McCann pushed the button on the door handle that lowered the passenger window by Toomer's head.

"Hey," Toomer said, "why'd you do that? Did you fart or something?" He looked back to see if Sheila, his new pal, would laugh at his joke.

"No," McCann said, pulling the .38 out of his jacket, "it's so your brains won't splash all over the glass."

Toomer's mouth made an *O* and McCann fired into the left lens of his sunglasses, and then the right. The sounds were sharp and deafening. The ex-sheriff slumped back, his mouth still open, a string of saliva connecting his upper and lower teeth.

Sheila screamed, *"Clay! Clay! Clay! Oh my God!"* her hands to her face, her knees clamped together.

McCann said, "I'm really sorry, honey," and shot her three times. One bullet passed through her necklace and sent pearls flying all over the inside of the car.

AT DUSK, TEN minutes before he'd close the office for the night, B. Stevens heard the clump of a shoe on the wooden stairs outside the Bechler ranger station and looked up as Clay McCann opened the door and came in. He looked flushed.

The ranger was stunned. "You ..." he said.

"It happened again, can you believe it?" McCann said as he wearily dropped a snub-nosed revolver on the counter. "I was giving a couple of locals a ride to Idaho Falls and they pulled this damned *gun* on me."

Stevens was speechless.

McCann held his arms out, wrists together, making it as easy as possible to put cuffs on them. The lawyer shook his head, said, "They're out there in the car. I guess they didn't realize who they were dealing with."

19

D EL ASHBY AND Eric Layborn drove Joe and Demming back to Mammoth after the initial crime-scene procedures were accomplished at Sunburst Hot Springs. They left at mid-afternoon while more and more rangers arrived until the basin was packed with them. The flood of vehicles to the scene attracted what few visitors were still in the park, who assumed that so much ranger action must mean bears had been spotted. Families in cars and RVs lined the narrow road into the area, causing a snarl of traffic that forced Ashby to break regulations and drive on the side of the road.

Joe listened as Ashby and Layborn complained about the quality of the crime scene, how the pathway had been trampled by Joe and Demming, thus obscuring the foot-prints of the killer or killers, how the condition of Cutler's body was such that it would be nearly impossible to tell if he fell, was pushed, or was murdered and then thrown in.

Demming defended their actions. "We did nothing wrong," she said.

"Of course not," Layborn said, rolling his eyes. "It's just the small things. You know, like getting into a confrontation with an Iowa mountain man who gets shot up and flown to the hospital at our expense. Or getting forced off the road by the likely killers, not getting a description or a plate number, walking all over the crime scene throwing up, getting your vehicle destroyed, not giving chase *or* calling it in, letting the third member of your party go on a walkabout, and delaying the initial investigation of the crime scene by three hours because you had to hitch a ride with a road maintenance crew. Other than that, you did real well. Did I forget anything, Del?"

"I think you covered it," Ashby said. "Except maybe the fact that Joe Pickett and his mystery buddy have been flashing their weaponry out in the open every place they go against Park Service policy."

"Oh, that too," Layborn said.

"You two are poised to become media stars," Ashby said, biting off his words. "We've got more calls for comment than all of us can handle. Just exactly what we didn't want—more attention on the Zone of Death and now a fully cooked Zephyr employee."

"I think you're out of line," Joe said. "Both of you." He wondered which of them, or if both, had sent the black SUV to intercept Cutler that morning.

Layborn fixed him with a cop stare, except that one of his eyes peered at something to the side of Joe's face. "We might just have to pull over and settle this."

"Maybe so."

"Let it go, Joe," Demming said. "This is a Park Service thing, you know?"

"That's right," Ashby said. "You have no say here. In fact, I'm thinking of punching your ticket and sending you back home to your governor."

Demming shot Joe a desperation glance, pleading with

her eyes for him to keep quiet. For her sake, he did. He thought that while he could go home, she couldn't.

AS THEY PULLED into the parking lot of the Pagoda at dark, Joe was plotting his moves that evening. Call Chuck Ward, tell him what was going on and what had happened, let him in on his suspicions. Beg for a new vehicle. Apologize for the last one. Call Marybeth. Drink.

"I want your full written statements by tomorrow morning," Ashby said. "I'm meeting with the chief ranger and want to be fully briefed. Plus, I would expect we'll be getting some calls from Washington wanting to know just what in the hell is happening to our park."

Ashby said to Demming, "When I asked you to come back yesterday, I meant it. But no, you wanted to continue to play cowgirl to John Wayne here. If you would have, maybe Cutler would still be alive."

Demming turned ashen.

Joe said, "That was low." He sort of liked being compared to John Wayne, though.

HE AND DEMMING followed Ashby and Layborn into the Pagoda. Demming looked pale and on the verge of tears she was fighting to hold back. Joe resisted the impulse to put his hand on her shoulder, to reassure her. He thought if he did that it would make her look weak to Ashby and Layborn.

The night dispatcher threw open the door to the lobby, his headset dangling from where he'd jerked it out of his phone. His eyes were wild.

"Chief," he said to Ashby, "you've got to take this."

"Take what?" Ashby said, grimacing.

"Stevens from Bechler."

253

"Wait here," Ashby told Demming and Joe, and followed the dispatcher.

Five minutes later, he came back. He was seething, his face bright red: "That son of a bitch Clay McCann did it again!"

20

J OE FINISHED WRITING his report—including the news of Clay McCann killing two more people in "self-defense" within the Zone of Death—and had it faxed from the front desk. While he watched Simon feed the pages through, something nagged at him. He needed to talk to Demming.

Lower-level federal housing was down the mountain from the Mammoth Hotel, a half-mile walk nearly straight downhill. The moon was full and lit the sagebrush-covered hillside. A small herd of elk grazed in the moonlight. Joe could smell their familiar musky smell in the air. He noticed blue parentheses on either side of the moon. Snow was coming.

The cluster of Park Service housing was built on a plateau on the mountain. The houses were packed tightly together with fenceless common yards. The density of the houses was claustrophobic, Joe thought, compared to the vast, empty hillsides in all directions. It reminded him of a government-built anthill in the middle of a prairie. He found Demming's house by the brown wooden sign outside that said LARS AND JUDY DEMMING and crossed the postage-stamp lawn. A BMX bike leaned against the wall. The house was small and looked exactly like every other one on the street.

The Park Service had even painted them all the same light green color. Demming's cruiser was parked next to a jacked-up Ford 4´4 pickup that looked formidable as well as well taken care of.

A man answered the door. Joe expected someone named Lars to be tall, strapping, blond. Instead, he was short, pudgy, with long sideburns and an acne-scarred face. Smile lines at the corners of his mouth suggested he was always of good cheer. He wore a baggy T-shirt with a silk screen of a wolf on it.

Joe introduced himself. "Hope I didn't get you at dinner," Joe said.

"Not at all," Lars said, looking over Joe's shoulder for his vehicle. Lars was the kind of man who judged other men by what they drove, Joe guessed. "Come on in. You *walked*?"

"Yup."

"Oh, that's right," Lars said, chuckling. "I heard about your Yukon. Quite a story."

The television was on in the living room and the house smelled of the fried hamburgers they had had for dinner. It was modest, almost spare, except for the elk heads and antlers on the wall. Joe didn't know what he'd been expecting. Maybe more books, he thought.

Lars introduced Joe to Jake, who was watching television. Jake, ten, was a younger, fitter version of Lars, and he self-consciously got up and shook Joe's hand and returned quickly to the couch. A teenage girl looked out from her room, said hello, and ducked back in.

"Erin," Lars said. "Fifteen and surly."

Joe nodded with empathy.

"So, Judy tells me you're a game warden."

"Yes."

"What do you think of those heads on the wall?"

"Nice."

"I got seven more of 'em in the garage. I was thinking you might want to take a look at them."

People always wanted to show Joe their game heads or hunting pictures. He was used to it. To be polite, Joe said, "Sure, you bet."

Judy intervened, coming from the kitchen, drying her hands on a towel. She was out of uniform, and she looked like, well, a mom.

"I think Joe's seen plenty of elk heads before, honey," she said.

"That's okay," Joe said.

"Really," Demming said to Lars.

Lars did a barely noticeable man-to-man eye roll, asked, "You want a beer?"

"You bet."

"Turn the television off, please, Jake," Demming said. "Time for homework."

"I don't have any," Jake said.

Demming gave him a look.

"Maybe I do," Jake said, peeling himself off the couch. As he went down the hall, Jake stopped at Erin's room just long enough to dart in to do something that made her squeal, "Mom! He flicked my ear with his finger again!"

"Jake, leave her alone," Demming said, half-heartedly.

Joe smiled. Just like home.

Lars returned with three opened bottles of beer.

"I didn't really want one," Demming said.

"I'll drink it," Lars said. "We don't want to see beer go to waste, eh, Joe?"

"Right."

Joe sat on the couch. Demming and Lars settled in well-worn overstuffed chairs.

257

"Too bad about Mark Cutler," Lars said. "He was a real nice guy. I met him a few times at Old Faithful."

It seemed oddly uncomfortable, Joe thought. No doubt both Lars and Demming felt the same. Demming did, he was sure, by the way she lowered her eyes while Lars told story after story about every time he had met Mark Cutler. Most of the tales had to do with Lars's road crew fixing the potholes around Old Faithful. Demming didn't interrupt when the stories got too long, deferring to her husband.

When Lars went to get Joe another beer, Demming said, "Ashby called. I've got a meeting with him and James Langston tomorrow. I won't be with you anymore either, providing they even let you stay. I've been reassigned to traffic if they don't decide to suspend me."

"I'm sorry."

She shrugged. "It gives me an excuse to quit. I wish I could. Maybe I can really try to get into interpretation now."

Lars came back and resumed telling stories about each of the elk on the wall, the circumstances in which he'd killed them.

Joe wanted to ask her how she was doing, but it seemed like the wrong time and place. Instead, he finished the beer because he thought Lars would want him to.

"I better get back," Joe said, standing. "I need to call my wife."

"Yeah," Lars said, grinning. "Don't forget *that* or there'll be hell to pay."

Joe said, "Marybeth's not like that."

Lars gave him a man-to-man wink, as if to say, *They're all like that.*

"Do you need a ride?" Demming asked.

"I don't mind walking."

"I'll drive you back."

"Jeez," Lars said, "haven't you two spent enough time together?"

He was joking, Joe thought, but he wasn't.

IN THE CAR, Demming said, "You wanted to ask me something."

"I wanted to see how you were doing."

"Besides that. What was it? I could tell."

She was Demming again, the ranger.

"Last night, after I left you the message about the meeting with Cutler, who did you call?"

"Ashby. Why?"

"I'm trying to figure out who knew about the meeting ahead of time."

"Do you realize what you're asking? What you're saying?"

"Yes."

She drove in silence the rest of the way.

When he got out, he said, "Be careful."

"You too," she said. "Maybe you ought to go home."

"What?"

She looked over, concern in her eyes. "You seem to have a nice family, Joe, and obviously you care very much about them. This isn't your fight."

"It's my job," he said. "Same thing."

JOE MISSED HIS family, missed them more than he thought possible, more than he should have given that it had been only four days since he left. When he really thought about them, really dug deep, he wondered if, in his heart, he felt out of his depth and therefore wanted them near him for comfort. Two more days, he thought. Two more days. But should he welcome them to a place where just that morning he'd seen a man boiled alive, had his state car destroyed, and come to a nagging realization that it was very likely that someone on the inside murdered Mark Cutler and could just as easily come after *him*?

Maybe that's what it was, Joe thought. The thought that Cutler had no one to mourn him. No wife, no kids, and a sort-of fiancée he'd made a fleeting mention of. If whoever got Cutler came after Joe ... he tried to imagine how Marybeth, Sheridan, and Lucy would mourn him. Would it demolish them, change them forever? He hoped so as much as he hoped not. Or would they figure out a way to go on? They were tough, he knew. He wished he were that tough. And now, he thought, sitting in his room at the Mammoth Hotel at midnight on a vacant floor with the half-empty Jim Beam traveler on his tiny desk, he was crossing over a line into a kind of morbid depression he hadn't felt since, well, since his brother died and his father left them.

And he realized what the root of his dark meditation was—the reunion with his father. It had brought everything back, most of all feelings of inadequacy, of not being properly rooted. He had forgotten that those feelings dwelled within him.

That, and the inevitable replaying of what he'd seen that morning as Cutler's flesh came off his body and floated away.

Oh, and Clay McCann. The lawyer who had upped his body count to six. The man who would very likely get away with his latest double homicide as easily as he had the first four.

What, was he losing it?

He needed Marybeth to tell him he wasn't.

And another drink. That would be okay too.

260

*

HE BROACHED THE subject of her not coming when he called home. "Marybeth, there's so much going on that I can't figure out," he said. "The last thing I want to do is put you and the girls ... into this mess." He almost said, "in danger" but rephrased it clumsily.

She paused a long time before saying, "Joe, I'm a little disappointed in you."

"Why?" He was puzzled.

"How much have we been through together?"

"A hell of a lot," he said. "Too much. That's why—"

"That's right," she said. "We're good together. Maybe I can help you out. Besides, I'm just about done with that research you asked me to do. I'll print everything out and bring it along."

"Anything interesting?"

"Not that I can tell. I still have a couple of companies to go. I should have it all done by the time we get there."

"I'm thinking of Sheridan and Lucy," Joe said. "I still feel so damned guilty about what they went through last spring. I don't want any more of that happening."

"Joe, what happened, happened. It's not your fault."

"If my job puts them into situations like that, it's my fault," he said.

She didn't argue, although he wished she would.

"Sheridan can't stop talking about going to Yellowstone," Marybeth said. "Lucy has already packed so she'll be the best dressed tourist in the park. You want me to tell them we're not going?"

Joe thought about it. "No."

"Good."

"I miss you," he said.

"It's only been a few days," she said. "But I miss you too."

261

"Besides," she said, laughing, "my mother is driving me insane."

IDLY, JOE REREAD Hoening's e-mails, hoping that something new would come to him now that he'd spent some time in the park. The exchange between Yellowdick and Samantha Ellerby drew him, and he studied the e-mails and tried to figure out why.

It was 8 P.M. in California, an hour behind mountain time. Joe used directory assistance to find her number. He caught Samantha in her apartment. She had a flat, bored tone to her voice he found slightly irritating.

"Who did you say you were?" she asked.

"My name is Joe Pickett. I'm investigating the murder of your friend Rick Hoening on behalf of the governor of Wyoming," he said, hoping that would impress her enough to keep her on the line.

"He wasn't really my friend, more like just a guy I knew back in Minnesota. I'm surprised Wyoming is big enough to have a governor."

Joe thought, *Airhead.*

"Still, I'm sure you'd like to help us clear up a few questions."

"I guess so. But I don't have a lot of time to talk. I'm going out."

"It won't take long," he said.

"Better not."

"Okay, I'll get to it. I take it you visited Yellowstone last summer."

"Yeah." Her voice was cold. "Geysers, like, big whoop."

"Didn't have a good time, then?"

"It was cold. There were bugs and way too many animals that can eat you. Not at all my idea of a good time. Plus,

262

Rick's idea of a great party is, you know, *outside*. I'm sorry he's dead and all but, God, like, what a loser."

"I wanted to ask you specifically about what you did with him."

"I'm hanging up."

"No, please," he said, wanting to smack himself in the forehead. "Let me rephrase that. Sorry. I want to know what places he showed you around the park. He knew the area really well, from what we understand. We think if we know where he went it might help us in our investigation." He hoped that last bit made more sense to her than it did to him.

She seemed to be debating whether or not to terminate the call.

"Look," he lied, "if it would be easier, we can send somebody over to your place to talk about this. It might be more comfortable for you." Hoping she wouldn't call his bluff.

"I said I was going out. No, okay. It's okay, I thought you were asking—"

"No."

"We saw all the sights, I guess. Some big canyons, some trees, a bunch of geysers. Old Faithful. Way too many fat people in shorts. I think Yellowstone ought to have some kind of fitness test you have to pass to get in. I mean, gross."

"Did you go to a place called Sunburst Hot Springs?" Joe asked casually.

"Hmmm, I'm trying to remember the name."

"Did you go hot-potting there?"

"Yeah, yeah. Sunburst. That was actually kind of a cool place. Except it's illegal, you know. They keep you from going to the really cool places."

"Okay," Joe said, "I'm going to ask you a question but

263

before you answer I want you to know that however you answer it, you will not be incriminated in any way."

"Huh?"

"Was Hoening involved with drugs? I'm not asking about you, I'm asking about him."

She seemed relieved and said, "Alcohol only. But lots of it. He was really backward in his thinking. I couldn't get him to … never mind."

"So he never used drugs in your presence?"

"Alcohol. It's a drug, you know."

"Then can you tell me what he meant when he wrote to you"—Joe fished out the e-mail—"*'We'll have some cocktails and laughs, watch the sun set over Yellowstone Lake, go hot-potting and light a couple of flamers.'*"

"Ooooh," she said, enthusiasm gushing for the first time, "those things were the coolest of all! Flamers, yeah. They were, like, *great*."

21

TWO POINT TWO million acres, Joe thought. Yellowstone was *that* big. And while he now had a plan, he didn't have a car.

There was a layer of light snow suspended on the grass and melting on the pavement in front of the Mammoth Hotel. He could see his breath as he walked to the restaurant for breakfast. The morning was achingly silent. Rising columns of steam from the hot spring terraces on the hill muted the sun, making it seem overcast despite the cloudless blue sky. Although it could, and did, snow any month of the year in the park, it definitely felt like summer was spent and had stepped aside in utter exhaustion to yield to fall and winter.

His mind was on something else, though.

Flamers, they called them.

Like the snowflakes that hung in the air, turning into floating sparks by the morning sun, thoughts and facts seemed suspended too. While it might be folly to connect them, Joe felt the need to try. It was more of a hunch than a theory, and he'd made mistakes going with his hunches before. But somehow it felt right. It was the new knowledge of the flamers that did it.

Flamers. The Gopher State Five. Clay McCann. Sunburst Hot Springs. Bob Olig. The black SUV. What Mark Cutler figured out but never got a chance to explain. And now Clay McCann again, with more blood on his hands. Somehow, they were all connected.

Samantha Ellerby had described flamers as streams of gas coming from tiny quarter-sized holes in the ground that could be lit with a match. She said the flame reached at least six feet into the air, sometimes higher, and provided both heat and light for hot-potting. She said there were at least seven of them near Sunburst Hot Springs, and when they were all lit up at night surrounding the hot pool the atmosphere was "way cool." She said when it was time to leave, Hoening smothered the flames by covering the holes with a thick wet blanket.

The Zone of Death was a diversion, he thought. This wasn't about the Zone of Death at all. The murders were a means to an end, a way of dealing with those facts that hung in the air and were somehow, some way, connected.

He hoped that a revelation would come to him while he ate breakfast, that the indiscriminate facts would somehow connect and cling to one another, form a pattern, create a story line.

They didn't.

WHEN SIMON SAID there were no messages for him at the front desk, Joe used the payphone in the lobby to call Chuck Ward. He needed to know what the governor thought of his reports thus far and how he could get a new vehicle, and he wanted to advise them of the new information about Cutler, flamers, and Clay McCann's latest crime.

Ward wasn't in.

"Can you tell me how to get ahold of him?" Joe asked the secretary in the governor's office.

"No. He took a few days' personal leave."

"Personal leave? Now?"

"Yes."

Joe was annoyed. This meant Ward hadn't received his reports and had no idea what was happening.

"When will he be back?"

"Monday."

"That's three more days!"

"Correct." She sounded bored.

Joe tried to think. There was no way Ward would be out of touch completely. He was the governor's chief of staff, he couldn't just vanish. It didn't work that way. He knew the secretary probably couldn't give out Ward's number, wherever he was. But he knew who could.

"I need to talk to the governor, then. It's important."

"What did you say your name was?" she asked before putting him on hold.

Joe waited. The hold music was Johnny Cash singing "Ghost Riders in the Sky." Joe assumed the governor had had something to do with the choice.

Finally, she came back on the line. "The governor says he's never heard of anyone named Joe Pickett."

Joe clenched his jaw, closed his eyes, said, "It's so good to be back in the system. Please have Chuck Ward call me immediately if he happens to check in. And please tell the governor things are happening. Three more people are dead. I'm sure he's heard about them—two murdered by Clay McCann, the other a Zephyr employee who we made contact with. That one might be an accident but I doubt it."

"I'll pass that along," she said in a tone suggesting she had no intention of doing so.

"He'll be interested," Joe said. "Trust me on that."

"Hmmmppf."

JOE WALKED TO the Pagoda, stepping through a television news crew from Billings that was setting up in the parking lot at the side of the building. A pretty blond correspondent who looked all of twenty-four was applying makeup to her sharp cheekbones, ready to do a stand-up report on the fact that Clay McCann was back in the Yellowstone jail.

The receptionist looked up as Joe entered. Layborn sat in a chair behind her, and he shook his head with clear disgust when he saw Joe.

"Thanks to you," Layborn said, "I get to spend the morning fending off the press instead of doing my job."

Joe ignored him. "Did you find anything out about the black SUV?"

"You mean the one you didn't get a plate number on? No. It was probably out of the park by the time we put out the APB at all the gates."

"But you've alerted the cops in all of the gateways, right? Jackson, Cody, West Yellowstone, Bozeman, Cooke City?"

"Gee," Layborn said, curling his lip, "we never even thought of that. Good thing you're here to advise us." He snorted, "Of course we did that. Christ. But we've got nothing so far. Do you know how many SUVs there are in this area? Everybody has 'em."

Joe nodded. True. "So McCann is here again, huh? Are charges being filed?"

Layborn looked quickly away. Joe could see that the ranger's face and neck were turning red. "We're holding him while the prosecutors try to come up with something," he said through clenched teeth. "This time, we can't even get him on a gun charge, since he claims the victims had

268

the gun and he took it away from them in self-defense. That son of a bitch is going to get away with it. *Again!*" he spat the word out.

"So he'll be released?" Joe asked, incredulous.

Layborn shifted in his chair, finally looked back at Joe. "We had to tell him this morning he could go."

"He's gone?"

Layborn shook his head. "That's the thing," he said. "He refuses to leave. He says he's staying in custody until we either bring a case against him or not. In the meantime, he's demanding to be moved to another federal facility. He says he doesn't care where—Boise, Billings, Casper—anywhere but here. Claims he fears for his life in Yellowstone, which really pisses off the brass. They don't want that getting out, as you can imagine."

"I can imagine," Joe said. He wondered whom McCann was scared of, who he thought could get to him in the Yellowstone jail.

"That's not all," Layborn said. "He says if we don't press charges, he's not leaving until the secretary of the interior issues a public apology to him for arresting him in the first place and talking about him to the press. He claims his house was vandalized and he can no longer earn a living because his reputation's been ruined. He says he'll sue us if the apology isn't made."

"You're kidding," Joe said.

"Jesus," Layborn said, "I wish I was. I also wish I could just take the weasel out in the woods, put a bullet in his head and end this."

Joe thought, *I know a guy who would be happy to do that.*
"Can I see him?" Joe asked.

"No visitors. Orders of the chief ranger."

"I've got some questions for him."

"Too bad. The chief thinks if he has no public contact he'll get bored and leave. McCann likes attention. So no press, no visitors at all. Direct orders. That's why I'm here this morning—to keep everybody away from him."

"I'm on your side," Joe said.

Layborn grinned viciously. "Somehow, I have trouble believing that."

"Can I at least look at him?"

Joe could see Layborn thinking about it, wanting to come up with a reason why he couldn't. Finally, he gestured to the door. "We've got cameras in all the cells. The monitors are down the hall. You can look at him there, but nothing else. Then you need to leave, and I mean it."

As Joe passed him, Layborn said, "I don't know what you think you'll see."

Joe wasn't sure either. Nevertheless, he went down the hallway into a small room with a bank of four black-and-white video monitors on the wall. Two showed empty cells. One revealed two disheveled men sleeping on cots. A Post-it note read "Zephyr, DUI." On the fourth monitor, a pale, pudgy man sat motionless on a cot with his hands on his knees, staring intently at a blank wall. McCann.

There was nothing threatening about him, Joe thought. He looked like an overripe accountant, or the lawyer that he was. He looked lonely, pathetic. Not the murderer or schemer he obviously was. He looked almost like ... a *victim*. Joe had been around several evil men in his life, and had felt a darkness inside himself when he was near them. Not this time. Strangely, it bothered him more than if McCann exuded menace. Here sat a man who assassinated six people in cold blood, who wanted an apology from the government for being arrested. This man, Joe thought, was beyond understanding. In a way, he was probably the most dan-

270

gerous man Joe had ever encountered. Joe wanted desperately to bring him down.

DEMMING WAS OPENING the door of a Crown Victoria when Joe came out of the Pagoda, ruining the taped stand-up for the Billings television station.

"Cut!" the producer growled to the reporter. "Jenny, you'll need to do it again."

"Sorry," Joe said, stepping out of the shot.

"Damn it," Jenny said, "I was on a roll."

"I'VE BEEN ASSIGNED to traffic," Demming said, as Joe climbed into the cruiser with her. "Suspension is still pending, though. I'll know by Monday if I still have a job. I've never seen Langston so angry. Ashby actually defended me, though. A little, at least. Enough to keep me employed through the weekend."

Joe didn't know what to say.

"It may all be for the best," she said, looking out the windshield at Jenny the reporter starting her stand-up again. "Lars will be out of town at a road engineering conference in Billings. I'll be around for the kids, which is good."

"I could use your help," Joe said. "You're a good partner."

She smiled. "It makes me happy to hear you say that, Joe."

"I mean it."

Joe told her about the flamers. She was interested, and he could see her thinking.

"She says they lit them with a match," Joe continued. "It sounded like she was describing a propane torch or something. Does this make any sense to you?"

"None. I've never heard of anything like that in the park."

Joe nodded. "There's no oil or gas here, is there?"

"No. And if there was, nobody could drill for it anyway. Are you sure this connects to any of the pieces?"

Joe shook his head. "I'm not sure about anything. But when I think about oil and gas, I think of Wyoming. That's how the whole state is funded. Hoening made a reference to *'something going on here with the resources that may deeply impact the State of Wyoming, especially your cash flow situation.'* Remember that? This new information could sort of go to that, and it might be what Cutler figured out and never got a chance to tell us."

Demming nodded. "Let's not forget, Joe, that we have no evidence Cutler was murdered. We're assuming it but have nothing to go on. The forensic guys on the scene are describing it as an accident, that Cutler lost his footing checking on the thermal and fell in."

Joe shook his head. "I don't believe that. I saw how careful he was out there."

"I agree. But we've got nothing. We've asked the FBI to take a look at what's left of his body and … the pieces they could find. They're FedExing it all to Virginia. Maybe we'll find out he got hit in the head or shot or something. Until then, we can't jump to conclusions."

"I've already jumped."

"So have I," she sighed.

"What about Hérve and the message?" Joe asked.

"He checks out," she said. "The message was left in his inbox and he simply delivered it. There's nothing to suggest he told anyone about the meeting, and he claims he never even looked at it. The investigator who interviewed him said he was clean."

HE TOLD HER what Layborn had said about the black SUV.

"I'm not surprised."

"If we could find that car and who was driving it, we might get somewhere."

"How do we do that now?" she asked.

"The surveillance tapes," he said. "Doesn't the Park Service get a shot of every vehicle and plate that enters at the gates? I've seen the cameras. We could look at the tapes for yesterday and see where the SUV came from. If we can't find it, we can go back two days and find out where it came in. We might even get a picture of who was driving it."

Her eyes widened with excitement. "That's right."

"So we need access to the tapes. Are they in the Pagoda?"

She frowned. "It's not as simple as that, Joe. The tapes are on site at each entrance gate. They're not compiled and sent to headquarters, and you can't watch them at any central place. To see them, you've literally got to go to each entrance and download the tapes from the day before and watch them there or bring it back. And if I remember correctly, we only keep a three-day record before the cameras record over the old tape."

"Which means we've got to move on this," Joe said.

Demming hesitated, and Joe felt suddenly guilty.

"You don't have to do it," he said. "You've been reassigned. You could really lose your job if you're seen hanging out with the likes of me."

"I'll take the North and West entrances," she said. "Don't worry, I'll be there as part of my patrol anyway. That gives you the South, Northeast, and East entrances. I think if you flash your badge and sweet-talk them, you'll be able to download the tapes. But if they call in for permission, you're sunk. We're sunk."

"I'm willing to try if you are."

"I am," she said.

What wasn't said between them was the implication of

them working independently, out of view of Layborn, Ashby, or Langston. Because, Joe thought, one or all of them knew more than they were letting on. Then something clicked into place: maybe McCann thought the exact same thing.

Joe wondered which one frightened McCann enough to make him request a transfer. It made sense now, Joe thought. McCann wanted to stay in very public protective custody so no one could silence him. His request for a transfer suggested that someone with access to the jail—someone on the inside—could get to him. He decided not to share this with Demming so as not to implicate her any further with her superiors.

"I know what you're doing," he said. "All I can say is that I appreciate it very much."

She nodded but didn't want to talk about it.

"I've been where you are," Joe said. "You're doing the right thing. But I have to confess that it usually gets me into trouble."

She laughed. "Like I could get into any more trouble."

As he opened the car door, she reached out and gripped his arm.

"Here," she said, handing him a set of keys.

"What's this?"

"Keys to Lars's pickup. You'll need a vehicle. How do you expect to get around?"

"I can't take these," Joe said, remembering Lars's obvious pride in his tricked-up 4×4.

"Take them," she insisted. "He likes you."

"I'm hard on cars," Joe said.

"Yeah," she said, dismissing him. "I'm kind of worried about that, I admit."

*

274

IT WAS EASIER than Joe thought it would be, despite the suspicious looks the gate rangers gave him when he pulled up in the jacked-up pickup with the loud glasspack mufflers and got out. He found they were lonely in the last days of the season and didn't mind taking the time to show him how to plug into the video units in their gatehouses and download three days' worth of taped entrances and exits. Only at the Northeast gate did he have to show his badge.

He hoped Demming would have the same good fortune.

ON THE WAY back to Mammoth, Joe turned off at Biscuit Basin. Although yellow crime-scene tape was stretched from tree trunk to tree trunk across the pathway to Sunburst, no rangers had been left to guard it. He looked around to make sure no one was watching and ducked under the tape.

The trail had been trampled into muddy goo by dozens of rangers and investigators from the day before. The runoff stream ran clear. As he approached Sunburst and felt an almost imperceptible increase in temperature and humidity from the pool, he noted the pink microbes waving in the water and the driftwood where the thermister was still hidden.

Now that he thought about it, he recalled the tickle of air on his ankle the first time he came to the pool with Cutler. Moving step-by-step, he backed around the thermal until he felt it again.

It came from a mouth-sized hole in the ground. He knelt down and put his palm out. The gas emitting from it was odorless and made no sound. But he could feel it licking his hand.

He stepped back and lit a match, held it out.

With a muffled *whump*, flame raced up the stream of gas and danced on the tip as if waving. He felt heat on his face and hands. It burned cleanly and nearly six feet into the air before dissipating.

He found another mouth and lit it too. And another. The three flamers undulated slightly as they burned. He imagined how they'd look at night, illuminating the trees surrounding the thermal. "Way cool" was how Samantha had described them.

He agreed.

He found four more holes that marched in a line toward the timber but stopped short of the loam and lit them all. There was now a wall of flame, each spout of fire licking silently in the air. It looked strangely tropical, Joe thought. And there was something else. The holes ran parallel to the dark line in the ground that Cutler had said was one of the few exposed coal seams in the park.

After watching them for a half-hour, he soaked his fleece vest in the hot pot and extinguished them.

"Way cool," he said aloud.

JOE RETURNED TO the Mammoth Hotel to wait for Demming and to make arrangements at the front desk for a cabin for Marybeth and the girls the next night. He didn't want to subject them to rooms in the empty hotel that even he found lonely. He used his credit card, knowing the state would likely not reimburse the cost, and wondered as Simon ran it when exactly his first new paycheck would arrive.

When Simon returned his card and said he could pick up the keys in the morning, he said, "There have been a couple of older gentlemen asking for you. I hope you don't mind, but I asked them to wait outside the lobby for you to return."

"Wait outside? Why?"

Simon looked apologetic.

Joe got it. "They were stinking drunk, right?" he said with despair.

"Beyond stinking," Simon said. "They reeked. And one of them had a little accident on the couch. He dropped his bottle of cheap whiskey."

Joe turned to see that the cushions on the overstuffed couch near the fireplace had been removed.

"Son!" George Pickett shouted as he staggered into the lobby from outside. "Son! My boy! Fruit of my loins!"

Doomsayer remained outside so he could throw up on the sidewalk.

Joe angrily intercepted his father. "What do you want?"

"To see my boy. Do you know how good it makes me feel to say I'm going to visit my son? Is there something wrong with that?"

His father hadn't shaved or changed clothes since he'd seen him at Old Faithful, as if their meeting had been the catalyst for the bender he was on. He stunk of whiskey and something rotten he'd eaten. His eyes shone with a giddy brand of happiness that bordered on the manic. His smile was forced, and as he stumbled, Joe reached out to hold him up.

"We have nothing to talk about," Joe said.

"But you're my son!" George said loudly. "The only one I have left."

Joe glanced over his shoulder to see Simon look away discreetly.

"You can't just stand here and yell," Joe said. "You're sure as hell not driving anywhere. Don't you have someplace to stay?"

"With you!" George slurred. "We can bunk with you! We can stay up late and tell stories and catch up. That meeting we had, that was no good. We need a new start."

Joe felt like smacking him, and instantly felt guilty for even thinking it. George *was* his father, wasn't he? But he was so much less than that, even though he'd come to Mammoth to see him.

Joe handed George the keys to room 231.

"DON'T WRECK IT," Joe said, getting both men into the room.

"You aren't staying with us?" Doomsayer asked.

"Never," Joe said. "And get out tomorrow when you two can walk."

"Ah, tomorrow," Doomsayer said, watching George stagger toward the bed and collapse into the middle of it. "We don't speak of tomorrow up here. It may never come."

IN THE CABIN he had rented, Joe sat at a small table and surveyed the accommodations. It would do, although it was dark and close. He'd hoped there would be a private bedroom for him and Marybeth. He missed his wife, and recalled their last moments together by the fireplace. Instead, there was a double bed and two singles in a long room. Maybe they could send Sheridan and Lucy out for some ice or something, he thought.

He hoped George Pickett would do as he was told and be out of the area by morning, when his family was due to arrive.

Tossing his bags into the small closet, he wondered when Demming would get back. He'd need to leave a note at the hotel about his new location.

And speaking of location, Joe thought, where in the hell was Nate?

22

W ITH ELECTRIC PEAK to the north-west, Bunsen Peak to the east, and Swan Lake ahead on her left, Demming's tires sang on the thin strip of roadway across the meadow with the peculiar, discordant note that came from the chips of sharp black obsidian that had been mixed into the asphalt by a long-ago road crew that probably included her husband, Lars. It was twilight, twenty minutes from Mammoth and home. She was headed north; it was an hour past the end of her shift but she wouldn't claim the overtime because she didn't want to explain to anyone why she was running late.

Her laptop was on the seat next to her in the cruiser, filled with downloaded videotapes from the West and North entrance gates. She hoped Joe had been as successful.

Because she was driving the only car on the road, she goosed up her speed to fifty, five miles over the park speed limit. The brilliant flashes of white on the leaden surface of the lake ahead were, in fact, trumpeter swans. Thus, Swan Lake. She'd be good at interpretation, she thought. She *noticed* things.

Like the black SUV with the smoked windows ahead of her. It was headed north also, and she could feel her heart race as she slowly closed the gap between them. She hadn't seen where the SUV came onto the road, and could only assume the driver had seen her because he was careful to keep to the speed limit as she neared.

There was no way to determine if this was the black SUV she had seen the day before, other than the fact that the hairs on her forearm and the back of her neck were standing up. She got closer.

Wyoming plates, County 22. Jackson Hole. On closer inspection she could see a sticker on the back window from Hertz. A rental. So the driver could be from anywhere and likely chose Jackson since it had the biggest airport of the park gateway cities and the most arriving flights.

When the last shafts of the sun hit the SUV just right she could see two people in it. Men. She recognized neither of them by profile, but noticed the driver had his head tilted up and to the right as he drove. He was watching her approach in the rearview mirror. She wished she could see his eyes or part of his face but the glass was too dark.

She slowed to maintain a cushion of a hundred feet and plucked the mike from its cradle on the dash. She tried to speak calmly.

"Dispatch, this is YP-twenty-nine, requesting backup. I'm in visual contact with a black SUV that matches the description of the vehicle reported yesterday near Biscuit Basin. I think it's the same one we issued the BOLO for yesterday. Repeat: requesting backup. I'm northbound to Mammoth at Swan Lake. I'd like to pull it over and see who's inside."

"Roger that," the dispatcher said. "Backup is on the way."

"ETA?"

"Five minutes."

She let out a long breath in relief. Five minutes was good. Because of the distances in the park and two-lane traffic, it wasn't unusual to receive ETAs of fifteen and twenty minutes. She eased the cruiser ahead, narrowing the space between them to fifty feet, sending a signal. There would be no doubt now to the driver of the SUV that he was being pursued.

Trying not to make rapid movements, she reached up and unsnapped the buckle of the twelve-gauge pump mounted on the console. For reassurance, she patted her handgun on her belt, rubbed the leather of the holster with her thumb. Then unsnapped it for quick access.

As the two vehicles slowed to round a corner, she looked ahead on the highway as far as she could see for headlights, assuming that her backup would arrive head-on, dispatched from Mammoth itself. The highway was clear.

She was both pleased and surprised when an NPS Crown Vic cruiser appeared suddenly in her rear-view mirror. The backup had arrived much sooner than she anticipated, and she was now ready.

Snapping the toggle for the wig-wag lights on the roof light bar, she said, "Let's see who you are."

Behind her, the backup cruiser did the same, flooding the inside of her car with explosions of blue and red.

The black SUV continued on, without speeding up or slowing down. After thirty seconds, she began to worry. Of course, it had happened before. Citizens who were straining to look for wildlife or simply unaware of their surroundings sometimes claimed they hadn't seen her behind them. But she knew the driver had been watching.

As she reached up to whoop the siren, the brake lights flashed on the SUV and it slowed. She did the same, closing to within twenty yards. Finally, the vehicle swung into a pavement pullout. The driver was courteous enough to park at the far end of the pullout, leaving enough space for both NPS cruisers to park off the road.

"Okay, then," Demming said to herself. She was trained to emerge slowly, keeping part of her body in the cruiser in case the driver ahead decided to gun his engine and make a run. She paused, as trained, behind her open door while she fitted her hat on. The parking lights lit on the SUV, a good sign. The tailpipe burbled with exhaust, meaning the driver hadn't killed the motor. Not such a good sign.

At once, the driver and passenger doors opened and a man swung out of each.

"*Get back in the vehicle*," she said, surprising herself with the force of her command.

The driver wore glasses and had silver hair and an owlish look on his face. He was tall, probably mid-fifties, dressed in jeans, a white shirt, and a blazer. He didn't look like a man on vacation. The passenger was shorter, with a smaller build, an eager, boyish face and dark, darting eyes. He looked vaguely familiar and seemed to know it by the way he avoided her.

Then things happened rapidly, but with absolute, terrifying clarity.

The driver turned and reached for his door handle, but the passenger didn't. Instead, he fixed his gaze on Demming's backup, behind her and to her left. Demming fought the urge to look over her shoulder, but she did when the passenger seemed to signal something to her backup with an almost imperceptible nod of his head.

They knew each other.

Demming snapped a glance over her left shoulder, saw the ranger she recognized with a gun leveled on her—not his service weapon but a cheap throw-down—heard the sharp *pop*, and felt as if she'd been hit in the ribs with a sledgehammer. She didn't feel her legs give out but knew they had when all she could see were the dull black glints

282

of obsidian chips in the pavement inches from her face. A flash of white—her hand—on the cold asphalt, scuttling across her vision like a crab for the weapon she'd dropped when she was hit. Where was it?

"Again," the passenger said. His voice was clear.

Demming turned her head to see the black hole of the muzzle of the weapon two feet from her face and the coldly determined look on the face of the shooter. She wanted to ask, "Why you?" Closing her eyes tightly, she clearly saw Jake and Erin at home, watching the clock, waiting for dinner.

PART FIVE

National parks are the best idea we ever had. Absolutely American, absolutely democratic, they reflect us at our best rather than our worst.
Wallace Stegner,
1983

23

T HIRTY-FIVE MINUTES LATER, a caravan of law enforcement vehicles and the EMT van coursed through Mammoth with lights flashing, sirens on, turning the quiet night into a riot of outrage, angry colors, and grating sound. Joe stepped outside his cabin into darkness to see what was going on. The few other visitors in the cabins were doing the same, either parting curtains or opening their doors.

The caravan blasted through the village and down the hill toward Gardiner, leaving a vacuum in its wake. It took five minutes before he could no longer see the lights flashing on the sagebrush hillside of the canyon or hear the scream of sirens.

Given the inordinate number of emergency vehicles, their display of lights and sound and the dearth of visitors remaining in the park, Joe immediately thought something bad had happened to a ranger—maybe *his* ranger—and a chill shot through him.

He jogged to a payphone near the utility building, called Demming's home. Erin answered crying.

"My mom's been shot!" she sobbed. "Somebody called for Dad and said my mom's been shot."

"Is she still alive?" Joe asked, his head swimming.

"I don't know, I don't know ..."

"Erin, stay calm," he said, not feeling very calm himself. "Let's not get upset until we know how badly she's hurt. Don't assume the worst. People get shot all the time and live through it."

His words seemed to help, even though he felt like he was lying.

THE TINY CLINIC in Gardiner was popping with activity when Joe arrived. NPS cruisers and SUVs filled the parking lot, and the EMT van that had delivered Demming was parked under the emergency entrance overhang, doors still open.

Ashby, Layborn, and a half-dozen rangers Joe didn't recognize crowded the small lobby. Layborn was in full dress, Ashby in sweats and running shoes, his hair wild, as if he'd just been called from a run or a workout.

"Is it true?" Joe asked.

"Damn right," Ashby said. "They found her on the road next to her car. At least two gunshot wounds, maybe more. We don't know yet."

"Is she alive?"

Ashby nodded. "Slight pulse, I guess. But her breathing was so shallow the first on the scene thought she was dead."

"Who was the first on the scene?"

Ashby nodded toward Layborn, who had been watching Ashby and Joe with obvious interest.

"Who did it?" Joe asked Layborn.

The ranger shrugged, said, "Last we know, she called for backup to pull over a black SUV matching the description of the vehicle you saw yesterday. I was on my way but by the time I got there she was already down. I never saw the other vehicle. We found a weapon, though, a thirty-eight tossed on the pavement. We've sent it to ballistics and should get some prints."

288

Joe shook his head. "If you found it that easily it's probably a throw-down. My guess is it'll turn out clean and untraceable."

Layborn and Ashby exchanged looks. Ashby said, "That's what I'd guess too."

"Man oh man," Joe said, running his fingers through his hair, then angrily rubbing his face. To Ashby, "Have you alerted everyone at the exit gates so the son of a bitch can't get out?"

Ashby's face fell. "We don't man the gates after dark this late in the season. There's no one there to stop them."

Joe turned away in frustration.

A few moments later an emergency room doctor wearing jeans, Teva sandals, and a sweatshirt reading WILDERNESS, SCHMILDERNESS opened the door and addressed the rangers.

"She's in critical condition," he said, glancing down at his clipboard. "We're trying to stabilize her but it doesn't look good. I called off the Life Flight chopper to Billings for now because I'm concerned about moving her at all. If we see some progress, I'll call them back."

Layborn asked, "Is she going to make it?"

"Didn't you just hear what I said?"

"But if you were to guess ..."

The doctor shook his head, said, "I'll keep you posted."

Joe found Ashby staring at him. "What?"

Ashby stepped close to Joe so he could speak in a whisper. "I just keep thinking that Judy would be okay now if you hadn't showed up," he said.

"CAN WE SEE her?" Jake asked Joe. Erin stood behind her brother in the living room of their house, her face drained, her hair stringy.

"I don't think so," Joe said. "The doctor wouldn't allow anyone in."

Jake said, "I'd like to get one of my dad's guns and find whoever did this." He said it with such controlled fury that Joe reached out and put his hand on the boy's shoulder.

"We'd all like to do that," Joe said. "But we don't know who did it yet. All we know is that he was driving a black SUV."

"Will they find him?" Jake asked, challenge in his voice.

"Yes," Joe lied.

He made sure they had food in the house and promised to call them the minute he knew something and to come get them if they would be allowed to see their mother.

"Can you get in touch with your dad?" Joe asked. "Does he know what's going on?"

"We tried to get him on his cellphone," Erin said. Her eyes were vacant, wounded. "He didn't answer."

"Keep trying," Joe said. "He needs to get back here."

Joe wrote down Lars's cell phone number and put the slip in his pocket, thinking he would try later himself. Maybe it would be best if Lars heard the news from him instead of his children, he thought.

As he left, he looked hard at Jake. "Keep the guns in the closet, okay?"

Jake said, "They're in a gun safe in my dad's bedroom."

"That's good."

"It would be if I didn't know the combination," Jake said.

"But you won't let him open it, will you, Erin?" Joe said.

"No."

Jake turned on his heel, punched the air, and strode angrily to his room, where he slammed the door shut.

"You're in charge," Joe said to Erin.

"Don't worry," she said. "Just help my mom."

ONE BY ONE, the rangers left the clinic throughout the night. Several to go out on patrol, searching for the black

290

SUV, several to simply go home and get some sleep so they could take over the search in the morning. Ashby left around midnight, after sending a message to the doctor through the receptionist that he was to be called at any hour if there was progress or "any kind of news." He left with Layborn, who lingered at the door longer than necessary. When Joe looked up, he got Layborn's coldest cop glare.

"You going back to the hotel soon?" Layborn asked.

"In a few minutes," Joe said.

Layborn nodded, left. Joe wondered why the ranger cared where he spent the night.

Joe sat on a worn faux-leather couch, trying to read a *Field & Stream* magazine but finding himself reading the same page over and over without absorbing it. He called Jake and Erin to tell them there was no news.

"Have you gotten ahold of your dad?" he asked.

"Nope," Jake said. "But we've left about a thousand messages."

Erin took over the phone. "You're staying at the hospital, right? So you can come get us when we can see Mom?"

Joe immediately dismissed the idea of going back to his cabin. "I'm staying," he said.

AT 2.45 IN the morning, Joe sat on the couch staring blankly at a washed-out photo on the clinic wall of Old Faithful erupting, copies of *Bugle*, *Fly Fisherman*, and *Field & Stream* at his feet like discarded playing cards. He was miserable with guilt and lack of sleep, and growing angrier by the half-hour as he thought it through. If he'd told Demming his suspicions about McCann's request for protective custody and a transfer, maybe, just maybe, she would have approached the black SUV differently. Possibly, instead of

291

pulling it over, she would have shown more caution and followed it to wherever it was going—which just may have been the Pagoda. Joe thought of Ashby and Layborn in the lobby of the clinic, Ashby upset and pinning the blame on Joe, Layborn furtive and suspicious, eyes darting around guiltily. He should have told her, he thought. By "protecting" her, he may have put her in greater danger. And was he protecting her, or himself? That was a tough question. She had shown nothing but loyalty to Joe, even though she wore the uniform of a park ranger. Had he shown her that same loyalty when he withheld information but accepted her offer to download video from the entrance gates, thereby jeopardizing her job?

His stomach surged angrily, growled loud enough to hear. He stood and stretched, tried Lars's cellphone number again and left yet another message, then went outside for some cold air.

He was surprised to see the only NPS cruiser in the parking lot was Demming's. One of the attending rangers must have driven it down the canyon in the caravan and gone back with someone else. Joe walked up to the car, saw the blood-flecked driver's door and winced.

It was unlocked. Joe opened the driver's door and looked inside. Demming's daypack, jacket, and lunch box were on the front seat and floor. The mike was cradled, the shotgun unbuckled for quick access.

He shut the door and started back to the clinic when it hit him: Where was her laptop?

He turned and searched again, making sure it wasn't under her seat, in the trunk, or under the jacket. He clearly remembered seeing it that morning on the seat between them. It was possible one of the rangers in the caravan had taken it back for evidence, but very unlikely since on the surface a laptop has nothing to do with a roadside bush-whack. And if they took the computer as part of evidence gathering, why would they leave all her belongings in the unlocked car?

No, Joe thought. Somebody involved in the crime—or one of the crimes, there were so many—had taken the laptop. And whoever had it was likely the inside man in all that had happened, the man McCann feared as well.

JOE ENTERED THE lobby to find the emergency room doctor bent over the counter, scribbling on his clipboard. He looked up as Joe came in.

"I thought everyone was gone," he said.

"It's just me."

"Are you the husband?"

"No," Joe said, "just a friend. A colleague." Joe tried to read something, anything, into the stoic expression the doctor showed.

There was an excruciating silence and Joe felt his fear build to a crescendo.

To his surprise, the doctor said, "It isn't as bad as I'd thought."

"Really?"

The doctor nodded. "There are two gunshot wounds, one of them serious. The bullet entered here"—he demonstrated by raising his left arm and reaching across his body with his right until his palm rested on the back of his ribs—"and angled up. There's extensive organ damage and her left lung is collapsed. The slug itself is lodged in her sternum beneath her left breast. She's lucky as hell it angled to the left instead of to the right, into her heart. But she's starting to stabilize. Blood pressure is getting better, and her right lung is compensating for the damaged left lung, so she's breathing almost normally. Based on what I can see, she has a very good chance to pull through."

Joe almost asked the doctor to repeat himself, to make sure he'd heard right.

"But wasn't she shot in the head?" Joe asked.

The doctor flashed a grim grin. "That's what we thought. It sure looked like it when they brought her in, based on the blood in her hair and powder burns on her face. But once we got her cleaned up, we found out that the bullet creased the skull just above her right ear and never broke through the bone. It made a hell of a scratch and it bled a lot because of the location, but all she needed on her scalp were a dozen stitches. It was a fairly small-caliber weapon, thank God. The bullet was diverted by her skull. Up here, most of the gunshot wounds are from heavier weapons, hunting rifles and the like."

Joe felt a rush of joy, smiled. "Her hard head saved her."

"I guess you could say that."

He breathed a long sigh of relief.

"I agree," the doctor said. "I see no need to send her by chopper to Billings, really. She should go there for observation, of course, since we don't have the greatest facilities here. We're more like a MASH unit than a real hospital. I can ask the EMT driver to take her later today. But if I were a betting man, I'd bet on a recovery. Not to say she'll ever be arresting bad guys again or wrestling bears, whatever park rangers do."

"I should call her family," Joe said, but suddenly had second thoughts.

The doctor nodded. "I'll advise Ranger Ashby."

Joe said, "I'd suggest you don't do that."

The doctor did a double take. "Excuse me?"

"I'd advise you to send her to the hospital in Billings as

soon as possible. Call in the Life Flight helicopter so everybody knows she's gone from here. They'll assume she's still in critical condition. That is, unless you want someone to come into this clinic and finish her off, I'd advise getting her out of here as fast as you can."

The doctor tossed the clipboard aside and sat heavily in a visitor's chair. "Explain," he said flatly. "I'm listening, but I've only got a minute before I need to go back and check on her."

Joe told the doctor why he was in Yellowstone, who he worked for, what had happened at Bechler and Biscuit Basin. The doctor nodded, listening, but also stealing quick glances as his wristwatch. "None of what you've told me gives me a reason to withhold information."

"Think about it," Joe said. "You showed me where she was hit. *In the back.* Not straight on, where you'd assume the guy she pulled over would have shot her. No, she was shot by someone she assumed was her backup. She was shot by a ranger, and probably someone she knew well enough to keep her back to. And whoever did it used a throw-down gun that can't be traced. Cops think about things like that, believe me. Your average bad guy would have taken his gun with him and tried to get rid of it far away from the scene, or more likely just kept it with him."

The doctor arched his eyebrows, as if not wanting to buy into Joe's theory.

"Demming and I got too close to what's going on up here," Joe said. "Even though we're not exactly sure what it is yet. I think one or more of the men in this room tonight pulled the trigger and followed her here. I don't want him coming back, do you?"

The doctor shook his head, but in a way that indicated he wasn't too sure.

"She had a laptop in her car," Joe said. "There was

295

information on that laptop that might have implicated some people in the Bechler murders and the Cutler death. The laptop is gone. Somebody took it from her car tonight."

After a few beats, the doctor said, "Do you know who it is?"

"I can't be sure yet," Joe said. "But I think I've got a pretty good idea."

"Does he have only one good eye? Like maybe his vision is impaired just enough to miss a headshot by a few inches?"

"Bingo," Joe said, impressed with the observation.

Their conversation had been so intense he hadn't noticed the burring of the telephone in the receptionist's office. She appeared at the counter holding the receiver and gestured with it toward Joe. "He says his name is Lars Demming. He wants to talk to you."

"I've got to take this," Joe said to the doctor.

"And I guess I need to call the chopper," the doctor said, rising wearily. "But you better be right about all this. Can you promise me you're right?"

Joe started to, then shrugged. "Nope. I'm pretty much guessing, as usual. But I'd rather have her in Billings than here, just in case. Wouldn't you?"

The doctor sighed and shook his head, and went to call for the Life Flight helicopter.

Lars was drunk, shouting and crying. *"I leave for one night and my wife gets shot! Shot! I'll KILL the son of a bitch who did this, I swear to God!"* Joe held the phone away from his ear and grimaced. *"I'm out with my friends and forget to turn my phone on, and when I get back to the room I have twenty messages! Twenty! My kids crying, you calling. I feel like shit warmed over! Jesus, poor Judy, poor Judy, poor Judy, poor me, poor Erin, poor Jake …"*

The receptionist looked at Joe with sympathy. Lars was

hysterical, but Joe thought he needed to cut Lars some slack. Finally, he raised his voice, *"Lars!"*

Lars stopped abruptly.

"Lars, you need to stay calm. And you need to stay where you are because they'll be flying Judy to Billings in a few hours. She'll be there where you are and you can go see her. It will all be all right, Lars."

"Will it?"

"Yes."

"Promise me?"

Joe thought he was being asked for too many promises, but he said, "Yes."

"Which hospital?"

Joe asked the receptionist, then relayed the information.

"I'll be there," Lars said. "I'll fucking be there. My life will mean nothing if she's gone."

Joe felt sorry for him and knew he meant it. In his peripheral vision, he saw the receptionist staying close enough to overhear most of the conversation.

"Pickett?" Lars said.

"Yes, Lars."

"I want you to stay away from her," he said, his voice catching with a sob. "Don't ever come near her again, or my family. I blame you for all of this."

"I understand," Joe said, feeling as though he'd been kneed in the gut.

"None of this would have happened if you didn't show up."

"You're right," Joe said.

"And if I see you again, I'll kick your ass."

"Kick away," Joe said. "But in the meantime, call your kids and tell them what's going on."

"I mean it," Lars shouted.

297

"I know you do *now*," Joe said, handing the phone to the receptionist.

"Tough," she said.

Joe agreed.

"Maybe you should go home and get some sleep."

Joe shook his head. "I'll go home after the helicopter takes off with her in it. Not before."

He went outside again to get more air. The stars pounded down on him like hammers. The night sky seemed to press on him as if to drive him into the pavement. He'd never smoked but thought he'd like a cigarette right now.

AT 4 IN the morning, Joe snapped awake, surprised that he'd fallen asleep on the couch in the clinic lobby. He sat up quickly, tried to clear his head, wondered what had startled him.

He realized what it was when the receptionist cradled the telephone and looked over the counter at him. "Another emergency call and the EMTs are on their way," she said in explanation. "Busy night."

"What about the helicopter?" Joe asked.

She checked her wristwatch. "It should be here by five. Another hour and you can go home."

Joe thanked her, asked, "What is the new emergency?"

She shook her head. "An assault victim, apparently. I didn't get many details. Now if you'll excuse me, I need to alert the doctor so we can prep the room."

JOE WAITED UNTIL the receptionist and the doctor were in the receiving station before slipping unnoticed into the room where Demming lay waiting. The light was dim but he could see the spider's web of tubing that dripped fluids into her, smelled the sharp smell of antiseptic and soap and fear. She looked younger and smaller in the bed, which was propped up to raise her head. She was slumped a little to the side. Her eyes were closed and she looked serene, but the china whiteness of her skin jarred him, since it made her look cold. He reached up and gently touched her cheek with the back of his fingers to make sure she was warm. She didn't react to his touch, but he was reassured by the slight puff of breath on his skin, which reminded him of the sensation produced by the flamers.

He leaned over her. "Judy, can you hear me? It's Joe."

Did her eyes flutter? He thought he saw something but couldn't be sure. Maybe she could hear him but not wake up. Maybe inside she was shouting, but he just couldn't hear her.

"Who did this to you, Judy? Try and give me a name."

He thought he saw a slight purse of her lips, but couldn't tell if it was deliberate or an unconscious tic.

"Give me a name, Judy, and I promise I'll get him. That's a promise I will absolutely keep. I'll get him."

She didn't, couldn't, or wouldn't respond.

He brushed her hair back, kissed her forehead, and told her Lars would be waiting for her in Billings.

JOE WAS OUTSIDE in the predawn, leaning against the brick building, listening for the sound of the helicopter in the utter stillness. His breath billowed with condensation. He remembered how he and Victor used to strike tough-guy poses against the fence in the backyard and "smoke" lengths of twig, blowing the steam out like he was doing now. The stars in the eastern sky were losing their pinprick hardness due to the mauve wash of the coming sun.

Four-thirty. He'd decided to wait until 6 to call Marybeth and tell her not to come. It was too dangerous. He simply couldn't let her take the chance now, as much as he wanted to see her and his girls.

In the distance, the EMT van sped down the canyon, headlights strobing, but with none of the fanfare or sirens that accompanied Demming's arrival. Assault victim, the receptionist had said. The van slowed abruptly, with a screech of brakes, and Joe saw a coyote in the middle of the road, in no hurry, loping down the center stripe. Finally, the coyote ran into the brush and the van could continue down the hill until it turned off the highway and wheeled to a stop beneath the alcove.

The driver and assistant bailed out, the assistant filling in the doctor who had come outside and nodded at Joe. Joe nodded back.

"What do you mean there's two of them?" the doctor said, annoyed. "The call said one. We prepped inside for one."

"There's two, all right," the assistant said, lighting a cigarette while the driver strode to the back and threw open the door. "One's in bad shape. The other one might just be passed out."

Joe froze as they pulled the gurney out and the legs unfolded, snapped into place, and locked. He saw the assault victim's face clearly, recognized him despite the lumpy, misshapen appearance and all the blood. It was his father. And the second man, the one still slumped in the back of the van, moaning like a steer, was Doomsayer.

The assistant rolled the gurney toward the entrance door, the doctor alongside, reaching under the bloodied sheet to find a pulse.

"Somebody entered with a key or they let him in," the assistant told the doctor. "The rangers said there was no sign of forced entry. Then whoever it was just beat the shit out of these two old guys with a billy club or a baseball bat. Luckily in this case, both of these birds were too drunk to resist or it might have been worse. It was probably like

300

hitting rag dolls—they just flopped around. But whoever it was just whaled the holy hell out of them ..."

STUNNED, JOE IDENTIFIED the victims and confirmed that the assault had taken place in room 231 of the Mammoth Hotel.

By the time he talked to the doctor, Demming had left in the helicopter and the sun had long ago burned off the frost.

His father was in a coma, severe brain damage likely. The chopper was coming back for real this time. Doomsayer had a concussion but would live, and was being left behind for observation.

Joe said, "The beating was meant for me."

The doctor simply looked at him and shook his head.

IN THE CONFUSION, Joe had forgotten to call Marybeth and by the time he did, no one was home. He tried her cellphone and got the recorded message that she was unavailable, out of range. He thought of trying to send a message to stop his family at the gate, but thought he was likely too late. He thought, *What a night*.

As they rolled the gurney toward the helicopter, Joe walked alongside. His father was nearly unrecognizable, his lips swollen like overripe fruit, eyes swollen shut, eyebrows bulging like melons. Joe fished under the sheet for his father's hand, squeezed it. No response.

The hot tears came from nowhere as the chopper lifted off for Billings, and he angrily wiped them away.

JOE WAS BONE-TIRED as he drove Lars's pickup through Mammoth village to the cabins. He was having trouble thinking clearly and was unable to stop his left eye from blinking furiously with stress.

MARYBETH'S VAN WAS parked in front of his cabin, doors open. Nate was helping her carry suitcases from the van into the cabin. They appeared to be chatting happily. Neither recognized him as he drove up in the pickup, although Nate shot an annoyed glance in his direction because of the burbling noise of the glasspacks. He could see Sheridan and Lucy wearing sweatshirts, their blond hair tied back in twin ponytails, sneaking up on a cow elk and her calf eating grass in a meadow that bordered the cabins.

When he parked and got out, Marybeth saw him, beamed, then switched to a fake angry face. Joe could tell she was about to say: *How nice of you to be here to greet us,* or *Thank goodness Nate was here to show us our cabin* … when she saw the expression on his face and became instantly, visibly concerned.

"Dad!" Lucy cried, turning and running toward him with Sheridan just behind her.

"One big happy!" Nate said, oblivious.

24

WHEN THE TRUSTY brought his breakfast, McCann said, "I want to talk to the man in charge of the jail."

"You mean Ranger Layborn?"

"Exactly."

"I'll tell him."

"You do that. And take the food back. I can't eat that crap. Leave the coffee, though."

HE WAITED FOR twenty minutes, sitting on his cot drinking weak coffee until the plastic carafe was empty. His stomach hurt and he wondered if he was getting an ulcer. He tried to ignore the video camera aimed at him through the bars outside his cell. It was strange how, at times, he felt people watching him. Like yesterday, when he felt the presence of someone quite strongly, someone new. When it happened he did his best not to move so as not to provide his watchers with anything to see. He wanted to look comfortable, and content, even though he wasn't. His goal was to show that he could wait them out, drive them crazy. Of course, he knew, as they did, he could walk out anytime. But that was the last thing on earth he wanted to do.

Out of his view, a metal door opened and closed and he

heard footsteps coming. He took a deep breath, straightened his back, set his cup aside.

Layborn stopped short of the front of his cell and leaned forward, his face an annoyed mask. "What now?"

"We need to talk."

"I'm busy."

"I promise you this will be the most important thing you hear today."

"You're an asshole."

"And you, Ranger Layborn, need to know on which side your bread is buttered. Grab a chair," McCann said. "Let's raise the level of discourse. Which means I talk, and you listen with your mouth shut for once."

Layborn's good eye bulged, and McCann thought for a second that Layborn was going to come in after him. Something made the ranger think twice about it, and instead he withdrew his head, turned angrily while muttering curses, and marched back toward the door.

"If you leave right now without hearing me out," McCann called after him, "I swear to God I'll blow this whole thing wide open and you'll go down with them."

Silence. Layborn had stopped. He was thinking about it.

"I'm not bluffing," McCann said.

"*Fuck,*" Layborn hissed.

McCann heard the legs of a chair scraping against the concrete. Layborn reappeared reluctantly, raised the chair and slammed it down, sat heavily in it, said, "You've got five minutes." McCann noted Layborn placed the chair far enough from the cell that it couldn't be seen on the video monitor if anyone looked. He knew there was no sound accompanying the live video feed, so they couldn't be overheard either.

"That's all I need. Are you listening? I mean, really listening?"

304

Layborn's good eye bored into him. His mouth was set; a vein throbbed angrily in his temple.

"So," McCann said, "were you the one they were going to send after me? I'd guess so, since you have nothing else to contribute to the deal except your willingness to bash heads. I mean, I wouldn't guess you'd have much to invest with a park ranger's salary, right? And they're not the types who do the dirty work themselves, so they need someone like you, a Neanderthal with a badge. Your trusty told me about the two old men who got beaten last night. He said they were in a room registered to Joe Pickett, but no one knows who they were. That was your handiwork, right?"

"I don't know what you're talking about."

"So when it comes to me, what were you going to do? Come to my office in West Yellowstone, shoot me in the head? Blame it on the angry locals? Was that the plan? Or were you going to bushwhack me somewhere?"

Layborn glared at him, then raised his watch to signal that McCann's time was quickly passing.

McCann said, "When they didn't pay or communicate, I knew they went to Plan B. Problem was, they didn't have a Plan B so they had to come up with one. They're schemers, but they're not from the street like I am. I was ten steps ahead of them, as usual. By the time they figured out they had to get rid of me, here I was under protective custody. Maybe they're finally realizing they're just not smart enough to proceed without me. That's something I knew all along."

While McCann talked, he watched blood drain from Layborn's face, even though the ranger tried hard not to react to anything that he said. But the lack of reaction was a reaction in itself, McCann knew. He'd seen it in witnesses on the stand, and in his own clients. Outrageous accusations should be met with outraged denials if the person accused was innocent. Lack of reaction meant guilt. He had him.

McCann paused, said, "I need you to get a message to them, and you need to get it right."

"Who are you talking about?"

"I think you know. In fact, I know you do."

"You're wasting my time. I don't like talking to lawyers. Lawyers are the problem, not the solution, is the way I think about things."

"Until you need one."

"I don't plan to."

McCann chanced a smile. "No one ever does."

"You guys are like wolves. You work the edges of the herd and go after the sick and weak."

"Wolves are an important part of the ecosystem, Ranger Layborn."

"I hate wolves."

"Like the ecosystem, our laws are far too complex for mere mortals to understand. That's why we need lawyers. It's not like our laws are moral codes—they're just a set of rules dreamed up by politicians to keep themselves in power and placate their contributors. I'm a lawyer, and I help powerless mortals cope with the rules and sometimes circumvent them. It's part of *our* ecosystem."

Layborn started to speak, then shook his head, sputtered, "That's bullshit."

"No it isn't, and you know it," McCann said softly. "If our laws were honest and based on universal truth, I'd be on death row for six murders. Instead, I can walk out of here any damned time I please."

"I wish you would," Layborn growled. "See how far you make it."

"Ah, now we're getting to the crux of it."

"Crux of what? I don't like this word-game shit."

"Of course you don't," McCann said. "You're a simple man of the law. And when I say that, I mean it in the worst possible way."

"Are you insulting me?"

McCann snorted, "Me? Never!"

"I'm leaving," the ranger said, rising to his feet.

McCann leaped up. "Stop!"

Layborn froze.

"Tell them the slate is clean again. Tell them. No one knows except us. I took care of that for them yesterday. No charge."

Layborn showed no expression.

"Tell them they have one choice, and one choice only. They can pay me what they owe me or I call the FBI tomorrow and work out a deal for immunity. Got that?"

Layborn hesitated. "I have no idea what you're talking about."

"Oh, come on. Sure you do. Repeat the terms to me so I know they sunk in."

Layborn stared back with what looked like fear in his eyes. Thank God, McCann thought.

"Repeat it," he said.

"Pay you what they owe you or you talk," Layborn muttered.

"Good! And when I say *pay*, I don't mean another empty promise about sometime in the future. I want it all, every penny plus the penalty, now. *Now!* I don't care what they do to get it. The transfer should be made immediately, in full. Do you understand that?"

"I guess."

"If my banker doesn't confirm that the transfer has been made within twenty-four hours, I call in the FBI. Simple as that. If they want to negotiate, it's the same as saying the deal is off. No more delays, no more Plan B's. Tell them," McCann said.

"Tell who?" Layborn asked weakly.

The lawyer rolled his eyes and snorted. "Too late for that. I can tell you know exactly what I'm talking about, and you know exactly who to talk to. Why pretend you don't? It's just us pals now, Ranger. Just us buddies. And we'll all get rich, won't we? In the meanwhile, I want you to personally start working on transferring me out of here to a federal facility. I've spent more than enough time in the Yellowstone jail."

Layborn shook his head. His face was pale. "All hell has broken loose out there," he said, mumbling. "You've got no idea what's happened in the last twelve hours. That game warden and the ranger, they've done all kinds of damage."

McCann thought this was interesting. The game warden? What was it with that guy? Suddenly, he knew who had been watching him the day before. The game warden *should* have gone away by now, it seemed. The park was about to close, and he was just a state employee. His business card wasn't all that impressive, after all.

"I really don't care," McCann said after a moment. "I've got more important matters to contend with. So do you, I suspect. And so do your bosses, although I'm sure you'd rather I call them your business partners. I hope they're smarter now than they've been so far, don't you? They need to forget about some stupid game warden and think about me. *Me*."

Layborn looked up. "The whole world doesn't revolve around Clay McCann, you know."

McCann arched his eyebrows, said, "Actually, right now it does. You forget, I'm free to go. All I have to do is walk outside and talk to the first reporter I see. I know they're out there, Ranger. Imagine what a scoop I can provide! It'll make the story of the Zone of Death and my first incarceration here seem like small potatoes."

Layborn took a long breath, then blew it out. His shoulders slumped; he looked beaten down.

McCann thought, *That was easy.*

For the first time in two days, he allowed himself to visualize himself on that beach with a drink in hand, millions in his account, a girl at his side. Not Sheila, though. Too bad, he thought, he was really starting to like her. Killing Sheila was the only thing he really felt bad about.

25

Like any family on vacation in Yellowstone National Park, the Picketts did the sights. First the Upper, then the Lower Loop; Yellowstone Falls; Hayden Valley; Fishing Bridge; Old Faithful (where they ate cheeseburgers for lunch in the snack bar because Old Faithful Inn was closed); Fountain Paint Pots. Winter was held off for yet another day although it didn't even attempt to hide its dark intentions anymore, and the weather was cool and clear. Pockets of aspen performed maudlin technicolor death scenes on the mountainsides while brittle dry leaves choked the small streams and skittered across the road with breaths of wind. Sheridan and Lucy were delighted with the park, Marybeth was cautiously relaxed. Oncoming fall brought out the wildlife. Sheridan kept track of The Animal Count in a spiral notebook, noting elk (twenty-four), coyotes (one), bald eagles (two), moose (one), wolves (two), trumpeter swans (seven), Ridiculous-Looking Tourists (five), and buffalo (eighty-nine and counting). Lucy claimed to have seen a bear but it turned out to be a tree stump, thus was docked ten points in Sheridan's counting system, which she seemed to be making up as they drove along to ensure that she would win.

Marybeth played referee and awarded Lucy five points back for "looking cute," despite Sheridan's protests.

Joe tried to join in, tried to relax, but he felt like an impostor. The .40 Glock was clipped to his belt and felt uncomfortable. He felt his heart race every time he felt another vehicle, and his palms broke out in a sweat at the sight of a dark one.

AT NORRIS GEYSER basin, the girls ran in front on the board-walk. Joe and Marybeth dawdled, holding hands, letting them get ahead.

"Your heart's not in this, is it?" she asked him once the girls were far enough away not to hear the conversation.

"It's not that," Joe said. "I really want them to have a good time. I want *you* to have a good time. This is such a great place."

"You're wound tight," she said. "I feel like if I let go of your hand, you'd unravel. Is it because your father is here somewhere?"

He tried to laugh but it sounded like a cough. "It's not about my father. Well, maybe a little. He's a distraction, but that's all he is."

"Cold," she said.

"He's nothing to me. I don't want him involved in our girls' lives, or in ours. I don't want them to even meet him."

"It might be unavoidable."

"Not if I can help it."

"And that's not all, is it?"

"Nope."

"Don't think I haven't noticed," she said softly. "You've got your gun with you even though you're trying to hide it, and you keep checking the rear-view mirror to make sure Nate's Jeep is still behind us."

312

"You saw him back there, huh?"

"I don't miss much."

They walked along in silence, until Joe said, "It's hard to believe so many bad things can happen in such a good place."

"Stay strong, Joe."

"I'm trying," he said. "There's so much going on, and so little I'm able to change or figure out. I want Judy to recover. I want my father to recover. I want to know what causes a flamer, who killed Mark Cutler, and why Clay McCann assassinated six people. I want to talk to Chuck Ward and make sure the governor is still engaged and that I'm still employed. And I want to talk to you alone, and to Nate. He's hovering, as you know. He knows something and he's waiting for the right opportunity to tell us."

Marybeth nodded toward Sheridan and Lucy, who had paused at the railing to stare into the depths of a hot pool. Lucy shouted for them to hurry up so they could see the bones deep in the water. After seeing Cutler's body, Joe didn't think he wanted to see any more bones.

"We're not here at the best time, are we?" she said.

Joe pulled her close. "I wouldn't have it any other way. Having you and the girls here helps me focus. But after what happened last fall ..."

"Enough," she said, but squeezed his arm in appreciation.

He said, "So I hope you don't mind that I slipped the desk guy Simon fifty bucks before we left this morning and asked him to move all our stuff to another cabin during the day but not to reflect it on the register. I know that sounds paranoid ..."

"Yes, it does, but I appreciate it." She looked up at him, smiled. "I hope we can find a little time together before I have to get the girls back."

He laughed. "Me too."

"But we have these darned girls with us."

"You're the cleverest person I know," Joe said. "You'll think of something."

"Where there's a will," she said, letting her hand slip from the small of his back into the back pocket of his Wranglers.

"YOU HAVEN'T SAID much about your mother lately," Joe said. "Are things going okay?"

They drove on the road that connected the upper and lower loop toward the headwaters of the Gibbon River. Joe had noted how pleasant it looked a few days before when he passed, and observed trout rising in the evening. He thought Sheridan and Lucy might like to try fly-fishing there, although both were napping in the car at the moment.

"I've deliberately not said anything," Marybeth whispered, checking to make sure their daughters weren't listening, "because all the signs are still there for a train wreck coming."

Joe grimaced.

"She's had two"—Marybeth made quote marks in the air with her fingers—"*arts council* meetings in the past week. I asked around and confirmed that Earl Alden just happened to be at both of them. And," Marybeth said, lowering her voice even further and leaning into Joe's ear, "they left together both times. The meetings ended at eight. Mom got back to the ranch at midnight."

"Uh-oh," Joe said.

"Uh-oh is right."

"Poor Bud," Joe said.

"What's wrong with our parents, anyway?" Marybeth asked rhetorically. "Is it because they're *of that generation*?"

"I believe so," Joe said. "The first of the Baby Boomers. It's all about them."

"Poor *us*," Marybeth said. "We have to put up with those people for a lot more years."

JOE BEAMED WITH pride as Sheridan and Lucy assembled their fly rods, tied on tippet, selected their own flies, and marched toward the headwaters of the Gibbon River. He could tell by the set of Sheridan's jaw that she was determined to out-fish her little sister.

"Stay in sight," Marybeth called after them. She'd found a flat grassy spot near the pullout to spread a blanket. There was a bottle of wine in the cooler.

"If you catch some fish," Joe said, "don't keep more than two each for dinner. Release any more than that like I showed you."

"That won't be a problem for Lucy," Sheridan said over her shoulder, "since she won't catch anything."

"But I still get points for looking cute," Lucy said, throwing a dazzling smile over her shoulder at Joe, "which won't be something Sheridan has to worry about."

"She's right, you know," Joe said.

"Aaaauuugh!" Sheridan howled.

NATE PARKED HIS Jeep behind the van as Joe pulled the cork out of the bottle of wine.

"I guess we need another glass," Marybeth said.

"And look," Joe said, feigning sarcasm, "you just happen to have three. How convenient."

Marybeth shot a sly glance at him. "I always have an extra."

"Just in case Nate shows up, I know."

"It doesn't have to be Nate."

"But he's the only one who shows up," Joe said, pouring.

"True."

Joe warmed with the realization that Marybeth now felt comfortable joking about her obvious but now harmless attraction to Nate. They were long past all of that, Joe hoped.

"Good timing on my part!" Nate said, coming down the hill. The fact that he wore his shoulder holster jolted Joe back into the situation he was in. For a moment, while he watched his daughters walk through the grass toward the stream and his wife unfurl the blanket and unpack the wine, he'd forgotten.

MARYBETH LISTENED CAREFULLY as Joe filled Nate in on what had happened since they'd last talked. Nate was particularly interested in the flamers and asked Joe to describe them more than once. As Joe did, Nate nodded, rubbing his chin, looking inscrutable.

"It seems like it's coming to a head of some kind," Nate said. "Whoever they are decided to go after you and Demming on the same night. You must have hit a nerve."

Joe nodded. "It had to be the videotapes."

"Have you looked at them?"

"I haven't had a chance," Joe said. "I've got three entrances. I may have something worthwhile there, but as I said, Demming had the other two entrances and her computer is missing."

"We'll need to take a look," Nate said.

"Yup."

"I've got something too."

Joe and Marybeth looked over the rims of their glasses at him.

"Cutler was holding out on you."

"Meaning what?"

"Olig was a Geyser Gazer. He and Cutler were best friends and colleagues, and apparently Olig went along on most of

Cutler's forays into the thermal areas. Hoening only went along a couple of times."

Joe was puzzled. "Why didn't Cutler tell us that?"

"Two reasons," Nate said. "One, he and Olig figured something out that could result in murder. Two, Cutler knew where Olig was hiding all along. I think Cutler was about to tell you both things when we went to meet with him but never got the chance. My guess is Olig is still here."

"Where?" Joe asked.

"Guess."

"The Old Faithful Inn."

"Right," Nate said. "Remember how I told you about all the secret rooms and hallways in that building? The ones that were designed for who knows what? They've all been sealed off, but that doesn't mean someone couldn't live there if the manager showed him how and gave him permission."

"But it's closed," Joe said.

"Officially, yes," Nate said, "but I saw a light last night on the top floor, toward the back. As I watched, a figure passed in front of the light, then it went out. It's in that area called Bat's Alley. That's a spooky damned place, but a great place to hide."

Joe looked over at Marybeth.

"I guess I know where you two will wind up," she said.

"Not tonight," Joe said.

"Good, since we have dinner reservations at seven." She turned to Nate. "Reservations are for five, Nate."

"How did you know I'd be here?" Nate asked.

"I guessed," she said.

"Enough," Joe cautioned.

From a distance, Sheridan whooped "Got one!" Joe saw the trout flash on the end of her line in the setting sun, looking more metallic than alive, confirming once again that there were few things more beautiful in the natural world than a rainbow trout—or his daughter catching one.

26

Saturday night, the Mammoth Dining Room was a quarter filled with the last visitors of the season and a few people passing through. Joe had made a deal with the chef to prepare the three trout Sheridan had caught after he cleaned them and brought them to the kitchen. Sheridan couldn't stop smiling.

They had returned at dusk to find that their possessions had been moved, as arranged, to a larger cabin a quarter mile from the one they had in the morning. The girls thought it strange.

"It's like we're Saddam Hussein," Sheridan said, "moving to a new house every night. Like we're a mafia family or something." She looked to Joe and Marybeth for an explanation.

"This cabin is bigger," Marybeth said, as if it were the most natural thing in the world. "We wanted a little more room."

Lucy nodded her assent, but Sheridan eyed Joe with suspicion. He looked back stoically.

In the dining room, Marybeth said, "This is our big night. Let's all behave and just enjoy it." It wasn't necessary to point out that since Joe had lost his job there had been very few nights where they ate out, and when they did it had been fast food.

"This is elegant," Lucy said, touching each piece of silverware (three forks!) and glassware at her place setting with the tips of her fingers. "I was born for this."

She was, Joe agreed, while Marybeth and Sheridan laughed and rolled their eyes.

Nate watched the exchange the way he always did, with a combination of disbelief and sentimentality.

THE MAIN COURSES had just been served—pasta for Marybeth, steaks for Joe and Nate, the fresh-caught trout for Sheridan and Lucy—when Joe saw the young, casually dressed couple making their way through empty tables toward them. The couple carried white foam containers of leftovers. The woman looked vaguely familiar.

"I thought that was Lucy!" the woman said, grinning, stepping up to the table between Joe and Marybeth.

"Mrs. Hanson!" Lucy cried. She was both excited and embarrassed, the way children are when they see their teachers in surroundings other than the classroom. "What are you doing here?"

"Josh and I are on our way to Bozeman to the recycling center," Mrs. Hanson said. "We thought we'd stop for dinner on the way through. How are you, Lucy?"

"Great! We caught these fish we're eating."

Joe saw the shadow of judgment pass over Mrs. Hanson's face but it didn't dent her smile. He thought it telling that the teacher didn't introduce herself to anyone else at the table and talked only to Lucy.

"We like to leave the fish in the stream," Josh said, cheerily but with admonishment, "where they belong."

"But it's okay," Mrs. Hanson said, "not everyone feels the

same way about nature. We know Lucy's dad is on the *other end* of that viewpoint."

Joe started to argue when he felt Marybeth place her hand on his thigh and she shot him a *"Calm down"* look.

Nate leaned back in his chair, studying the Hansons with a Clint Eastwood-type grimace.

"You'd change your mind if you ate this," Sheridan said to Lucy's teacher. "It's really good. I wish I could have another one. I wish I could catch and eat five more."

"How are you, Mrs. Hanson?" Marybeth asked pleasantly, trying to move the conversation past Sheridan's overt challenge.

To Joe's annoyance, Mrs. Hanson and her husband pulled over chairs from the next table, sat down, and proceeded to tell Lucy how they were.

JOE COULD HAVE kissed Simon when he came to the table and interrupted the conversation with the Hansons. Instead, he followed him from the dining room to the lobby near the bar.

"I'm sorry to disturb you, sir," Simon said. "But one of those men is back to see you."

"Believe me," Joe said, "I don't mind."

As they walked out of the building toward the hotel, Simon asked about the new cabin.

"It's great," Joe said. "Thank you for doing that."

DOOMSAYER SAT ON a bench outside the Mammoth Hotel. A wide bandage covered most of his head and glowed white in the moonlight, and his left arm was in a sling. Joe . sat down next to him.

"How's my dad?"

Doomsayer shook his head sadly. "I talked to the doctors

in Billings. He may not make it, Joe. And if he does, well, he may not have use of his brain. He's a goner, Joe."

Joe looked away.

"It's not so bad," Doomsayer said. "The last thing he did was have a hell of a good toot and reconnect with his son. It could be worse."

"How could it be worse?"

Doomsayer smiled. "He could be like me. Sore as hell and knowing the end could come at any time."

"Tell me what happened."

He shrugged. "There's not that much to tell. The lights were out, and I think we were both sleeping. Passed out, actually. I know I was, anyway. I never heard anyone come in, which leads me to believe they had a key. But to be honest, someone could have knocked and George could have answered the door thinking it was you. I don't know. All I can remember is hearing some heavy blows in the dark, and your dad sort of grunting as they hit. I sat up and asked him what was going on when I got hit in the head. That's all I know."

Joe said, "So you never turned the light on? You never saw who did it?"

"No."

Joe shook his head. In his mind, he pictured Layborn swinging his club at a form on the bed, connecting with bone and flesh, spattering the white walls with blood. "He assumed it was me," Joe said. "But he didn't know it wasn't until he realized there were two people in the room."

"I guess."

"Is that what you told the rangers?" Joe asked.

Doomsayer nodded.

"Who interviewed you?"

The old professor withdrew a business card from his

pocket and handed it to Joe. Layborn. No surprise there.

"Can you feel it?" Doomsayer asked softly.

Joe looked over, saw the man looking at his feet. "What?"

"Tremors. They're very soft, but if you make yourself still and concentrate on the ground, you can feel them."

Joe felt nothing.

"It takes practice, and patience. But I can feel them. They've been getting stronger over the past hour. We've got some definite seismic action brewing. If you don't believe me, you should call the federal seismology centers. They'll confirm that we've got a little dirt dance going on right now."

Whether it was real or because of Doomsayer's suggestion, Joe thought he felt a slight vibration through his boots.

"George is lucky," Doomsayer said. "He'll not even know what hit him when the caldera blows."

"Stop it," Joe said, pointing toward the Mammoth restaurant. "My family is in there eating."

"I'd advise you to get them home," Doomsayer said, making his eyes wide, "as long as home is the South Pole. That's probably the only place they'll be safe."

Joe snorted and stood up. He couldn't take any more of the old man.

"Thanks for the update on my dad," he said. "I'll try to get up to see him soon."

"That's nice," Doomsayer said with a hint of sarcasm. "Better hurry."

Joe strode away upset. Why had he let Keaton get to him this way? Maybe because, he admitted, there was something to it. He stopped on the sidewalk in the dark, thought he felt a slight tremble, as if the ground shuddered. He thought how in the entire day of sightseeing with his family, they'd never left the inside of the Yellowstone caldera—that's how big it was.

He turned. "Professor, have you eaten dinner tonight?"

"I'm really not hungry, but that's a very nice offer. I could use a little drink, though."

"Follow me," Joe said, suppressing an evil grin. "I'm buying."

INSIDE, MRS. HANSON was telling Lucy she'd read recently that measurements between rings of the trees within Yellowstone were proving to scientists, beyond doubt, that the ecosystem was dying, being tortured to death by carbon monoxide emissions from snowmobiles and snow coaches. Lucy listened wide-eyed. Marybeth feigned interest. Nate and Sheridan ate dessert and acted as if the Hansons weren't there. Joe broke in, said, "Wasn't that study written several years ago by Dr. Miles Keaton?"

Mrs. Hanson and Josh looked up. "Why, yes," she said, "I'm surprised you know that."

"I do manage to read when I'm not driving my gas-guzzling four-wheel drive around the ranch," Joe said, which elicited a sharp glare from Marybeth. "Would you like to meet him?"

"Dr. Keaton? He's here?" She flushed. "I'd be honored!"

"I just ordered him a drink at the bar," Joe said. "He's in there waiting for you."

Mrs. Hanson excused herself, telling Lucy, "It was great to see you, Lucy, but sometimes the teacher needs even more education, if you can believe that."

When the Hansons were gone, Marybeth looked suspiciously from Joe to Nate and asked, "What are you two smiling about?"

THE IMAGE THAT would stay with Joe as he glanced into the bar after paying for dinner was Mr. and Mrs. Hanson's bloodless, horrified expressions as Doomsayer wagged his finger in their faces.

AS THEY WALKED back to their cabin, Nate dropped back from Joe and Marybeth and asked Sheridan and Lucy if they'd like to go hot-potting.

"With swimsuits," Nate added, for Marybeth's benefit.

Joe watched his older daughter carefully. Nate and Sheridan had once been master falconer and apprentice, but the relationship had been severed. There had been a time, two years before, when Sheridan announced quite clearly that she didn't care if she ever saw Nate Romanowski ever again. Nate tried to apologize to her for his transgressions but she'd hear none of it. Nate let it ride, biding his time. Now he was asking her and her sister to join him.

"What's hot-potting?" Lucy asked.

Nate said, "It's like sitting in a hot tub outside, only this hot tub is natural."

"Isn't it illegal?" Marybeth asked.

"Yes," Nate said.

Joe nudged his wife, and she got it. Nate was not only mending fences with Sheridan, he was working it so Joe and Marybeth could have some time alone together.

"I've got a new pink suit," Lucy said. "I was hoping I could use it. Sheridan, you brought yours, right?"

Sheridan hesitated. "Yes."

"Can we go?" Lucy asked.

"As long as you don't get thrown in the Yellowstone jail," Joe said.

"So let me get this straight," Sheridan said. "It's legal to shoot and kill people in Yellowstone Park, but it's against the rules to pick up a rock or go hot-potting?"

325

"You've got it," Nate said. "Thus begins your enlightenment and understanding of our federal government."

Marybeth laughed nervously, started to object, but again Joe nudged her.

"Don't be gone long," Marybeth said.

But long enough, Joe thought.

"Okay," Sheridan said, sighing, "I'll go."

As they left the cabin, Sheridan paused at the door, rolled her eyes at her parents, and sighed again before leaving.

"She knows," Marybeth said.

"No, she doesn't," Joe assured her.

"Yes," Marybeth said, "she does."

THEIR LOVEMAKING WAS furious and seemed dangerously illicit, as they kept expecting a knock on the locked cabin door when the hot-potters returned. Both feared either Sheridan or Lucy asking, "What are you two *doing* in there?"

As usual, Joe overestimated his staying power and was up, dressed, and scanning the entrance gate videotapes when Nate and his daughters returned.

27

WHILE SHERIDAN AND Lucy got ready for bed in the cabin, Joe and Nate sat outside under the porch light sipping bourbon and smoking Cuban cigars Nate dispensed from a box beneath the seat of his Jeep labeled "Fuses and Toilet Paper."

"I've never smoked a Cuban cigar before," Joe said, marveling at its fruit-tinged smoothness. "I think I could get used to 'em."

"Don't," Nate said. "They're illegal."

"Quintero Brevas," Joe said, reading the label of his cigar, "Habana."

"Yup."

"I'm not going to ask how you got them," Joe said. "Just like I'm not going to ask you what you do to make a living."

"Wiser that way," Nate said, nodding in agreement, the red cherry of the cigar bobbing in the dark. "That way you've got plausible deniability. You need that. You're a man of the law. At least you used to be. I'm not exactly sure what you are now."

"I'm beginning to wonder that myself."

"Governor Rulon's private detective," Nate said. "Range Rider Number One."

WHILE NATE READ over the thick printouts Marybeth had brought from her Internet search, Joe fast-forwarded through the entrance gate videotapes on his laptop from the East, Northeast, and South gates, looking for black SUVs.

"Thanks for taking the girls hot-potting," Joe said.

"My pleasure."

"You mending fences with Sheridan?"

Nate smiled. "She's tough. But we're getting there."

"Did you two talk about falconry?"

"Let's put it this way," Nate said. "As I was handing her a towel when we were done, she asked about the peregrine."

"That's not nothing."

"You're right. Once those birds get in your bloodstream, they never get out."

JOE STRUGGLED TO concentrate on his screen and the images. He felt as if he were running on fumes. He was beyond tired from the full day of sightseeing and the night before spent in the hospital, but he was determined to see this through. If he stopped for even a minute, he thought, he would collapse with exhaustion. That wouldn't do, because he felt he needed to keep the investigation moving forward. He'd learned over the years that often the thing that solved a case, especially one like this, with so many aspects and floating facts, was simple and unrelenting forward motion. By pushing ahead, even if he didn't know exactly where he was going, he sometimes forced a reaction from the conspirators that might reveal them.

The moon was a perfect thin slice of ice-white in a thick soup of stars that hardened as the temperature dropped near freezing. Although Nate was still warmed to the core from hot-potting and wore a fleece vest over his denim shirt, Joe was bundled in the hooded Carhartt coat he had worn on the Longbrake Ranch in the winter. He could feel exploratory fingers of cold pushing up his pant legs and down his collar. The cold helped him stay awake.

By his estimate, he had looked at more than three hundred vehicles thus far on his screen. Although that was a lot of cars, he knew he was lucky that the three days he was viewing were so late in the season and the number of visitors was at its lowest. Yellowstone received 3.5 million visitors in the summer, and he could only imagine the traffic count in mid-July. Of the three hundred-plus he had looked at, there were thirteen dark SUVs. Of the thirteen, six were black. Five of the six had Wyoming plates. He bookmarked each of them before proceeding, since he had no idea how many target vehicles he'd end up with after looking at the whole tape.

The camera angles from each gate were different, he noticed. The focus from the Northeast and East gates was more on the license plates, so the vehicle and registration could be identified later if the driver failed to pay the entrance fee or had commercial cargo and didn't declare it. The South Gate camera had a wider field of vision and included not only the plate but also the grille and front window. If the glass wasn't tinted in the vehicle, he could see the driver and passenger, and sometimes faces peering over the front seat from the back. Joe had no idea what the vantage points at the North and West gates—from Demming's missing computer—were. He was under the assumption that whoever had bushwhacked her had entered the park from one of those two entrances, which is why they took her computer.

Which meant that he was probably wasting his time.

Nevertheless, he continued until he was through. Then he went back to study the shots he'd marked. All were from the South gate, via Grand Teton Park and Jackson. He remembered a ranger in the Gardiner clinic lobby saying Demming's call specified that the SUV she pulled over had Wyoming plates and a rental sticker. Maybe, he thought, he had something.

The first of the five black Wyoming SUVs had a single driver and no passengers and the plate WYO 22-8BXX. County 22 was Teton County, or Jackson. The driver was male, mid-fifties, silver hair, serious. That in itself was interesting, since most of the shots Joe saw were of harried tourists with a carload of family members. But a single driver didn't match the profile. He forwarded.

The second and third matches were families. A pudgy man in an Australian drover hat manned the first, his anxious wife at his side, kids and dogs peering over the front seat. Joe discounted them, as well as the second shot of an enormously fat contingent of five, two of whom were gnawing on what looked like turkey legs.

The fourth black SUV was WYO 22-8BXX again, which got Joe's attention and he sat forward in his chair. This time, there were two profiles in the vehicle, which he could now identify as a GMC Yukon. Unfortunately, the sun hit the wind-shield and obscured any identification of the driver and passenger. Joe checked the date. Two days before. The day Cutler was killed. He searched for the time stamp and found it: 5:15 A.M.

"Nate," Joe said, "I may have something."

Joe did a quick calculation based on spending a week in Yellowstone driving the figure-eight road system. If WYO 22-8BXX entered the park at the South entrance at 5:15 A.M., it could have been at Sunburst Hot Springs by

6.30, a half-hour before they were to meet Cutler. *It worked.*

"Oh man," Joe said.

"What?" Nate asked.

"I may have them," Joe said, puffing furiously on his cigar. "They may have taken the wrong computer. I may have them right here, coming up from the South entrance."

"Jackson," Nate said, snorting. "That figures."

Joe fast-forwarded to the fifth and last bookmark.

There it was, WYO 22-8BXX again. From the day before, the day Judy Demming was shot. They had come back. There were two of them again, and despite the sun on the windshield and the smoked-glass windshield, this time he could see their profiles. The driver matched with the first shot: lean, silver-haired. Whoever it was was back again, three times in three days. The passenger was harder to see because of glare on the glass, but there was something about his silhouette, the tilt of his head, the jut of his jaw, that seemed strangely familiar to Joe. Inside his head, alarm bells went off. He realized he was shaking not only with the cold but also with excitement.

"I know this guy," Joe said.

"Who is he?"

"I'm not sure. But there's something about him. I've seen him before. I just can't make him out on the screen." Joe wondered if he could send the image to the Wyoming DCI in the morning for enhancing. He didn't know if they worked on Sundays. He doubted it.

The cabin door opened and Marybeth came out.

"It's cold out here, guys," she said. "You can come in now. The girls are in bed."

"Joe thinks he's figured something out," Nate said.

"Maybe," Joe said.

"Aren't you going to offer me a cigar?" Marybeth asked, looking from Joe to Nate. Joe couldn't believe it.

Nate opened his "Fuses and Toilet Paper" box, and she took one. Joe watched in amazement as she clipped off the tip, lit it, and blew out the smoke.

"Good," she said.

"You're smoking a cigar," Joe said, dumbfounded. Marybeth raised her eyebrows at him as if to say, *Why not?*

"This is real interesting," Nate said, holding up a sheaf of paper. "I might have found something too."

"Sounds like we'll be up for a while," she said.

"I ALMOST MISSED IT," Nate said once they were inside and had spread the documents out on a table. Sheridan and Lucy were in bed sleeping, lumps amid strewn covers. "I was concentrating on this Swiss company called Genetech. They're the ones who have the bio-prospecting permit in Yellowstone Cutler told us about. Judy couldn't remember the name. Remember the 'million-dollar slime' they found at Sunburst that's used for genetic typing? They've made millions off of it, according to these documents and what Cutler said."

Joe took the cover sheet from the Genetech file and read it over. Based in Geneva, the company was partially owned by the Swiss government but had majority private financing. Genetech's bioengineers were also researching hot springs microbes in New Zealand and Iceland to try to mine more useful microbe thermophiles, but as yet could not find a match for the particular specimen they'd found in Yellowstone.

"Would the microbe be worth killing over?" Joe asked rhetorically.

"Absolutely," Nate said. "The company's made a fortune so far exploiting it."

332

"So we have a suspect?" Marybeth asked. "A Swiss bio-engineering firm?"

"That's what I was thinking at first," Nate said, "but I've changed my mind. I don't think this has anything at all to do with Genetech, other than they were the company that originally found the microbe and obtained the permit to harvest it from Yellowstone."

Joe explained to Marybeth what Cutler had told him about the permitting process—how sloppy and controversial it seemed to be, how environmental purists like Rick Hoening and others were opposed to it.

"I tend to agree with them," she said. "If it's illegal to dig a mine, hunt, or do any logging in a national park, how can you justify taking microbes for commercial purposes? I don't know enough about it to have an opinion either way, but it's not consistent with their policy, is it?"

"Nope," Nate said.

"Then why would the Park Service grant permits to companies to do this kind of prospecting?"

"Bucks," Nate said. "Parks always need more money."

Joe was beginning to get what Nate was driving at.

"So we've got Genetech, who has a permit extending another five years to exclusively harvest this particular microbe," Nate said, digging out a copy of the agreement. He showed them where it was signed by the superintendent of the park as well as the chief ranger. "But it seems there's another company in this pile of papers Marybeth brought with her that desperately wants a permit as well."

Nate turned to Marybeth. "Where did you get this particular list of companies?"

She nodded to Joe.

"I saw the names on binders in Clay McCann's office," Joe said.

"Okay," Nate said, his voice rising, "that's the connection—Clay McCann. Now we come to a company called Ener-Dyne."

This was the file Nate had waved in the air earlier. He summarized it: "EnerDyne was incorporated just last year in the State of Colorado. The incorporation papers are filed with the secretary of state there, and Marybeth was smart to print out the documents when she did her search. EnerDyne has several floors of offices in downtown Denver, a pretty large payroll, but no income as yet according to the records."

"How can they stay in business?" Joe asked.

"I'm getting to that," Nate said, excited.

"Please get to it with your voices down," Marybeth cautioned, gesturing at her sleeping daughters.

ACCORDING TO THE papers filed with the Colorado secretary of state, Nate said, EnerDyne was a research, development, and engineering firm created to implement coal gasification projects throughout North America.

"Coal what?" Marybeth asked.

"Gasification," Joe said. "Turning hard coal into gas that can be transported in pipelines and distributed. I remember reading about it back when we had the mineral rights dispute around Saddlestring. Energy companies have been trying to figure out how to do it economically for years. The technology is there, but it's too expensive to do in a cost-effective way, at least so far. They'd have to build big plants to turn the coal into gas, and since coal only costs pennies per ton to mine and ship, it doesn't make financial sense."

"That's right," Nate said. "Wyoming and other states have billions of tons of coal in the ground. There are seams of coal in the West that are miles thick and stretch across half the state—the largest deposits in the world. If that coal could be made into gas, it could solve all of our energy problems and change the face of the economy. We could be energy independent."

"My God," she said.

"If it could be done cheaply," Nate said, "it would be what everybody wants."

"But nobody has figured out how to process coal into gas that way," Joe said.

"Which is why it's significant how EnerDyne plans to do it," Nate said. "It says here their plans are proprietary, but they do have to leak a little the general concept of it to the SEC in order to be listed as a public company and to attract investors. And what it says here is 'EnerDyne is the leading company in the world in a new method to *organically* gasify coal.'"

"Organically?" Joe said.

"Think about it," Nate said.

Joe and Marybeth exchanged looks, and it seemed to hit them both at the same time.

"Microbes," Joe said. "They want to find a microbe that will react naturally with coal to produce gas."

"They think they can find it in Yellowstone," Marybeth said.

"And maybe they have," Nate said.

"Flamers," Joe said. "Free fire."

Marybeth looked at him.

"There's a little seam of coal near Sunburst geyser. It's next to the flamers Hoening talked about and I went and lit."

"Oh, man," Nate said, and whistled.

"Maybe someone figured out that the microbes in Sunburst were reacting with that stream of coal to produce

335

gas just under the surface. And if that particular thermophile was introduced to one of those miles-thick seams of coal Nate was talking about ..."

"It would be worth billions," Nate said.

Marybeth said, "But they'd need a permit to do it. And if they thought there would be a protest by environmentalists to block any new permits, that might definitely be worth killing for."

It took a few minutes to sink in. As Joe thought about it, many of the previously floating facts started to drop into place, to become links in a chain of a new theory.

"Who are the company officers?" Marybeth asked softly.

Nate found the incorporation papers. "Layton Barron is the CEO. I've never heard of him. In fact, I've never heard of any of these people except for the last one. We'll have to do more research, I guess."

"Nate ..." Marybeth prompted, "I'll do the research as soon as I can get to a computer. But in the meanwhile, what are the names?"

"Oh. Okay. Layton Barron is the CEO. Michael Barson is the CFO. Katherine Langston, VP of development. C. T. Ward the Third, VP of operations. Any of those names ring a bell?"

"Nope," Joe said.

"This last one will. Guess who's the attorney of record?"

"Clay McCann," Joe said.

"Got him," Nate said.

Marybeth started to say something but stopped abruptly and cocked her head. "I hear someone coming," she mouthed. Joe sat back and stopped breathing. He heard it too. Gravel crunching. Footfalls outside the cabin, getting closer.

Nate had his .454 out, cocked, and aimed at the door in one liquid movement. Instinctively, Marybeth rose and moved into the shadows between the beds of her sleeping daughters.

The knock on the door was light, barely audible.

Joe stood, Nate behind him and to the side.

"Your weapon," Nate whispered.

Joe drew the Glock out of the holster, worked the slide as quietly as possible, then kept the gun pointed down in his right hand as he approached the door. He hated being in a situation where his family was right there, behind him, exposed.

"Yes?" Joe asked, keeping his voice calm.

"Mr. Pickett, it's Simon. I saw the light on ... I'm sorry to bother you, but you've an urgent message at the hotel from Mr. Lars Demming. He thought you were still in the hotel, and insisted I come get you."

It *sounded* like Simon, Joe thought. Nevertheless, he motioned for Marybeth to get down and checked with Nate, who had his pistol raised in two hands, eye level, ready to fire if necessary when Joe cracked open the door.

Joe pulled it open quickly and stepped back, keeping the Glock loose at his side, ready to raise it.

It *was* Simon, off-duty in jeans and a hooded sweatshirt, and the desk clerk looked into the muzzle of Nate's .454 with absolute terror.

"Sorry," Joe said to Simon. "You can put the gun away, Nate."

"Are you sure?" Nate asked.

"I'm sure."

JOE APOLOGIZED TO Simon as they crunched through the gravel on the way to the hotel. Several times, Joe had to reach out to steady the desk clerk, who was shaking so badly he had trouble walking.

"That's a first," Simon said. "Like something out of a Western movie."

"You get used to it out here," Joe said, distracted, his mind racing with what he'd learned about EnerDyne and Clay McCann.

The old-fashioned black telephone sat ominously on the front desk, and as Joe approached it he tried not to think the worst. Maybe Judy had taken a bad turn, maybe she died. Maybe someone had gotten to her in Billings ...

"Joe Pickett," he said as he picked it up.

"Joe!" Lars sounded unexpectedly buoyed. "I'm damned glad they found you."

"Me too. How's she doing?"

"Much, much better. The doctor said a full recovery is pretty likely. I'm just so ... happy."

"Thank God," Joe said, feeling weight he didn't know was there lift off his shoulders.

The line was silent for a moment, and Joe thought perhaps the connection had been lost. Then Lars spoke softly. "I've really got to apologize to you. I said some bad things to you, and I'm sorry. Judy has been filling me in on what happened, how you stayed with her and made sure she got sent here so no more harm could come to her. I didn't understand before. I'm just real damned sorry I said what I said."

"Don't worry about it," Joe said, knowing how hard it was for a man like Lars to say those words. "Apology accepted. I'm just glad she's doing all right."

Lars said, "Better than all right. She's sitting up, talking, eating even. Except for those damned tubes, she looks pretty good. Beautiful, even. Yes, she looks beautiful."

Joe smiled. He could hear Judy's voice in the background saying, "Oh, stop it, Lars."

"She wants to talk with you," Lars said. "That's why I called and woke you up. Well, that and to apologize."

"I was awake," Joe said. "No problem."

"Oh, one more thing. Judy says she gave you my truck to use."

"Yes," Joe said, not expecting what would come next.

"Keep it as long as you need it," Lars said. "I don't mind. We'll be here another couple of days. I got one of my road crew guys to pick up Jake and Erin to bring them here."

"Thank you. I'll take good care of it."

"Watch the transmission," Lars said. "Sometimes it slips. I need to replace that pressure plate in the clutch—"

"Lars," Judy said in the background.

"Okay, okay," Lars said to Joe. "Here she is."

Joe waited.

"Hey there." Her voice sounded tired but strong.

"Welcome back," Joe said. "I was worried."

"I'm tough," she said, which made Joe smile again. He was surrounded by tough, good women.

"When we were in the clinic," Demming said, "you came into the room and asked me who the shooter was. I could hear you but I couldn't talk."

"Yes."

"I can now. It was James Langston."

"The chief ranger?" Joe was stunned, but it made sense now why Langston had been so interested in where Joe was staying while at the same time making a point not to meet with him.

"I saw him clearly. I thought he was there for backup, obviously. The dispatcher didn't say who was coming, so I assumed …"

"Wow," Joe said. "And you'll testify to it?"

"Of course. But I still can't believe it."

339

"Neither can I," Joe said, "but this thing is big. And it just got bigger."

"What should we do?"

Joe looked around the empty lobby, trying to sort it out. Should she contact someone else with the information? If so, whom? Should he?

"I'm thinking," he said. "Sometimes, it takes me a while."

"I know it does," she said, chiding him.

"First," Joe said, "make sure you're safe there. As long as you're alive, you're a threat to him and everyone he's involved with, even though he thinks you're dying. We've learned a lot in the last hour, Judy. None of it is good. Your life is still in danger, so call the Billings PD. If you have to, make up a story, but make sure they send some men to the hospital to stay outside your door. Make sure no one comes to visit you except your kids."

"Okay …" she said, almost in a whisper. The giddiness she'd started the conversation with was gone.

"Make a deposition," Joe continued. "Get your statement down on tape and on paper. If nothing else, it will make it less likely they'll try to get to you if they know you've got a statement with the police."

"And if they do get to me," she said, "Langston will still go to jail."

Joe didn't want to say it that way, but Demming was sharp. And when he said the name Langston aloud, it triggered a question. "What's James Langston's wife's name?"

"Hmmm … I met her a couple of times. Tall, skinny, cold. Katherine, I think."

"Katherine. Are you sure?"

"I think so."

"Katherine Langston is listed as VP of development for

340

EnerDyne. Either she's involved or James is protecting himself by using his wife's name. Probably both.

"Oh," Joe continued, "I nearly forgot to ask you. Did you recognize the men in the black SUV?"

"I didn't recognize the driver," she said.

"Could you pick him out in a photo? Like from the entrance gate video?"

"Absolutely."

Joe nodded. "Good. I'm pretty sure I've got a couple of pictures of him." Joe described the driver.

Demming said, "That's him."

"What about the passenger?"

"He looked familiar."

"In what way?"

"I've been trying to figure that one out," she said. "I know I've seen him before, but I don't know his name. It seems to me he was up here a year or so ago with your governor."

Joe felt a chill shoot through his spine.

"He stuck to your governor like glue," she said. "He seemed like a nice guy but real intense."

The profile from the video, Joe thought. He knew now why it was familiar to him too.

The name should have struck a nerve when Nate said it. Vice president of operations for EnerDyne, but under his formal name. James Langston wasn't the only officer at EnerDyne playing name games.

"Joe?"

"I'm here," he said weakly.

"What's wrong?"

"His name is Chuck Ward," Joe said, "aka Charles Ward, aka C. T. Ward the Third. He's Governor Rulon's chief of staff. Now I know why he didn't want the governor to send me up here, and why he had to take some personal leave."

"He's the guy you're working for?" Demming asked, disbelieving.

"He was," Joe said.

"Does the governor know?"

Joe started to say, *I'm sure he doesn't* but his world was turning inside out. Given the implications of free fire, he was sure of nothing.

Instead, he said, "I have no idea what the governor knows."

"Get out of there," Demming said. "Get out now."

Joe mumbled that he understood her, told her to call the Billings PD right away, said he'd come see her as soon as he could.

"Meaning what?" she asked.

"Meaning I've got to go."

JOE DID FOUR long circuits around the outside of Mammoth Hotel in the dark, rubbing his face, running scenarios through his head, stopping once to throw up. He had a headache from lack of sleep and too much thinking and his mouth tasted of stale smoke and regurgitated dinner. As he walked, it got darker and colder. Storm clouds rolled across the black sky, extinguishing the moon and stars, covering Yellowstone Park like a lid on a boiling cauldron.

Winter had arrived.

On his fifth circuit, little pellets of snow strafed the ground, hitting so hard on the pavement they bounced. In the darkness, it looked like the road was awash with waves. He thought he felt tremors through his boot soles, and concluded that he probably did.

He stopped in front of the Pagoda. A single light was on from within a cell on the second floor. Clay McCann was awake.

"McCann!" Joe shouted.

After a few moments with no reaction, he shouted again.

The shadow of a face appeared at the window. Joe recognized the lawyer's profile. The thick window was frosted so McCann couldn't see who had called his name outside.

"I've got you now," Joe called, "you son of a bitch!"

BACK IN THE Mammoth Hotel lobby, Joe dug a worn and faded business card out of his wallet that he'd kept with him for three years. On the back, handwritten, was a number. He dialed, let it ring eight times before it was answered.

"What?" Tony Portenson said, groggy.

"It's Joe Pickett."

Joe heard a clunk as the receiver was dropped on the floor, then picked up. "It's fucking three-thirty in the morning," the FBI agent growled. "How'd you get my home number?"

"You gave it to me," Joe said. "Remember?"

"I remember nothing. It's too early. Can't this wait?"

"No, it can't."

"Jesus Christ. *What?*"

Joe could hear a woman's voice ask, "Who is it, honey?"

Portenson said, "A fucking lunatic."

"Quit cursing," his wife said.

"Yes, quit cursing and listen," Joe said. "I've got a conspiracy for you that's so big you'll be famous for blowing it open. It's so big, you'll be able to name anywhere in the country you want to be transferred to."

"Okay," Portenson said. "I'm awake now."

"Before I tell you anything more, you've got to agree to a deal."

"I can't do that."

343

"Then hang up and I'll call someone else," Joe said. He had no idea who else he would call.

"What?" Portenson said sarcastically. "I can't agree with anything if I don't know the terms."

"Fair enough. Here's the deal. I can deliver the biggest arrest you've ever made in your career by far. We're talking national, international headlines. It'll shake the foundation of both federal and state government, but don't worry; it's no one you like. It'll affect national energy policy, and you'll probably receive a medal from the president. Oh, and it will completely break the Clay McCann case."

After a few beats, Portenson said, "Jesus. What do you want from me?"

"You've got to get a team together and get up here by tonight. It needs to be in complete secrecy. You can't notify anyone or you'll blow the collar. And when the arrest is made, you have to look the other way when it comes to one individual involved on our side."

"One individual?" Portenson said.

"Yes."

"Oh fuck, you mean Nate Romanowski, don't you?"

"Yes."

"I *knew* he was there."

"He helped figure this thing out. He saved our lives in the Zone of Death. Besides," Joe said, "he's a friend of the family."

"He *killed* two men!" Portenson yelled. "An ex-sheriff and a federal agent!"

"Allegedly," Joe said.

"Allegedly my ass."

"Do we have a deal or don't we?"

Portenson moaned and cursed.

"Well?"

"We have a deal."

AS JOE WALKED back to his cabin in the snow at 4 in the morning, he thought, *Another night without sleep.*

In his stupor of sleeplessness and putting together the fledgling plan for the coming night, he didn't pay any attention to the work crew and pickup parked next to the first cabin in the complex. But he smelled the strong rotten-egg whiff of gas and could hear a powerful hissing sound from inside.

The front door flew open and a man staggered outside, ran a few feet, and crouched with his hands on his knees, breathing deeply. Another man in a hard hat appeared from around the side of the cabin, yelling, "Get me a wrench!"

Joe stopped, trying to figure out what was going on.

The first man finally stood after filling himself with several lungfuls of fresh air.

"Are you okay?" Joe asked.

"I'll be fine in a minute," the man said, wiping his eyes with his sleeve. "There's a gas leak inside there, and I got a big breath of it."

The second man snatched a toolbox from their pickup and carried it to the back of the cabin.

"I don't know if I can fix this," the second man shouted. "It's like somebody broke the fucking valve off. We'll need to turn the whole system off before somebody lights a match and blows us all to hell."

The first man shook his head. "Good thing the park is nearly closed. There was enough gas in there to kill a herd of buffalo."

Joe listened as the second man cranked on a shut-off valve. The hissing stopped.

It took a moment to realize the cabin they were fixing was the one he had moved his family from earlier in the day. Whoever had broken off the valve didn't know that.

"EVERYBODY UP!" JOE shouted as he entered the cabin. Marybeth sat up in bed. Nate had curled up in some blankets on the floor.

"What's going on?" Lucy asked.

"It's snowing," Joe said. "You've got to get out of the park before the roads close."

"Snowing?" Marybeth said. "Since when are we scared of a little snow?"

"As of now," Joe said, knowing he sounded like a maniac.

28

CLAY MCCANN COULD not stop pacing. the only time he paused was at the window, and only for a few seconds. There was something different outside. The dawn light through the mottled glass was white and muted, and the sounds of cars on the road outside the jail were more hushed than usual. He could tell it was snowing, although he couldn't see it.

He had not been able to get back to sleep, ever since that man outside had stood beneath his cell at 4 in the morning and yelled, *"I've got you now, you son of a bitch!"*

Who *was* he? What was he doing out at that hour? The incident disturbed McCann immensely. He knew the voices of his partners, and it wasn't any of them. Had they brought in someone else, or was the owner of the voice an independent threat? Or a local crank?

McCann wanted out. This had been going on too long, he thought. Layborn should have delivered the threat the night before, and action should be taking place. Would they be stupid enough, once again, to try to outflank him? Would they convene another of their meetings? What the hell was going on?

And now it was snowing. *Great*.

*

WHEN HE HEARD the sounds downstairs, McCann's first assumption was they had come to meet with him. There was a muffled conversation, a long pause, and the sound of the front door being shut. He stopped pacing and stood still, listening. He could feel his heart beat faster, and he clenched and unclenched his hands.

Footfalls on the stairs, the sound of a key in the lock, the door swinging open.

"Good morning, asshole."

The tall man on the other side of the bars had long blond hair in a ponytail, sharp, cruel blue eyes, and the biggest gun McCann had ever seen. Snowflakes melted on the man's shoulders.

"You're coming with me," the man said, opening the cell door.

"No," McCann said, his voice weak. "I'm staying right here."

This caused the man to pause. His mouth twisted into a grin that made McCann's blood run cold.

"All right, then," the man said, and shot his hand out, grasping McCann's left ear and twisting so hard the pain made his legs wobble. Then he pulled the lawyer out of the cell, still twisting on his ear, and guided him down the stairs into the lobby of the building.

Although he was cringing with pain, McCann saw the lobby was empty. "Where's my guard?"

"He decided to take a walk and get some air."

"And just *leave* me here?" McCann said, blinking through tears.

"You're not exactly Mr. Popular in this neck of the woods. Sit," the blond man said, shoving McCann into a chair by an empty desk. McCann sat, rubbing his ear. When he pulled his hand away there was a smear of blood on the tips of his fingers.

"That's right," the man said, "I'll rip it right off next time if you don't do everything I tell you. Believe me, I've done that before."

"You can't do this," McCann said.

"I just did."

"What do you want with me?" McCann tried to place the man and couldn't. His voice was not the same one that had called to him from under his window.

The blond man raised the gun, the muzzle not more than three inches from McCann's face, and cocked it. McCann watched the cylinder rotate, saw the huge balls of lead turn.

"You're going to make a call to James Langston. Tell him you're going to the FBI, and you're bringing Bob Olig along with you."

"What?"

"You heard me."

"Bob Olig?"

"They'll figure it out."

As McCann punched the numbers on the phone with a trembling hand, the blond man said, "Somehow, I thought you'd look more impressive, considering you gunned down six people. But you're just a fat little weasel with pink hair, aren't you?"

29

"So," JOE ASKED McCann, "who figured out that the microbes at Sunburst react with coal to produce gas?"

"Mmmf."

"Nate, would you mind taking the duct tape off of Mr. McCann's mouth?"

"Happy to," Nate said, reaching over the front seat of Lars's pickup. McCann tried to turn his head but Nate grabbed a corner of the tape and ripped it off hard. Red whiskers and a few pieces of skin came with it. McCann howled.

They were headed south from Mammoth, climbing the canyon out of the valley, the snow a maelstrom. Joe was driving and McCann was wedged onto the narrow back bench seat, hands and feet bound with tape.

Joe was still angry that he had had to send his family away, that someone had tried to harm them. Seeing his daughters look back at him from the windows of the van as Marybeth pulled away had torn his heart out. It hadn't helped seeing the grim look on Marybeth's face as she drove, determined to get her girls out of there while at the same time upset over leaving her husband. Joe blamed McCann because he didn't know whom else to blame and McCann was in the truck. "You can't do this," McCann sputtered, tears in his eyes from the sting. "I'm technically innocent. This is kidnapping and assault."

"Nate, can you put fresh tape on his face and rip it off again, please?" Joe said.

"Happy to," Nate said.

"No!"

Nate stripped six inches of silver tape from the roll with a sound like fabric tearing.

"I asked you who figured out the microbes," Joe said.

Nate started to lean over the seat.

"Genetech people!" McCann said quickly, "but they didn't realize what they had."

Nate shot a glance to Joe, who nodded back. Nate lowered the tape but glared at McCann with menace.

"Talk," Joe said. "It's the only thing that might save you right now. And don't start in on kidnapping and assault. You murdered six people. Putting a bullet in your head will not cause any crocodile tears up here, I'd say."

McCann breathed deeply, worked his mouth since he couldn't rub it with his hand. "Why should I talk?"

"Because," Joe said patiently but with an edge, "it's the only chance you have to stay alive."

"Why should I trust you?"

"Because you have no choice. We don't even have to kill you. All we need to do is stop and let you out, which I'm more than happy to do. The bears and wolves will take care of you. That's the disadvantage of living in a place where there are so many animals that can eat you. And with this snow, your bones won't be found until spring."

"I recognize your voice," McCann said. "You were the one who yelled at me this morning outside the jail."

Joe watched McCann's face in the rearview mirror. The

lawyer seemed to be calculating his odds on the fly. He saw McCann shoot a quick glance out his window at a coyote nosing into the snow after a gopher. *Good timing*, Joe thought.

"Genetech has a little branch office in West Yellowstone," McCann said. "They hired two local guys who do no more than drive to Sunburst every couple of weeks, harvest the pink microbes, and send them in a special incubation container to Geneva. They're not engineers, just local boys. One of them got into trouble a year ago, DUI. He asked me to represent him, since I'm also local counsel for Genetech."

"Stop," Joe said. "What does that mean? What do you do for them?"

"Very little," McCann said. "I file the annual extensions for their permit with the Park Service and meet a couple of times a year with James Langston to assure him the company is complying with all of the environmental regulations. I'm on a retainer to keep an eye out for my client in case something goes wrong or there is a challenge to their permit."

"Ah," Joe said, now knowing how McCann and Langston had met. "Go on."

"Anyway, this Genetech guy with the DUI was telling me about something that happened when they were at Sunburst getting the microbes. He's a smoker, and he said he tossed a cigarette aside while they were working and suddenly flame was shooting out of the ground. He said it singed his jeans. At the time, I thought it was just one of those weird Yellowstone things, and I forgot about it.

"Then I was approached by the CEO of a start-up company out of Denver. They knew about my familiarity with Genetech and the permitting process, and they were interested in getting a permit from Langston to harvest thermophiles."

"Who is the CEO?"

McCann sighed. "His name is Layton Barron. He's a con artist, but I didn't know it at the time."

"What's he look like?"

"Mid-sixties, thin, gray hair. An arrogant prick."

Joe turned to Nate. "Sounds like the driver of the black SUV."

Nate nodded.

"Anyway," McCann said, "Barron asked me to meet with Langston to try to secure a permit for them. He said he had investors lined up all over the world who would put up big bucks if EnerDyne got the permit. It had to do with bioengineering or something I don't really understand. It was later when I realized Barron was a fucking con man. He was fishing, is what he was doing. He was just hoping that if his company could start harvesting microbes that maybe, just maybe, his engineers could figure out a use for them. Since the microbes from the park are unique compared to anywhere else, he might have been right, but who knows?"

"Did you get the permit for them?" Joe asked.

"I'm getting to that."

Nate stripped off more tape.

"Okay, okay," McCann said. "I found out that some Zephyr employees were up in arms about the harvesting permits. They were environmental extremists, and they planned to start letter campaigns to newspapers and politicians and some kind of online fund-raising movement to wage war on Genetech and anyone else who was harvesting microbes. *Legally* harvesting microbes, I might add."

"That's where Rick Hoening comes in," Joe said.

"He was their leader. He made no bones about what he planned to do, and he was getting a buzz going in the park and within the environmental community all over the country and internationally. They wanted a moratorium on any new permits, and an investigation into who they'd been given to in the past and why. Langston was beside himself, to say the least, since he was the guy who signed the permits in the first place. Genetech slipped him a little something on the side, you see. I know that because I delivered the envelopes of cash."

"Bastard," Nate said.

"Barron and EnerDyne were even more up in arms when they found out about Hoening's plans. If he was successful, they'd never get their piece of the pie."

"That's where you saw your opportunity," Joe said.

"Being a lawyer is all about recognizing opportunities."

"And here I thought it was more than that," Joe said. "Silly me."

"I really didn't care how it came out," McCann said. "I looked forward to the fees that would come from litigation. But I did contact Hoening on behalf of Genetech. That's when he told me about the flamers. He thought Genetech's activities were causing some kind of disturbance, and he was damned mad about it. I remembered what the Genetech employee had said, and I gave this information to Barron. He sent a couple of his engineers up here, and they were the ones who made the connection between the microbes and the seam of coal. Barron was out-of-his-mind happy, and knew he really had something. The information was worth billions.

"See, the problem with coal gasification is the huge expense of building the plant, and the fact that Western coal is soft and might require so much coal to get gas that the dollars just wouldn't work. But if these Yellowstone microbes could be injected into the ground, into that coal, a big plant wouldn't be necessary. The coal gasification would occur

355

underground, naturally. All EnerDyne would need to do was tap it and pipe it out. And I was the only person outside of his company who knew it. So we made a deal. They retained me as their counsel. Barron started working the inside, finding players who could help him get exclusivity in exchange for positions and stock within the company.

"But before we could get everything into place, Rick Hoening started causing trouble."

"So you had to stop him," Joe said.

"Yes, I had to stop him."

"But why kill the others? Why didn't you quit with Hoening that morning?"

McCann shrugged. "Two reasons, Game Warden. If I'd walked away after Hoening went down, the investigation would have centered on him and me, and no doubt someone prior to you would have put the pieces together long before now. Plus, I had no doubt Hoening had recruited his friends to his cause. They would have carried out the campaign against bio-mining and made Hoening into some kind of martyr. Taking them out eliminated the effort entirely, and cast everything in the light of the Zone of Death instead of Hoening."

"But," Joe said, "four innocent people …"

"No one is innocent," McCann said definitively.

Joe just stared at him, hatred building.

"Joe …" Nate cautioned.

Joe took a breath. "What happened next?" he asked McCann.

"Barron recruited Chuck Ward from your governor's office so Ward would be available to head off any action that might stop EnerDyne at the state level. And he got Langston to buy in, knowing Langston was a few years from retirement and wanted a huge payoff."

"Those bastards," Joe said.

McCann shrugged. "It's amazingly easy to buy public officials. Everybody knows that. Barron was a master of it, and quite a salesman."

Joe was disgusted. The governor's chief of staff and the chief ranger for the park had exchanged their positions of trust for big personal payoffs. Worse, they'd gone off the deep end to protect their interest, including the ambush of Judy Demming, the likely murder of Cutler, and targeting Joe and his family. As much as he despised McCann, Langston and Ward were as bad or worse.

The snow was building up on the road and Joe had to slow down. At least four inches had fallen and stuck. Park policy was not to plow the roads in winter, but to let the snow build up until only snowmobiles and snow coaches could use them. That meant if he got stuck, it could be days before someone found them. And, based on what they were learning, there were no guarantees that whoever found them would be friendly.

"Okay, so EnerDyne wants to harvest the microbes," Joe said. "That I understand. But how did it happen that you turn into Rambo?"

For the first time, McCann smiled. Joe could see him in the mirror, and he thought McCann looked smug.

"That came about by happenstance. One of my clients is an elk poacher. He kills the elk, cuts off their antlers, and sells them to Asian firms who grind them up and sell it as an aphrodisiac."

"I hate poachers," Joe said, "nearly as much as bureaucrats who go bad."

"I'm a lawyer, I don't make moral judgments."

"Which is why you're an asshole," Nate growled.

"Anyway," McCann said, gaining in arrogance as he went

357

on, Joe thought, "his hunting ground is near Bechler ranger station, technically in Idaho. He was contacted by the Idaho Fish and Game, who told him they were watching him. He came in to see me to find out whether Idaho could arrest him or not, since he was doing his poaching on federal park land. So as I researched his question, I found the loophole. I couldn't believe it when I found it. I told Barron about it and said I'd take care of his Hoening problem if he'd make me financially secure for the rest of my life. You see, I'd learned about the annual reunions of the Gopher State Five from Hoening himself. I knew where they'd be, and when they'd be there."

"You sound proud of yourself," Joe said.

McCann shrugged. "Why shouldn't I be? I committed the perfect crime."

"So why didn't you just leave with the money after you killed Hoening and the others?" Joe asked. "Why stay around to be caught?"

"First, I'm not caught," McCann said. "Second, Barron reneged on me. It turned out he'd filed false financials with the SEC, and all that public money he promised was tied up in regulations. He simply didn't have the cash. He lied to me."

"Imagine that," Joe said.

"Worse than that," McCann said, "they panicked. They really are amateurs. Instead of concentrating on ways to get me the money, they screwed everything up by lying and delaying further. I knew they had decided to get rid of me somehow, so I stayed ahead of them and got myself put in their own jail where I'd be high profile and safe. Meanwhile, they tried to eliminate all of the witnesses, or anyone who might potentially be a witness. I want no part of them anymore, or EnerDyne. I just want my money."

"But they want you," Joe said, "so you won't talk and implicate them."

"Yes."

"Why did you kill that woman and the ex-sheriff?"

"They knew too much. If someone got to them, they might have exposed me."

Joe said, "So you lured them into Idaho to kill them. You've admitted to kidnapping."

McCann said, "Sure, I talked under duress. Under the threat of torture from your friend here. After being kidnapped and assaulted. Sorry, my confession won't stand since I'll claim I said whatever I had to, so I could save my life. It would be your word against mine."

He beamed at Joe.

Joe dug his microcassette recorder out of his pocket and held it up.

"Want to bet?" Joe said. "Anybody who hears this tape will hear how proud you are of what you did. None of it sounds forced out of you."

McCann went white and his mouth sagged open.

"Shut him up," Joe said, and Nate eagerly dove over the seat with the tape and stretched it across the lawyer's mouth.

"You'll get death," Nate said, smoothing the tape.

"Assuming he lives long enough to get to trial," Joe said, turning and looking into Clay McCann's wide, panicked eyes.

And seeing that less than a hundred yards behind them was a park ranger Ford Explorer with wig-wag lights flashing, gaining on them by the second, snow flying from the tires in twin plumes of white.

"UH-OH," JOE SAID.

McCann turned, saw the vehicle, and whimpered. He sagged in the seat to hide. The Explorer closed the gap, fishtailing a little in the snow as the driver accelerated.

"Who is it?" Nate asked, squinting. "Can you tell?"

"My guess is Langston and Layborn," Joe said, reaching behind his back and gripping the Glock, putting it on the seat next to him. "Here we go."

"I can put a bullet into the grille," Nate said, "knock them out." He ran the window down so he could lean outside. The cab of the truck filled with swirling snow.

"Hold it," Nate said, "there's only one guy inside."

Joe concentrated on driving because it was getting harder to see where the road was in a sea of white. He shot a glance in his mirrors. Yes, there was only the driver, and Joe recognized him.

"Don't shoot," Joe said. "It's Ashby."

"Are you sure?"

"Ashby's not involved, is he?" Joe called to McCann, who grunted something back.

"What did he say?" Joe asked Nate.

"I think he said no."

"Let's pull over and take our chances," Joe said. "We can really use Ashby's help if he'll cooperate. Be ready."

JOE DIDN'T DARE pull off the road and chance getting stuck in the snow, so he gradually slowed down. The Explorer stayed with him, a few feet behind, until both vehicles were stopped. Because of the way the wind-driven snow moved steadily across the meadow on either side of the road, it seemed to Joe as if they were still moving.

"Cover me," Joe said, opening his door and jumping down. Snow lashed him in the face.

Ashby was out of the Explorer, his hand perched on his holstered gun.

Joe held up his hands to show he had no weapon.

"Up against the truck and spread 'em!" Ashby yelled. "And tell your buddy to get out and do the same."

Ashby was wearing sweats beneath his parka, and had apparently jumped out of bed to pursue them.

"Hold it," Joe said. "I'm on your side."

Ashby withdrew his gun, held it with both hands in a shooter's stance, aimed at Joe.

"Del," Joe said, feeling his belly clutch up, "calm down. We have McCann. We're using him as bait. Before you try and arrest me or pull that trigger, there's something you need to listen to. We've got new information and you're not going to like it."

Ashby wavered, Joe could see it in his eyes.

"Five minutes," Joe said. "Just listen to McCann's confession. Then you'll want to help us out."

"Confession? Everybody knows what he did."

"But not why he did it," Joe said.

"He'll tell me?"

"He doesn't need to. I've got it on tape."

Ashby seemed to weigh what Joe said, and while he did he glanced toward the pickup. His face dropped with shock and fear. Joe quickly followed Ashby's sight line. The muzzle of Nate's .454 aimed straight at the ranger.

"He'll blow your head clean off with that," Joe said.

"Tell him to lower the gun," Ashby said. "I'll listen."

"You can tell him," Joe said, able to breathe again. "He speaks English, you know."

WHEN HE PUT Lars's truck in gear and plowed forward in the untracked snow, Joe had trouble getting the image of Ashby's face out of his mind from a few minutes before, when the ranger sat in the truck and listened to the tape. It was the stricken face of betrayal, and what he heard

361

caused Ashby to slump against the door as if all the fight had been punched out of him.

"I know how you feel," Joe said.

"Langston doesn't surprise me as much as I would have thought," Ashby said. "But Layborn ..."

"Really?" Joe asked, surprised.

"I thought Layborn, despite his faults, was a true believer in the Park Service, in our mission here," Ashby said. "I thought he was loyal to me."

"Sorry," Joe said, meaning it. "Why is it some bureaucrats always think they deserve more?"

Ashby shook his head. "I don't," he said.

Nate said, "That's why you'll always be poor like Joe. And I say that with compassion."

Ashby still had the look on his face when he got out and trudged back to his Explorer to follow Joe, Nate, and McCann to the Old Faithful Inn.

"DO YOU THINK this plan is going to work?" Nate asked Joe as they picked up speed again and steered straight into the maw of the storm.

"Maybe not," Joe said truthfully. "A lot of things could go wrong. And I didn't count on this weather."

Nate jerked a thumb at McCann. "Do you think they want him bad enough to follow us?"

Joe said, "I do. He's their loose cannon, and they can't afford to let him follow up on his threat to talk. Especially if they think he's somehow hooked up with Bob Olig, who can corroborate much of his story."

"That's a hell of a wild card to play, isn't it?" Nate said, referring to Olig. "We don't even know for sure if he exists."

"I'm trusting your instincts," Joe said.

362

"Remind me not to play poker with you, Joe," Nate said, grinning.

Joe shook his head. "You might want to rethink that. Both Sheridan and Marybeth always clean me out."

30

J OE WAS THANKFUL for the high clearance of Lars's pickup by the time they took the turnoff to Old Faithful. It was early afternoon, completely socked in, ten to twelve inches already on the ground, the lodgepole pine hillsides looking smoky and vague in the falling snow. When they cleared the rise they could see the Old Faithful Inn below—a boxy, hulking, isolated smudge on the basin floor.

His growing fear that Portenson didn't or couldn't make it due to either bureaucracy or the weather was relieved instantly when Nate pointed out the single Suburban in the parking lot with U.S. Government plates. The agents— Joe counted six—huddled under the portico of the inn near the massive front door. Joe pulled up under the overhang as if he were a bus disgorging tourists. Portenson was there, nervously inhaling a cigarette as if trying to suck it dry. Butts littered the concrete near his feet. His team of five wore camouflage clothing with black Kevlar helmets and vests, and looked competent and alert. Cases and duffel bags of weapons and equipment were stacked against the building. Two of the assault squad were smoking cigarettes and squinting through the smoke at Nate Romanowski, as if sizing up an adversary. Nate nodded at them without blinking as Joe shut off the motor of the truck.

"Glad you made it," Joe said to Portenson, getting out. "I'm not sure that camo stuff will work all that well in the snow, though. You guys look like a bunch of bushes."

Portenson was instantly around the truck in front of him, his face red. "Do you realize what will happen to me if this doesn't work out? I put my career on the line for you and brought these men up here without authorization. This kind of operation requires sign-offs all the way to the director of Homeland Security himself."

Joe nodded. "We couldn't risk that. If it went federal up the chain of command, somebody might tip off Langston, since you're all in the same happy family."

"We are not," Portenson said hotly.

"Sure you are," Joe said.

Ashby had pulled up behind Joe and was watching the exchange closely.

Joe asked Portenson to send one of his men to drive the Suburban up and hide it behind the inn, out of sight. He asked Ashby to do the same with his Explorer.

"They won't come in if they get any kind of indication that anyone is here besides us and Clay McCann," Joe said.

"How do we get in?" Portenson asked, nodding toward the massive front door of the inn.

"I have a key," Ashby said, handing it to Joe.

"Will you leave your Kevlar vests?" Joe asked Ashby.

INSIDE, IT WAS dark except for the tiny red glow of dots from the emergency backup system mounted high on the walls. Normally, Joe found the lobby of the inn impressive, but with the lights out and the snow covering up any sunshine leaks, it was oddly intimidating. As the men entered,

with every footstep echoing, Joe felt as if he were dese-
crating a cathedral. All the windows had been boarded up
for the winter, and the temperature was colder inside than
outside. There was no power or water. The building was
completely winterized.

Nate went about starting a fire, rolling logs the length of
small cars into the massive stone fireplace. Within twenty
minutes, the fire threw sheets of orange light on the walls
and started to warm the place. The FBI assault team
unpacked their weapons and equipment using the light
from the fire and from headlamps they'd brought. Several
of them scrambled when a deep-throated *whoosh*ing sound
seemed to shake the walls, and Joe said, "It's just Old
Faithful erupting outside."

Joe noticed how the assault team spoke to one another
in whispered voices or via radio mikes strapped to their
shoulders, even when they were all in the same room. He
got the distinct feeling that despite Portenson's overall command of the operation, these men were in their own tight
universe. The squad commander, a beefy and intense man
with a breast patch that read "McIlvaine," kept up a low
monologue with his men while flashing quick, suspicious
looks at Nate, Joe, and Portenson.

After pulling a dust sheet off a table, Joe sat down at it
with Portenson, Ashby, and McIlvaine. McCann, still bound
and gagged, was seated across from Portenson. Nate hovered
nearby, pretending to tend the fire. He fed it with wood the
length and girth of rolled-up Sunday newspapers.

As the fire crackled and the snow fell outside, Joe outlined
his plan to Portenson and played back sections of the
recording of McCann that implicated Langston, Ward, and
Layborn. While he listened, Portenson rubbed his hands
together. At first, Joe thought the agent was warming them.

Then he realized Portenson was growing more excited the more he heard, apparently confirming that the case was solid after all and soon he would be making headlines, receiving commendations, and requesting a transfer to Hawaii. McIlvaine, meanwhile, shook his head. The assault commander smiled wolfishly, obviously not surprised by the corruption of his brethren. McCann looked bored as he heard his own words played back.

"So we can arrest them in one fell swoop," Portenson said, nodding. "That's the part I like. We've got video and audio equipment with us, so we'll get it all down."

"I assume they'll all arrive together," Joe said, ignoring the camera crew comment.

"If they can get here at all," McIlvaine said. "The weather's gotten worse, not better."

"What kind of lead do you think we've got on them?" Portenson asked Joe.

"I'm guessing a few hours," he said. "It would take a while for them to get together and talk this all through. They're big talkers, according to McCann. They like to have meetings to decide what to do. So they'll know McCann is gone, and they'll have his call about Olig and going to the FBI. There have been rumors up here all summer that Olig is alive and hiding out around here; no doubt they've heard them too. That's why we mentioned Olig, so they'd draw their own conclusions. We wanted to get them to come here, but we didn't want it to be too obvious."

McCann rolled his eyes, said, "Mmff."

"He wants to say something," Portenson said.

Joe reached up and pulled the tape away, much more gently than Nate had done it.

"What if I don't cooperate?" McCann asked. "There's a big assumption being made here."

"Why wouldn't you?" Portenson said. "This is the best chance you're going to get. If it all works out, you can cut a deal and testify against your buddies. You might even walk … *again*."

Joe sat back and said nothing. The idea that McCann would once again go free bothered him nearly as much as his plan falling apart. He vowed that it wouldn't happen but kept his mouth shut. When he glanced up at Nate, he saw Nate studying him as if reading his mind. Nate nodded slightly, as if to say, *"McCann won't walk."*

There had been no discussion about the arrangement Joe had made with Portenson, and Joe found it odd that after the initial acknowledgment, the agents had conspicuously ignored Nate. Again, Joe got an inkling something was going on beneath the surface with McIlvaine and his assault team that might or might not involve Portenson.

"I want some assurances," McCann said to Portenson in his haughtiest manner. "I want a piece of paper that says if I cooperate to make the arrests, the federal prosecutor will give me immunity."

Portenson simply stared. Even in the poor light, Joe could see that blood had drained from the agent's face.

Ashby looked from Portenson to Joe, concerned.

"I can't get a piece of paper here in time," Portenson said. "You know that. We're in the middle of fucking nowhere. It's Sunday night."

"Then forget it," McCann said, sitting back. "No paper, no cooperation."

Portenson, Ashby, and Joe exchanged looks. To Joe, it seemed as if the other two were in the first stages of panic. McCann was playing them the way he'd played his partners, played the Park Service, played a jury, played the system.

"No paper, no cooperation," McCann said again, firmly.

Out of the corner of his eye, Joe saw Nate suddenly rear back and throw a length of wood, which hit the lawyer in the side of his head, making a hollow *pock* sound. Before McCann could slump off his chair, Nate was all over him, driving him into the hardwood floor.

McCann gasped, and Nate reached down and twisted his ear off, yanking it back so the tendons broke like too-tight guitar strings.

"No cooperation, no fucking *ear*!" Nate hissed, holding it in front of McCann's face like a bloody poker chip.

Ashby said, "My God!"

"Fuckin' A!" McIlvaine said, approvingly.

Blood spurted across the floor, ran down McCann's neck onto his shoes. Nate reached down and grabbed McCann's other ear, growled, *"You want to make another threat, law boy?"*

"Please, no! I'll do what you want! Please, somebody get him off me!"

Joe grimaced, stood, said, "Nate."

McCann shrieked, "I'll help! I'll help! I'll help!"

As Nate pulled McCann to his feet, he flipped the severed ear onto the table like a playing card he no longer needed. McIlvaine picked it up and inspected it, whistling to himself.

Portenson looked at Joe, raised his eyebrows, shook his head. "We don't do this kind of crap, Joe."

Joe winked. "Sure you do."

ONE OF THE assault team was placed in the woods near the highway interchange with a radio so he could call ahead if anyone was coming. Inside, Joe had watched with interest as McIlvaine efficiently placed the rest of his men throughout the cavernous lobby: two on the second-floor veranda with automatic weapons and a full field of vision of the lobby and door, one in a room on the side of the front desk with a view of the door, another behind the glass in the darkened gift shop, next to the hallway that was the only means of escape.

While the commander checked in with his team, Ashby bandaged McCann's head and cleaned up the blood on his face and neck. McCann looked terrified and never took his eyes off Nate, who prowled around the fireplace like a big cat.

"Is this the way you do things in Wyoming?" Ashby asked Joe.

"When Nate's helping me, it's the way we do things," Joe said. "This wasn't his first ear."

"I've been meaning to ask you about that guy."

Joe shook his head, said, "Don't."

WITH THE INN set up for an ambush, Joe and Nate prepared to go find Bob Olig. They strapped headlamps on their heads and Portenson handed Joe a radio.

"We'll call you the second we see a vehicle coming," Portenson said, "although you'll probably hear it from the chatter. We want you back as soon as you hear because we need you to help set the trap."

Joe nodded, clipped the radio to his jacket breast pocket, and put the earpiece in.

As they climbed the stairs into the absolute darkness of the inn, Joe could hear the assault team checking in with one another. It was pure business, he noted. He wondered again what they'd been discussing among themselves earlier.

NATE LED JOE up set after set of ancient, twisted knotty pine staircases into the upper reaches of the inn. The only

371

light as they climbed was from Nate's bobbing headlamp and his own. It got slightly warmer as they rose, but never warm enough that their breath didn't escape in clouds of condensation. They stepped over or ducked under the chain barriers on each floor to prevent visitors from using the staircases. Joe didn't like the way the old wooden steps creaked, and he felt a wave of sweat break over him when one of the steps cracked sharply under his boot but didn't give way.

They paused to rest on the top landing. The ancient weather-stained boards of the ceiling were right above them. Joe looked around by rotating his head so his head-lamp would throw light. At the end of the landing to their left was one of the bizarre Old Faithful crow's nests that extended perilously over the expanse of the lobby. It looked rickety and diabolical, something designed in a fever dream. He took a step toward the crow's nest, felt the planks of the walkway sag, and stepped back. Below them, what seemed like a mile down, was the muted orange light from the fireplace. The combination of fear, darkness, and height made Joe swoon and lose his balance, and he bumped into Nate.

"Careful," Nate cautioned.

Joe grunted. He didn't realize he had a fear of heights and had never experienced this feeling before.

To their right was a heavily varnished door with a painted sign on it reading NO ENTRANCE.

Nate said, "Look." The orb of his headlamp illuminated the rusted steel doorknob and lock. The lock looked rusted shut and wouldn't give when Nate gently rattled it.

"I wonder where we can get a key," Joe said. "Do you want me to call down to see if Ashby has one?"

Nate shook his head, examining the lock more closely.

He ran his finger down the lock plate.

"See these gouges?" Nate whispered. "They're new."

Joe leaned over and could see them, a series of horizontal scratches that revealed bare metal. "Try this," Joe said, handing Nate his pocketknife.

Nate thrust the three-inch blade between the edge of the door and the jamb, levered it down, and pulled back sharply. There was a click and the door opened an inch.

"Somebody's oiled it recently," Nate said, handing the knife back to Joe.

Before they opened the door and continued, Joe turned the volume down on his radio and unsnapped his holster. Nate already had his .454 out, loose at his side. The last thing Nate said before opening the door was, "Don't shoot me."

The hallway was narrow, twisted, completely dark. Joe's shoulders almost touched both walls in places. The ceiling was low and the floor uneven. This was Bat's Alley, the mysterious passageway built for no apparent reason by the architect of the inn at the turn of the last century. Nate dimmed his headlamp and Joe did the same.

Joe followed Nate twenty yards until the hallway took a forty-five-degree turn to the left and the floor rose slightly. There were several closed doors on either side now, the openings misshapen and heights uneven. A single small porthole allowed a blue-tinged shaft to fill the hallway with just enough light to create dark shadows. As they passed the porthole, Joe stopped to stick his head into the opening and look out through an oval of thick, mottled glass.

The scene outside was dark and haunting. The snow on the ground far below was tinted blue, the timber black and melded with the inky sky. There wasn't a single light outside, only the falling snow. In the distance, in the geyser basin, rolls of steam punched their way into the night like fists.

Another turn of the hallway, and then a distinct smell of food cooking. Another turn, and they could see a band of yellow light from beneath a door at the end of Bat's Alley.

Nate turned in the darkness, whispered, "We've got him."

Joe nodded, his shoulders tense, heart thumping. He slipped his Glock out and, as silently as he could, worked the slide. From behind the door, he could hear hissing and something boiling or bubbling. And someone humming. Joe recognized the tune as "Mambo No. 5." Joe hated that song.

At the door at the end of the hallway, Nate paused, mouthed, "Do we knock?"

Joe nodded yes, and Nate rapped on the door. Although he did it gently, the sounds seemed startling and rude. The humming stopped.

Nate knocked again.

Joe heard shuffling and saw the knob turn and the door swing open.

A man stood there wild-eyed, his mouth agape. He looked like a well-fed yearling bear—short, stout, heavy, with long hair sticking out at all angles from a perfectly round bowling ball of a head. He wore a walrus mustache that had taken over most of his cheeks. There was a gun in his hand but it was pointed down.

"Bob Olig, I presume?" Joe said.

Olig worked his mouth but no sound came out. His eyes were fixed on the gaping muzzle of Nate's .454, which was six inches from his eyebrow.

"Drop the weapon," Nate hissed.

Olig dropped the gun with a clunk, and Nate kicked it across the room.

"You don't get a lot of visitors, I'd guess," Joe said.

"I get *no* visitors," Olig said, his voice throaty, as if he hadn't used it for a while. "Who *are* you?"

"My name's Joe Pickett. I'm a Wyoming game warden. This is Nate Romanowski."

Olig shifted his eyes from Nate's gun to Joe. "I've heard of you. Cutler told me."

Joe nodded. The connection was made.

"I'm making some moose stew," he said. "Would you like some?"

"No, thank you," Joe said, thinking that any other time he would have accepted because he liked moose.

They went inside, but there was barely enough room for the three of them. The room was narrow, with an extremely high ceiling. Two Coleman lamps hung from metal hooks, hissing. A camping stove burned in the middle of the floor, heating a dented aluminum pot filled with the bubbling dark moose stew. A cot and sleeping bag took up a wall on the inside, and there was a college dorm-like bookcase built with planks and bricks. Tacked to the walls were a map of Yellowstone, a laminated cover sheet of the Kyoto Accords with a red circle drawn over it and a slash through it, and several ripped and puckered magazine pages featuring the actress Scarlett Johansson.

"I get lonely," Olig said, flushing. Then, "I don't get it. What are you guys doing here?"

Joe said, "We came for you."

"You need to come with us," Nate said.

Something passed over Olig's face, and he stepped back as far as he could in the small room. "I'm not going anywhere," he said.

"Sure you are," Nate said, growling.

"We've got Clay McCann," Joe said.

Olig's eyes flashed. "He's here?"

"Downstairs," Joe said.

"I want to kill that prick."

Joe nodded. "I assumed that. Otherwise, I'd guess you would have been long gone by now."

"Damned right."

Nate shot a puzzled look at Joe.

"You were friends with Mark Cutler, weren't you?" Joe asked. "He gave you the room up here while you two tried to figure out why McCann shot your friends from Minnesota, right?"

Olig nodded.

"And you two figured out that there were people in the Park Service in on the crime, right?"

He nodded again.

"So you stayed here until the two of you could get enough evidence on who was on which side and you could turn them in. But they got to Cutler, and you figured you were next."

"I thought you might be them," Olig said, gesturing to his gun on the floor.

"Nope," Joe said. "We want to get them too. And we've set up a trap here tonight using McCann and you as bait. We want them to come in and incriminate themselves so we can throw the whole lot of them into prison."

"This is a dream come true," Olig said, rubbing his bear-cub hands. "But you need to leave me alone in a room with Clay McCann. Five minutes. That's all I need. I've been dreaming of this for months."

"You'll need to stand in line for that," Joe said.

"I should be first. He killed my friends."

Joe shrugged, conceding the point.

Nate turned from Olig to Joe. "We can't stand here talking all night."

"I know," Joe said. "I want to make sure Mr. Olig is with us."

Olig said, "You bet your ass I am."

AS THE THREE of them went down the hallway, Joe asked, "Besides revenge, why did you stay?"

Olig sighed. "Guilt. Then fear. I should have been at Bechler with my friends that day, but I was pissed at Rick. I didn't like his idea about going national with the bio-mining protest. Since I've been up here I've found myself thinking of things differently. The black and white I used to see when it comes to environmental issues had turned gray. I figured, shit, we might find a cure for cancer with those microbes, or something. We shouldn't automatically oppose everything. I mean, what makes us so fucking smart? We're the beneficiaries of people before us figuring out shit that makes our lives better or helps us live longer. Why stop now, just because we think we know it all? The last thing I thought about, though, was that those microbes could be used for energy development."

"So you figured that out, huh?"

"Not me," Olig said. "Cutler had his suspicions. We all knew about the flamers, but Cutler was a geologist and thought about *why* they burned. He also told me he was going to show you. That was the night before he was killed."

"So you saw the message to us?" Joe asked.

"Yeah," Olig said. "I prowl around at night when everyone's sleeping. Otherwise, I'd go crazy in that little room. I scared some guests a few times though," he said, chuckling at the recollection.

"Do you know how far the conspiracy goes within the Park Service?" Joe asked.

"No. But Cutler was starting to think it went pretty high. At least to the chief ranger."

"Bingo," Joe said.

"And of course Layborn is involved, that prick. He spent *way* too much time asking about me around here after my friends got killed. He has informants, but luckily none of them knew to give me away. But I'll tell you, I spent a lot of sleepless nights in that room back there."

"Was this before or after your dates with Scarlett Johansson?" Nate asked.

"Hey," Olig said, "that's cruel."

"I'm a cruel guy," Nate said.

"So here's what we need you to do," Joe said, interrupting.

THEY WERE NEARLY to the lobby when Joe heard the radio crackle on his jacket. He plucked it off and turned up the volume slightly.

"I see someone coming," the FBI ranger stationed on the road said. "They're driving one of those snow coach things they use in the winter up here. ETA is ten to fifteen minutes."

"Joe, did you hear that?" Portenson asked from somewhere.

"Got it."

"We need you down here now." His voice sounded shaky.

"On our way," Joe said. "And we've got Bob Olig with us. He's agreed to help."

"*Jesus Christ,*" Portenson said.

31

In the darkness of the gift shop adjacent to the lobby, Joe crouched down behind shelves of stuffed bears and snow globes and watched through the window as the snow coach descended the hill from the highway interchange toward the Old Faithful Inn. The boxy vehicle ran on steel tracks and was lit up with red running lights. Its headlights illuminated the swirling snow in front of it. Soon, he could hear the motor and clanking of the tracks. He got a close glimpse of it as the snow coach maneuvered under the overhang, but he couldn't tell how many people were inside. While he doubted there was enough snow accumulation outside to make the snow coach essential, he guessed they had erred on the side of caution when they chose to bring it.

Portenson, Nate, Ashby, Olig, and McCann also huddled in the gift shop. One of McIlvaine's assault team crouched behind the front counter, watching the black-and-white video monitor, switching smoothly between cameras one, two, and three. Joe couldn't see the snipers behind the railing on the second level, but he knew they were there. McIlvaine checked in with each of them, and they either whispered or clicked a response on their radios.

Joe thought, *The bad guys don't have a chance in hell to get out of this one.*

He looked over to see Olig glaring at McCann with naked hatred. McCann seemed oblivious to it. He looked bulky and nonthreatening in his parka. They'd both been briefed; both had agreed to perform their roles.

As if finally feeling the intensity of Olig's death stare, McCann turned to him, asked, "You must be Bob Olig."

"The only one you didn't kill that day," Olig said.

McCann shrugged. "It wasn't anything personal."

Olig started to reach for McCann but was stopped by Ashby. "Later," Ashby said.

Portenson said to McCann, "Don't fuck this up or I'll do more than rip your ear off."

Again, McCann shrugged. Joe watched him carefully. If anything, McCann looked calm, which unnerved Joe. Was the lawyer planning something, trying once again to stay ahead of everyone around him?

McIlvaine's voice came over the radio: "Everybody ready? My guy in the woods says they're getting out of the vehicle. He counts four men."

McCann smiled at Olig. "Showtime," he said.

With that, the lawyer sauntered across the lobby toward the blazing fireplace. Olig walked stiff-legged behind him. Joe guessed Olig was scared out of his mind, as Joe would be in the same circumstances.

The lawyer turned one of the big rocking chairs around and sat down, his back to the fire, framed by it. Olig stood nervously off to the side where, if necessary, he could duck and hide behind a stone column.

Joe felt his heart race and tried to keep his breathing steady. He flicked his eyes from the monitor to the lobby outside the window, as if trying to decide whether to watch what was about to happen for real or on TV.

The heavy front door squeaked as it opened a few inches. A curl of snow blew in.

"Come on in," McCann called. "It's warmer in here."

The brain trust of EnerDyne Corporation entered the Old Faithful Inn.

Layborn was first, slipping through the door rapidly and flattening himself against the wall near the door, weapon drawn and aimed at McCann with two hands. The ranger flicked his eyes around the room, trying to see if anyone else was there. As planned, he could see no one else in the dark.

"Clear," Layborn barked. James Langston, Layton Barron, and Chuck Ward followed. All wore heavy winter suits. All glanced around suspiciously. When Langston recognized Bob Olig standing near the fireplace, he cursed.

"Yeah," Olig said, "I'm still here."

"So," McCann said, "did you finally bring my money?"

Barron said yes at the exact same time Ward said no. Joe cringed at their lack of coordination.

"What was that?" McCann said.

"We brought it," Barron lied, as Ward deferred. "Does this mean you haven't contacted the FBI?"

"Oh, I contacted them," McCann said. "They're on their way. I was hoping we could come to terms before they get here."

The FBI microphones were good, Joe thought. These guys were good at this kind of technical stuff. He could even hear Langston mumble to Ward out of McCann's earshot, "Not in this storm they aren't."

"It can all still work, gentlemen," McCann said cheerfully. "It's not too late to come to terms."

"What do you mean?" Ward asked. Ward looked anxious,

scared, looking for a way out, something he could grasp. Joe stared at him with morbid fascination. It seemed so odd to see him in this light.

"You pay me what you owe me and let me run the operation from here on out," McCann said. "You guys have really screwed everything up with your endless plotting and meetings. You're like the worst kind of mid-level managers trying to launch some crappy brand of soap. You overthink everything and make poor decisions, like isolating me. I'm your best asset, and always have been. That you couldn't see that shows you're a bunch of amateurs, that you're out of your league in a game played for keeps. None of you has ever faced a jury or a judge when it's just you, naked, standing there. None of you knows how to think on your feet."

The four of them were momentarily entranced by him. Joe was too. McCann had decided to take this in another direction.

"That bastard," Portenson whispered. *"He's out of control."*

In the lobby, whorls of fire roiling behind him, McCann said, "If we're going to get all of this behind us and make a lot of money, which is all I've ever cared about and the only reason I associated with dolts like you, I need you idiots to shut up, quit having meetings, and listen to me. We're going to do things differently, which means smarter. For once."

He paused to let his words sink in. Joe tried to read the four men both through the glass and on the monitor. Langston looked angry, defensive, struggling with his first impulse to pull rank and ream someone out. Barron tried mightily to distance himself from Langston without physically moving, and appeared ready to concede. Ward stared at the floor, confused and resigned to the bad choice he'd made. Layborn sneered at McCann's words.

382

"He's fucking us," Portenson moaned.

"Hold on," Joe said, "I think he knows where he's going."

Clay McCann said, "No more accidents like Mark Cutler."

"We had no choice," Langston said. "He was about to—"

"No more ambushes of park rangers like Judy Demming."

"That wasn't planned," Langston said, stammering. "It just happened."

"Okay," Portenson whispered inside, clearly relieved. "We're back on track. He just got the bastards to incriminate themselves."

McCann changed the subject. "When we agreed that I would take care of Hoening and the Gopher State Five, you agreed to pay me for it. I did my part. You didn't do yours."

Barron said, "The SEC—"

"Fuck the SEC," McCann said. "My deal was with you."

"We can still pay," Barron said. "If we can get things back on track like you say. If we can make an announcement to attract investors—"

McCann exploded: *"That's what you should have done months ago!"*

Layborn said to Barron, "Why are you letting this asshole dictate to us? Can't you see what he's doing?"

Ward looked terrified, Joe thought. He almost felt sorry for him.

"So," McCann said, "I'll ask you one more time. Did you bring me my money?"

Silence. Ward looked as if he was about to break down. Joe saw Langston make eye contact with Layborn, giving him a prearranged signal.

"Even better," Layborn said, unleashed, narrowing the distance between him and McCann. "I brought you this," and before Joe could react, he raised his weapon and fired twice, *pop-pop*, the gunfire splitting the silence. The impact of the bullets sent McCann toppling straight over backward in his rocking chair.

"Jesus!" Ashby shouted, scrambling.

Suddenly, Layborn swung his pistol toward Bob Olig, saying, "And you—"

Through the radio, McIlvaine barked, "Pull!"

And Layborn's head exploded from automatic gunfire. His headless body stayed erect for a second before crumpling to the floor.

"Freeze!" McIlvaine shouted from the dark. *"All three of you, down on the ground, hands behind your heads, now!"*

Ashby threw open the gift-shop door. Joe, Nate, and Portenson ran out behind him. Joe felt adrenaline shoot through him like electric currents as he scrambled, the afterimage of Layborn's death seared into his vision.

Everything was happening at once: agents were thundering down the stairs in their heavy boots; Olig was screaming and cursing from where he was now hiding behind the fireplace; Langston, Ward, and Barron were dropping to their knees and flopping onto their bellies as ordered.

Within half a minute all three were cuffed and searched. Only Langston had a weapon. Barron was pleading, saying he had no part in anything, was an innocent businessman. Langston hissed at him to shut up, but Barron was already offering to testify in exchange for a lighter sentence.

Ward was in apparent shock, staring at a river of Layborn's blood as it snaked across the floor toward him.

As Joe walked toward the still-living triumvirate of Ener-Dyne, he saw something white and blood-flecked rolling slowly across the hardwood floor and reached down and snagged it as if spearing a lazy grounder at shortstop. Layborn's glass eye looked at him accusingly from his palm. He remembered what Demming had said and rotated the eye. Yup. The National Park Service logo was on the other side.

JOE'S HEART WAS still beating hard when the agent from the gift shop came out beaming, said to Portenson, "We got it all on tape. It's perfect."

"Then shut the system down," McIlvaine said, with a menacing smile.

By then, McCann had been helped to his feet and was standing there gasping for air. Despite the Kevlar vest under his parka, the impact of the bullets had punched the breath out of him, and he wheezed raggedly. Olig had stripped off his vest and thrown it across the room as if wearing it another second insulted him somehow. He was furious, he said, about how close he'd come to death, how long the agents had waited.

Joe squatted next to Chuck Ward. Ward still had the distant, almost animal look of shock on his face. Joe had seen many game animals in the back of pickups with the same look.

"How could you do this?" Joe asked. "How could you betray the governor like this? Worse, how could you betray Wyoming?"

Ward studied the hardwood floor inches away, tears forming in his eyes.

Joe repeated his question, and this time it got through. He absentmindedly worked Layborn's glass eye in his hand like a big prayer bead.

"He knows everything, Joe," Ward said.

"Who?"

"The governor. Our boss. Nothing gets by him when it comes to revenue."

"I don't believe you."

"Then don't. You're so naïve."

"You're lying."

Ward turned away with a bitter smile. He was lying, Joe thought as he stood up. Of course he was lying. Of *course* he was lying.

PORTENSON SKIPPED OVER and gave Joe a bear hug, almost lifting him off the ground. "It was perfect," Portenson said. "Your plan, it was perfect! Even better, it's federal prosecutor—proof! This is the biggest arrest we've ever made in our office, and I was in charge! I'm going to get the hell out of this fucking state after all."

He kissed Joe sloppily on the cheek, and Joe looked away.

"I'm next," McIlvaine said, stepping up after Portenson let go. He wrapped his arms around Joe and clamped hard, nearly squeezing Joe's breath out.

"Okay, okay," Joe grunted.

But McIlvaine didn't let go. Instead, he squeezed harder. Suddenly, what was about to come next hit Joe like a hammer. The realization was worse than McIlvaine's grip.

"Get his weapon," McIlvaine ordered one of his men, who plucked the Glock out of Joe's holster.

Across the room, before Joe could shout out a warning, two agents clubbed Nate to the ground with their rifle butts. They took his .454 and cuffed him behind his back, shouting at him to *"stay the fuck down."*

Joe tried to get loose, arching his back in a wild jerk, attempting to take McIlvaine to the ground with him, but the FBI commander was too strong. After Nate was bound with an agent on top of him and a gun jammed into his temple, McIlvaine pressed his mouth to Joe's ear.

"I'll let you go now, but don't try to save your friend. There are way too many of us, and you saw what happened to Layborn."

When McIlvaine released him, Joe staggered away, sucking in racking breaths. He saw Portenson staring at him, shaking his head sadly.

"We had a deal," Joe said, gasping.

"Yes we did," Portenson said, "and I honored it. But you didn't have a deal with *him*." He gestured toward McIlvaine.

"He's been on our list for quite a while," McIlvaine said, confirming without saying what the whispering campaign on the radios had been about.

Joe threw himself at Portenson and his fist caught the FBI agent square in the nose, hard, smashing it flat against his face in a concussion of dark red blood. Portenson dropped to the floor, unconscious. Joe tumbled on top of him, cocked his arm back for another blow, when McIlvaine and two other agents tore him away.

Before cuffing Joe around a knotty pine stanchion to keep him out of the way, McIlvaine leaned into his ear again and said: "Don't you know by now? *Never trust a Fed.*"

THROUGH A FOG of rage and betrayal, Joe watched as the assault team read Miranda rights to James Langston, chief ranger of Yellowstone Park; Layton Barron, CEO of EnerDyne; Chuck Ward, chief of staff for the governor of Wyoming; and Nate Romanowski, ex-special forces officer and outlaw falconer. Layborn's body had been rolled up in dustcovers taken from tables in the restaurant. Portenson moaned from where he lay on the couch near the fire, holding a handkerchief to his head.

McIlvaine had ordered up another snow coach from the South entrance to take everyone away. It would be three hours before the tracked vehicle could get to Old Faithful, he reported to his men.

Across the room, Joe and Nate locked eyes.

"I'm sorry," Joe said.

"Don't worry about it," Nate mouthed, "it's not your fault."

"It is," Joe said. "I'll get you out. I promise."

"You promise?" Nate said, arching his eyebrows, the words visibly relaxing him, making him smile.

With every fiber in my soul, Joe thought but didn't say, because McIlvaine stepped between them to block the exchange. The commander winked at Joe, then wheeled and kicked Nate in the ribs so hard Nate curled up into a ball, his face purple from pain.

"Stop it!" Joe screamed, but at the same time he felt incredibly indebted to Nate, wondering if he could possibly come through with his promise and thinking, *I have to.*

THAT'S WHEN DEL Ashby shouted, "Hey! where'd McCann go? And where is Olig?"

The room froze with silence. Even Joe turned from Nate and looked around.

The front door burst open, and the FBI agent who had been stationed in the woods entered, shook the snow off his coveralls, and said, "Who just took the snow coach?"

388

32

THE FLAMERS WERE being lit one by one, the whole line of them, columns of angry fire reaching as high as six feet into the snowy night sky, melting the falling snow with sharp sizzles that sounded like *zzzt*, warming the air around Sunburst Hot Springs so much that Bob Olig felt comfortable taking off his parka and tossing it aside.

Clay McCann leaned back against the trunk of a lodgepole pine, noting how the flames played on Olig, made him look bigger and meaner than he really was, making him look like some kind of biblical avenger. The handcuffs bit into the flesh of McCann's wrists.

"Just take them off for a minute," McCann said. "Please? I need to scratch my ear where that maniac tore it off. It really hurts and I need to scratch it."

"Gee," Olig said, roaming around looking for more flamers to light, "I really feel for you."

The stolen snow coach was parked in the trees at the edge of the firelight. McCann could see a reflection of flame in one of the side windows. The pain in his chest had steeled into a steady throb and he was just now able to speak. He recalled how he'd tried to shout as Olig attacked him earlier and hustled him out the front door of the Old Faithful Inn, but the impact of the bullets had kicked not only the breath out of him but also his ability to talk.

Finally, Olig walked over to where McCann was sitting.

"I've been thinking of you for a long time."

McCann sighed. "Why weren't you there that day?"

"Rick and I had a disagreement. I decided to pass on the reunion this year. I wish I was there."

McCann smiled malevolently. "I wish you were there too."

Olig said, "I wondered for months what it could possibly feel like to kill someone. It's beyond my understanding how someone like you could be so cruel. Someone supposedly with education, like you."

McCann thought about it for a moment. "It isn't as hard as you think. It was a means to an end. Nothing personal, like I said earlier."

Olig seemed to be studying him, his mouth curling with revulsion.

"That makes it worse," he said.

"Maybe it does," McCann conceded.

"Get up."

McCann felt a trill of pain in his groin, and he squirmed. "I'm sure we can work something out if you'll let me try."

"Nope," Olig said. "No deals. Especially with a lawyer who killed my friends."

"But you'll be a murderer," McCann said. "You'll be as bad as me."

Olig smiled. "I'll never be as bad as you."

"I'm not moving."

Olig reached out and grabbed McCann's good ear, asking, "Do we have to go through this again?"

McCann felt the flames on his face as he was pulled toward the hot springs. He thought about running, thought about fighting, thought about trying to negotiate.

The surface of the water smoked with roils of steam, looked oddly inviting. He thought of Sheila, hoped he'd see her again wherever he was going, hoped she wasn't too angry with him.

He felt a massive, two-handed shove on his back and he was flying forward. The water was so hot it seemed cold.

It was quick.

33

J OE DROVE LARS'S pickup back toward Mammoth with Ashby in the passenger seat. It was 2.30 in the morning, the snow had stopped, and the FBI agents had left an hour before with their prisoners en route to Jackson Hole. The snow was deep and soft, but the oversized tires bit well and Joe had no doubt that if he held the vehicle steady and kept it moving forward, he wouldn't get stuck.

As quickly as they'd come, the storm clouds dissipated, leaving a creamy wash of stars and an ice-blue slice of moon that lit the snow blue-white. Joe didn't even need his head-lights.

He and Ashby hadn't talked about what happened. Ashby seemed lost in his own thoughts and loyalties, and Joe certainly was. Joe replayed his brief conversation with Ward. Of *course* Ward was lying about the governor. If Rulon knew about the microbes and the motive for the murders, why would he have sent Joe to investigate?

Unless, Joe thought darkly, Ward and Rulon expected him to fail. Unless they figured Joe Pickett, shamed ex-game warden, was too bumbling and incompetent to crack the case, thus giving them the political cover of claiming it had been investigated but nothing was found. And, eventually,

Ward would be rich personally and the State of Wyoming would have yet another source of revenue.

Could Rulon possibly be that manipulative? Yes, Joe thought, he could. But was he? Joe wasn't sure.

The only thing he was sure about, as he drove, was that he'd use the relationship he'd established with the governor to press for Nate Romanowski's release. The governor owed him that, Joe figured.

Joe was so deep into rehashing his situation and what had happened that he didn't notice that Ashby was gesturing frantically, pointing at something through the window, sputtering as he tried to put words together. "My God, Joe, look! It's Steamboat!"

Steamboat Geyser, which Cutler had said was by far the biggest and most unpredictable geyser in the world, was shooting up in a massive white column of water and steam, the eruption far above the tops of the trees to their left. Joe didn't understand at first how big it was until he stopped the truck and realized that the geyser was miles away, that the eruption they could see pulsing white into the night sky was so huge it would drench—and possibly kill—anyone or anything around it.

"All my years up here," Ashby said, "and I've never seen Steamboat go off. Hardly anyone has. My God, just look at it."

Joe ran his window down. The geyser speared into the sky, blocking out a vertical slice of stars. Its roar rolled across the landscape, a furious, powerful, guttural sound as if the earth itself was clearing its throat.

And that wasn't all, as the truck began to vibrate. A pair of Lars's sunglasses on a lanyard started to swing back and forth from where they hung on the rearview mirror. Old cigarette butts danced out of the tray. Joe could feel the springs in the truck seat tremble, and ahead of them in the dark trees, snow came tumbling down from branches as the ground shook.

"Earthquake," Ashby said, his voice thin.

"Big one," Joe said, watching the snow crash from the trees to the ground like smoke pouring in the wrong direction.

"Jesus," Ashby said, reaching out to steady himself on the dashboard. "This is huge."

Out on the sequined meadow, a herd of elk emerged from the trees and ran across the virgin snow, hoofbeats thumping, sets of antlers cracking against one another as the bulls scrambled to separate themselves. The herd, more than eighty of them, thundered across the road in front of the truck, leaving a wake of snow, snatches of hair, and a dusky smell.

"Maybe this is it," Ashby said.

Joe didn't want to think that.

"Something really upset the balance," the ranger said, pointing toward a sputtering spray of superheated water that was shooting through the snow in the meadow the elk had just vacated. "It's affecting the whole park. That geyser wasn't there even two minutes ago. Now look at it."

Joe had an impulse to call Marybeth, wake her up, tell her that he loved her. Tell her goodbye.

But the trembling stopped.

As did Steamboat Geyser. The new little geyser in the meadow spat out a few more gouts of water, then simply smoked, as if exhausted.

Joe realized he'd been holding his breath, and he slowly let it out. His grip on the steering wheel was so tight his knuckles where white. "I think it's over," he said. "I think we're okay."

"I hope so," Ashby said.

Joe inched the truck forward, crossed the trail the elk had made, eased out into the meadow.

"I was just thinking I should start going back to church," Ashby said. "Or put in my papers for a transfer to Mount Rushmore or someplace like that. The Washington Monument. Maybe Everglades."

It took until they could see the lights of Mammoth Village for Joe to fully relax. He wanted to know what had caused the eruptions and the earthquake, what had upset the underground plumbing system.

"We'll probably never know what caused it," Joe said.

"That's the thing about this place," Ashby said. "It's so much bigger than us. We're nothing here."

EARLY THE NEXT morning, as the sun came up, Joe walked through the still and silent Gardiner cemetery. The snow was untracked until he got there. It took twenty minutes to find the gravestone for Victor Pickett. He couldn't think of anything to say.

BEFORE DRIVING TO Billings to see Judy and his father and return Lars's pickup and meet Marybeth, who would take him home, Joe called the governor's office. Rulon took the call and listened without comment as Joe outlined what had happened. Rulon's only reaction was to curse when Joe told him about Chuck Ward.

"That sneaky son of a bitch," Rulon said.

"So you had no idea what he was up to?" Joe asked, trying to sound casual.

"Of course not. What are you implying?"

"Nothing, except the last thing he told me," Joe said, trying to swallow except his mouth was dry, "was that you knew everything."

There was a long pause. Then the governor said, "Of course he'd say that. And he'll probably say more and try to implicate me in order to cut a deal with the Feds. But he can't prove anything, not a damn thing. Why would I send you up there after the fact to investigate if I had a role in anything?"

"Maybe because you thought I would fail," Joe said.

"Well, I did think there was a pretty good chance you'd screw things up," the governor said breezily. "That's what you do. But no, I didn't know about the microbes, although I'm fascinated by the possibilities. We've got to own them. They belong to us ..."

Joe could hear the excitement in Rulon's voice. He listened as the governor speculated about the possibilities of gasification, of transforming the world of energy production.

"Do you realize what you've found?" the governor finally asked.

"I think so," Joe said.

"Can we get those microbes?"

"I have no idea," Joe said. "The secret will soon be out."

"Then we have to move fast," Rulon said, and Joe could picture the governor gesturing to his underlings to come into his office. "I've got to go," he said.

"I understand," Joe said, "but there's something else."

"What?" Rulon said impatiently.

"My friend Nate Romanowski. The Feds took him."

"I told you I didn't want to know about him," Rulon said. "In fact, I think our connection is going bad."

"Governor—"

"I'm losing you! Damn! You're fading away! Goodbye, Joe. And damned good work. Let's keep in touch!"

"Governor ..."

*

397

INSTEAD OF GOING North into Montana, Joe drove south into the park. It was hard to believe that the night before was the first major snowstorm of the season. By mid-morning, the roads had melted and were merely wet, and the sun blasted off the snow in a white-hot reflection.

He could see the tracks of the snow coach Olig had stolen going in and out of the Sunburst Hot Springs turnout, but Olig was gone. So was Clay McCann, Joe thought, so was Clay McCann.

Sunburst was dry, likely a result of the earthquake the night before. The pink microbes in the runoff stream were flat and turning gray as they died. Joe ran his bare hand over the flamer holes that once expelled natural gas. Nothing. He lit a match and waved it over the holes until it burned down to his fingertips.

YELLOWSTONE, JOE THOUGHT, as he drove out of it, was the most beautiful place on earth. It was the beginning and the end of everything he knew. He couldn't wait to get home.

AFTERWORD

Since Free Fire was written, three things have happened:

Scientists and geological engineers have begun serious research into whether microbes introduced to coal seams can produce natural gas or liquified fuel;

The National Park Services in Yellowstone has begun public hearings regarding the exclusive contracts to research firms for the bio-mining of unique thermafiles;

U.S. Senator Mike Enzi of Wyoming has contacted fellow lawmakers with the purpose of future federal legislation to close the Yellowstone "Zone of Death" loophole.

And now
an exclusive preview of
Blood Trail
the next Joe Pickett novel
by acclaimed mystery writer
C. J. Box

1

I AM A *hunter, a bestower of dignity.*

I am on the hunt.

As the sun raises its eyebrows over the eastern mountains I can see the track through the still grass meadow. It happens in an instant, the daily rebirth of the sun, a stunning miracle every twenty-four hours so rarely experienced these days by anyone except those who still live by the natural rhythm of the real world, where death is omnipresent and survival an unfair gift. This sudden blast of illumination won't last long, but it reveals the direction and strategy of my prey as obviously as a flashing neon OPEN sign. That is, if one knows where and how to see. Most people don't.

Let me tell you what I see:

The first shaft of buttery morning light pours through the timber and electrifies the light frost and dew of the grass. The track made less than an hour before announces itself not by prints or bent foliage but by the absence of dew. For less than twenty seconds, when the force and angle of the morning light is perfect, I can see how my prey had hesitated for a few moments at the edge of the meadow to look and listen before proceeding. The track boldly entered the clearing before stopping and veering back to the right toward the guarded shadows of the dark wall of pine, then

*continues along the edge of the meadow until it exits between two
lodgepole pines, heading southeast.*

I am a hunter.

*As a hunter, I'm an important tool of nature. I complete the
circle of life while never forgetting I'm a participant as well.
Without me, there is needless suffering and death is slow, brutal,
and without glory. The glory of death depends on if one is the
hunter or the prey. It can be either, depending on the circumstances.*

I KNOW FROM *scouting the area that for the past three mornings
two dozen elk have been grazing on a sunlit hillside a mile from
where I stand, and I know which way my prey is headed and
therefore which way I will be going. The herd includes cows and
calves mostly, and three young male spikes. I'd also seen a hand-
some five-by-five and a six-by-five bull, and a magnificent seven-
point royal bull who lorded over the herd with cautious and stoic
superiority. I'd follow the track through the meadow and the
still-dark and dripping timber until it opened up on the rocky crest
of a ridge that overlooked the grassy hillside.*

*I walk along the edge of the meadow keeping the track of my
prey to my right so I can read it with a simple downward glance
like a driver checks a road map. But in this case, the route I am
following—filled with rushes, pauses, and contemplation—takes
me across the high wooded terrain of the eastern slope of the
Bighorn Mountains of Wyoming. Like my prey, I stop often to listen,
to look, to draw the pine and dust scented air deep into my lungs
and to taste it, savor it, let it enter me. I become a part of the whole,
not a visitor.*

*In the timber I do my best to control my breathing to keep it soft
and rhythmic. I don't hike and climb too fast or too clumsily so I
don't get out of breath. In the dawn October chill, my breath is
ephemeral, condensating into a cloud from my nose and mouth
and whipping away into nothingness. If my prey suspects I am on*

it—if it hears my labored breathing—it might stop in the thick forest to wait and observe. If I blunder into him, I might never get the shot, or get a poor shot that results in a wound. I don't want that to happen.

I almost lose the track when the rising terrain turns rocky and becomes plates of granite. The sun has not yet entered this part of the forest, so the light is dull and fused. Morning mist hangs as if sleeping in the trees, making the rise of the terrain ahead of me seem as if I observe it through a smudged window. Although I know the general direction we are headed, I stop and observe, letting my breath return to a whisper, letting my senses drink in the scene and tell me things I couldn't just see.

Slowly, slowly, as I stand there and make myself not look at the hillside or the trees or anything in particular, to make the scene in front of me all peripheral, the story is revealed as if the ground itself provided the narration.

My prey had paused where I pause, when it had been even darker. It looked for a better route to the top of the rise so as not to have to scramble up the surface of solid granite, not only because of the slickness of the rock but because the surface was covered with dry pockets of pine needles and untethered stones, each of which, if stepped on directly or dislodged, would signal the presence of an intruder.

But it couldn't see a better way, so it stepped up on the ledge and continued on a few feet. I now see the disturbance caused by a tentative step in a pile of pine needles, where a quarter-sized spot of moisture has been revealed. The disturbed pine needles themselves, no more than a dozen of them, are scattered on the bare rock like a child's pick-up sticks. Ten feet to the right of the pocket of pine needles, a small egg-shaped stone lies upturned with clean white granite exposed to the sky. I know the stone has been dislodged, turned upside down by an errant step or stumble, because the exposed side is too clean to have been there long.

Which meant my prey realized scrambling up the rock face was too loud, so it doubled back and returned to where he started. I guess he would skirt the exposed granite to find a better, softer place to climb. I find where my prey stopped to urinate, leaving a dark stain in the soil. I find it by the smell, which is salty and pungent. Pulling off a glove, I touch the moist ground with the tips of my fingers and it is a few degrees warmer than the dirt or air. The prey is close. And I can see a clear track where it turned back again toward the southeast, toward the ridge.

On the other side of the ridge will be the elk. I will likely smell them before I see them. Elk have a particular odor—earthy, like potting soil laced with musk, especially in the morning when the sun warms and dries out their damp hides.

Quietly, deliberately, I put my glove back on and work the bolt on my rifle. I catch a glimpse of the bright, clean brass of the cartridge as it seats in the chamber. I ease the safety on, so when I am ready it will take no more than a thumb flick to be prepared to fire.

As I climb the hill, the morning lightens. The trees disperse and more morning light filters through them to the pine-needle-covered forest floor. I keep the rifle muzzle out in front of me but pointed slightly down. I can see where my prey had stepped, and follow the track. My heart beats faster, and my breath is shallow. I feel a thin sheen of sweat prick through the pores of my skin and slick my entire body like a light coating of machine oil. My senses peak, pushed forward asserting themselves, as if ready to reach out to get a hold on whatever they can grasp and report back.

I slow as I approach the top of the ridge. A slight morning breeze—icy, bracing, clean as snow—flows over the ridge and mists my eyes for a moment. I find my sunglasses and put them on. I can't risk pulling up over the top of the hill and having tears in my eyes so I can't see clearly through the scope.

I drop to my knees and elbows and baby crawl the rest of the way. Elk have a special ability to note movement of any kind on the horizon, and if they saw me pop over the crest, it would likely spook them. I make sure to have the crown of a pine from the slope I just climbed up behind me, so my silhouette is not framed against the blue white sky. As I crawl, I smell the damp soil and the slight rotten odor of decomposing leaves and pine needles.

There are three parklike meadows below me on the saddle slope and the elk are there. The closest bunch, three cows, two calves, and a spike, are no more than one hundred and fifty yards away. The sun lights their red brown hides and tan rumps. They are close enough that I can see the highlights of their black eyes as they graze and hear the click of their ungulate hooves against stones as they move. To their right, in another park, is a group of eight including the five-by-five. He looks up and his antlers catch the sun and for a moment I hold my breath for fear I've been detected. But the big bull lowers his head and continues to chew, stalks of grass bouncing up and down out of the sides of his mouth like cigarettes.

I let my breath out.

The big seven-point is at the edge of the third park, at least three hundred yards away. He is half in the sun and half in shadow from the pine trees that border the meadow. His rack of antlers is so big and wide I wonder, as I always do, how it is possible for him to even raise his head, much less run through tight, dark timber. The big bull seems aware of the rest of the herd without actually looking at them. When a calf moves too closely to him, he woofs without even stopping his meal and the little one wheels and runs back as if stung by a bee.

The breeze is in my face, so I doubt the elk can smell me. The stalk has been perfect. I revel in the hunt itself, knowing this feeling of silent and pagan celebration is as ancient as man himself but simply not known to anyone who doesn't hunt. Is there any kind of feeling similar in the world of cities and streets? In movies or the Internet or video games? I don't think so, because this is real.

407

Before pulling the stock of the rifle to my cheek and fitting my eye to the scope, I inch forward and look down the slope just below me which has been previously out of my field of vision. The sensation is like that of sliding back the cover off a steaming pot to see what is inside. I can feel my insides clench and my heart beat faster.

There he is. I see the broad back of his coat clearly, as well as his blaze orange hat. He is sighting the elk though his rifle scope. He is hidden behind a stand of thick red buckbrush so the elk can't see him. He's been tracking the big bull since an hour before dawn through the meadow, up the slope, over the ridge. Those were his tracks I'd been following. He is crouched behind the brush, a dark green nylon daypack near his feet. He is fifty yards away.

I settle to the ground, wriggling my legs and groin so I am in full contact. The coldness of the ground seeps through my clothes and I can feel it steady me, comfort me, cool me down. I thumb the safety off my rifle and pull the hard, varnished stock against my cheek and lean into the scope with both eyes open.

The side of his face fills the scope, the cross-hairs on his graying temple. He still has the remains of what were once mutton-chop sideburns. His face and hands are older than I recall, wrinkled some, mottled with age-spots. The wedding band he once wore is no longer there, but I see where it has created a permanent trough in the skin around his finger. He is still big, tall, and wide. If he laughed I would see, once again, the oversized teeth with the glint of gold crowns in the back of his mouth and the way his eyes narrowed into slits, as if he couldn't look and laugh at the same time.

I keep the crosshairs on his temple. He seems to sense that something is wrong. His face twitches, and for a moment he sits back and looks to his right and left to see if he can see what, or who, is watching him. This has happened before with the others. They seem to know but at the same time they won't concede. When he sits back, I lower the crosshairs to his heart. He never looks directly at me, so I don't have to fire.

408

I wait until he apparently concludes that it was just a strange feeling, and leans forward into his scope again, waiting for the seven-point bull to turn just right so he offers a clean, full-body shot. My aim moves with him.

I raise the crosshairs from his heart to his neck just below his jawbone and squeeze the trigger.

There is a moment when a shot is fired by a high-powered hunting rifle when the view through the scope is nothing more than a flash of deep orange and the barrel kicks up. For that moment, you don't know if you have hit what you were aiming at or what you will see when you look back down the rifle at your target. The gunpowder smell is sharp and pungent and the boom of the shot itself rockets through the timber and finally rolls back in echo form like a clap of thunder. There is the woofing and startled grunt of a herd of elk as they panic as one and run toward the trees. The seven-by-seven is simply gone. From the blanket of trees, birds fly out like shooting sparks.

Here's what I know:

I am a hunter, a bestower of dignity.

2

J OE PICKETT WAS stranded on the roof of his new home. It was the first Saturday in October, and he was up there to fix dozens of T-Lock shingles that had blown loose during a seventy-five-mile-per-hour windstorm that had also knocked down most of his back fence and sandblasted the paint off his shutters. The windstorm had come rocketing down the eastern slope of the mountains during the middle of the night and hit town like an airborne tsunami, snapping off the branches of hoary cottonwoods onto power lines and rolling cattle semitrucks from the highway across the sagebrush flats like empty beer cans. For the past month since the night of the windstorm, the edges of loosened shingles flapped on the top of his house with a sound like a deck of playing cards being shuffled. Or that's how his wife Marybeth described it since Joe had rarely been home to hear it and hadn't had a day off to repair the damage since it happened. Until today.

He had awakened his sixteen-year-old daughter Sheridan, a sophomore at Saddlestring High, and asked her to hold the rickety wooden ladder steady while he ascended to the roof. It had bent and shivered while he climbed, and he feared his trip down. Since it was just nine in the morning,

Sheridan hadn't been fully awake and his last glimpse of her when he looked down was of her yawning with tangles of blond hair in her eyes. She stayed below while he went up and he couldn't see her. He assumed she'd gone back inside.

There had been a time when Sheridan was his constant companion, his assistant, his tool pusher, when it came to chores and repairs. She was his little buddy, and she knew the difference between a socket and a crescent wrench. She kept up a constant patter of questions and observations while he worked, even though she sometimes distracted him. It was silent now. He'd foolishly thought she'd be eager to help him since he'd been gone so much, forgetting she was a teenager with her own interests and a priority list where "helping Dad" had dropped very low. That she'd come outside to hold the ladder was a conscious acknowledgment of those old days, and that she'd gone back into the house was a statement of how it was now. It made him feel sad, made him miss how it had once been.

It was a crisp, cool, windless fall day. A dusting of snow above treeline on the Bighorns in the distance made the mountains and the sky seem even bluer, and even as he tacked the galvanized nails through the battered shingles into the plywood sheeting he kept stealing glances at the horizon as if sneaking looks at a lifeguard in her bikini at the municipal pool. He couldn't help himself—he wished he were up there.

Joe Pickett had once been the game warden of the Saddlestring district and the mountains and foothills had been his responsibility. That was before he was fired by the director of the state agency, a Machiavellian bureaucrat named Randy Pope.

From where he stood on the roof, he could look out and

see most of the town of Saddlestring, Wyoming. It was quiet, he supposed, but not the kind of quiet he'd been used to. Through the leafless cottonwoods he could see the reflective wink of cars as they coursed down the streets, and he could hear shouts and commands from the coaches on the high school football field as the Twelve Sleep High Wranglers held a scrimmage. Somewhere up on the hill a chainsaw coughed, started and roared to cut firewood. Like a pocket of aspen in the fold of a mountain range, the town of Saddlestring seemed packed into this deep U-shaped bend of the Twelve Sleep River and was laid out along the contours of the water, until the buildings finally played out on the sagebrush flats but the river went on. He could see other roofs, and the anemic downtown where the tallest structure was the wrought iron and neon bucking horse on the top of the Stockman's Bar.

In the back pocket of his worn Wranglers was a long list of "To-dos" that had accumulated for the past month. Marybeth had made most of the entries, but he had listed a few himself. The first five entries were:

Fix roof

Clean gutters

Bring hoses in

Fix back fence

Winterize lawn

The list went on from there for the entire page and half of the back. Joe knew if he worked the entire day and into the night he wouldn't complete the list, even if Sheridan was helping him, which she wasn't. Plus, experience told him there would be a snag of some kind that would derail him and frustrate his progress, something simple but unanticipated. The gutter would detach from the house while he scraped the leaves out of it, or the lumber store wouldn't have the right fence slats and they'd need to order them. Something. Like when the tree branches started to shiver and shake as a gust of wind from the north rolled through them with just enough muscle to catch the ladder and send it clattering straight backward from the house to the lawn as if it had been shot. And there he was, stranded on the top of the roof of a house he really didn't even want to live in, much less own.

The wind went away just as suddenly as it had appeared.

"Sheridan?"

No response. She was very likely back in bed.

"Sheridan? Lucy? Marybeth?" He paused, *"Anybody?"*

He thought of stomping on the roof with his boots or dangling a HELP! message over the eave so Marybeth might see it out the kitchen window. Jumping from the roof to the cottonwood tree in the front yard was a possibility, but the distance was daunting and he visualized missing the branch and thumping into the trunk and tumbling to the ground. Or, he thought sourly, he could just sit up there until the winter snows came and his body was eaten by ravens.

Instead, he went to work. He had a hammer and a pocketful of nails in the front of his hooded sweatshirt. And a spatula.

As he secured the loose shingles he could see his next-door neighbor, Ed Nedny, come out of his front door and stand on his porch looking pensive. Nedny was a retired town administrator who now spent his time working on his immaculate lawn, tending his large and productive garden, keeping up his perfectly well-appointed home, and washing, waxing, and servicing his three vehicles—a vintage Chevy pickup, a Jeep Cherokee, and the black Lincoln Town Car that rarely ventured out of the garage. Joe had seen Nedny the night before when he came home applying Armor All to the whitewall tires of the Town Car under a trouble light. Although his neighbor didn't stare outright at Joe, he was there to observe. To comment. To offer neighborly advice. Nedny wore a watch cap and heavy sweater, and drew serenely on his pipe, letting a fragrant cloud of the smoke waft upward toward Joe on the roof as if he sent it there.

Joe tapped a nail into a shingle to set it, then drove it home with two hard blows.

"Hey, Joe," Ed called.

"Ed."

"Fixing your roof?"

Joe passed a beat, discarded a sarcastic answer, and said. "Yup."

Which gave Ed pause as well, and made him look down at his feet for a few long, contemplative moments. Ed, Joe had discerned, liked to be observed while contemplating. Joe didn't comply.

"You know," Ed said, finally, "a fellow can't actually *fix* T-Lock shingles. It's like trying to fix a car radio without taking it out of the dash. It just can't be done properly."

Joe took in a deep and waited. He dug another nail out of the pocket of his hooded sweatshirt.

"Now, I'm not saying you shouldn't try or that you're washing your time. I'm not saying that at all," Ed said, chuckling in the way a master chuckles at a hapless

415

apprentice, Joe thought. The way his mentor-gone-bad Vern Dunnegan used to chuckle at him.

"Then what are you saying?" Joe asked.

"It's just that you can't really fix shingles in a little patch and expect them to hold," Ed said. "The shingles overlap like this," he held his hands out and placed one on top of another. "You can't fix a shingle properly without taking the top one off first. And because they overlap, you need to take the one off *that*. What I'm saying, Joe, is that with T-Lock shingles you've got to lay a whole new set of shingles on top or strip the whole roof and start over so they seat properly. You can't just fix a section. You've got to fix it all. If I was you, I'd call your insurance man and have him come out and look at it. That way, you can get got a whole new roof."

"What if I don't want a whole new roof?" Joe asked.

Ed shrugged affably, "That's your call, of course. It's *your* roof. I'm not trying to make you do anything. But if you look at the other roofs on the block—at my roof—you'll see we have a certain standard. None of us have patches where you can see a bunch of nail heads. Plus, it might leak. Then you've got ceiling damage. You don't want that, do you?"

"No," Joe said defensively.

"Nobody wants that," Ed said, nodding, puffing. Then looking up at Joe and squinting through a cloud of smoke, "Are you aware your ladder fell down?"

"Yup," Joe answered quickly.

"Do you want me to prop the ladder back up so you can come down?"

"That's not necessary," Joe said, "I need to clean the gutters first."

"I was wondering when you were going to get to that," Ed said.

Joe grunted.

"Are you going to get started on your fence then too?"

"*Ed...*"

"Just trying to help," Ed said, waving his pipe, "just being neighborly."

Joe said nothing.

"It isn't like where you used to live," Ed continued on, "up the Bighorn Road or out there on your mother-in-law's ranch. In town, we all look out for each other and help each other out."

"Got it," Joe said, feeling his neck flush hot, wishing Ed Nedney would turn his attention to someone else on the street or go wax his car or go to breakfast with his old retired buddies at the Burg-O-Pardner downtown.

Joe kept his head down, and started scraping several inches of dead leaves from his gutter with the spatula he'd borrowed from the kitchen drawer.

"I've got a tool for that," Ed offered.

"That's *okay,* Ed," Joe said through clenched teeth, "I'm doing just fine."

"Mind if I come over?" Nedney asked while crossing his lawn onto Joe's. It was easy to see the property line, Joe noted, since Ed's lawn was green and raked clean of leaves and Joe's was neither. Nedny grumbled about the shape of Joe's old ladder while raising it and propping it up against the eave. "Is this ladder going to collapse on me?" Ed asked while he climbed it.

"We'll see," Joe said, as Nedny's big, fleshy face and pipe appeared just above the rim of the gutter. Ed rose another rung so he could fold his arms on the roof and watch Joe more comfortably. He was close enough that Joe could have reached out and patted the top of Nedny's watch cap with the spatula.

"Ah, the joys of being a homeowner, eh?" Ed said.

417

Joe nodded.

"Is it true this is the first house you've owned?"

"Yes."

"You've got a lovely family. Two daughters, right? Sheridan and Lucy?"

"Yes."

"I met your wife Marybeth a couple of weeks ago. She owns that business management company—MBP? I've heard good things about them."

"Good."

"She's quite a lovely woman as well. I've met her mother, Missy. The apple didn't fall far from that tree."

"Yes it did," Joe said, wishing the ladder would collapse.

"I heard you used to live out on the ranch with her and Bud Longbrake. Why did you decide to move to town? That's a pretty nice place out there."

"Nosy neighbors," Joe said.

Nedny forged on, "What are you? Forty?"

"Almost."

"So you've always lived in state-owned houses, huh? Paid for by the state?"

Joe sighed and looked up. "I'm a game warden, Ed. The game and fish department provided housing."

"I remember you used to live out on the Bighorn Road," Nedny said. "Nice little place, if I remember. Phil Kiner lives there now. Since he's the new game warden for the county, what do you do?"

Joe wondered how long Nedny had been waiting to ask these questions since they'd bought the home and moved in. Probably from the first day. But until now, Nedny hadn't had the opportunity to corner Joe and ask.

"I still work for the department," Joe said. "I fill in wherever they need me."

"I heard," Nedny said, raising his eyebrows man-to-man, "that you work directly for the governor now. Like you're some kind of special agent or something."

"At times," Joe said.

"Interesting. Our governor is a fascinating man. What's he like in person? Is he really crazy like some people say?"

Joe was immensely grateful when he heard the front door of his house slam shut and saw Marybeth come out into the front yard and look up. She was wearing her weekend sweats and her blond hair was tied back in a ponytail. She took in the scene: Ed Nedny up on the ladder next to Joe.

"Joe, you've got a call from dispatch," she said. "They said it was an emergency."

"Tell them it's your day off," Nedny counseled, "tell 'em you've got gutters to clean out and a fence to fix."

"You'd like that, wouldn't you, Ed?"

"We all would," Nedny answered, "the whole block."

"You'll have to climb down so I can take that call," Joe said. "I don't think that ladder will hold both of us."

Nedny sighed with frustration and started down. Joe followed.

"My spatula, Joe?" she asked, shaking her head at him.

"I told him I had a tool for that," Ed called over his shoulder as he trudged toward his house.

ORDINARY MAN EXTRAORDINARY HERO

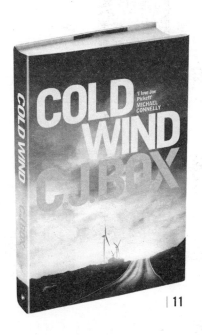

| 11

JOE PICKETT, Wyoming game warden, has taken on eco-terrorists, rogue federal land managers, animal mutilators, corrupt bureaucrats, crazed hitmen, homicidal animal rights advocates – all in the pursuit of justice.

Through it all, he has remained true to himself and his family.

COLD WIND available in hardback Christmas 2011

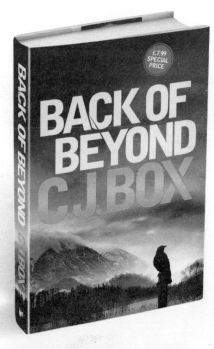

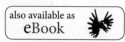